HUMAN PUNK

John King is the author of *The Football Factory*,
Headhunters, *England Away* and, most recently,
White Trash.

ALSO BY JOHN KING

John King

HUMAN PUNK

V

VINTAGE

Published by Vintage 2001

2 4 6 8 10 9 7 5 3 1

First published in Great Britain in 2000 by
Jonathan Cape

Vintage
Random House, 20 Vauxhall Bridge Road,
London SW1V 2SA

Random House Australia (Pty) Limited
20 Alfred Street, Milsons Point, Sydney
New South Wales 2061, Australia

Random House New Zealand Limited
18 Poland Road, Glenfield,
Auckland 10, New Zealand

Random House South Africa (Pty) Limited
Endulini, 5A Jubilee Road, Parktown 2193,
South Africa

Random House UK Limited Reg. No. 954009

A CIP catalogue record for this book
is available from the British Library

ISBN 0 09 928316 6

Papers used by Random House UK Ltd are natural,
recyclable products made from wood grown in sustain-
able forests. The manufacturing processes conform to the
environmental regulations of the country of origin

Printed and bound in Great Britain by
Bookmarque Ltd, Croydon, Surrey

FOR AMANDA AND SAM

The place to look for the germs of the future England is in the light-industry areas and along the arterial roads. In Slough, Dagenham, Barnet, Letchworth, Hayes — everywhere, indeed, on the outskirts of great towns — the old pattern is gradually changing into something new. In those vast new wildernesses of glass and brick the sharp distinctions of the older kind of town, with its slums and mansions, or of the country, with its manor houses and squalid cottages, no longer exist. There are wide gradations of income but it is the same kind of life that is being lived at different levels, in labour-saving flats or council houses, along the concrete roads and in the naked democracy of the swimming pools.

'England Your England', George Orwell

I clambered over mounds and mounds of polystyrene snow,
Then fell into a swimming pool, filled with Fairy Snow,
And watched the world turn dayglo, you know,
You know the world turned dayglo, you know.

'The Day The World Turned Dayglo', X-Ray Spex

SATELLITE

Slough, England
Summer 1977

Boots and braces

IT DOESN'T SEEM right somehow, seeing that kid run across the football pitch with his head sprayed gold, turned into a robot, knowing he has to get home and scrape the paint off before his brain boils and head explodes. He reaches the fence and climbs over, hurries towards the high street. It's not nice, not nice at all, Delaney shaking the can while the others hold him down, covering his face and neck, big blobs in his hair. He'll probably laugh about it later, when he's scrubbed clean and having his tea, safe and sound. And it's a good life when you're not on the receiving end, us lot in our own little corner, sitting in the sun on the last day of term, Johnny Rotten banging out of the cassette player, six weeks of summer holidays drifting into the future. I lean my head into the bricks and stare up at the sky, a pure blue dome with no clouds in sight, the only smudge the thin white trail of a single Heathrow jet, hot and cold air clashing, leaving a long line of fizzing crystals behind. The Pistols chop through 'God Save The Queen' as the flakes slowly melt, and I come back to earth when police bells ring in the 45-version of the Clash's 'White Riot'.

I'm showing off a new pair of DMs today, turning the right boot one on its side so it catches the sun, a warm patch of white light, and they're ten-eye, two over the eight worn by most kids round our way, and the fact I've got them and Dave hasn't is doing his head in. He likes to be one step in front when it comes to clothes, but I worked hard for these boots, stacking shelves at night after school, pricing baked beans and peas while everyone else was at home watching the telly, listening to the radio waiting for John Peel to come on and play some decent music, wanking off over Debbie Harry and Gaye Advert. Soon as I got these Martens home I went out back and rubbed them up with a brick, added big dollops of cherry-red wax then polished the leather till my arm hurt. So I'm getting my money's worth, specially when it comes to this prize tosser Dave Barrows, who's doing his best to ignore the new boots, keeps telling his story.

– So Ali's standing there with Wells holding this knife against his belly and he's shitting it, and all the time there's this little wanker running a bike in his legs. There's four of them, and they're fresh off the train, back from the races, and I suppose they've seen Ali and thought, right, we'll have a laugh and do some Paki-bashing. Ali doesn't know what to do, if he should leg it or wait and see whether he gets let off. The knife makes this some serious aggro and he's got tears in his eyes, but doesn't want to show himself up and start crying. He's handing over the two quid he's got in his pocket when Alfonso comes strolling round the corner.

Chris laughs and Dave stops for a second, gives himself away. He kicks at my right foot, but I'm too quick, stick out my jaw, tell him to come and have a go if he thinks he's hard enough. He sucks deep down in his throat and fills his mouth, gobs at the same boot. Again I'm too quick for him and this massive greeny hits the concrete. I feel sick just looking at it, move over and take my chips with me.

– You should've got steel toecaps, he says. That's what I'm saving up for. A proper industrial pair off a building site.

I shrug and tell him to go ahead and buy steel toecaps if he wants. Doesn't bother me what he does. Can never work out why he takes these things so serious, and anyway, the coppers will have the laces off him soon enough, when he goes to football. Offensive weapons.

– You going to eat those chips? Chris asks. I'm fucking starving.

I say I don't know yet. I'm still thinking about it.

– So what happened next? Smiles asks. Did Ali get his head kicked in or what?

Dave goes on, doing his best to ignore the ten-eye Doctor Martens staring him in the face, shining bright, out on parade.

– Alfonso doesn't say a dicky bird, just goes over and nuts Wells between the eyes. Wells goes down, and the others don't move. Now it's their turn to brick it as the knife falls on the ground and Alfonso bends down, picks it up, admires the blade and tucks it in his dungarees. He pats the div with the bike on the head like he's nothing, while Wells lays there spark out, spread all over the pavement. Alfonso takes the two quid and stuffs the notes in his pocket. He tells Ali to have a kick if he fancies it, but Ali says no thanks, thanks anyway, and Alfonso says to get off home. Ali reckons two pound's a bargain to see Wells get done like that, but there was no point sticking the boot in, specially with the others watching. That would be asking for worse trouble later on.

– Makes sense, Chris says. Must've been tempting though. I'd have kicked the bloke in the head and worried about it later.

Ali made the right choice. There's no point making problems for yourself.

Nobody says a word, not till Smiles pipes up.

– I thought Alfonso and Gary Wells were mates.

Chris nods and Dave grins.

– Not any more they're not.

I think of Ali, trapped in a corner with no way out, mugged by Wells and his poxy bumper-boy mates, all baseball boots and striped T-shirts, wankers picking on an easy target. It's just bullying, same as the kid getting his head sprayed gold. Wells is nineteen, four years older than Ali, and that's a big difference at our age, plus it's four on to one. Least Ali didn't get a kicking.

– You shouldn't waste those chips, Chris says, smiling.

This boy's always eating, stuffing his face with crisps and chocolate, the cold pork pies and Scotch eggs he nicks down the shops, grabbing anything he can get his hands on. He always helps himself to two school dinners, three puddings. Doesn't matter what's on the menu. Could be roast, could be liver. He's always tapping us for chips. He should be fat, but instead he's tall and skinny. Maybe he's got a tapeworm.

– Ali and his brother had to run from Alfonso and Wells when they were out Paki-bashing last year, Smiles says. Wonder what happened.

Fuck knows, but it's a beautiful day and we've got six whole weeks away from this shithole. I tell the others to have a look at the sky, how it looks as if it goes on for ever. Time doesn't matter. It's good to be alive.

They all look at me. Dave laughs.

– You fucking bum boy.

But he can't resist having a peek himself, even though he tries to do it on the sly. He's like that. Always has to have one over on you.

– I hate this place, Chris says, turning angry. It does my fucking brain in. One more year . . .

The fifth form are leaving today, and the lucky ones will be fixed up already, off down the trading estate in the next few weeks, straight into the factories and warehouses, shop floor and offices, full-time jobs with proper full-time wages. We can't wait till next summer when we'll go the same way, maybe get an apprenticeship and learn a trade. There'll be no more skiving when we start work, and we'll have to clock-in on time, learn to do what we're told by some manky old git with a clipboard, but it doesn't matter. We want to earn decent money so we can afford all the records and go to the sort of places we've only read about in the *NME* and *Sounds*, London venues like the Vortex and the Roxy, treat the girls to a film and a drink instead of shinning up the Odeon drainpipe the whole time.

– I've got a surprise for tonight, Chris says, lighting a fag.

He blows a ring in the air, then pumps smoke out of his nose like he's a Rastaman smoking the old ganja. All he needs is the dreadlocks.

– What's that then? Dave asks.

– Wouldn't be a surprise if I told you, would it?

– Come on you wanker, what is it?

– Fuck off cunT, Chris laughs, spitting out the T.

It's a game we play, doing what the teachers tell us, not dropping our Ts, taking the piss out of the same teachers who call us lazy, hooligans, thick. So we make the T stand out, but for one word only.

– Wait till tonight and you'll find out then.

Smiles stretches over and takes one of my chips. They're cold and hard, the fat turning solid, but he puts it in his mouth and starts chewing. Chris, who's scoffed his portion in half a minute and been sitting around looking sad as the rest of us enjoy ours, has this look come over his face. He's been waiting patiently, staring at the chips, imagining the taste, and now Smiles has strolled right in and helped himself. I laugh as Chris stubs his fag out on the concrete, puts it back in the pack, leans forward and grabs a big handful, stuffs them in his gob. He munches away, grinning, cheeks packed with chips, then suddenly frowns and almost spits them out again. It's the salt. He's forgot I covered them with salt. We're pissing ourselves. Dave waits for Chris to stop choking and tries again.

– Come on, what's the big surprise?

Chris shakes his head.

– He's probably bringing Tracy Mercer round, Smiles says. We all like Tracy.

– Dirty cow, Dave says, and looks across the playground, his face changing from pretend disgust to surprise.

We follow his eyes and there's another kid running along with a gold-plated head, same as in the James Bond film *Goldfinger*, when 007 gets knocked out and comes round to find the girl he's been shagging is dead, painted from head to toe so she suffocates. A real waste of decent fanny. But this kid's alive, head glowing in the sun. Delaney and the boys have been busy.

– Who do you reckon it is? Chris asks.

The kid jogs across the playground, past the metalwork room with its mesh fence, off over the football pitch, all professional like. The grass is turning from dark green to a burnt-out yellow, and small clouds of dust kick up as he goes. When he gets to the fence he's straight over, teacher's pet lapping the field, lungs clean, no fag smoke slowing him down.

– Jennings.

Mark Jennings, the school's top sprinter, long-jumper and football captain. Clever as well. Top of the class in all his subjects. Worse than that, he's a big-head. Thinks he's better than the rest of us, which I suppose he is really. Thing is, he shows it, so there's always someone looking to punch him in the mouth.

– He won't be able to breathe, Dave says. He'll drown in his own sweat.

– Only if his whole body's sprayed, Chris says, the expert on these things. They've only done the head.

Five minutes after Jennings disappears, a load of older boys walk across the playground and over the pitch, Delaney near the front. We get up and follow. I turn the cassette player off and jam it under my arm. Dad bought it off some bloke at work for my birthday, and there's this microphone you plug in and prop up in front of the speakers of a record player or radio. That way you can record songs you can't afford to go out and buy. We take turns buying. Share stuff around. The radio plays shit most of the time, and you never know if something decent's going to come on, so records are your best bet.

– Have some of this, Chris says, pulling a small bottle of whisky out of his jacket pocket.

He's been saving it and I feel bad not giving him my chips now. He still passes it over and I take a swig. It burns the back of my throat and I want to spit it back out, but swallow and make sure my face doesn't move.

– Let's have some. Come on, you fucking wally.

I pass the bottle to Dave.

– Not bad. Not bad at all.

I don't want to take the cassette down the bus station, but I've got no choice. Other boys our age start coming over, and I suppose we're a shadow really, trailing the older kids. By the time we reach the fence there's about twenty of us, and Delaney and the others are waiting, hands in pockets, gobbing on the ground, screwing us, checking the faces, nobody smiling. It's not a bad little crew now, and everyone turns and the fence gets a heavy-duty kicking, all these DMs smashing home, the wood cracking into long pink shards, two whole panels kicked to fuck in under a minute. This is the sort of aggro we like, where there's no pain and no comeback, where you can stick the boot in hard as you want without hurting anyone.

– Wonder what the surprise is, Smiles says, as we march along, on our way to the high street.

I don't know, the only thing I'm thinking about is my cassette player and if it's going to get smashed up. I've got three tapes in the side pockets of my trousers, halfway between knee and waist, and make sure the buttons are done up so they don't fall out. One day I'm going to buy a proper hi-fi system, with quality speakers, but it's a long way off.

– Come on, what do you think Chris has got lined up?

Maybe he's used some of that charm he's always going on about and chatted up a prostitute, conned her into coming round to visit us at Smiles's house, seeing it's the last day. Maybe she's going to give us a blow job each. Just so she can enjoy our company.

– Wonder if she spits or swallows, Dave asks, his voice rising as he tries to work out if I'm telling the truth, sticking close to Chris just in case, his brain racing.

I bagsy first go and the others think about it for a minute.

– I'm not going after you, Dave says. No fucking chance. Dirty fucking Arab.

We keep walking. Me and Chris snapping our hands so the fingers crack together. Dave starts laughing at us, joins in and drowns out the sound with the sort of cracks that mean he has to be double-jointed, same as Ian Hutchinson with his windmill throw-ins. I've got the Martens and Dave's got the wrist action. Too much wanking, that's his problem. When he leaves school he could be a professional tosser.

– Fuck off cunT, he laughs.

And we're feeling good, looking forward to the summer, keeping up with the others, going with the flow, like you do.

The big boys are at the front as we trip down the steps leading into the subway, leaving the artificial glow of the precinct behind, some kid's Blakeys echoing down this long dark tunnel with the prick of light at the far end, millions of miles away out of reach, the conversation dipping as our words are punched back from the sort of grimy walls you normally find in a train station bog, the reek of stale piss and sweat replacing the shopping arcade's disinfectant. And because the blokes leading us are leaving school today we know it's going to be a bigger bundle than usual, that they want to go out with a bang, that this is the day they sign on with the adult world and start following another set of rules, snotty-nosed juveniles shifting up a gear leaving childhood behind. And because leaving school opens things up there's this party atmosphere rippling along the high street, through Queensmere and down into the subway where Charlie May's trying to hold the family Alsatian back with a chunk of thick silver chain, we've picked the dog up on our way, Charlie's mum looking out of her front window and spying us lot hanging around by her gate, gobbing all over the pavement as we boot her broken wall with our DMs. And Charlie's fighting to control a dog who's gagging for some aggro, snapping jagged teeth and bubbling white froth, pulling on his arm and a new tattoo that's covered in brown crust, a thick scab hiding the colours of the Union Jack and army dagger. And we've walked into an echo chamber down here, with that coat of Gents slime smoothing the cracks, and because there's nowhere for the sound to go our voices get distorted, turn all fuzzy like some smelly hippy's been pissing about with his drugs and feedback, kaftan coats and cheese-cloth shirts, no punk chords, no edge, the flavour and colour rubbed right out, everything dead and forgotten. And it's like we're stuck in a sewer, floating along in the shit and blown-up rubbers as long-distance lorries rattle over our heads, HGVs driven by tired men who don't know we exist, don't give a toss, want to get home to their families, have a bath and some food, play with their kids, plug into the telly same as my dad. And I suppose we're nothing special, nothing at all, just your everyday garden boot boys out on the prowl wondering if the Langley boys are going to turn up, us younger kids bouncing along feeling like nothing can touch us, floating on air, Doctor Marten's special soles, and even though we don't say it we know we're safe at the back, acting hard, lots of mouth and not much muscle. And before we know it we're turning left and going up the ramp leading into the bus station, and a few seconds later a brick comes flying and bangs into the wall where it cracks in three, quickly followed by a milk bottle that smashes into tiny silver nuggets, just missing Khan's head, and we look up and see their front-row troops leaning over the railings giving us wanker signs as a second brick hits Butler square in the face, blood blowing down his clothes and specking the ground, and we don't hang about, keep following our leaders, let them decide what's best, the Alsatian barking his head off and flashing those razor teeth, gums pulled back same as grown men when they're rowing, and the dog's going mental, his bark roaring back down the ramp where it gets under the skin of china walls sprayed SLOUGH TOWN

BOOT BOYS and CHELSEA NORTH STAND, washes into the tunnel where someone has gone to the bother of carrying a pot of tar through the streets of Slough at four in the morning just so he can splash IRA SCUM and TEDS KILL PUNKS in massive capital letters. And we're not going to stand still waiting to get bricked to death, not with Butler down on his knees holding his face and trying to stop the blood, a surge flushing us into the open where we surface in the middle of the Langley boys, and it's obvious they don't fancy the look of the May family mutt, moving back but keeping an eye on the fangs, Charlie pulled forward by a dog who loves a punch-up and, seeing this, we pile in as they shift further down the walkway towards the cafe, some of their younger boys jumping over the railings to get away, dodging a bus as the driver hits his brakes and adds burnt rubber to the trapped diesel fumes, and the big boys are getting stuck in now, Delaney next to Charlie May, backed up by Mick Todd and Tommy Shannon, and this lot don't give a fuck about anything, punches and kicks swapped till Todd pulls out the hammer he carries around with him and takes a swipe at this fat kid who's already got the Alsatian digging its teeth in his arse, ripping the trousers, catching the boy on the funny bone so he screams like a disco dancer. And it's the dog that makes the difference, the rest of the Langley boys climbing over the railings that box off the different bus stops, shoppers scattering but making sure they take their bags with them as a man in greasy overalls tells us to fuck off out of it, that we're a bunch of bleeding yobs, our heads battered by the fumes and roaring engines, smoke rising till it can't go any further and settles along the roof, the first clouds I've seen all day. And the fat kid goes down on the floor and curls up as the boot goes in, some kicks to the body and Todd and the others move on, job done, everyone except Khan who kicks the boy hard in the head with the stacked shoes he's wearing, one of only two or three boys not wearing Martens, thick wood that makes a loud cracking sound against the skull. And the bang makes me feel sick, when I look at Smiles I know he's thinking the same thing as Khan grins and goes to kick the boy again, least till Todd turns and shouts at him to pack it in, that's enough, leave it out, the wooden handle of the hammer topped by a thick steel head, a rounded back to the flat front. And Khan goes to say something, stops, knows better than to muck Mick Todd about, knows that upsetting Todd means upsetting his three older brothers who are all well-known headcases, the oldest a Royal Marine serving in Germany who's just done six months for beating up a GI, so instead Khan shrugs his shoulders as Langley open a sports bag and start lobbing bottles, must've brought them down on the train, and this kid comes running over at me and tries to grab the cassette so I punch him hard as I can in the face, and he's bigger and older but spins back and gets booted up the arse by Tommy Shannon, thumped with the hammer by Micky Todd, punched by Delaney so he stumbles and almost goes down, tries to run, falls over and gets up, goes along the walkway as I tuck the cassette deeper under my arm. And I look at the fat kid who's still on the ground and he's been knocked clean out, but before we can go over and see if he's alright everyone freezes, a police van bombing along the main road with its siren going, and the aggro's forgotten as eighty or so boys leg it in different directions, nobody wants the coppers coming round your house causing trouble, and the van disappears, then comes barrelling into the station Sweeney-style, except Regan and Carter would be in a Jag, could be Kojak, except it's a van so it must be Ironside, and even though it's summer the van's lights are on, full beam, spotlight eyes. And me, Smiles, Dave and Chris stick together, leave this pressure cooker behind and run into the scorching summer sun, sucking the fresh air down as we blink, getting used to the bright, keep going towards the front of the train station, the Langley boys ahead of us pegging into the ticket hall, the bloke I hit at the back, if one of them turns round now we'll be in trouble, they'll think we're after them, but they keep going, disappear, and when we get to the station we turn left towards the bridge that crosses the tracks, where Delaney, Todd and some of the others are walking the opposite way as if they don't have a care in the world, and when we get near enough I can see they're eyeing us up like we're little kids who are fine when they need the numbers but an embarrassment any other time. A panda pulls round the bend and they start whistling the *Z Cars* tune, till the driver puts his foot down and the light starts blinking, and they sprint back the way we've come while we run up to the bridge, cross over the tracks, slow down near the Printer's Devil as a Paddington train pulls into the station. We stop and watch through the railings as the Langley boys climb aboard, and once the train starts moving light bulbs come flying out the windows, pop on the platform, like they're on a football special. They're on their way home, Langley one stop away, the traditional end-of-term punch-up forgotten as the carriages get smaller and disappear under the gasworks bridge. And we start walking, nice and slow, sweating our bollocks off, it's really hot this summer, same as last year, taking our time and mucking about, snapping our wrists, clicking the fingers, a haze rising off the tarmac same as fumes from a lorry. We turn down Smiles's street with its COCKNEY REDS graffiti crossed out and replaced with the boxed SHED logo that covers most of the desks at school, in letters twice the size, FUCK OFF sprayed on a garage door. And we're laughing, looking forward to tonight, this is where the summer really begins, wiping the water from my face, nodding to Major Tom trooping up the middle of the road like the Grand Old Duke of York himself, the local loony out on patrol, the sort of mental patient who'll do a citizen's arrest on you for gobbing on the pavement, and I look at Dave who always has to go and take the piss out of the bloke, and he bites his lip, wants to laugh but knows it'll mean a row that could go on for hours. The Major should be at home, sitting back and enjoying the weather. I feel sorry for him, same as I do for that kid Khan kicked in the head, and Smiles of course, everyone feels sorry for Smiles, and it's shit how things work out, because when one person starts laughing at the Major everyone else joins in. Like they can't make their own decisions. And we pass by the Major and go in Smiles's house. He points us into the living room, the crack of the boy's skull echoing as Chris bangs the front door shut, and I start thinking about the way Delaney and the others look at us like we're a bunch of wankers, and it just shows all that look-up-to-your-elders, follow-the-leader, go-with-the-flow thinking is bollocks, that you've got to work things out for yourself instead of playing Simon Says for the rest of your life.

★

I look out of the front window and think about Debbie, wonder what she's doing, what she's thinking, Dave coming back from Smiles's room with the Vibrators' *Pure Mania*, *Damned Damned Damned*, Dr Feelgood's *Malpractice* and *The Ramones Leave Home*. The Major's standing at the end of the street, a proper scarecrow off the allotments, dressed in his Sunday best, the jumble-sale jacket and grey trousers, staring at what looks like a pile of dog shit, his face turning red at this latest crime against the community, going purple, almost gold now, as if he's been held down and spray-canned.

The Major might be off his rocker, but he's harmless. He's thirty or thereabouts, but never had a proper job in his life. Dad says it's not that he doesn't want to work, because he does, he'd love a nine-to-five like nothing else, to hold his head up a proud working man, but no company will give him a start. Instead of sitting in the precinct drinking meths with the dossers, or hanging around the job centre begging one of the Gestapo down there for an interview, he patrols the streets on our behalf. There's no wage or paid holidays, no sick pay if he has a cold, but he's glad to be busy. If he spots anything dodgy, something that's not quite right, he's straight over to investigate. Under-age smokers and grown-up drunks get a stern lecture off Major Tom, while shoplifters and vandals are nicked straight away. Thing is, it's easy to get one last chance off him, even if you've had twenty last chances already.

Sometimes he'll issue an official warning, the serious look on his face making it hard not to piss yourself laughing. He lives by the rules of the land, but doesn't let his work run his life. Five o'clock on the dot he's off home for his tea. Even if he's just nicked a boy for smashing up a phone box, he'll be off in mid-sentence if it's his teatime. The Major might be a bobby on the beat, but his mum doesn't like her boy being late in. Sometimes he goes out on night patrol, but Dad says it depends on the weather. This is when the Major gets stick, coming out of a doorway after the pubs kick out and tapping a man on the shoulder when he's having a piss down an alley, or like that time he tried to nick Tommy Shannon's old man for blasphemy, saying Jesus because the Major made him jump. Mr Shannon knocked him out. Broke his glasses as well.

The Major doesn't seem to mind the stick too much, keeps his feelings to himself, maybe accepts it as part of the job, but deep down he must wonder, the anger bottled up inside. His thoughts are buried deep, expression firm. He can't be planning his next Milky Bar wrapper arrest or Curly Wurly raid twenty-four hours a day, seven days a week, every single month of the year. I don't know. Nobody knows. That's the trick, I suppose, getting inside the other person's head, seeing things from their point of view. That's the thing about music, specially the new bands, because they're putting into words what we're thinking. It's like *The Clash* album. The songs on there sum up our lives. That LP was already inside us, waiting for someone to write it down.

Charlie May and his Alsatian pass the top of the road, followed by Delaney, Todd, Khan and a few others. The silver rings on Delaney's fingers and ID bracelet on his wrist catch the light. A bell rings in Major Tom's head when he sees the dog. I can hear it, sitting by the window with Lee Brilleaux belting out 'Going Back Home'. The dog stops, cocks a leg, and pisses a fountain of yellow syrup against a lamp-post. It's thick and dark, from the sun and excitement. He needs a drink, wags his tail and moves on. The piss rolls across square concrete slabs, losing its colour, something wet in a dry street, the boys, dog and piss the only movement in between dozing houses. The Major pushes his glasses into his face and takes two steps before stopping. He's thinking. Working things out. Knows he's only ever going to get trouble off this lot. They're the hooligan element, up-and-coming, just about old enough. The Major's got to behave. He turns his back and returns to the evidence, takes his notebook out, starts writing, turning pages. Maybe he gives these notes to his mum when he gets in and she studies his report as he tucks into his fish fingers and chips.

– Fucking· hell, Smiles says, sitting down on the couch, masking tape holding the stuffing into the arms, putting a Harp tray down on the carpet, four glasses of orange covering the picture of a yellow pint of lager, dog piss in a glass.

– I thought we were going to get done when that car came round the corner. Dad would murder me if the police came knocking on our door. You know what he's like.

Smiles's mum killed herself when he was eight, and his old man has never been the same since. That's what they say, and Smiles goes along with this idea. His dad makes the headmaster at our school look like a vicar, or at least the priest who comes in once a week for the Irish kids. The headmaster, Hitler, doesn't fuck about when it comes to discipline. He loves his cane. He's got three hanging on the wall of his office, and makes sure he keeps the wood vibrating, specially after Charlie May crept in and had a shit on his chair, an expensive-looking effort with armrests and a padded seat. Hitler never found out who did it, so made us all suffer. He would've expelled the boy and, if possible, had him sent to borstal.

Hitler loves taking revenge on the scum mucking up his life, and after he found the shit things got worse. It was same as the war films. One person in a village does something wrong and the Germans come along and machine-gun the lot. He stands there in assembly and tells us the fighting and vandalism is bad enough, that we're a bunch of guttersnipes, lower than the lowest animal, but now someone had sunk even further down the evolutionary scale. We're looking at the floor trying not to laugh out loud, whispering 'the truth is only known, by, guttersnipes', from 'Garageland' by the Clash, making sure the missing Ts stand out, same as Joe Strummer sings it, another game we play, fitting song words to what's going on in front of us. The whole school knows Charlie May has left a turd in Hitler's office, that he went and splashed out on a plate of baked beans down the cafe before school to make sure things happened fast. He had to get in and out commando-style, but Hitler isn't giving us the messy details.

He goes off his trolley for a few weeks, and even canes Smiles for having a fag in the bogs, which is a scum thing to do, seeing the sort of boy Smiles is and what's happened to him in life. Bowler, the poof who teaches PE, even goes and complains. Hitler should've called in the Major and put him on the case. I wonder if he's CID material, or just a beat copper, if he really sees what's going on around him, remembers faces, builds up a picture over time, whether the notes he makes in his notebook are for show or part of a bigger plan, if every case stays open till justice is done. I just don't know. And he's still out there, sweating in the boiling heat, chewing his pencil, splinters in his teeth and lead on his tongue. Maybe it's the lead doing him in. I heard it gives you brain damage.

– Getting nicked would be the end of me, Smiles says, stuck on the flashing blue light.

He shakes his head.

Smiles's old man is as bad as Hitler, so we call him Stalin, because, though we don't know much about Stalin, there was these two men down the Friday disco last month telling us how Stalin was worse than Hitler, killed more people, how the communists are trying to destroy our culture, that they want to take away our right to earn a living, the unions run by hardliners who've brought British industry to its knees with their endless strikes, it was them gave us the power cuts and food shortages, trying to shut the country down, so we couldn't even collect our rubbish, and when it comes to the Labour Party it's all university-trained benders handing the working man's taxes to queers and scrounging rich-kid hippies, flooding the country with coons and wogs, middle-class traitors selling the ordinary man out to the Reds. They say socialists want to corrupt British children and turn the country into a Russian slave state. They give us a National Front leaflet and we move on, find a corner where we can listen to the music. There were two bands playing that night, and there was all these different people turning up from nowhere.

Soon as we get away this long-haired bloke comes up and tells us we shouldn't be talking to those two, what's the matter with us, are we stupid, don't we know they're NF and want to set up concentration camps and exterminate women and children. This hippy says people who love their country live in the past, we should be ashamed of the empire and our role in world politics, that we are all equal and new laws are needed to help immigrants, that only with the help of decent white people can the coloureds climb the social ladder. The English have no culture, and what we do have is rubbish, and he goes on for ages in this posh voice so in the end you feel closer to the NF who at least have the same accent, and he says we're responsible for the starvation in Africa, the potato famine in Ireland, is it any surprise the IRA let off bombs and kill British soldiers. He smiles same as one of your teachers, looking down his beak at us, hands us a Socialist Worker's Party leaflet, says laws are needed so homosexuals can get better jobs. Now we might be a bit thick, but we're not stupid, know that a homosexual is same as a benny, and with this last one we leg it into the crowd, try and find some peace.

So we christened Smiles's old man Stalin, to match Hitler.

– What's the Major up to? Dave asks, looking out the window.

I tell him he's found a pile of dog shit. That Charlie May just went past with his mum's Alsatian and he's been putting two and two together. I ask Dave if he heard the crack of that kid's skull when Khan booted him?

– It made me feel sick, Smiles says.

I nod and Dave does a wanker sign in front of my face.

– You're a couple of poofs, Chris laughs.

Skinny cunt.

– What's the Major going to do, scoop it up and carry it home as evidence? Dave asks, opening the window and leaning his head out, getting ready to take the piss.

– Don't do that, Dave, Smiles says, worried. He'll tell my old man, and then he'll know you've been round.

It's not right being afraid of your own dad. Dave shuts the window. Understands. We never use the name Stalin in front of Smiles, seeing as with his mum dead his dad's the only family he's got, apart from Tony, his brother, who's older and either out working or down the pub. There again, up against Khan's old boy, Stalin's peace and love, so I suppose there's always some poor git worse off. It's not hard to work out why Khan's a nutter, his dad running a cash-and-carry, a snob businessman who has to have top end-of-term marks from his sons. Khan never gets those sort of results and his dad uses his belt, head to toe, buckle end. He was even supposed to have fag burns in the showers after football, but he's a year older so I never saw that. Bowler was there, watching, making sure the boys wash under their arms, and he asks about the burns, but Khan makes up some excuse and Bowler isn't going to get too close. You'd think some of the other teachers would notice, but the PE lot are a bunch of cunts, fancy themselves too much, more bullies.

But it's not nice having that sort of thing done to you by anyone, let alone your own flesh and blood.

– What time's your dad get back? Dave asks.

– Half-eight. He's doing overtime tonight.

– Good, we can have some of this, Dave laughs, taking a small bottle of rum from his pocket.

Stalin works a lot of extra hours, so Smiles and Tony have more freedom, can look after themselves when it comes to cooking and washing clothes, the sort of things your mum does. If they step out of line Stalin knocks them about, but never uses his belt. If the dishes aren't washed and in the cupboard when he gets in they get thumped, or if anything is out of place in the living room he'll bounce his fists off their heads, really battered Tony once when he got sick and messed up the bathroom.

Tony is old enough to fight back now, and Stalin knows it, both of them keeping away from each other. With Tony out so much, Smiles cops more than his fair share of aggro. He's an easy target and you learn from the first time you go down the rec to play football, or walk in a playground, that the easy targets are the ones people attack. You don't have to be brainy to work that out. The way I see it, Stalin is another bully, same as old man Khan. Me, Dave and Chris agree. Sometimes I imagine getting a shotgun and blowing his head off, but know I'd never do it. Don't have the guts for a start, and anyway, it would make Smiles an orphan.

– This tastes like piss, Chris shouts, spitting rum on the carpet.

– Fucking hell, says Smiles. What did you go and do that for? It'll leave a dirty great mark.

He goes in the kitchen and comes back with some rags, gets down on his knees and starts rubbing at the rum. Chris takes one and joins him.

– What did you do that for?

– It's horrible that stuff. I didn't think.

– Come on. Dad will see it when he comes in.

They rub harder.

– How do you know what piss tastes like, Dave asks, sitting back, feet up, laughing.

Chris and Smiles spend the next ten minutes working on the

carpet, me and Dave giving them advice as we pass the bottle back and forward. It doesn't seem to be going down much. Chris was right. It tastes bad. I raise the rum to my lips and pretend to take a swig, give the bottle to Dave. He's been trying to impress, nicked it off his dad, but Chris is the robber here, anything from Smarties and Crunchies to Morris Minors and Ford Capris. He fancies himself as a crook, likes the reputation.

– I've got something a bit better than that, Chris boasts, once the carpet has been rubbed clean. Something much better.

He digs in his underpants and Dave asks if he's going to get his knob out. Chris grins and produces a small packet. He puts it on the table and opens it up. There's this powder inside, and at first I think it's cocaine, something we've read about, but know it can't be. Coke is the rich man's drug and carries a bad image for kids like us, boot-boy punk rockers. Could be heroin, but that's hippy drugs, a loser's drug, has nothing to do with us. It's bad enough going to the doctor's for a blood test and seeing the needle he uses. We all hate stuck-up wankers and smelly hippy students, so that leaves speed, cheap and cheerful, fast and furious, and Chris says that's what it is when we move forward for a closer look. None of us has tasted sulphate before, but know it's the punk drug.

– Where did you get it? Smiles asks.

Chris taps his nose, keeping secrets, and we stand around with our mouths wide open, doing goldfish impressions.

– Let's have a bit then, Dave says at last, leaning forward too quick.

Chris backs him off.

– Later on. We've got to make it last. There isn't much. We'll have it before we go out tonight.

He tucks the sulphate back in his pants, down by his bollocks, and I'm glad it's wrapped up, specially with the heat and how my own nuts are sweating. I go back to the couch and look out the window, see the Major leaving the scene of the crime. He hasn't drawn a chalk line around the dog shit, which is a surprise. I think how Smiles found his mum's body in the bath, her wrists slit, blood drained. He sat there with her naked body and had a long chat. He never told me what he said, and I never asked. He doesn't talk about his mum much. Poor old Smiles.

Poor old Tony. Even Stalin's had a hard time. Have to remember that as well. Talk about bad luck. And we go and sit in the back garden where I lean against the wall under the kitchen window, stretch my DMs out for Dave's benefit, look forward to tonight as I click the cassette player on and Gaye Advert speeds her way through 'One Chord Wonders', all thick black mascara and an old leather motorbike jacket, and if I was at home I'd be lining up my second wank of the day.

We're punk rockers, brick chuckers, finger fuckers – fifteen-year-old boot boys with little chance of a bunk-up even though we know we look the business with our chopped hair and straight-legs, sleeper earrings and cap-sleeve T-shirts, standing on the edge of this disco darkness sucking at crumpled cans of lager pretending we love the horrible taste of alcohol, making the dregs last a little bit longer, eyes drifting from one pair of bouncing tits to the next straining for an eyeful of anything over a 32B as Slade shake the speakers with 'Cum On Feel The Noize', singing along as we line the wall by the bar shifting our attention to the girls on the far side of the dance floor, real quality crumpet this lot with their pencil skirts and stockings, tight black material wrapping skinny bums and legs, forcing short steps, C&A tops stained with rum-and-black and halves-of-sweet-cider, balancing on too-high heels slowly moving foot-to-foot careful they don't snap an ankle, hanging around the turntables watching the smug git spinning records, a right wanker with his Elvis sideburns and wrap-around Starsky cardigan, and we're watching from a distance because these girls prefer 12-inch disco imports to 7-inch home-grown punk rock, they don't have a fucking clue when it comes to good music, but the thing is, we don't have much choice because there's not a lot of places to go and listen to music round here, and these girls have the power to pull the blokes in so they'll get their shitty music later, the DJ thinking with his prick like every other bloke in here, wants to keep the girls happy, and they let the older boys chat them up leaving us lot to lick our lips at the fishnets and stilettos, skirts riding up their legs keeping us staring, our brains full of pictures from the porno mags we nick down the market, suspenders boxing small strips of pale skin as the UV light shows off low-cut bras and dandruff, thin front-loading Playtex straps and oversized collars, Tracy Mercer pushing up close to Barry Fisher back home on leave from Belfast, glad to be alive, hoping to get his leg over with a local scrubber, least that's the way he sees things, Tracy dressed up nice with Soldier Barry in his neat clothes and squaddie crop, regimental wages burning a hole in a brand-new pair of jeans as he runs his hand over Tracy's bum, tracing his fingers along where the crack should be, if the material wasn't so tight, and she gets in even closer, like she's going to disappear down his throat, and I'm thinking poor old Tracy, the girl everyone calls Iron Gob for the blow jobs she's famous for as much as the dental work, and Chris says he knows some kid who knows this other kid I've never heard of, a friend of a friend, and this boy says she's a right goer who'll suck off anything in a pair of trousers, a fucking slag, but from where I'm standing it doesn't seem fair she gets this gossip going on behind her back, she's always friendly enough sitting in the station cafe or the BHS canteen with a cup of tea and a packet of biscuits, whispering like girls do, four or five of them giggling and nattering, watching the boys, and she always smiles and says hello if she knows your face, a friendly girl who deserves better, seems like the stroppy ones get the respect, closed up and cold, maybe that's what it's all about, so Tracy gets a load of stick for smiling in public, but none of us have got off with her so who knows the truth, the only thing that's certain is that Fisher thinks he's the bollocks because he's in the army, filling the girl's head with stories, everyone remembers the IRA bomb in Birmingham, every night another explosion or killing on the news, and even though my head is racing from the speed I've had I think of that wanker of a careers officer who told me to join the army, not just me either, told everyone to sign up, the Clash's 'Career Opportunities' running through my head, the lines about hating the army and the RAF, about not wanting to fight in the tropical heat, mixing in with 'Pretty Vacant' coming through the speakers, and Fisher must know the DJ or he wouldn't be seen knocking around with a load of kids, but I suppose there's enough older people in here, when you stop and look, Fisher a teenager himself, off seeing the big wide world, getting away

from Slough and the everyday routine, but there's no way I'd
go to Ulster so snipers can pick me off from a high-rise, the
careers adviser another recruiting sergeant who can fuck off out
of it, that's all he knows, I'm going to do something with my
life, get a decent job and have an easier time than Mum and
Dad, enjoy myself, Dave leaning his head right in next to mine
so I can hear what he's on about, still moaning about the 10p
we've paid the JA outside, six and a half foot of Jamaican Aggro
with the usual lend-us-10p line, and we get this every Friday
night regular as clockwork so I don't know why Dave's going
on about it, that's what happens when you're a kid, people take
the piss, boys bigger and older are always looking for 10p to tide
them over, that's how it is, and my head is racing along trying to
keep up with the Sex Pistols, skin tingling, this is what life is all
about, telling Dave to forget it, listen to the music, tell him to
have a decko at Iron Gob's mates, one of them's a real beauty
queen with peroxide hair, ten times better than your boring
Miss World efforts, all perms and sparkling teeth, this one stands
out from the other girls, and right on cue the Ramones take
over from the Pistols, 'Sheena Is A Punk Rocker' getting
everyone's heads going, volume cranked up, and I wonder
where this girl goes to school and where she lives, if she's got a
boyfriend, if she takes it in the mouth, if she spits or swallows,
the same old lines we say over and over again filling my head,
but I suppose it's only the hair that's different, Dave's thumping
his heel against the wall in time to the music, Chris nodding as
he looks at the girl with the hair, I can feel the bang of Dave's
boot chipping into the plaster, and Smiles is right next to Dave
laughing like he does, suppose Smiles is my best mate out of this
lot, with his big grin and plastic razor-blade chain, happy to be
out with his mates, and he's got this easygoing nature, doesn't
have a bad bone in his body, and that's what you get off the
punk bands, they've got a sense of humour, busy taking the piss,
and some do it with the lyrics, throwaway words from the
Ramones and Vibrators, while others put something extra in,
and Smiles's real name is Gary Dodds, he got his nickname off
the *Sunny Smiles* books they used to give us in the infants,
photos of baby orphans we had to sell for charity, and Smiles
always asked for an extra book or two, spent hours flogging the

sad little pictures of laughing kids that always made me feel sad, seeing those happy faces knowing there was nobody there for them, but it was Smiles who made an effort, can see him growing up and doing something worthwhile, he's that sort of bloke, Mum calls him a little treasure, my best mate Sunny Smiles leaning back against the wall loving every second of our Friday night, happy to be alive, the speed and power of the music blocking out bad thoughts, and now it's Debbie Harry's turn to fill the speakers, fucking beautiful, but I need a piss and give Smiles my empty can to look after because it's handy having something to hold when you're skint, so you don't look like a wanker standing there with your hands empty, and I worm my way along the edge of the dance floor to the bog, go inside, stand up straight and let the piss flow, halfway through when Dave comes charging in and pushes me into the wall, nice and hard so I splash myself, piss soaking the front of my trousers, black moleskins that show the wet, and worse than the mark is the feeling in my Y-fronts, the wet soaking my knob and balls, piss running down my legs, and I turn round and try to spray him but he's too fast and legs it into a cubicle, slamming the door and jamming the lock, leaving me to finish, then I go and start booting the door, DMs rocking the hinges, but the wood's too strong and I've got no chance knocking it down, can hear Dave laughing inside, and I start worrying that I must stink, and even though I probably won't get off with anything tonight it's nice thinking you've got a chance, keeps the spirits up, and anyway, who wants to stroll around reeking like a dosser sleeping in the subway, a meths-drinking wino who should be in a loony bin, specially on Friday night, the last day of term, and no girl is going to fancy someone who smells like a toilet seat, so I leave Dave and walk over to the towel machine and take a big wad of paper, stick it down the front of my trousers, trying to soak up the mess, what did he go and do that for, he shouts that serves you right for when you did me last week, and I can tell by the strain in his voice he's trying to work out where I am and why the kicking's stopped, the door flying open and Chris and Smiles coming in, the voice of Bob Marley following them through with 'Punky Reggae Party', volume turned down again when the door snaps back, Chris asking me where

Dave's got to, dirty cunt's not having a shit is he, and I point to the bog where he's holding up and, hearing our voices and knowing I'm over by the sinks Dave piles out grinning, suppose he's got a point about last week, but he did me before that, and it goes right back, suppose you've got to let things drift same as Ali not kicking Wells in the head, but no, I'll get Dave when he's not expecting it, we're only having a laugh, and Chris starts scrunching up his face as he sees my trousers and works things out, wrinkles his nose, Dave laughing so hard I think he's going to join the club and piss himself, Chris shaking his head sadly and unzipping, stands there humming to himself as Dave takes the spray can from his jacket, rattles the ball-bearing and starts decorating the walls while I finish mopping up and go over for a turn with the paint, and in two minutes flat the toilet's been covered in graffiti, everything from ELVIS IS A WANKER to THE LOFT RUN FROM MOTHERCARE to that old chestnut VAMBO MARBLE EYE, and when I tell the others the can is almost empty they bundle out the door so I'm left holding the evidence, a bunch of wankers, and I give the can one last shake, add DAVE BARROWS IS BENT AND SUCKS OFF SOLDIERS in dirty great letters before lobbing the empty into one of the bowls and leaving the scene, head down, quickly merging with the mob of boys and girls filling the dance floor, the whole place going mental to 'God Save The Queen', the real number one during Jubilee Week, and I get over to the bar, back in the crowd, spot Soldier Barry on his own, blown out by Tracy Mercer and probably narked by the song, Chris taking money off us and pushing in for our second and final cans of the night, and we all have a shot of lime which is 1p extra but worth it to kill the tang of the lager, none of us is going to admit we don't like the taste, say it's just for a change, Chris handing the drinks out then pointing at another one of Tracy's mates, look at the fucking tits on that, and we follow his finger to a girl who's clearing a section of dance floor, Dave's eyes popping in his head, and we watch this girl in action, the gentle bounce of her tits and the line of her stockings till a bundle starts and everyone backs off as the two sides swap punches and kicks, the music shifting into Bowie's 'Life On Mars', and I'm waiting for that great line about cavemen fighting on the dance floor, strobe light flashing, and maybe the DJ's not such a wanker after all, because I know punk means we've got to get rid of all the music we've listened to in the past, start fresh, but Bowie is magic as far as we're concerned, and nobody believes the stories about Bowie being a poof, it's just that singers saying they're bent is fashionable and gets them noticed by the papers, and it's the Jeffersons causing trouble as the bouncers jump in and drag the three brothers outside, and as they go through the door the music stops dead and the tosser at the controls makes this big deal out of nothing and says some cunt has sprayed the bogs and when he finds out who it is the bouncers are going to cut their nuts off, and there's a cheer for the paintwork and boos for the knife job, but most people don't take a lot of notice as we're concentrating on the aggro that's flaring up outside, the DJ asking will Dave Barrows please step forward and take his punishment like a man, and one or two people look Dave's way but not enough to cause a stir, and he's sharp enough, starts looking round himself which confuses the people who think they know his name and he's worried and I hope the joke doesn't go too far, except the bouncers have got other things to worry about as they pull the Jeffersons through the second door and stick the boot in, the brothers game and big for their age, the old man's well known for wrecking pubs and knocking out coppers, the oldest of the three brothers belting the biggest bouncer who's off balance and topples back through the plate-glass window, and there's this screaming from the girls and the DJ gives up trying to find out who's sprayed the bogs, has a go at calming things down by putting on some brain-dead love song, and these blokes who are mates with the bouncers get stuck in as well, looking through the broken glass I can see the Jeffersons legging it across the car park, well outnumbered now, disappearing in the dark, the bouncers right behind, and I check the time with Smiles and know that from now on the music is going to be shit, slow dances for the smarmy boys to move in and pull, and Dave asks me how the DJ knew his name, but I smile and shrug my shoulders, nothing to do with me, leaning against the wall watching the girls from a distance, stupid slags dancing around their handbags, fresh air coming in through the broken window, people laughing and

28

joking, hot and sweaty, all sorts catered for, building up for Alice Cooper's 'School's Out', and we sip our cans, lined up getting bored now, wish they'd play something else, agreeing this sulphate's not bad, not bad at all.

We walk down to the hot-dog van, the men in front of us blocking out the counter they're so big, but I can hear the bacon sizzling, smell onions frying over the dust of their road building and layers of bitter. The man running the van is even bigger than his customers, dressed in a funny striped apron with a frilly belt, a tiny chef's hat growing out of his head. He looks a right state, but none of us is taking the piss, calling him Nipple Head or Noddy or anything that's going to set him off. Everyone's on their best behaviour, seeing as how a month back this drunk told him he was a big, fat Turkish cunt when he ran out of crisps, ten seconds later the bloke picking his front teeth up out of the gutter. We're sitting on the wall sipping our tea, minding our own business, and end up with front-row seats as Chef delivers a lesson in manners, better than the Thriller in Manila or the Rumble in the Jungle.

Thing is, Chef's Greek, and he isn't too happy being called a Turk, doesn't seem to know what cunt means. His English is a bit iffy, but he's learning fast and, anyway, he knows the word Turk. He's out of the van swinging a pickaxe handle before the pisshead can say Muhammad Ali. There's blood everywhere, and we've learnt that the Greeks and Turks hate each other, that Chef fought the Turks in a war in Cyprus. We get this information off another of his regulars. Chef gets all emotional, says he should have waited until the children had finished their tea and gone home to bed, tells us he's very sorry. It takes us a minute to realise he's talking about us, and in the meantime he goes in the van and comes back out with a Mars bar for each of us. We're not exactly happy being called kids, but keep our mouths shut, eat the Mars bars.

Since he did that bloke, Chef hasn't had any trouble. There's stories going along the brick wall where everyone sits eating their hot dogs and bacon sarnies, drinking cocoa and tea, munching crisps and chocolate, that Chef killed three Turks during the war in Cyprus, hacked them to pieces with a sword, cut their arms and legs off, chopped their bollocks off and stuffed them in the dead men's mouths. The killing is bad enough, but it's the mutilation that really upsets people. Don't know if this is true, but nobody's going to take a chance and get lippy with Chef now. Even the men in front, the sort of full-time knuckle merchants who don't usually care who they upset, are nice and polite, put their pleases and thank-yous in all the right places, share a joke and some old-fashioned banter with the big Greek in the apron and frilly belt, the butcher of Cyprus.

These men move to one side of the counter and we get to watch Chef as he puts their orders together with a flourish, showing a serious pride in his work, thick fingers working with the same delicate moves as Oliver Hardy. The bacon is nicely crinkled and pushed into buns, topped with thick slices of onion, ketchup and brown sauce added according to the wishes of his customers. Once they've got their food, they go over to the wall and sit down, while me, Smiles, Dave and Chris step forward and order four cups of tea. Wouldn't mind some food, but as usual we're skint, take our plastic cups and sit on the bricks after Chef's asked us about school, what we're learning, what we want to do when we grow up. It's like slow torture, something the SS do in the films, the speed almost worn off and this Greek nutter putting us in our place.

When we finish our tea we decide to walk back instead of hanging around waiting for something to happen. There's always the chance that a carload of beautiful girls is going to pick us up and take us home, all spiky hair and PVC miniskirts, safety pins and suspender belts, gagging for sex, but it never seems to happen somehow. Smiles has to be in by twelve anyway.

– Or he turns into a fucking pumpkin, Dave says.

We stroll along talking and taking the piss, like you do, running through the girls who were out tonight, how we'd love to knob every single one of them, except the pigs, or at least finger them, or get inside their bras and stroke their tits, through the material if we have to, or maybe have a snog, or if that's not on then get a quick kiss on the cheek. Truth is, we'd settle for anything. A smile would be fine, set us up nicely, something to think about till next Friday, building it up, till by Thursday you know you're going to get your end away. Just watching the girls dance gets you going, and with a couple of cans of lager in your belly you start believing you're going to end the night pulling something more than your knob.

– See you, lads. I'm going home for a long, slow wank, Dave shouts as he turns off the main road with Chris. That Tracy Mercer won't know what's hit the back of her throat tonight. Dirty fucking cow.

I keep walking with Smiles, do a right turn, and we're almost home when we spot the black outline of a man standing dead still, lurking in the shadows. It makes me jump at first, but then I see it's the Major. He comes out into the light and salutes, steps forward and produces his wallet with the Joe 90 identity badge. He asks if we're alright and I tell him things couldn't be better. He wants to know if we've seen anything suspicious. I tell him we haven't. The Major nods and says that we must keep our eyes peeled at all times, watch out for subversive elements, plus the murderers, rapists and muggers that plague every democratic society. He nods again, moves back into the darkness.

– He's barmy, says Smiles, when we're out of range.

I tell him it doesn't matter if he wanders around at night, he's not hurting anyone. He's just a bit simple.

– I suppose so. I'll see you then.

When I get indoors Mum and Dad are still up, sitting in the living room watching telly. I go in the kitchen looking for something to eat. There's two fish fingers left from earlier and I shove each one in a slice of bread and add HP, put the kettle on for a cup of tea. I go in the living room and see Mum's fallen asleep, her head at a funny angle on the back of the couch, an empty box of Quality Street on the floor, wrappers in a pile. Dad is busy watching Dracula sink his teeth into a blonde in a white nightie, doesn't turn his head till he hears me chewing. Christopher Lee's eyes are cracked and bloodshot, and I know Peter Cushing is lurking somewhere, with his cross and wooden stake ready, hiding in the shadows, ready to stamp out the evil threatening the local serfs, who are busy getting pissed in the pub.

– Give us a bite, Dad says, smiling when he sees the brown sauce oozing through the white of the bread.

– I hand him one of the sandwiches and he sticks half of it straight in his mouth so a blob falls on the carpet.

– Fucking hell.

He scoops it up and pops it in his mouth.

– No harm done. Have a good time, did you?

I tell him it was alright, that they played some decent music for a while, but a lot of rubbish as well.

– Any trouble down there?

I shake my head.

– Good.

Dad goes back to watching the film, and I keep eating, lean back in the chair. It seems funny now, having six weeks off. Usually you've only got the weekends, and most Saturdays I work, either that or go to football, so that leaves Sunday, and it's quiet then with the shops shut and roads empty. And I get pulled into the film, Dracula sitting pretty in his castle, living for ever, drinking to stay alive, hunted by vampire killers who are so stuck-up and boring you want Dracula to get away with his murders. Another blonde virgin starts screaming as the Count moves in and Mum opens her eyes, takes a second to realise where she is, smiles when she sees I'm in. She kisses Dad and goes up to bed, and he stretches out on the sofa, kicking his slippers off.

– Make your poor old dad a cup of tea, will you.

I remember I've boiled the kettle and go back in the kitchen, make us one each, take it in the living room and put Dad's on the carpet, next to his feet.

– What's that smell? he asks, twitching.

I shrug my shoulders and tell him I don't know, that it's probably his socks seeing as he's just taken off his slippers.

– You cheeky little sod. They were fresh on this morning.

I forgot about the piss down the front of my trousers. I've got the tea to drink and sit back down, hurry and finish so I can get out of the room. I'm at an angle and he hasn't noticed the wet patch, that has mostly dried up now. He sniffs his cup of tea, looks around, puts his slippers back on. I'm alright for a bit, till he starts sniffing again, so I yawn and say I'm going to bed. Dad nods, concentrating on the mob of villagers marching towards Dracula's castle, their burning torches held up in the darkness, looking for revenge.

– Don't wake your mum or sister up, he says.

I go in the bog and have a piss in the dark, try not to miss the bowl or hit the water. I take off my trousers and have a quick wash, tiptoe along the landing and lie on my bed. It's hot, and it's going to be ages till I get to sleep, my head racing. I run through today and wonder if the Major is still out on patrol. I think about the kid getting kicked so hard in the head I could hear the bang and the brain damage it could've done, Ali having a knife pulled on him. Best of all I think of the great songs, the thump of the music, imagine myself standing on a stage chugging away at a guitar, beating fuck out of a drum kit, writing my own lyrics and getting someone to sing them to a packed crowd. You never know. The others might take the piss, but it's good to be alive. Don't care what anyone says.

After a while I want to sleep, but it won't come. The downstairs light turns off and Dracula has been spiked in his coffin. I hear Dad's feet on the stairs, hear the splash of his piss following mine into the bog, and Mum's a light sleeper so we don't flush it, unless someone has a shit of course, and the floor creaks as he goes in their bedroom, the click of the door, the mumbling of voices and a long shush from Mum. The walls are thin and you can hear most of what goes on in this house. I cover my head with a pillow, then take it off because I can hardly breathe. There's no noise. I get up and pull the curtains apart, open the window and lean on the sill, look at the houses and gardens, the street lights and shadows. Everything's quiet out there as well, now and then the sound of a car.

After a while I lie back down on the bed, sweating into the sheets, play the faces of tonight's girls through my head, think about Debbie and wonder when I'll see her again. Tracy Mercer's mate with the hair was alright, the best girl there. Thing is, you don't get the dressed-up punk girls round here. Nobody's got the money for a start, and this isn't the King's Road, just a new town full of houses and people instead of shops and clubs. I leave the locals and concentrate on Debbie Harry's face pinned to the wall, the high cheekbones and blonde hair lit up by a street light, and I imagine her between my legs, lipstick rubbing off on the end of my knob, don't have enough imagination for the impossible, go back to porno mag memories, the German and Swedish models who set off for Hollywood but took a wrong turn somewhere and ended up in the backstreets of Slough.

Dodgems

MUM YANKS THE curtains open and I jump up when she tells me the time, get dressed quick and take the toast she's burnt, run to the bus stop. I spot the bus rattling down the road and speed up, but the driver sees me and does the same, grinning as he flattens the accelerator. Luckily I beat him to the corner and his smile fades as he's forced to brake and turn. I jump on and go upstairs, sit at the back in the corner with a view of the passing houses, a line of bedrooms and frosted bathrooms. The conductor hauls his stiff old legs up after me and props his arse against the back of an empty seat. I sort out my coins as he moves the cogs into position, cranks a lever, riding the bumps, the dodgems of life, years of experience making sure he stays on his feet. He rips the ticket across copper teeth and pins it in my hand, peers down the aisle and asks for any more fares. He frowns when nobody answers, smooths the Brylcreemed sides of a greying quiff, scratches a Brillo Pad chin, and goes back down.

Once the conductor's left I finish the toast tucked in my jacket. Some of these blokes get stroppy if you eat on their bus, think they're back doing their national service. They love showing off with kids, but leave the older boys and men alone. Maybe it's the uniform that does it. But the marg has only gone and leaked into the lining of my jacket. Can't fucking believe it. There's nothing to wipe away the stain. I take my Harrington off and suck at the red-and-white tartan, spitting fluff on the floor. This old biddy three seats in front turns her head, thinks I'm spewing and looks like she's going to be sick herself, puke up her boiled egg and soldiers. Don't know what she's doing up here anyway. Pensioners usually sit downstairs. I don't want to upset the woman, so make do with a fuzzy mouth, suffering in silence.

The glass is cold when I press my face on it, looking into the houses, the unmade beds and empty mirrors, Formica wardrobes and football-team posters, dirty washing and plastic guns, a blonde in red stockings kneeling in front of a naked man, head moving, four quick thrusts and she's gone. I stand up and look out the back window, but the room is three, four, five houses back. The picture sticks in my head. This is just what I need, that old dear lurching back and spotting her first hard-on since the war. I have to forget the blonde, ignore the upright tits and curvy bum, drive her right out of my head. I try and concentrate on something boring, but it's difficult. It's another brilliant day, the sun shining so bright that even the pebble-dash seems smooth, while the slate roofs sparkle like they're lined with silver. The bus stops by the gasworks, a pile of rusty tanks and glistening pipes, the Grand Union Canal by the side, out of sight. Traffic crosses the bridge, lorries pumping out fumes that drift down to the canal and seep into the big banks of nettles, the brambles and brown metal, smoke settling on thick green water. The canal's covered in scum, cartons and tins stuck solid, billions of tiny green leaves fighting for a place in the sun, soaking up the light, growing and spreading, forgotten. There's frogs along the canal, big croakers with bulging eyes and thick leathery skin, safe with the brown and dark green leaves.

The lights change and we turn left along the main road, heading towards Uxbridge, picking up speed, the Drill Hall a solid block against the uneven spread of bricks, a centre for the Territorials, past the allotments, green fields on both sides of the dual carriageway, quickly replaced by the pine trees of Black Park, that blonde trying to sneak back in my head. And this is a great ride, the fields and trees easing things, and I'm going back to the same work I did last summer, picking cherries a million times better than the job I've jacked in, stacking shelves for 48p an hour for that wanker shop manager Keith Willis. I hate him like nothing else, with his whining voice and favourite workers, the neat suit and royal manners. I'll have him one day. When I'm older and strong enough. I'll go banging on his door and drag him round the shop, up and down the aisles for the shelf-stackers and checkout girls, out back with the rubbish and breeding rats. I'll make sure he gets the smell of broken mustard jars and rat shit, the rotting cabbage and poison pellets, just so he has a sniff of what it's like being lumbered with the shit jobs, stuck on the bailer crushing cardboard boxes while some cocky fucker takes the piss. I'll kick his head in. One day.

Suppose I shouldn't waste time thinking about him now I've left, he's the one stuck in a poxy shop, strutting around like Adolf Hitler. When I left I filled a big bag with aftershave to sell and chocolate to eat, stuffed it out back next to the bins and went back Sunday morning, a bonus for a year of hard graft, but ended up giving most of it away. You can't make a profit out of your mates. And working in the orchard is another world from the shop. For a start you're outdoors, and you get paid for what you pick. It's mostly cherries, but I've done apples, and want to have a go at the strawberries. The cherry trees are best. Apples are alright, but you get a lot of maggots. You can be stretching for that big juicy clump at the end of the thinnest branch on the tree, hanging on with your legs and risking a broken neck, doing a good monkey impression, and then when you pick it and bring it back to the trunk you find they're full of holes. Cherries smell better, taste better, and I end up stuffing my face. It means I don't earn as much as I should, but it's a good laugh.

The farmer's from Wembley originally, has this haystack hair and wears thick rubber boots, a shotgun tucked in next to the seat of his tractor. He sees himself as a land-owning country squire now he's two miles outside the London Borough of Hillingdon. Because he pays you for what you pick, he doesn't care if you have a slack day and only turn in one box. There's no aggro. I was getting paid every night last summer so always had a pound or two in my pocket. If I was sensible and had no pride, didn't mind getting treated like shit and wanted to keep a job past the summer picking, I would have stayed in the shop stacking shelves, but I had to get out. I could try and get in one of the factories on the trading estate, lie about my age or something, regular work sweeping floors, or make tea on a building site, that's supposed to be good money, but maybe fifteen is too young. The orchard means no questions asked, do what you want when you want, away from the town and the crowds, doing my own thing.

I ring the bell and go downstairs, stand on the platform with warm air rubbing my face, kicking the pole and feeling it shake in my hand. There's a lorry right behind and the driver is swearing his head off as the bus slows down, indicating right to overtake. I jump off before we stop, wait to cross the road, then stand on the central reservation as cars whizz past. One mistake and I'm a goner. I watch the traffic till it thins, go down the lane leading to the orchard, past football pitches on one side and nice detached houses on the other, trimmed plants growing up the bricks, windows sectioned by strips of lead. There's a bird singing and a squirrel scratching, jaw chewing and eyes blinking. I keep going, the houses set back from the road, and it must get lonely living down here. In a terrace you feel safe somehow, hearing people next door, the laughing as well as the arguments. At night I can hear everyone breathing, snoring, tossing and turning, getting up for a piss, put a pillow over my head when Mum and Dad are on the job. We're all together. No loony could break in and kill you without being heard, but out here nobody would know. It would be alright during the day, in the summer, I'd love that, have a massive garden and everything, but at night and in the winter you'd be the only person in the world. Being alone is fine, as long as there's people nearby, things going on so you can join in if you want.

I turn left at the first lane and go in the farm, grab a couple of boxes from the shed, more a corrugated-iron barn really, go to the cherry orchard and get lost in the trees. There's three sparrows hanging upside down on a wire fence, feet tied with string, eyes wide open. Last year there was a bloke going round hunting birds, and he shot one in the tree I was in. It was a tiny little thing, and he picked it up and bashed its head on a trunk, feathers spraying everywhere. He looked at the crushed brain and threw it away like an old crisp packet. I shouted down to him, said he could've killed me, and he looked into the branches till he found where I was, and said maybe next time, walked off laughing. I climbed down and had a look at the bird, saw the face all broken up with bits of skull sticking out. The rest of the summer I imagined having a gun, nicking his and blowing his legs off. I'd never do it, but it's one of those daydreams that make you feel better. It's the same with Willis.

The smell of the grass and bark takes me back to last year, and

it was David Bowie all the way for us lot, with *Diamond Dogs,
Ziggy Stardust, Hunky Dory* and *Aladdin Sane.* It's a chance to get
away from things down here, and even though it can take a
while to fill a box I get the same rate as everyone else, instead of
being ripped off for the same work just because I'm younger.
There's no taxes and if you work hard you can make decent
money. I haven't really cracked it yet, but it's up to me to speed
up. There's a ladder by the side of the path and I carry it further
into the orchard, right over near the back fence, find a tree
that's loaded with ripe cherries and wedge it into the trunk. I
take my jacket off and climb the moss-covered rungs, balance a
box between the top of the ladder and the tree, get stuck in. I'm
soon back in the swing of things, eating as many cherries as I
pick, climbing along the branches and getting used to how
much weight they can hold, always tempted to push my luck
and stretch another inch or two. I'm moving, quickly fill the
first box, start on the second. I'm getting ready to climb down
with this when a voice makes me jump.

– You getting rich up there?

I see two feet but not the rest of the body, move forward for
a better view, see it's Roy from last year. He must be forty or so,
a huge gypsy in thick-soled boots. He travels around the south
of England, parks on the Denham roundabout when he's
working here, or over in Burnham where his brother lives. He
makes a living doing all sorts, a jack of all trades, a friendly man
who always has time to talk. Wouldn't think he'd bother with
the likes of me, but he doesn't put people in the normal blocks.
Suppose he's a bit of a loner, his own boss, does what he wants
when he wants, has this freedom I wouldn't mind having one
day. It's a different life, but he grew up in a house and doesn't
have a caravan, just a car. I lug my box down the ladder, making
sure I hit the rungs, moss slippery from the dew, the leaves of
the tree keeping the sun off. By the time I reach the ground
Roy has flattened a patch of grass and is sitting against a stump,
tobacco tin open as he works on a roll-up. He doesn't look at
me trying not to spill the cherries, too busy trying not to spill his
tobacco.

– What happened to your hair? he asks, when I sit on another
stump and help myself to a handful of cherries.

– Didn't recognise you coming in from the lane, picking up your boxes without saying hello. I was over in the strawberries talking to the ladies, wondering who the new boy was. Then I guessed it was you from last year.

I tell him I got rid of the Ziggy Stardust cut, except it wasn't the proper job, no dye, just the shape. There was a kid three years ahead of us who had the works. Red hair and pale white skin, as if he was painted or something, fresh out of *A Clockwork Orange*. He was a proper Bowie freak, a nutter as well. One day he picked up a fork in the dinner queue and stabbed this other kid in the bollocks. He was expelled, and the boy ended up one ball short, same as Hitler during the war. But things change. I tell Roy we're listening to punk rock now, that all the other music is shit. He nods and scratches his head.

– You still look like a bog brush. New boots as well. You must be doing well. Where's the safety pins then?

We're not dressing much different to how we've always dressed, just shorter hair and straight-legs. Suppose there's kids with safety pins, but that's more fashion. No, it's the music that's changed, become tougher and more to do with everyday life. I never understand the stuff they write in the papers about punk being nothing more than loud noise that doesn't mean anything. The best bands have a lot to say, and at least they don't spend their time singing about love non stop. I hate that long-hair hippy music and emptyhead disco. Never trust a hippy. Load of bollocks, dressing up in psychedelic clothes and playing hours of feedback, getting excited over Genesis and Yes. Punk has changed things for ever. Same goes for the Beatles, all that horrible tinny sixties wank. I ask Roy what he's been doing for the last year.

– Moving around, same as usual. Making a living. I went across to Ireland for six months. I've got friends there and stayed with them for Christmas. They live outside Galway and I worked behind the bar in their mate's pub, a quiet boozer in the country. It's proper countryside as well, not like you get in England. Real wild land, same as Scotland. It's a hard life. Six months was enough. There's more going on over here.

I offer Roy some cherries and he takes a load, pulls the stems off one by one, popping them in his mouth. It's good to be working back here. It's not proper countryside, but it's good enough. You only need a small strip of green to feel different.

– Life's no easier over there, he says. People make life hard wherever you go. They've got the priests and we've got the politicians. They're all laying down laws and telling us how to behave.

If everyone saw things through the other person's eyes, there wouldn't be any arguments.

– That's the secret, but it won't ever happen. If everyone always saw the other person's view, we'd all end up acting the same, turn into machines. Same customs, food, music, everything. It's differences that make life interesting, and there's always going to be some organisation trying to make things the same. Doesn't matter if it's religion, politics, big business, royalty. They're all at it. A bit of friction keeps you on your toes, but I know what you mean, and it's true when it comes to people. You can have both. Differences and respect.

The cherries taste good. Nice and ripe. He smokes his roll-up not saying much else as he enjoys the flavour, then goes off to the apple trees. Roy's like that, slow and easy. I go back up the ladder and start filling the box again, lean into the branches and pick cherries for the rest of the day, glad I'm on my own. Every time I take my boxes back to the shed I look over at the rows of strawberries. Must be thirty people working there, mostly women and kids. It's supposed to be harder work, and you're out in the sun more with no shade, but I'll give it a go one day. Right now the cherries are fine and I've always liked being alone, doing things when I want. I'm not one of these people who has to have company the whole time, talking non-stop, walking the streets for hours on end. And I've got that first-day energy, glad I'm away from Willis and the bailer, the shelves and price gun, the tins and flickering lights. If I can concentrate hard enough I could crack this. I know I could.

The time passes quick, as it always does when you're busy, or interested in what you're doing. I fill six boxes and earn three quid. The farmer comes down and dishes out the money, the woman who counts the boxes during the day handing him the book she keeps. I look around for Roy but don't see him. The farmer just grunts as he gives me my cash, nods and moves on. I stand outside the shed, next to his tractor, and he's left the shotgun where anyone could stroll along and nick it, get lost before he knows what's happened. I try and see how much the strawberry pickers earn, and the first woman collects well over double what I've got. But I've done alright, and walking back up the lane I'm feeling pleased with myself, even though my arms and legs ache. My DMs are dirty and need a polish, clothes covered in green burns, stains off the bark.

Thing is, like Gran says, you have to count your blessings, and I know I'm lucky, feel sorry for the people stuck in the shop, missing the summer as they build tin pyramids and shift boxes in the warehouse. I think back to the time when I marked the carrots up wrong, did them as baked beans. I got a bollocking for that, and had to peel every single label off, then start again. Worst of all was Willis slagging me off in front of Carol, one of the full-time girls who works on the till, her boyfriend this Cockney Red who showed us the scar he got outside Ninian Park before the game with Cardiff, a line of stitches binding his gut together. She's alright Carol, a nice girl, and good looking as well. She could be a model I reckon, if she had the connections. She was good as gold, didn't laugh at Willis's piss-taking, just stared at him as he tried to make me look stupid in front of her, showing off. She didn't say a word, and in the end he got the message, saw the hate in her eyes, shut up and walked off.

I reach the main road in time to see my bus flash past. There's no one at the stop and so it isn't slowing down. I see the driver's face, a square head man in his mid-twenties, a bulldog jaw and red cheeks. I'm tired and want to get home for my tea, stick my hand out hoping he'll pull over and wait for me to catch up, but he looks straight back with this big happy smile and slowly shakes his head side to side. It's the same bloke from this morning and he's well chuffed. The bus roars past the stop and keeps going, disappears round the bend. This is London Country, so we only get a part-time service. Nobody gives a toss about us lot out here. I stand by the side of the dual carriageway, thumb out for a few minutes, give up and sit down against the bus stop, Martens stretched out on the gravel, dig in for a long wait.

Debbie comes back into my head, and I don't know why really. It's not even the sex, more like this sad feeling when I think about her. She said she loved me but I know she doesn't mean it, not really, wants to get engaged soon as we leave school. She has to get married and settle down, have a home, but same as Tracy Mercer she ends up getting called a slag. Last time I saw her was a week ago, bunking off school, her mum and dad at work, the room orange from the curtains, boiling hot indoors, and she's on the bed with her pencil skirt up round her waist, rubbing her fanny, acting the adult, giggling like a kid, silver rings and black stockings. She wants to have it off in time to one of the records I've brought round, the flip side of 'Anarchy In The UK', a great song, 'I Wanna Be Me'. She was going on about Fisher doing it to the Rolling Stones. This pissed me off, and she starts sulking, thought I didn't like her any more. Her dad came home and I had to jump out of the window, run like the clappers. It doesn't matter now.

There's the sound of a car horn and I look up, see a Cortina in the lay-by, motor revving. This bloke leans out and asks if I want a ride. At first I think it's a bum boy or something, look closer and see Smiles's brother on the other side, behind the steering wheel. I get in and Tony pulls away, burning rubber and spitting up gravel.

– You working in the orchard again? he asks.

The passenger passes me a bottle of cider and I have a drink, a big bloke with very short hair.

– Gary should be going down there instead of working with the old man. He's been acting funny lately. Don't know what's wrong. You should have a word with him.

If Tony's ever out of work he could have a go as a racing driver, and I sit back, half listening to the news on the radio, this posh voice raving on about law and order, how our police are the greatest in the world, the country on the verge of anarchy, punk rockers, muggers and football hooligans laughing in the face of authority, unions and socialists conning people with their lies. We race down the outside lane, a few minutes later back in Slough, stopping at the lights. There's some sort of discussion going on in radio land, and unwed mothers, drugs and under-age sex are mentioned. I don't take much notice. It's nothing to do with me, leave all that stuff to Dad talking to the telly after work. I'll be seeing Smiles on Wednesday, listen to Tony and Billy laughing about when they went up to Wolves for the promotion game. The lights change and right now I'm hoping Mum's made something nice for tea. Tony drops me off and I go in, smell the sausages cooking and hope we're having mash as well.

We keep our voices down, me and Smiles sitting in the bus-station cafe, concentrating hard, dealing with a serious matter. The place is nearly empty, a lot different to when we come in here after school, when the tables are packed with kids nursing mugs of tea and coffee. There's two mums nearby, eating egg and chips, telling their kids not to play with the food. Three men sit by the door, their boiler suits specked with creosote, talking quietly, heads low over their plates, laughing and looking over at the women to make sure they can't hear. One of the mums catches the bald man's eye and blushes, starts making a fuss of her son. The man goes back to his food, putting pie on his fork, working his way back into the story, adding beans, quickly looking at the woman, a puff-faced blonde with a shaggy perm and pushchair, plastic white sandals and red nails.

Today was my third day in the orchard and I'm feeling fitter and stronger. There's cakes lined up along the counter, going cheap, but Smiles isn't looking for a bargain. He's off his food, got other things on his mind right now, like how he's gone and made this girl Linda pregnant. He got off with her at a party two months back, and now she's turned up and told him she's in the club. She's found out where he lives and ambushed him in the street. She's not hysterical or anything, but wants to know what to do, needs to share the problem, which is only right. Smiles isn't smiling any more. It's the first time he's got his leg over and, typical for him, she's expecting. That's Smiles all over. Doesn't get the luck. If something is going to go wrong, then it'll go wrong for him. Drop a piece of toast, and it'll land butter-side down. Poor old Smiles.

— She told me she was on the pill, he says, leaning over an empty cup, dropping his voice even lower so I can hardly hear what he's saying. I was going to use a johnny, but she said it was okay.

He looks bad, water in his eyes, but still remembers to lift the empty mug to his lips so the miserable cow running the cafe doesn't come over and tell us to buy another one or get out. The tea in here is weak and tastes the same as hot water, and I'm not wasting my hard-earned cash on another one. It's a place to sit, nothing more, built into the station, without much character, more a canteen than a proper bacon-and-eggs cafe. It stays open later than most places, and works out cheaper than a pub.

– She could've been lying, or maybe she just forgot to take it, I don't know. What would she go and lie about it for? It's not as if she wants a kid. She's only fifteen, same as me. What am I going to do? We don't even know each other. I can't believe this is happening. It's a fucking nightmare.

Smiles is looking at me as if I know something he doesn't, but the thing is, I don't have a clue. You never think of sex and babies going together. It was different when our mums and dads were young. They didn't have the pill in those days, and VD could kill you. Imagine being able to die from having sex. Things have moved on. None of this helps Smiles. He's been caught out.

– She says it's definitely mine. She doesn't want to get rid of it, doesn't want to have an abortion. Reckons they suck the baby out with a hoover and stick it in a bucket, turn its brain to mush with an injection or something. Do you think that's true?

Never thought about it, just imagined they did abortions with a tablet, made the body vanish. All that stuff is for when you get older. They never tell you about hoovers and injections at school. I keep my mouth shut, wait to see what happens next, if an answer will suddenly come out of nowhere. I'm trying hard to think, but nothing's happening.

– Two minutes of sex and she's in the club. Why me?

Smiles got off with Linda at this party in Langley. Took his chance after a slow dance to Bryan Ferry, something he felt bad about next day. Not that he minds Roxy Music or Bryan Ferry, but dancing is for wankers, and we were taking the piss out of him, doing a poof routine, selling out so he could get his leg over. It was the dance that helped him shag her, and the dance that's got him in trouble. Never danced in my life, except at a couple of weddings, when Gran forced me to join in the hokey-cokey – left foot in, left foot out, in out, in out, shake it all about – but that doesn't count. Like Smiles says, it's not fair. You get these studs who go round knobbing everything that moves and nothing ever happens to them, they never get caught out. Maybe their spunk's no good, duff-quality duff, but it's not that, not really. They're more professional and less romantic. Suppose you hear the stories and believe the lies, start thinking life's all roses. Smiles is going to have to come up with a plan.

He nods and closes his eyes.

– I might have to get married.

There's a long silence, in the background the sound of laughing from the men and crying from one of the kids. Smiles looks at the men enjoying life, eating their food and telling jokes, off work and looking forward to a pint, then at the little boy with a yellow mess streaking his shirt, chunks of egg white covering his chin, snot dripping from his nose. There's a layer of the stuff smothering his lips. His mum should sort it out. It's going in his mouth with the toast. How she can eat with that sitting opposite I do not know. The kid's probably still in his nappy. Sitting in his own shit. I'm glad I'm not Smiles right now, facing that sort of future. Me, I'll never get caught out, never marry or settle down. No chance.

– What's going to happen when Dad finds out?

It's hard to see Smiles having to get married, but his old man will go mental when he finds out. Mind you, any excuse. It depends on what the girl's mum and dad do. If she's got brothers it isn't going to matter that Smiles is the same age as her, and I wonder if they do under-age boys for shagging under-age girls, or whether it's just proper grown-up men who get locked away. I don't want to see Smiles in borstal getting the shit kicked out of him, marching around in a uniform. That would be worse than having a kid, stuck in borstal, same as being buried alive. You have to have your freedom or you might as well be dead.

– It's like I'm stuck in a horror film and can't get out.

The woman behind the counter has started peering down her

nose at us, like we're scum. I pick up the empty mug and take a sip of air, look out the window and watch the traffic thinning, everyone on their way somewhere else, leaving their fumes behind. There's a smear of what could be lard, the print of a hand, sunlight giving it this weird X-ray effect. When a tipper passes the glass rattles so much I think it's going to cave in, the roar of the HGVs harder than the drone of Cortinas and Capris. That's what we need. Wheels to get us around.

– Think of it, being a dad when you're still at school. Come on, let's get out of here. There's no point sitting around.

We walk through Queensmere, looking in shop windows, dossers in the square sipping their bottles of cider, arguing with each other over a fag end. Two coppers stand outside a shoe shop, arms crossed, watching the alkies. The shops are closed and there's not many people about. We go down the high street and in the front bar of the Pied Horse. I buy Smiles a light and bitter to cheer him up, and we sit in the corner. This is a lively pub at the weekend, but quiet now, seven o'clock on a Wednesday. The back bar gets busy with a hard soulboy crew that boasts some well-known faces from the surrounding areas, and they pull in some dirty old disco girls. Smiles's brother Tony comes down here, even though he's still a bit junior in comparison.

We make the drink last, sitting in silence again, same as the older family men who've stopped in on their way home from work, ground-down blokes in their forties and fifties. At least they're working, I suppose, have wives and kids, a warm bed at night, better off than the dossers in the arcade. We leave after one drink. Go to the fair.

– That's what having kids does to you, Smiles says. You spend your life working and then you're too knackered to even talk. Look what it's done to my dad. Turned him into a machine.

Music rolls over from Upton Park, Gary Glitter and the sound of church organs. The Stranglers would do well here, and Mum hates their *Rattus Norvegicus* album, doesn't know how we can listen to that sort of stuff. Her and Dad prefer Elvis. He's their hero. Gene Vincent and Eddie Cochrane are others they like, plus the Who and Stones.

– Think, I could be bringing my child down here one day, Smiles says. Maybe it would be a laugh, but it's all the other stuff. Getting the money to pay for its clothes, the rent and food. That sort of thing. There's going to be people putting their oar in, causing trouble. If it was the kid and no aggro, I could live with that.

He laughs.

– I could call him Bryan, after Bryan Ferry.

We pass the usual stalls, the darts and air rifles, house of horrors and coconut shy, a sign pointing to Sheri who'll tell our fortune for 25p, half a box of cherries. What's the point of knowing the future anyway? There'd be nothing to look forward to if you knew what was going to happen next. There's the smell of candyfloss and toffee apples, excited children chasing each other around, gangs of kids our age over by the dodgems, hands in their pockets, DMs primed, shoulder-length boot boy cuts and shorter crops where the sides have been chopped off. The girls eye up the gypsy boys working the bumper cars, while the local boys make jokes, try and act like they don't care, can handle anything, and I know that look, because it's what I do as well. The Todds, Delaney and Charlie May are over there. Two coppers come along and have a word with one of the Todd brothers, who peels away and stands there bouncing foot to foot.

The music's cranked right up as we get on the big wheel, pay our money and wait for it to fill up. We move slowly and get a view of the roof tops, Windsor Castle on the horizon, over the other side of the river, Slough to our right, waiting for the machine to speed up. It doesn't sound too healthy, and it's taking its time, and bang, something snaps. We're left sitting right at the top.

– What else can go wrong? Smiles asks, shaking his head. You can see for miles up here.

It's a long way down, a killer drop, so I sit back and close my eyes, only open them when Smiles leans forward to catch what the bloke on the ground is saying. He leans right into the bar and we rock forward, this massive pikey cupping his mouth and shouting at us to stay where we are, keep still, that they'll have it going in a minute. Must be off his head if he thinks I'm going anywhere. The gasworks and the floodlights of the greyhound stadium stand out, the concrete blocks of the shopping centre in the middle of town, grey slabs of stone and steel, small glass squares, the factories and warehouses of the trading estate, the spread of houses and Matchbox cars.

– Can you see my brother? Smiles asks, leaning forward. Tony said he was coming down here tonight.

I tell him to stop moving otherwise he's going to tip us out. He nods and grins, sits still for a minute, waiting for the part-time mechanics on the ground to get us going. I turn my head away from Slough towards the castle in Windsor, and it looks smart enough, postcard-style, except outside the walls the pubs are packed with off-duty squaddies who'll kick your head in for fun, even if you're five or six years younger, and then there's the hardest Hell's Angels chapter in the country, the sort of men who'd never waste time on the likes of us. Smiles starts rocking, gently at first, then faster, for a laugh. A voice comes up from below.

– Stop fucking about up there.

Smiles does as he's told, and here we are, stuck in the air like a couple of muppets, have to wait half an hour till the motor starts and we jump forward, stop again as people unload two by two. We stay patient, wait our turn, coming down to earth in slow motion, finally push the bar off and get out. Someone asks for a refund and the owner tells him to piss off.

– Could've given us another ride, Smiles mumbles, as we walk away.

We have a go shooting airguns at Jam targets, throw darts at rings on playing cards, for goldfish we don't want, splash out on a toffee apple each, stand around, couples walking along holding hands, lost in their love zones while the lights flash and some healthy speakers pump out the hits of Alvin Stardust, Showad-dywaddy, Hot Chocolate, Mud, the Bay City Rollers, Sweet. There's the steady hum of generators behind the scenes, and the cables running back behind the caravans are old, the casing cracked, but it's good down here, the stalls packed with David Essex lookalikes, and there's an edge, something in the air. It's got the smells and sounds, the hard feel of a football match, a mix of people, all sorts turning out, from gangs of teenage hooligans to pensioners and babies, one or two Paki families, a couple of coloured kids. The music never stops and people shout to get heard, the smell of grease and burning electrics rising and falling with the rides, girls screaming their heads off.

– Come on, Smiles says, let's have a go on the bumper cars.

We're halfway through our ride, smacking into the side of these two birds, one of them a ginger nut with buck teeth, the other a blonde with big firm tits, and they're giving us the eye, laughing and smiling, and I'm just about to clatter into them again and line up a night at the pictures and maybe a wank in the back row when the kid I hit in the bus station last week shows up and rams into the side of us, and if a boy does this on the dodgems, a boy round about your own age, it means trouble, and he's taking the piss driving with one hand as he uses the other to give us a wanker sign, the two girls looking back wondering where we are, waiting for a shunt up the rear, but there's a choice to be made, love or hate, and love has to wait a minute as I dodge past a jam of cars and cut back inside the loop hitting the bloke in the side, and it's a good one as well, enough power to send him and his mate snapping sideways, and I pick up the current, swerve away so I can get after the girls before they forget our faces and someone else gets in there, Smiles coming over all shy when we smack into the girls again and spin them sideways, back in the flow, doing the circuit, and I'm glad I'm driving, feel like a Spitfire pilot, or James Bond in his Aston Martin, the one with the ejector seat, just need the machine-guns, bouncing into the girls, going for love and romance now, forgetting about that tosser and his mate, the ginger nut screaming and waving, the blonde concentrating on her smile, tits jutting out of her tank top so I think the material is going to burst, and it's a good way to chat up a bird, just bang her with your car, means you don't have to come up with any clever lines, I never know what to say to a girl, and those two wankers are back again, trying to ram us but just nicking the front, the driver leaning over.

– We're going to have you two, you fucking cunts.

He gets two fingers back and we keep going, enjoying the ride, Gary Glitter's voice worming its way under the roof from outside, cracking with the flashing electricity above us, running

down the pole, a Shed favourite, HELLO, HELLO, CHELSEA
AGGRO, CHELSEA AGGRO, HELLO, same as every other
end, and Gary's the king of the terraces, king of the fairground,
king of the discos, singalongs for boys and girls everywhere. It's
good to be in the driving seat, can't wait to get a car one day, a
bonus spying Alfonso standing on the side with Smiles's brother
Tony, a stroke of luck when the current snaps off and the
ceiling goes dead. Those two blokes come straight over, red in
the face they're so wound up, and this pikey steps in and tells
them to get in a car or fuck off to the side, no fighting here
sunshine, he's got a living to make, so they go over to their
mates. Now there's six of them screwing us out, snapping their
hands, clicking the fingers, waiting to kick our heads in.

– Look at that, Smiles says, as we leave the car behind.

The two girls we were chasing are busy talking to two other
boys. We've got no chance now, and head over to where Tony
and Alfonso were standing, but they've gone. We get to the side
and see them over by the chip van. The kid I punched starts
slagging me off and there's no way you can get out of these
things sometimes, so I tell him to come on then. He hits me in
the face and I hit him back, using my knuckles, and next thing
we're on the ground rolling around in the dirt. A man steps in
and pulls us apart, says to behave ourselves, then goes back to his
goldfish stall where he hands an excited little girl a ping-pong
ball, her dad leaning forward to help her win a pet. I want to see
if she gets a fish, but Tony and Alfonso have come over now,
and when these other boys see the size of Alfonso they walk off
with their heads down.

– What was all that about? Tony asks.

I tell him and Alfonso laughs. Tony treats us to a bag of chips
each, doing his big brother act, and even though he's two years
younger than Alfonso they've started going around together,
work at the same place and play in the same football team.
Tony's sharp. A nice bloke. He's into reggae, same as Alfonso. I
reach for the salt.

– Fuck me, he says, you're not going to eat those now are
you?

– You've got enough salt there to blind the Devil, Alfonso
laughs.

Don't know what he's on about, but I laugh anyway, to keep him happy.

– Give us one, Tony says, reaching over.

He pops it in his mouth, chews, spits it on the ground.

– Fucking Ada.

He kicks the chip away, goes round to the side of the van and gobs.

– Tastes worse than the fish my old man used to make me eat, Alfonso says, after he's had a go.

It's a treat for us talking with someone like Alfonso and enjoying his banter. He's got a reputation, and any boy is the same, likes to be seen with a nutter occasionally. Not many people cross him. He did six months for glassing some bloke who called him a black bastard in a disco car park. And it must be hard for a coloured boy in a place like Slough, a town full of young whites, plus the Pakis who don't get out much. It's different in somewhere like Notting Hill, where they have the carnival riots, a big city area full of JAs.

We stand around listening to the music and watching the people, till Tony and Alfonso go off with these two girls they've arranged to meet. They're nice as well, near enough twenty and dripping sex. Me and Smiles share another portion of chips and hope those boys aren't hanging around, waiting to give us a kicking. Six on to two doesn't go. Smiles goes quiet again, thinking about the baby, and I can see him sitting in a doctor's waiting room, same as I was with Debbie a while ago after school. She went down to collect her pills from the family planning and wanted me to go, so I did, sat there surrounded by women, one other bloke in the place, a few teenagers scattered around, but it was mostly women with kids who couldn't afford or handle a bigger family. Debbie was so glad someone could be bothered to go with her I was pleased I went.

We haven't had a go on the coconut shy, and I fancy it, Smiles standing back as I knock one off with my last ball. The woman running the stall cracks it open with a hammer, and this thin liquid runs away. I share the coconut with Smiles, use my front-door key to break lumps off the shell.

We sit on the steps by the side of the bumper cars. It's getting on now, and people start drifting away. Those two coppers come back, stand near enough for us to hear the crackle of their radios, voices under the fizzy static, broken sentences that don't mean anything, and it's there in the background, same as the stuff Dad gets upset about, the fuzzy arguments on the telly, we get it non-stop, see the headlines, hear the speeches, don't care about the crime threatening society – the mindless hooligans – the white boys smashing up football specials – the black boys throwing bottles at the police – the scroungers and do-gooders – the muggers, pimps, drug dealers – the Irish boys bricking soldiers – the decent majority of law-abiding citizens – the bully boys who need a lesson – the rule of law – the social order – the best police force in world – the best legal system, best medicine, best education, best army, best democracy – best of everything – best music, best pubs, best girls, best football hooligans, best drugs – the call for hanging, flogging, stocks – the death penalty for the Birmingham and Guildford bombers – the young offenders crying out for a shock to the system – life far too easy in our prisons – far too hard for our rulers – it isn't like the old days – the good old days – 'The White Cliffs of Dover' – George Formby – punk rockers swearing on television – sticking their tongues out – taking drugs, taking the piss – punk rockers and bovver boys – scum of the earth – too much sex, too many skivers, too much freedom – too young, too old – unwed mothers, unwanted pregnancies – communism doesn't work – socialism doesn't work – jumped-up union barons are trying to destroy the country – turn us into a Soviet slave state – Moscow ready – nuclear warheads ready – three-day weeks, power cuts, food shortages, loss of confidence – our taxes going down the drain – immigrants, layabouts, anarchists.

Someone has gone and sprayed DIAMOND DOGS ROOL OK on the back of an old truck, and the song sums up the fairground in a way, coming out of the oxygen tent, a gritty fantasy world that sets up, does a job, moves on, keeps going, same as the bumper cars, the old dodgems of life. The police walk off and the feedback fades. They talk with the man running the house of horrors, all laugh at something. Sharing a joke. I finish my bits of coconut and wait for Smiles to finish his. It was a good shot as well. Bull's-eye.

★

After a week working, swinging through the trees like Tarzan, I'm feeling good, feeling rich, and get Dave and Chris out. Smiles wants to come, but his auntie's round for a visit so he has to stay in and eat sausage rolls. She's his mum's sister and Smiles likes her well enough, but she's not exactly a stranger, Southall three stops on the train. Stalin wants him to show respect for his mum's memory and keep the family together, so Smiles is lumbered. He could do with a drink to help forget the latest disaster clogging up his life. Dave and Chris have been busy sitting down the park and shoplifting in the arcade, for peanuts mostly, except Chris has got lucky and nicked himself a decent pair of headphones, for a hi-fi he doesn't have. I leave Mum and Dad sitting on the couch, watching telly, plates balanced on their knees, and go over to Dave's house. I skirt the dog shit and breathe in the sweet smell of mowed verges, cross hot tarmac and look at parked cars. In a couple of years I'll be old enough to drive, and I see myself cruising around in a customised Capri, the girls gagging for a length as I pull over with an elbow resting on the door, feeding them classic one-liners.

There's two girls sitting on a wall up ahead, bare legs dangling on the breeze blocks, a row of dandelions growing in a line below their feet. The tall one's wearing a bleached jean jacket, the arms cut off and cotton frayed, while the other has a black blouse. They're both looking straight at me, staring me out, and I know I'm going to fall over any second, tread in the sort of shit that's going to stick in the soles of my boots. I make an effort and try to walk confident, go the other way and start to swagger same as a pirate. I want to cross over, but it's too obvious, hope my face hasn't gone red. There's only us three in the world and they're taking the piss without saying a word. I wish I could think of something, but as usual there's nothing there. I have to keep going and pass the girls, staring at the slabs of concrete and strips of cement, trenches packed with ants. The girls show no mercy, follow me with their stares, whistle at my back.

— Give us a kiss, darling, one of them shouts, both girls screaming as they crack up laughing, falling forward off the wall.

I stop and they turn their heads away, climb back on to the wall. There's a row of garages behind them, the doors covered in graffiti – CHELSEA BOOT BOYS, TRACY MERCER IS A SLAG and PAKIS OUT, in three different colours. The second one has been painted over, but I saw it before and can still make out the words. Poor old Tracy. Probably some ugly cow jealous of her good looks and smile. There's a big pile of gravel that's been forgotten, and all these little flowers have taken over, the girls talking to each other, dock leaves and daisies along the curb, ivy weaving its way along a sagging mesh fence, twisting through the rusty diamonds, some sort of creeper running along the top, white petals and black seeds trimming the pattern.

– Come on, give us a kiss, they shout, both together, once I've started walking again.

I keep going this time, sit in Dave's room and wait for Chris to give us a knock. His mum and sisters are downstairs watching telly, his old man down the pub. I can hear them laughing. I tell Dave about the girls on the wall, and he wants to go that way when we walk to the club. He's got this new porn he's nicked down the market, off one of the stalls, digs under his mattress and spreads the magazine out on the floor. It's strange stuff. There's women with pigs, goats and donkeys, and a man shagging a chicken. There's a donkey with a huge cock spunking up over a blonde girl's face. There's gallons of the stuff. There's another with these five pigs on their backs, five women on top facing the camera. You can see where their cocks go in the women. There's another of a woman sucking off a goat, which has been done up to look like the Devil, the animal's horns painted bright red. Usually we see pictures of naked women pulling themselves open, showing off their tits and that, but nothing like this. I feel sorry for the animals, because they don't have much choice. It isn't exciting or anything.

– I can't work it out, Chris says, when he comes round.

– Maybe it's supposed to be a joke or something, Dave admits. I thought it was going to be men and women. There's nothing on the cover.

– You should leave the thieving to me. You always get it wrong.

Dave stuffs the magazine back under his mattress.

– Someone might buy it off me. You never know.

We take a long cut to the social club, pass the wall where the two girls were sitting. They're long gone, but Dave goes over and sniffs the concrete for a laugh, reckons it's still warm. This old codger comes round the corner walking his dog and sees Dave with his nose to the grindstone. The man watches as we walk off. And those pictures are stuck in my head. They don't make sense.

– You should chuck those photos out, Chris says, after we've signed in.

Dave nods, and Chris gets in at the bar, buys three pints of lager. We find a table over by the wall and sit down, enjoy the drink. The lager's nice and cold, and it's a lot cheaper in here than in a pub. The bar staff are more easygoing as well. This is a proper working-men's club geared for everyone, and we've never been asked our age.

– Cheers, Dave says.

The place is packed for the bingo, white-haired Gerry doing his best Bruce Forsyth impression as he pulls out ping-pong balls, a fixed grin all over his face. He's dressed up in a yellow blazer and tie, biros tinkling glasses for legs eleven, women right across the age groups busy with their cards, girls and pissed grannies side by side, squeezed in by the majority of middle-aged women, alive and happy and dressed up for the special vodka promotion, doing the extra cheap prices proud. The women laugh and shout, taking the piss out of Gerry and his balls, and every so often there's a scream as a hand bangs into a mouth, the shock of winning smudging lipstick. There's four or five old boys playing, but most of the men are over by the bar, or further back from where we're sitting, the other end of the club where younger men play pool, a bigger snooker table next to that, taken over by Tommy Shannon's dad and a load of his brothers, cousins, mates, measuring shots, Guinness lined up on a table.

– These girls were tasty then, were they? Dave asks.

I've told him already. They were alright. One of them whistled and asked me for a kiss. Don't know which one though.

– More like a fuck. Those sort are always begging for a bunk-up.

Dave's talking out of his arse, as usual.

– Come on, you wanker. If a girl shouts at a bloke in the street, or comes over and starts chatting him up in a disco, then you know she's asking for it, crying out for a fuck, a right old slag.

– It's true, says Chris.

Don't see how these two know so much. None of us is exactly shagging regularly, and I don't think Chris has even got his end away yet. Dave had some bird at a party, same as Smiles, except he won't tell anyone her name.

– Did they have big tits? Chris asks.

They were alright. Not much more than a handful.

– Small tits are the best ones, Dave says, the expert.

– Fuck off, cunT, Chris says. You're just a bum boy. Give me a healthy pair any day. Birds with flat chests look like boys. Who wants to touch up a girl with nipples instead of proper king-size knockers.

– You're the fucking bender. How can a´ bird look like a bloke just because she hasn't got massive tits? You've got queers on the brain, you fucking tosser.

– Fuck off.

I tell them both to shut up or we'll get kicked out. If you're still at school and drinking in a pub, even a club like this where the rules are lax, a place for families to come and enjoy themselves without any aggro, you have to behave. If you sit in the corner and keep quiet, spend your money and don't spew up over the tables, don't spray the bog and rob the johnny machine, they'll turn a blind eye. Start causing trouble and you'll be out on your ear, banned for life. The others know this and shut up.

– We still going into town next week? Chris asks. Like we said? Go to that pub in Camden again?

– It'll be nice to get away from this place, Dave says. I'm bored out of my skull round here. There's nothing to fucking do, nowhere to go. We'll make sure Smiles comes as well. Go up nice and early.

I tell them me and Smiles are working, so it will have to be when we've finished, that they should be as well, then they wouldn't get so bored. Both answer at the same time. Perfect Flowerpot Men routine.

    – Fuck off, cunT.

We finish the first drink quick, and I go up to the bar, wait my turn, watch the bubbles rise through the gold liquid, filling the glasses. The man serving is a professional, even turns the handles towards me. We drink light and bitter normally, because when you go up for another round most landlords give you more for your money. Each time the pint is filled a bit further over halfway, and with a bottle of light ale making up the measure you can end up getting a pint and a half for the price of a pint. It makes sense. We drink to get pissed, not because we like the taste. In here, because the drink's a lot cheaper than a pub, we can treat ourselves to lager. Dad says lager's a girl's drink, but a lot of the younger lads prefer it to bitter these days, specially during the summer when it's hot and a cold drink is refreshing. Not many men drink from a straight glass though. I bring two pints over to the table and set them down, go back for the third, sit down with the others.

    – Smiles was fucking miserable when I saw him the other day, Dave says. Wasn't his normal happy self. What's the matter with him?

I shrug my shoulders, look around the tables. We're the youngest in here, apart from the children playing by the glass doors. I spot Debbie's mum sitting with three other women, having a good time, laughing her head off. She looks more human down here, younger as well. Bet she was a raver in her day, a Teddy girl in a pleated skirt and stockings. I've got a pair of brothel creepers at home, two-tone suede. Thick soles and buckles. Haven't worn them for a while now, same as the fluorescent socks. Everything from lime green to bright orange. I've had a pair of DMs since I was twelve, but used to switch them back and forward with the shoes. Now it's Martens all the way. Every normal kid wears Doctor Martens non-stop. Some younger boys end up with monkey boots, get it wrong.

    – That's Barry Fisher over there, isn't it? Chris asks, pointing at Soldier Barry, who's standing by a pool table, drinking lager, mouthing off about Paddies and the scum in the IRA.

I wonder if the Shannons can hear.

– He used to go out with Debbie, didn't he?

That's right, but I don't say much. He was the one who broke her in. It was a couple of years ago.

– He's a nutter, Chris says.

He's a squaddie serving in Northern Ireland. He's bound to be a nutter.

– Why is it . . .? Dave asks, lifting his glass and taking a mouthful of lager, almost choking because he's gulped too much.

– You fucking wanker, Chris says.

– Fuck off you string-bean cunt.

If I can hear Fisher going on about the Irish, then the Shannons must be able to as well, and while I don't suppose they have any sympathy with the IRA, they're still Irish.

– Why is it, that wherever you look there's always a nutter, Dave finishes. Think about it. There's Fisher over there, Gary Wells who mugged Ali and goes around tooled-up, Alfonso the giant jungle bunny who nuts Wells and glasses people, the Jeffersons who put bouncers through glass doors, the bouncers themselves, the Shannons who I've never seen do anything but look hard enough, and the likes of Mick Todd who uses a hammer, his brothers, Charlie May with a fucking police dog on the end of a chain, and even Khan, a headcase Paki who doesn't mind kicking some knocked-out kid's brains in. Those are the ones we know about. Let's face it, lads, we're surrounded by nutters. What's it all about?

Don't have a clue.

– It's because they're older than us, Chris says. That's the reason. If we were nineteen or twenty, or thirty, or forty, then we wouldn't worry about them. It's just they're older and bigger, and have more experience. It's the same with the older girls you see. They look dirty, but really they're no worse than your average fifteen-year-old.

– Fuck off. You telling me you'd say no to an older woman taking you in hand. Think of the tricks they'd know. You telling me that stripper we saw doesn't know more about sex than a schoolgirl.

We went to this pub that does strippers on Sunday, the

59

windows covered with thick curtains and the tables packed, standing room only, this bird onstage who must've been in her thirties, with the sort of body the likes of us will only ever see in a dirty mag. The landlord had a record player set up and went through a couple of songs before the strip. She was a real professional, the hundred or so blokes going mental, pissed out of their heads Sunday dinner time, and the stripper was spinning silver Christmas tree tassels pinned to her tits, taking them off, stripping out of her G-string and bending over for the punters to surge forward, a quick flash of her lips before this bloke buries his head between her cheeks and tried to lick her arse. She skipped offstage with a big smile on her face, and someone went round with a beer mug. She did alright as well, the coins quickly mounting up. The landlord pulled the curtains after the last bell, did afters for those blokes who didn't have a Sunday dinner to go home to, gave us a bollocking when he saw how old we were.

– That stripper was a beauty, Chris admits, love in his eyes.

– Dirty Arab, Dave says. Remember that wanker who stuck his tongue up her bum? It's enough to put you off sex for life.

– She had a lot of class.

– Fuck off. You should've been up there with that mong.

Debbie's mum, Bev, shouts and waves her numbers in the air. It's true what they say, every girl is someone's daughter, mum, sister. I was thinking that when we were watching the woman strip, and maybe she has kids somewhere, doing what she can to earn a living, and she has to have a mum. Imagine some bloke trying to stick his tongue up her bum. And those animals pictures. Those women aren't doing that by choice. Maybe they're forced into it. They can't make much.

– Never mind, says Chris. The thing about a professional stripper is that they show themselves but don't let the crowd touch. In other words, she's no tart, just a prick-teaser.

– Who told you that then?

– I read it in the paper. There was an interview with a stripper. Other girls shag blokes onstage.

We all think about this for a minute.

– I bet every bloke down there went home and had a wank over her, Chris says. I did.

– Dirty bastard, Dave says, pretending to be upset.
– You saying you didn't, Chris asks.
– No, I didn't.
Neither did I.
– I waited till the next day.
– What about you, Joe?
I tell them I never did.
– Bum boy. It's your round. Come on, you tight cunt.
I tell Dave I got the last one, and Chris bought the first.
– Must be mine then, he says, going up to the bar.
– What did you think of those pictures? Chris asks.
I tell him the truth, don't pretend it's a laugh.
– That's what I thought as well.

Dave brings the drinks back on a tray and we take the piss out of him as he tries not to spill them. The bingo ends and the night turns into a piss-up, things always friendly in here. We slow down, but end up having seven pints by closing time, chipping in for the last round. We talk about music, girls, getting pissed, the normal stuff, winding each other up over nothing. I keep quiet about Smiles. It's his business and he doesn't want the whole world knowing. It's his story.

– Come on then, Dave says when the first bell's gone. Let's get going. I've had enough.

We walk down to the crossroads, and Debbie's mum is standing on the corner outside the Nag's Head, saying goodbye to one of the women she was drinking with inside, looking around for someone else. Soldier Barry marches down the street with two other blokes, Blakeys clicking on the pavement. He goes up to this Irishman and nuts him in the face. The man goes down and one of Barry's mates kicks him in the face. Fisher stands back, arms crossed, polished brogues catching the headlights of a Cortina that mounts the curb and scatters the small crowd that's quickly gathered. The driver's door opens and bangs into Soldier Barry. Tommy Shannon's dad jumps out of the other side and runs round the car, punches Fisher in the head. The bloke that Fisher's nutted gets up and walks over to the pub wall, where he sits down and watches. Fisher recovers and nuts the driver who's out of the car now, a real beaut right between the eyes, his second of the night. It's a classic head-butt, but it doesn't have much effect. The man lifts his right knee into the squaddie's bollocks and the army boy stumbles forward, the first time he's bent over since he was potting pool balls earlier on. It makes me wince, and I think of the tennis balls I used to get in the bollocks playing football in the playground, but another part of me is glad to see his nuts take a pounding, sick of the stories Debbie used to feed into my ear. Seconds later a panda replaces the Cortina, which screeches away, two coppers jumping out, radio babbling as they swing their truncheons in the middle of an empty street.

– I hate this, Debbie's mum says, gripping my arm. What's the matter with them?

Everyone involved in the punch-up is on the move, and I catch the back of Soldier Barry marching away, flanked by his mates, eyes straight ahead, back straight. Debbie's mum is shaking, digging her nails into my arm.

– Will you walk me back? My friend's gone. I told her to wait, but she's disappeared.

I sober up quick, look round for a skinny kid and a flashy part-time punk, but Chris and Dave have legged it, not wanting to get nicked by mistake. I'm a grown-up now, with a full-size grown-up woman leaning against me. My head's buzzing from the drink.

– Let's go back along the canal, Debbie's mum says. It's quicker. And you can call me Bev.

We go over the road and work our way down to the towpath. This is the end of this stretch of the canal. It's dark, and we walk slowly, passing the backs of houses, the moon reflecting on the water. It's another world down here, and the air smells clean and musty at the same time. They taught us about the canal at school, how the Slough Arm was added to the Grand Union to help the railways which couldn't handle all the bricks being made here and shipped into London. The city was spreading and the brickfields supplied the raw material. When the bricks ran out, the barges took gravel up instead, and London sent back its rubbish to fill the holes. We helped build London, and they sent us the shit they didn't want. We had a good laugh at that. But today the canal is forgotten, and it's not the sort of place I'd normally come.

– Why do men always want to fight? It was the same when I was a girl. It doesn't turn women on, you know. It puts them off.

Bev brushes my arm and I jump. It's the second time. Her arm is on my shoulder and it's like she's oozing perfume the smell's so strong. I'm shitting it. What if she wants a bunk-up under the bridge? I see her lying back against the sloping concrete, rubbers left behind by Debbie and her squaddie boyfriend, Bev lifting her bum up for a schoolboy in ten-eye Doctor Marten boots, finding his winkle's shrivelled up from fear. I'm a kid, fifteen years old, just want an easy life.

– I can't see much down here, don't know where I'm treading. We don't want to fall in, do we?

It takes a while, and we're walking slowly, and it's a brilliant night out, and as it's darker down here we can see the stars, millions of dots in a clear sky. I'd never come down here on my own, and my fear goes, because Debbie's mum is old enough to be my mum as well. I laugh at myself, look at the water and watch my step, small ripples on the surface, where the canal isn't clogged with weeds. We finally reach the bridge and go under, and it's dark and smelly, dead beer rotting in cans, piss and shit, the smell of Bev's perfume banging into me again as her hand runs down my arm. She holds my hand and squeezes.

– Hold my hand, dear. I won't bite.

Before I can sort my head out we're on the other side of the main road and can see her house. Bev's hand goes and there's space between us. The light in Debbie's room is on, curtains shut. My head is spinning and I feel stupid. Bev looks at me, smiles.

– Thanks.

She turns and walks away, goes indoors without looking back. I stand by the bridge thinking hard, go up the steps and on to the road. I start walking, head down, feel like a wanker, cross the road to miss two drunks coming the other way, shouting their heads off and kicking parked cars. Fucking cunt this, fucking cunt that. But it was a good night and I've done nothing wrong, go in and find the old man asleep in front of the telly, the same old static fizzing behind the screen.

Sound of the Westway

CHRIS BREAKS THE Cortina's front window and slides his long rubber arm inside, opens the door and waves us out of the shadows. We move fast, me and Smiles bundling in the back, Dave climbing over the driver's seat to the passenger side, cutting his leg on the broken glass. Chris clicks the door shut and starts pissing about under the dash, while Dave tries to find the splinter digging in his knee, swearing as he runs his palm over the bone. Me and Smiles aren't bothered about Dave getting stabbed by a sliver of glass, seeing as we're too busy shitting it, hoping we don't get caught. The engine roars and Chris sits up straight, releases the handbrake and juggles the gearbox till he finds first. The car leaps forward and the engine cuts out. Dave forgets his knee and knuckles Chris on the back of the head, a loud crack ringing out.

– You fucking wanker, Dave says. You should stick to nicking lollypops and sherbet dips.

– Fuck off, will you, that hurt. You drive if you're so clever.

Chris turns in his seat, ready to have a go back, but Smiles shouts and gives us all heart attacks, points to the three men pegging down the middle of the road. Chris ducks down again and the engine flares up. He crunches the gears, slams into first and the car jumps, almost stalling as it clips the van in front, banging into the legs of the first bloke on the scene, a big horrible monster who slides off the bonnet. Chris stops, digs his foot into the clutch, keeps the engine running.

– Is he alright? he asks. I've fucking killed him. Is he dead?

No, he's alive, ugly and pressing his face into the glass inches from Smiles, shouting that he's got a screwdriver he's going to twist into Smiles's brain, and he looks past him and sees me, says he's going to rip my goolies off with a chisel. This carpenter dips into a pocket and starts jabbing at the window with a blade. Could be a screwdriver, could be a chisel, could be a knife. Doesn't matter. It's going to hurt.

– He's a nutter, Dave shouts. He's a fucking nutter and he's going to cut our fucking heads off.

I shrug my shoulders and smile, try to show the bloke that nicking his prize Ford is nothing to do with me. It's not my fault I ended up in the back seat of a car he's worked so hard to buy, done overtime to keep on the road. It's an accident I'm sitting here.

– Put your foot down, Dave screams. Fuck's sake. He's going to do us. What are you waiting for, you stupid cunt.

Chris accelerates down the road and it takes Dave two whole seconds to change from bottle to wind-up merchant. He rolls down his window, panic over, cocky now we're safe, hangs his hand out and gives the men two fingers, follows it with a long, trembling wanker sign. Chris stops at the junction and waits for a car to pass, a polished Triumph doing a good milk-float impression, a zombie granny at the controls. Dave's shouting at her to hurry up, but she's deaf as well as blind, peering over the steering wheel trying to find her bonnet. Suddenly Dave's back to being a shitter. I look round and the owner and his mates have almost caught up with us. They're old and nasty, and things are looking bad. Dave winds his window up and locks the door, everyone except Chris watching the beer guts getting bigger, the faces redder, the mood darker. The look on Dave's face is a real classic, because hanging his hand out of the window and taking the piss means he's the first one on the menu. The rest of us don't matter. YOU'RE GONNA GET YOUR FUCKING HEAD KICKED IN plays in my head, but I keep quiet.

– Just go, Dave shouts. Just fucking drive.

They've reached the car and are yanking at Dave's door, one of them drawing his fist back to smash the glass, and Chris does as he's told, slams his foot down and shoots across the road. We zoom off, cutting up the Triumph in one long swerve, Chris straightening the car, laughing his head off like a mental case. He stares in the mirror and laughs harder, says he's left marks on the road, now we're driving with bald tyres, and there's a smell of burnt rubber that quickly fades away. I look back and we're long gone, the three men specks in the distance, hands on knees, knackered.

– Did you see their faces? Chris shouts, pissing himself. Did you see their faces when we got away. They thought they fucking had us. And you, Dave. Talk about bricking it. You fucking slag. You could go out and build a wall with the bricks you've just laid. All you need is a trowel. Your face was fucking ace. I'll never forget that as long as I live. What a fucking cunt.

Dave's leaning his head back against the door frame. He keeps his trap shut and looks out of the window, breathing heavy.

– They saw who we were, Smiles says.

– Fuck them, Chris decides. They don't know us from Adam.

– They could find out, Smiles says. This is Slough, not London or Liverpool.

– Fuck off, will you, Chris shouts, getting angry suddenly, out of character, specially where Smiles is concerned.

Smiles goes quiet. Normally he gets special treatment. With his mum and that.

– Don't worry, Chris says. We'll be fine.

– They can't prove anything, says Dave, acting like a kid. Like it's going to turn into a court case.

– Fuck them all, Chris says, and leans into the wheel, racing past the houses and crashing a red light, missing a van coming across us by a couple of feet.

– Let me out, Dave moans.

– Fuck off.

We give Chris a bollocking and he promises to stop for the reds, and we're leaving Slough behind, passing the cider round, race past where I work, down the hill to where the Oxford Road meets the Western Avenue, the caravans and trucks parked in Denham, up the hill to Uxbridge Circus, crashing the lights by the Master Brewer, the crossroads empty, yellow lights lining the edge of the Northolt airstrip, working their way inside the screen as we share a bottle of cider, and Dave's stuffed a tape in the cassette, the Jam's *In The City* setting us up for the run into the middle of London, and Chris is really shifting now,

66

the Cortina riding well as we pile along the outside lane, burning up better cars than this, pissing all over a shiny Rover, slowing down for the roundabout by the Polish War Memorial, speeding up again, slowing for the next roundabout and roadworks, windows open feeling the rush of fresh air on our faces, more stops and starts till we reach Hanger Lane and dip into the tunnel, back out in seconds, twenty-five minutes after we nick the car in Slough getting ready for take-off.

– Fasten your seat belts please, Chris says, doing his best to sound like an airplane captain.

I've never been on a plane, but this must be what it's like, pelting down the runway building up speed, lifting into the sky, a gradual climb as the White City dog track eases past, the QPR floodlights in the distance, the Cortina taking us on to the flyover, and we're high above the city here, London spreading out around us. This is the Westway, and this is the moment we've been waiting for.

– Come on, Smiles says, worried Dave's going to muck it up.

Dave takes the cassette out and slots another one in. We wait for the Clash to stroll onstage. Mick Jones tuning his guitar and Joe Strummer testing the mic. This is what life is all about, the tingle of the cider and thousands of *Mary Poppins* rooftops, the concrete towers of Notting Hill and the glass blocks of the West End, the Post Office Tower lording it over thousands of Monopoly streets. Chris guns the engine as we sing along to 'London's Burning', and we're burning up this tosser in a Jag, a poofy wanker in a boating cap and one of those funny little playboy scarves you see on telly. Didn't know people like that really existed. The song gets a bit lost in the speakers, but it doesn't matter, it's just a laugh, in and out the lights, and even though the yellow lights over by Northolt are brighter these go with the song. It's right what they say, it's a great traffic system. We know the words off by heart and don't miss a beat. None of us can think of a better way to spend the night, London big and exciting compared to where we live, and we're left out in the cold with nothing to do while up here everyone's piled on top of everyone else, a major city where there's more of everything – rich, poor, music, shops, excitement.

Back home there's the pubs and a disco every now and then,

the social clubs and shopping arcade, football pitches and pinball machines, the Cat Balou for the Teds and the Odeon for kids looking for a back-row snog with the girlfriend, but apart from that it's houses and the trading estate with its maze of factories and warehouses, a new town that feeds the roads and lanes, bored teenagers stuck in the middle of nowhere. There's nothing to do if you're young round our way, but up here, in Soho and Camden Town, there's bands galore, all sorts of things happening, a bigger mixture of people, everything from massive estates to the sort of knobs and grand old houses you never see in real life. The kids in London get the works, training pitches with floodlights and flashy youth clubs, places to go and things to do. The houses are big, built to last, while ours are done on the cheap, quantity over quality. According to Dave, you get a lot of benders up here as well, whole pubs full of them. Don't know why, but you don't see any queers in Slough, that's for sure.

– Watch out, Smiles shouts from the back. You almost hit that cab.

Chris turns his head and grins, but I was worried too, Jackie Stewart behind the wheel taking the bend too fast. There's a grey-haired man behind the wheel of the cab and he flashes his lights. I can see us going through the barrier and hitting the ground down below, another sound of the Westway this Cortina smashing into a terrace. I don't want to end up the same way as that rock 'n' roll wanker James Dean.

– Nobody's going to make a poster out of you, Chris laughs. You ugly fucking cunT.

Dave's staring at Chris as if he's gone mad, and there's three of us in this car who want the rollercoaster ride to end, wishing someone would pull the plug. You get a smoother ride on the bumper cars, the smash-and-grab of the dodgems, but there's no telling Chris. He's been taken over by the excitement, turns the music up and slows the car down, the ride easier as we come off the flyover and glide along at street level, stopping and starting for the red lights, Baker Street tube on our left, buildings rising up on both sides, huge marble palaces fresh from a Michael Caine film, James Bond in a wood-panelled office testing a rubber johnny on Moneypenny, seeing if the poison works. We keep going, see Capital Radio, take the piss.

– In tune with nothing, Smiles says.

There's a sign pointing to Camden Town and we turn left before an underpass, race past greasy walls and dusty streets full of old codgers and Jack the Ripper loonies, a high-rise estate and Mornington Crescent tube, turn down a side street. Chris parks and we get out quick, leave the car and walk off, heads down. On the main road we're in the clear, well pleased with ourselves now, slow down, a meths drinker stepping out of a bookies doorway swinging a bottle, yelling at us, hair thick and twisted, same as a Rastaman. Her eyes are bleary and the skin on her face is peeling back, feet wrapped in newspapers, tied together with string. We dodge past her and keep going, don't look back, heads down again, and you don't get that in Slough, where people know each other, more local than this place, pass a pie-and-mash shop that cheers us up again, joking about chirpy cockneys and jellied eels, rhyming slang and cockles and mussels, alive alive-o, an Indian restaurant belching out curry powder, the dark cut glass of an Irish pub, the sound of banjos and fiddles inside.

– This is where you get the IRA pubs, Dave says. Here and in Kilburn. The Paddies come round collecting for the bombers and you have to put money in or you get your head kicked in.

– Fuck that, Chris says, gobbing on the pavement right outside the front door. You'd think someone would go and smash the place up. It's our fucking country. Scum going round bombing people.

There's some good pubs up here, big boozers that have been going for hundreds of years. The history is there in the wallpaper, the carved ceilings, the old stone and wooden bars. They're the best thing about London. After the music. The tube's opposite now, with its criss-crossing traffic and a mob of tramps standing around outside the entrance, tapping people for change. There must be twenty of them, men and women. They sound Irish, Scottish, Northern, smell the same as a jumble sale. We keep going towards the canal bridge, more pubs along the road, over and round to our right, under the railway bridge.

You can't see in the Hawley Arms from outside, but we've been here before, squeeze into the packed bar.

— It's your round, Dave tells Smiles.

— It's always my round.

I go with Smiles and we worm our way to the bar, wait for him to get served, weighing up the crumpet. There's some good-looking girls in here, most of them seventeen and over, out of our price range but nice to look at and dream about, quite a few punk birds with leather jackets and spiky hair, jet black or peroxide, but mostly it's everyday people, specially the blokes.

— How old are you? the barmaid asks, and Smiles puffs up, stands on his toes and drops his voice.

— Eighteen.

— You sure?

Smiles nods and she serves him four light and bitters, fills each pint past the halfway mark, being generous after showing him up. It's bad news being asked your age like that, and I feel sorry for Smiles. She didn't need to do it really. Nobody heard, the pub noisy and people with better things to do, but sometimes you think the whole world's looking at you. There must be a lot of under-age kids in here.

— Fucking slag, Smiles says, when we get back to Dave and Chris.

We stand by the wall and sip our drinks, served in straight glasses that feel funny, like they're going to slip out of your hand. I drink quick, so I can empty and dump the light-ale bottle. There's a couple of old boys in front of us, standing next to three girls in bondage trousers, sipping their bitter, don't know what's hit them. I wouldn't say no if the girls were offering, but they're the sort who probably go shopping down the King's Road, and they're older as well. We've got no chance. You've got to have money to dress like that. I've never been to the King's Road. It's funny how the papers go on about the clothes all the time, because nobody I know dresses in plastic trousers. We're not complaining. It's a good job these sort of girls are around. There's enough talent in here for five years of non-stop wanking.

— Look at the state of that, Dave roars.

The perfect woman squeezes past in the crush of bodies, more and more people jamming in the pub. She's about twenty, with peroxide hair, black fishnet stockings and a rubber miniskirt. Her top is red and black, her tits rock solid. She's wearing thin black gloves and a stud in her nose. Her eyes are painted black, same as a badger, and her lips are bright red. She's got high cheekbones, a pretty face, but I can see she's tough as well. She's not cocky, play-acting or anything. She's one hundred per cent, the sort of girl you dream about meeting. She disappears into the Ladies.

— Un-fucking-believable, Dave says.

The girl sticks in my head, and I keep looking down the pub to try and see her again, music thumping out, all the best songs, but we're more interested in the girls, from inner and outer London, out to the new towns, a bumpkin accent and something that sounds Scottish passing us. Doesn't matter where you come from, it's what you are, how you think. I reckon that's important, and punk does well in the charts when it's not really chart music, dips into every corner of the country.

— Look at the arse on that, Dave says.

We follow another girl with our eyes, this one with jet-black hair and a motorbike jacket. Proper leather by the looks of it, not your cheap copycat gear. Can't see us getting up to the bar for a while. Don't see how anyone else can squeeze in, but one bloke does, carrying a football bag, selling fanzines I think. That's another thing you get in London that you can't find in Slough. If you want donkey porn, no problem, you can have pigs, chickens and goats thrown in as well, a long line of women getting their faces creamed in a Devon farmyard, but try finding *Sniffin' Glue*.

— Anyone interested in badges?

— What have you got? Smiles asks, trying to look in the bag.

— The lot, and the bloke wedges it on the shelf behind us.

Smiles forks out for GOD SAVE THE QUEEN. Wouldn't mind one myself, but we're wedged up against the wall, and I can't get a look-in. The badge-seller is feeling the pressure. Smiles pays and he moves on.

— Put it on then, Chris shouts over the din.

Smiles does as he's told. It looks alright. I should've bought one.

– Not bad, Chris admits, leaning over.

It almost shines in the dim light. Same as the peroxide hair of the most beautiful woman in the world who's coming back down the pub, easing herself through the press of bodies, classy in the way she moves, in control. She passes us, the others concentrating on the badge as I watch her go. She gets lost at the other end of the pub, before the table football where a mob of older boys is playing, tipping the table up, Mott The Hoople's 'All The Young Dudes' slipping out of the speakers. I wash the drink around my mouth. It's going to be a good night.

– That's Tony's mate over there, isn't it? Dave asks Smiles.

We look where he's pointing and it's Billy, from Tony's car the other day. He recognises Smiles and Chris, maybe me, I'm not sure, stops with this half-caste mate of his and says a few words to Chris, who he seems to think is in charge for some reason, maybe because he's taller or something. Chris laughs. They stand close together, something passing between them, and I realise that's where he gets the speed. Billy turns back and nods to Smiles, on his way towards the table football. He looks at me and clicks.

– Alright mate. You still picking cherries for a living?

He seems to think this is funny.

– Couldn't knock us out some special rate, could you?

He laughs again.

– You won't get rich doing work like that.

They leave and we huddle round Chris.

– This is for later on, he says. You'll have to chip in. I only got a bit. It's cheap, but not that cheap.

Never mind the speed, someone has to get in at the bar, people four-deep waiting to get served.

It's nearly nine when we leave the pub, gobbing at each other as we cross the road under the bridge, taking the piss, six light and bitters setting us up nicely, snapping our hands as we go, clicking the fingers, Dave cracking away loudest of all, Billy and Leon walking behind well impressed, tell Dave he should be on a stage, must be double-jointed, and the road follows the curve of a massive brick wall and Billy and Leon go up some steps into this big building called the Roundhouse while we follow Chris into this takeaway that has a cone of meat hanging in the window, Chef's Brother standing behind the counter with a sword in his hand, a long thin skewer with a razor-sharp edge, and Chris is hungry as usual, starving, orders a large doner kebab, whatever that is, Chef's Brother slicing slivers of meat off the cone and sticking it in this doughy bread, adding cabbage and slices of onion, asks Chris if he wants chilli sauce, and Chris loves his food, dining out in style, exotic new dishes in exotic new places, pleased with his driving, Slough to Camden in thirty-five minutes, says why not, asks for more, another helping on top of that, and Chef's Brother looks at him funny, says the chilli is hot, very spicy my friend, and Chris says no problem, and he's feeling good, doing his hard man routine as Chef's Brother adds a healthy spoonful of pink mush to the meat and veg, and as we leave I see a map of Cyprus on the wall, next to it a poster showing some ruins, TURKEY written in red letters, so Chef is no brother of Chef after all, he's the man on the other side, the enemy, the man on the other side of the counter sharpening his blade, and back in Slough our Chef is in his van with a pickaxe handle, and I wonder if the stories are true, the chopping and hacking, it doesn't make sense to me, and we stand on the pavement arguing whether we're going in the Roundhouse, Dave's realised we're going to have to pay, and we could always go back to the pub and listen to the jukebox for nothing, but Smiles is keen, says it must be a proper punk club looking at the people going up the steps, and Dave's eyeing the girls, reckons it's worth a go as well, and anyway, everyone was leaving the pub to come here, what's the point coming to Camden if we're going to stand around in an empty pub, we could do that at home, and all the time Chris is biting into the kebab, munching away, the first kebab any of us has ever had, never seen one before to be honest, and he says it's tasty, shovelling it down, almost finished when his brain catches up with his teeth and he goes quiet, says his mouth is on fire, passes the rest of the kebab to Dave who has a sniff and lobs it down the road where it splits open and splashes cabbage across the pavement, and it looks like we're going in, looking for music, looking for girls, looking for a sink filled with cold water for the tall skinny boy who's always eating, Chris suffering now, hands stuck over his mouth, eyes scared, face covered in sweat, and once we're inside he goes looking for the bogs while we suss out the bar, buy four pints of cider in plastic glasses, stand together sizing the place up, and I reckon it was well worth the money for the music alone, never mind the girls, because there's this reggae shaking the ground under our feet, one or two kids dancing with their arms stretched out, as if they're ready for take-off, gliding along the Westway, and it doesn't take long for us to work out that there's a band playing soon, people facing an empty stage, and even though I'm into lyrics, words that tell a story, it doesn't matter with this reggae, it's pure sound, gets inside my head, everything slowing down, giving me time to think, and we get a bit of reggae at home but this is different, can't explain it, and because there's no words it's easier to get into, we're satellite white boys not inner-city dreads, the Rasta lyrics don't have anything to do with us, and against the speed and anger of punk this balances things, suppose you can't keep racing along all the time, have to stop and have a breather now and then, slow your thinking down, but it's hard sometimes, sorting out everything floating around your brain, making decisions, deciding what you believe in, Billy and Leon standing nearby sipping their drinks, and Smiles starts slagging them off in my ear, says Billy's a headcase, but he seems fine to me, doesn't have to be friendly with us younger lads, a lot of older boys won't bother if you're a year or two behind, and even though he takes the piss it doesn't mean anything, it's a way of being friendly without acting poofy like a smelly hippy, and Smiles isn't his usual self, not surprising with a baby on the way, noses to clean, nappies to change, bums to wipe, Chris coming back with wet hair and taking the cider I've been holding for him, says he's burning up, the sauce has done his guts in, says he's got the runs, shitting piss, maybe the meat was rotten and he's been poisoned, he lifts the cider to his mouth and drinks half in one go, throat swelling as it pours down, Dave says Chris is looking thinner than usual, starts taking the piss, and I tell Dave to fuck off, it's obvious Chris is suffering, and Dave has a go back, can't be bothered with him sometimes, Chris brings the cider back up to his mouth and finishes it off, drops the plastic on the ground where Dave breaks it with his foot, and Chris smiles, frowns, turns, legs it back to the bogs as the lights dim and people start cheering and moving towards the stage, and none of us has a clue who's come out and started with the guitars and drums, a surge forward same as on the terraces except there's some girls and there isn't the same edge, a different sort of excitement, and we're a bit higher up and can see the crowd moving, a V-shape coming through from the back, a thirty-strong football crew doing a boat impression right into the middle of the dance floor, and Dave reckons they've got to be Arsenal, seeing as this is Camden Town, and he might be right, but it could be anyone, and there's a good buzz, and the band's okay, but I don't know the words and make do with the atmosphere, and because the dance floor is flat and we're on a wooden terrace we can watch the crowd moving, on the edge looking in, and there's some gobbing, but not much, not like they say in the papers, and this is a real-life proper punk gig here, the first one we've ever been to, and it's by chance, a lucky dip, read the papers and you'd think it was all fashion dolls, but it's not, it's mostly everyday people same as us, and that's what makes it for me, it's not like we're in a hall full of long-haired students listening to Genesis and Pink Floyd, cross-legged on the floor smoking ganja, and a gap opens in the crowd, at first it looks like a punch-up, someone down on the ground, but instead of the boot going in the mob stops being a mob and backs up so the bloke who's landed on his arse can get up before he's trampled to death, and I sip the cider, rinsing my teeth and gums, wonder if Chris is alright, not much we can do for him, probably wants to be alone if he's on the bog, and the songs bang out one after the other, and the band aren't heroes or anything, that's a load of shit, our heroes are the bigger kids down the pub and fairground, local lads with a reputation, and on a bigger scale it's the names at football, those are a boy's heroes, how can someone in a band be a hero, the stage somewhere to face, and I suppose that's why there's some gob flying, putting them in their place, and whenever you see a picture of one of these cock rockers with long hair and leathers you piss yourself because they're all weedy-looking wankers acting hard for a camera, and the new bands are different to that, they dress up but take the piss, so we let them off, maybe some people take themselves seriously, think they're something special, and if they do then they're wankers same as the cock rockers, and really, the secret is not to have any heroes at all, to do your own thing and go your own way, otherwise you'll end up doing things you don't want to do, just so you won't get left out, and more of the crowd are moving with the music so people surge back into us, and three girls end up between me and the others, and the first one I look at is a chubby bird with a dog collar, five earrings through her ear, I count them, one-two-three-four-five, behind her a small girl with smeared lipstick and eyes that have been pecked out by crows, or if not they're buried in her skull somewhere, fuck knows, and when the other one turns and smiles at me I almost spunk up in my pants, Gran was right, there is a God, and this is heaven right here, the beauty queen from the pub standing next to me, with her peroxide hair and red lipstick, her arm brushing me, and she's even better close up, easy on her feet, no body to pull me away from the shape of her head, the bone under clear skin, she doesn't have acne or anything, and the light just nicks the tips of her eyelashes, the same black make-up's in there as well, and I start thinking about the smile and remember walking down the canal and how you have to understand who you are, what's possible and what's not, otherwise you'll make a fool of yourself, you have to know your limits but not give up, and this girl is older and wiser and I'm just a kid trying to get by while she's working and living in the grown-up world, and when she smiles a second time I smile back to be polite, wish I was a few years older, better-looking, and I stay here till the end, look at the girl's ears and neck, each hair standing out, least at the front where the light hits, waxed or something, I don't know, and before the end she turns and I see into her eyes and know she's the best-looking girl I've ever seen, feel bad that after tonight I'll never see her again, maybe this is what they call love at first sight, and punk is good because it blows away the sadness, gets on with things, goes straight in on a search-and-destroy mission, you'll never hear a punk love song, you can't sit around moaning, feeling sorry for yourself, have to get lost in the speed and anger, and this is one of the best days of my life, I want it to go on for ever, know it's never going to get any better than this, just hope the feeling stays, and when the band goes off the girls leave, I watch them fade into the crowd, and we go to the bar, Smiles thinking ahead and in already, passes the drink back, and I'm hot so it slips down, the reggae back again, calming things, the smell of sweat taking over from the smoke and drink, Chris nowhere to be seen, and we're wondering if one of us should go looking for him, I keep my eyes peeled, watching out for the beauty queen, Dave more pissed than me and Smiles, telling us not to worry about Chris, fuck him, there's nothing we can do about Chris, nothing we can do as Dave leans over to one of the two girls behind us and says something, and she smiles, listens so it looks like he's in, till she lifts her pint and tips it over his head, and me and Smiles crease up seeing Dave soaked and looking like a rat, wonder what he said, even he starts smiling, the girls walk off, Chris coming over eyes wide open, he's seen Dave get embarrassed and has enough strength to knuckle the back of the boy's head and call him a cunT, all of us laughing, and the three of them are shoulder to shoulder in front of me with this space music booming in the speakers, and I have to admit that we're a bunch of tossers, young and broke and without a decent chat-up line between us, wanking our lives away, miles away from the action, no fucking chance, we're useless, but at least we're making the most of things, know how to laugh, and maybe that's what it's going to be about for us, the failures of life, and at least we don't take ourselves too seriously, Chris polishing off his drink in one go, says he's going home, he's sick, been on the bog shitting his life away, he can't hang around, and Smiles says he'll go back with him, doesn't want to risk getting in after midnight, his old man will do his nut, he's in one of his moods, as per fucking usual, and it'll take them time to get down to Paddington, unless Chris nicks another car, and me and Dave decide to stay a bit longer, Smiles hurrying after Chris who's already on his way.

Billy pushes through the winos outside Camden tube and we follow him down the escalator, Leon holding the doors as we jump on a train to Leicester Square, the carriage packed. This is the first time me and Dave have been to Leicester Square, and Billy says there's loads of cheap Chinese restaurants there, and we're going to get something to eat, have a look around, then get over to Paddington. We've heard of Leicester Square, we're not farmers. We pay last stop and follow the older boys, and even though it's after eleven the streets are busy. When Dave sees an alley he goes and takes his T-shirt off, twists it like Mum does, tries to get it dry.

– Come on Dave, you're alright, Billy says.

His Martens are a couple of sizes bigger than mine and worn in, the sort of boots that get used on a regular basis. Tony goes up the North Stand, and knows Billy and Leon because they drink in the same pub, the Britannia. They live somewhere in London.

– How much money do you make a day picking cherries? I tell him.

– Not much is it, for all that work.

It's alright.

– There's money around, you've just got to know how to get hold of it. There's people around who spend what you earn in a year on a meal in a restaurant.

Grand buildings tower over us, human faces and crests carved into the red stone, day trippers crowding the tourists, the smell of boiled rice drifting down the alleyway. There's food everywhere, different smells mingling together, and you don't get this at home. We've got our chippies, the hot-dog van, a Chinese takeaway, an Indian. There's all these cinemas big as a multi-storey, and I realise what really makes London different. It's not even the age of the buildings, most stuff in Slough new, no, it's the height. At home everything spreads out, the town low-lying so you can see the sky and feel the cold blowing through, while here the concrete rises up and closes out the light. If you were stuck on top of a big wheel here you'd be still staring up at the rooftops. I'm looking forward to the Chinky they've been talking about.

– Let's go down here, Billy says, gobbing at a couple of scruffy students coming the other way.

– Fucking wankers.

He leads us off the main square towards an amusement

arcade. Leon gives us some coins and tells us to go and play one of the machines, and suddenly they're treating us like kids. We ask why, what happened to the food, but they tell us to go on, it's part of a plan they've got to make some cash, then we can order the works, get some king prawns in batter. We're playing for five minutes when these two blokes come over. They act poofy and talk funny, and I'm looking for Billy and Leon, see them at the end of the row making signs at us with their hands. The men give me the creeps, ask us where we live and do we fancy something to eat. We soon get fed up with this and are about to tell them to fuck off and leave us alone when Billy strolls up. He chats to the two men, one of them resting his arm on Billy's shoulder. He tenses, but the bender doesn't seem to notice, his bum chum smiling at Dave. Billy steps sideways with the poofs, and I tell Dave we should leave. We're missing something here. He looks worried. Thing is, we don't really know where we are, down this side street somewhere. The two men piss off and it looks like we're alright.

— Come on, boys, we're going over to Kensington, Billy says, an edge to his voice.

I ask why we're going there and he says to get some money. I ask him how we're going to do this.

— How do you fucking think? You thick or something?

— Leave it out, Billy, Leon says, turning to me. Look, those two blokes are bent, right, and they're loaded. Nothing bad is going to happen to you. We go round their place for a chat, maybe have a drink, and then they give us some money. It's simple. They're rich and we're not. We talk to them and they give us some pocket money. Did you see the cuff links the tall one was wearing? They must've been worth twenty quid on their own. That's how it works, boys. We all live happy ever after and have the biggest Chinese you've ever seen.

It seems easy, but doesn't make much sense. Don't want to get back too late either.

— Kensington is right by Paddington, Billy says. It's on the way home.

We won't have a Chinese then.

— Look, there's nothing to it, Leon says. Nothing bad is going to happen to you. It's just for a little chat. Poofs get lonely on their own.

Billy laughs. He's got a strange look in his eyes. Maybe Smiles was right after all. It's doing my brain in thinking about all this.

– You get ten pounds each up front, and you don't have to stay more than half an hour. You've only got to talk to them. Come on, lads, there's nothing to it, nothing at all. You'll get another tenner after we've had a drink, if everything goes well.

Twenty pounds is a lot of money. I could buy eight or nine albums with that, and records aren't cheap. Billy hands us a tenner each, and Leon waves down a taxi. We travel in style, a proper black cab with leather seats. We pass through streets lined with big white buildings trimmed by black railings, finally stop outside a red block. Billy presses the buzzer and talks to the wall. I have to say hello before the door is unlocked automatically. There's carpet in the hall, and a vase with roses. We get in the lift and whizz right up. Leon is quiet and thoughtful, Billy tapping his DMs on the steel wall. The lift stops and one of the bum boys is standing at the end of a corridor, next to an open door. We go inside and the tall bloke is sitting on a couch. There's some music playing quietly. They're old and boring, don't know what we're going to talk about, but it's true what Leon says, they've got money alright. The flat is plush and looks like it goes on for ever. I think of the peroxide girl from earlier on. Shame this isn't her place. I imagine her inviting me back.

– Would you like a drink? one of the benders asks.

I ask for a can of lager and he laughs.

– Bit young to be drinking aren't you, he smiles. How old are you?

I say eighteen and he frowns. Billy says we're fifteen, that we just want the lager, think we're in a pub and have to lie to get served. The bender gives me and Dave a can each. It's warm and tastes like shit, but I don't say anything. We sit on two chairs sipping the drink, while Leon talks to the man on the couch. I don't listen to what they're saying. Ten quid for sitting around is easy money. I was getting £4.95 for a full day stacking shelves and I'm lucky if I make three pounds picking cherries. These blokes don't do much, just sit around. One starts smiling at me, staring, and he's getting on my nerves. Don't know what we're doing here. Dave isn't saying much, looks clumsy, same as how I feel. Maybe something's going on we haven't twigged. Me and Dave might argue, but we stick together. We're mates.

– Go have a word with Reg, will you, Billy says, in this new polite voice. Over there in the corner, by the table.

I shrug my shoulders and go over to the man sitting at the edge of the room. We should be off soon. I'm trying to think of something to say to the poof, but he's not going to be interested in the same things as me. With him it's probably art galleries and theatre plays, while I prefer watching telly and listening to punk records. It's a big place, lamps everywhere, paintings on the walls. I'm almost up to the bloke when I see he's got his knob out and is having a wank. I stop, stuck to the floor, and he stands up, grabs me and pulls me forward. I shout at him to fuck off and leave me alone.

– What's the matter with him, I hear the other poof say, from over on the couch next to Leon, anger in his voice that wasn't there before.

The man has me by the arms. He grabs at my bollocks. I try and get away, but he's strong.

– Don't be shy, young man. I'm going to fuck you up the arse and you'll love it. That's what all you young boys want.

I draw my head back and nut him right in the middle of his nose. There's a crack and his conk explodes, same as Butler's head the other week in the bus station. His hands go up to his face and I move back, ready to boot him in the balls, but new hands grab my arms from behind. I hear Dave shouting to leave me alone. Billy has me in an iron grip and for a second I can't move. He lifts me out of the way and steps forward. He kicks the queer hard as he can in the nuts. The hands that were holding a bloody nose shoot down to a pair of cracked bollocks. Billy picks his spot and kicks the man in the face, planting his steel toecaps into the nose I've already splattered. I can see the mark, a cut right into the bone. I feel sick, but more from being touched than seeing the queer get a kicking. Fucking cunt.

– You dirty fucking cunt, Billy screams. You sick fucking nonce. They're only kids and you want to bum them.

My head has gone and I stagger back. My whole body is

shaking and I stand against the wall. I look at the other man and Leon is doing a number on him. He's down on the carpet and Leon is putting the boot in, kicking him in the head and body. The poof in front of me is busy pissing blood and trying to protect himself, but Billy doesn't give him a chance. He punches the face and smashes the skull into a concrete column. Blood specks the wall. When Billy finally lets him fall, he really gets stuck in, kicking the head around till he's worn out and can't kick any more. When he's finished, he unzips his flies and takes his knob out, pisses on the silent poof, blowing the blood off the side of his face.

– Fucking scum. They deserve everything they get, trying to fuck little boys up the dirt box. They think they own the fucking world, can do anything they want because they've got the money.

Billy is calmer now and zips up. Maybe that's what benders do, stick their knobs up you. Debbie said something about a friend of hers doing it up the bum once, but I never thought about it really. Doesn't make sense. That must be why they call them bum boys. Billy looks at me and sees I don't understand.

– You must be slow in the head, he says, laughing, but not in a bad way. That queer wanted to stick his knob up you. That's what they do. Get hold of children and have their way. They're fucking sick. Come on, it's time for some wealth distribution.

I sit down on a chair and look at the bodies on the carpet. Billy and Leon are in control, moving through the flat. They know what they're doing, find a couple of suitcases and start loading them with valuables. They empty the men's wallets and give me and Dave another twenty quid each. That makes thirty. I put it in my pocket. It's brilliant money, the most I've ever had, but I feel ill, lean forward and puke on the carpet. I think about cleaning it up, but realise it doesn't matter. Dave stands next to me. We wait for Billy and Leon to finish.

– This is called queer-rolling, Billy says, from a bedroom. Turning the dirty bastards over in their own homes. The poor fuckers you do for fun, in a bog, but it's better coming up here because you don't only have a laugh, you can make a few bob as well.

I watch him going through a chest of drawers, transferring things to the bag. Leon is in another room and whistles.

– We've hit gold, Billy boy, he shouts. There's rings and all sorts in here. One of them looks like a diamond.

– Some blokes hang around the Gents and they get bashed in there, Billy continues. That's queer-bashing as well. Then there's Paki-bashing, but that's a mug's game. Pakis hate queers as much as us, and they've got no money. Other poofs, scum like this, bring boys home. They're the mugs, because good boys like us pile right in and take over. We teach the nonces a lesson. We're doing nothing wrong, just upholding the law. You two are under-age, and they know it. They can't go to the old bill or they'll get done for molesting children. The other prisoners will kick their teeth in and then the screws will have a go as well.

Four suitcases sit on the floor, stuffed full.

– Shame about the hi-fi, Billy says. Must be worth a bit.

– Can't be helped, Leon laughs, unless you fancy carrying it down the road balanced on your head. We've done well. Come on. Let's get out of here.

Dave walks over and kicks the bloke who grabbed me in the head. Billy laughs and Leon looks at his watch, cool under pressure. We leave the flat and Leon pulls out a ring once the lift starts moving. We stare at it, wonder how much it's worth, if it really is a diamond, till the doors open and he stuffs it back in his pocket. Billy and Leon are quiet, loaded down with the bags. When we get outside, they tell us to go home. It's important we split up, and before we have a chance to say anything, ask where we are or what about a better share of the takings, they're in the back of a cab and off down the road. We're left standing on a corner like a couple of lemons.

– Bloody hell, Dave says. What do we do now?

Those two men could be dead for all we know. There's a bus coming and we run for the stop. It pulls over and waits, and we jump on. The conductor moans when I hand him a tenner, but says not to worry, we can ride for free. It's the last bus of the night and he's already bagged up. We press our faces against the windows and watch the streets, looking for somewhere with a name we recognise. When we spot Earls Court tube we jump off. All we've got to do now is wait till morning. The trains will start running in four or five hours, and Earls Court has places that are still open. At home the streets are dead by midnight, but here it could still be eight or nine.

– What a night, Dave says at last, when we're sitting in a cafe, run by these Arabs who serve us coffee and sweet cakes with nuts on top.

– I've never seen anything like that. I thought they were going to kill them. Billy and Leon went mental.

Maybe they did kill them.

– I fucking hope not. I don't want to end up in borstal for the rest of my life. How did you feel? I was bricking it in there. When you went over and he had his knob out, I couldn't fucking believe it.

I tell him I never thought about queers, what they did. I didn't know they stuck their knobs up each other.

– I thought they just talked funny, Dave says. Least men don't have to do that to women.

I think of what Debbie said. Funny how you don't know these things. I wonder why they go after kids. They were old enough to be our dads. That was a heavy-duty kicking Billy and Leon dished out. They got what they deserved, but Billy and Leon are wankers using us like that, pretending to be our mates when all they wanted was a way into the flat. Shows you have to watch yourself, that looking up to people because they're older is a mug's game. Least we're safe here. I start thinking about the bags they filled, and there must've been hundreds of pounds' worth of watches, clocks, cuff links, ornaments. Plus cash as well. Thousands even. We made thirty quid each, and that's good money, but they got a lot more. They took the piss out of us. Even if we'd earned a hundred quid, it wasn't worth all that.

– We'll keep away if we ever see them out, Dave says. Least Billy and Leon don't live near us. That's something. We'll know next time.

We sip our coffee and watch the people come in and out. Nobody bothers us, and the man running the place doesn't tell us to order another drink or get out, like that miserable cow in the bus station.

– We won't tell anyone what happened, Dave says. Not that we did anything wrong, but people will only take the piss. It wasn't our fault.

We have two more cups of coffee to keep ourselves awake, strong dark mud that rockets my head into space. We have a roll each at about five, talking for a while, repeating ourselves a lot, running through the night, what happened, shaking our heads with Camden in the past, feeling stupid, seeing the last hour out in silence.

It's gone seven by the time we get back to Uxbridge, tired cleaners and tube workers dozing on the seats around us as we roll along. After a long wait at Raynor's Lane, the bigger Baker Street service chugs along, past the semi-detached houses of Eastcote and Ruislip, long gardens reaching down to the track, paint flaking. Wouldn't mind a place like that one day. We should've gone to Paddington, but it meant hanging around for another half-hour and we wanted to get moving. There's no one on the gate at Uxbridge and we walk over to Woolies where the bus leaves for Slough. A 207 to Shepherd's Bush revs its engine at the top of the stairs, choking us with fumes. The timetable says we've got twenty minutes till our bus leaves, so we duck in the cafe built into the side of the station, splash out on a full breakfast. We eat fast, get back to the stop with time to spare. The same bloke who sells me a ticket in Slough is standing on the pavement, having a fag before the return journey. I don't see the driver, who's still in his cab, raring to go.

Up on the top deck, Dave takes out his felt pen and covers the back of the seat in front, the smell lingering, the usual stuff – ELVIS IS A WANKER, TEDS RUN FROM PUNKS and NEVER TRUST A HIPPY. He thinks for a minute, brain ticking, brings things up to date with CHRIS IS A SHITTER and POOFS ARE SCUM. I catch this bus most days, and the conductor's bound to notice, but I keep quiet, don't want to set Dave off. It'll only make him worse, and he'll do the other seats as well. He doesn't have to use this bus every day. He can't think of anything else to write and puts his pen away. Dave was there with me last night, when everything went wrong, and he kicked that bloke in the head like he wanted to kill him. We're always winding each other up, but he's a good mate. Still gets on my nerves, and he shouldn't do the seats like that, but there you go.

People hurry down the alley next to the DHSS, men and women with their heads down, the bus half full by the time we leave. We turn past the White Horse and down along the high street, the driver ignoring a boy running to the next stop, speeding up even though the kid gets there just in time and sticks his hand out. We turn left at the Odeon, go past the multi-storey and the Mahjacks roundabout, off past the Prince of Wales, Rockingham Arms, Dolphin, General Elliott, Pipe-makers. The conductor does our tickets in silence, stops at the top of the stairs to run a steel comb through his DA. I see his face in the mirror, and he's narked. He's seen the graffiti but kept quiet. Suppose we're growing up. The bus struggles along the hill to Iver Heath, axle rattling as we pass the Black Horse and another Prince of Wales. Must've been a proper pisshead, that prince. I ask Dave if he wants to come and pick some fruit, do a decent day's work for a change, instead of dossing in the precinct with the meths drinkers.

– Fuck off, cunT, he grins. I'm going home to bed. Have a good wank over one of those birds from last night and sleep till teatime. I've just earnt thirty quid, so what's a pound or two extra? Why bother? Come on you div, it's not worth the effort.

I tell him he's a layabout and get off the bus. Dave's at the back and opens the window, stands on tiptoe and turns his head sideways so he can gob at me, back to his old ways. His spit gets caught in the churn of air as the bus pulls away, hangs for a second, then flashes straight back in his face. I wave and carry on down the lane clicking my hand, snapping the fingers, and it's in the wrist action, just wish I could make more noise.

This is another world from Leicester Square and Camden Town, with the hedges and mesh fence, the chirp of a robin. I think of that bender last night and blank the picture of Billy trying to crack his skull open. That was some serious aggro and I don't want to think about it too much, concentrate on the trees that make a tunnel as they loop over the road, and when I get to the farm it's already busy. It's nearly eight now, and I don't normally get in till after nine. I go over to the shed and pick up two boxes, the woman there giving me a funny look, shoot off before she starts in.

I walk to the back of the orchard where it's easy to hide. There's a place at the end of the fence where the grass is long and seeding, a good place to doss. I'm knackered, plan to lay down for a bit, fill some boxes and get off home. If I take a bag of cherries back it'll sweeten Mum up. She loves cherries. Dad isn't bothered, hates fruit and leaves her to tell us off. She's handy as well. And I lay down and look at the sky, make shapes out of the clouds as they float along, imagine them as mountains, then cars, Ford Cortinas and Aston Martins. Winter goes on for most of the year so you have to make the most of the summer while you can, and I hope I don't end up stuck indoors all my life, when I leave school, working nine-to-five, under control. I'm not stupid, know that things are going to change when I leave, that I won't be able to come down here and do my own thing. Roy has got his life worked out, but I wouldn't want to be travelling around all the time.

It doesn't take long to close my eyes, just for a minute, then open them again and see that the sun is on the other side of the sky. I'm sweating and a bee's buzzing around my head, a great big one with fur. I leave it alone and it flies off looking for something more interesting. Don't know how long I've been asleep, but a lot has happened.

I've been back to a smart flat with the most beautiful girl in the world, sat with her through the night, happy in her front room drinking mugs of coffee, eating these cakes with nuts on the top. We're waiting for the sun to come up but the night goes on and on, and it's winter outside, the rain running across the windows. She has this expensive hi-fi system and shows me how to use it, has all these records I've never heard of, knows every word, tells me what the songs are about, and once she's told me everything I need to know, she puts on this other music that relaxes us both, lets the ideas float around in our heads. She moves in next to me listening as I tell her about my mum and dad, how Mum loves cherries and Dad loves watching the telly after he gets in from work, says he's worn out and wants to relax. She isn't bored, seems really interested, and for a second I think she's taking the piss, knows my life is boring, putting on a show, her hand going up to her mouth, amazed that the old man can watch so many programmes in one night, or that Mum can eat so many cherries, but she's really impressed, so I stand up in front of her and start clicking my hand, and the loudest cracks I've ever heard echo around the room, mingle with the music, sound effects that make her shiver and smile. She's dressed in fishnet stockings and a rubber skirt, with a red-and-black top, and she's kept her gloves on, but it's not about sex. She's interested in my mates, asks questions about Smiles's family, gets worried that Chris might die on the way home, that Dave will get done for a murder he never committed, says Dave is a good mate, one of the best. I lift one of my boots in the air, turn it on its side so she can see how well polished it is, her eyes shining, reflecting the outline of the DMs, and she says her hair is polished as well, peroxide wax instead of cherry red, and I know we were made for each other. She's tough, but melts when I slowly lift a trouser leg to show off my right boot, and she's counting as I go – one, two, three, four, five, six, seven, eight . . . nine, ten holes. She's well impressed, pulls me over so I'm sitting next to her on the couch again, presses her lips against mine, then sits back. She wants to know who's my best mate, and I tell her it's Smiles, who does she think. She asks me to follow her, and we go outside and look down into the street, see a police car pull up, the sun suddenly shining, four men in suits jumping out and looking up at me, smiling, slapping coshes into their palms, backed up by police with dogs. I move back and turn to the girl, but she's not there. I go inside and there's blood all over the walls, the smell of rotten meat and a skewer on the floor. Dave tells me to hurry up, we've got to get out quick, before we're caught and hung. I look around for the girl, but she's left with her mates. The buzzer goes and I brush a bee away, sit up in the grass and stretch, move my neck and go over to the boxes, start work.

I only do one box before I give up. I'm tired and can't get last night out of my head. I take the box over to the sheds, glad Roy's not around. I don't want to talk to anyone.

– What happened to you? the woman in the shed asks. You look like you've been up all night.

She's right.

– You're too young to be drinking and staying out.

I wasn't drinking.

– I can smell it on you. And look at this box. It's not even full.

She stares into me like she can see everything that's happened, and I say I'm off home. Ask her if she'll add the box on to tomorrow's list.

– Go on then.

The farmer's outside, shifting a trailer of horse shit, and I stand back to let his tractor pass, the wooden butt of the shotgun next to his leg. I follow the tractor, go through the apples, a man and woman hard at work, the woman holding the ladder and the man right at the top of the tree. There's a pile of bad apples next to the path, big holes where the maggots have got in and hollowed out the core, a sour smell of cooking fruit, same as when Chris nicked a home-brew kit and tried to make his own lager. Don't know how he got it out of the shop, but he's got the knack, even if he gets caught sometimes, and he added the yeast and that, then forgot about it for a couple of months. The bucket stank so much his mum went and opened the lid, and there was three inches of this cheesy fungus on top, with blue and green patches. He showed me before he got rid of it, proud of the pong. Out here, the apples boil down in the sun, mouldy white pimples dotting the brown mush. It's a rotten smell, but sweet as well as sour. You get some brilliant mushrooms in the shade, keeping out of the spotlight.

I climb over the fence and walk up to the main road, go along to the bus stop, looking over my shoulder.

Mum gives me a bit of stick when she gets in from work, but nothing like I expected, hopes I haven't been with any girls, makes me my tea early, Dad out, and it's good to be home with some proper food on my plate. She says she wants Dad to have a chat with me, about the birds and the bees, so I understand how babies are made and don't get caught out. I tell her I knew about all that stuff years ago and she seems surprised. I've forgotten the cherries, but don't need them. When I've finished eating I go round to see Chris, find out if he's alright. His mum lets me in and starts having a go, thinks we've been fighting, has one of her turns going on about how we'll end up in borstal if we're not careful, how do I think she feels having the police round the house accusing him of all sorts, she remembers when we were five and six years old, no trouble, no trouble at all. But she's getting upset about nothing. I tell her Chris had some bad food, that's all, and she wants to believe me but can't, doesn't want to be made a fool of, and I can understand that, specially after last night, and she's off again, knows it's drugs, thinks we're going round sniffing glue, and it's going to give us brain damage, look how thin her boy is, that's what drugs do to you, make people skinny and weak. She doesn't know what's going on these days, the whole world's gone mad. I tell her it isn't like that, Chris is fine, and it takes a while but she calms down, believes what I'm saying. We haven't been doing anything wrong, and it's true, the only thing that was our fault was the car, and I don't tell her this, just know it was wrong nicking off someone who's worked hard for what he's got. I feel guilty about that, but at least we didn't wreck it, and he should get it back soon enough. Chris's mum smiles and seems happy now, says she'll make us some tea. I go and sit with Chris out back, and he looks bad, like he's shrunk. He laughs when I tell him we're made mostly of water, and if he was shitting non-stop he better get some medicine or he'll disappear. He laughs, but says it wasn't funny, calls it the worst night of his life. The Gents was shut at Paddington and he couldn't hold it in any longer and had to go outside, behind a wall. These kids saw him and started throwing bottles. He says he'll never eat foreign food again, specially chilli sauce. He knows that's what did him in, not the meat, he's eaten worse than that, look at the tripe his mum makes, that's guts, bollocks, all sorts. Meat is good for you, no, it was that other stuff. He asks what happened after he left, and I say not a lot, ask if he's still got the speed, and he nods quickly as his mum brings me a mug of steaming tea, and she asks after Mum and Dad, says my sister's growing up fast, goes back indoors. I stay for an hour, then go round and see Smiles. His old man is working, and Tony lets me in. Smiles asks what happened last night, after they went home, and again I say not a lot, I'll have to make up a story with Dave, don't mention the queers. Can't believe any of that happened, just hope they didn't die. It's like a bad dream now. Smiles seems more cheerful than last night, and when I tell him there's another single from the Clash coming out soon he's even happier. We'll have to find out who was playing last night, the name of the venue, and when the Clash are in London we'll go see them. It was a good night, the first part, and he's wearing his new badge, even though he's at home. I stay for half an hour, start getting tired, go round Dave's and knock on the door, and when his mum opens up she tears into me, and I listen to it for a while trying to work out what she's on about, ask if I can see him or not. She calls me a dirty little bastard and tells me to piss off, she's not having my sort in her house, and she's got this mental look on her face, real hate. I can't be bothered with a mad old slag like that and head off home. A few minutes later Dave catches me up and says sorry about his mum, but he hadn't bothered thinking of an excuse when he got in, and since the coppers brought him home the other month, when he got caught thieving with Chris, she's been touchy. I don't see why she's having a go at me. He says no, it's not my fault. And he's got that look on his face. I've known him for years. I ask him what? What is it? He doesn't want to say, and I keep on at him, promise I won't get angry, and he checks my fingers to make sure they're not crossed, tells me to cross my heart and hope to die. And when Dave got in she was right on him, and it wasn't just because he didn't come home and she was worried, she'd only been making his bed and found the animal porn, and there was his mum standing in front of him holding out these photos of women sucking off donkeys and riding pigs. She rubbed them in his face. What was he supposed to say? I look at him, and he smiles, fights to cover it up. His head was spinning and he was knackered, had to think quick before she kicked him out of the house, he didn't want to spend the rest of his childhood sleeping rough, so it just came out of his mouth, how the magazines belong to me and he was looking after them, that he hadn't looked inside so didn't know what was in them, and the reason he was out all night was I went in a sex shop to get some more and we missed the train. He told her it was an accident I got animals in the first place, that I wanted some proper men-

and–women porn, and could only get the hard stuff in Soho. He tells me he's sorry, but it was the best he could come up with at the time. He couldn't have his mum thinking they belonged to him, could he? She's family after all, his own flesh and blood. I suppose not, but it's not nice. Dave smiles and says he owes me one. His face twitches and then he starts laughing his head off.

Kicking for kicks

THE WOMAN AT the next table asks a lot of questions and gets all the right answers, sipping a pint of Guinness as she talks to herself, frowning when she finds a hair in her drink. She's fifty if she's a day, but doesn't care about the creases, decked out in a polka-dot skirt that shows off her wrinkled legs and ironed panties. She turns and winks, holds a long red nail in front of her mouth and says she won't tell the barmaid we're too young to drink. When this Ted with a squashed Henry Cooper nose and thick brothel creepers strolls over, balancing a plate of food in each hand, her dentures flash and we're forgotten. She takes her tea and sniffs the pie and chips. She cuts into the pastry and smoke curls out, the smell of thawed steak and kidney filling the air. Her boyfriend slips in next to her and tips more pale ale into his mug. She's a stroppy cow, putting us in our place like that.

– I'll get another drink, Smiles says, counting his change. I've just got enough.

He goes to the bar, walking tall, that pub in Camden fresh in his head. Smiles is buying me a drink I can't get back, and it's like I'm poncing off him, but we've had six pints and need another. I'll sort him out next time. I've got money at home, didn't plan on coming down the club, that's all. Smiles has made his mind up about Linda. There's not much he can do really, except either help her or try and get out of it, and it's as much down to him as her. He's thought about it and reckons it's only the outsiders who are going to make things hard. They don't have to get married, live together or anything like that. It doesn't have to be the end of the world. He leans on the bar and waits for Stella to fill our glasses. She's in her twenties and pretty, everyone fancies her, but she's married with a baby so doesn't get the chat-up lines she deserves. People respect mums.

Normal people anyway. Don't see why it should matter if they're fifteen or twenty, single or married.

– Here you go, Smiles says, sitting down. I'm pissed. Didn't realise until I stood up. My head's spinning. Shouldn't have got so wound up about everything. It's going to be alright. Worse things happen in life. Look at Mum and what she did to herself. Nothing can ever be worse than killing yourself.

This is going to be our last drink, and we take our time, drinking a new lager, and it's alright, extra bubbles and very refreshing. Don't know how that woman can drink Guinness on a day like today. Don't know how she can drink it any time, even in winter. The club's quiet tonight, and last time I was in here Smiles was stuck indoors, Fisher and the Shannons kicking lumps out of each other down the road.

– What do you think's a good name for a boy? Smiles asks, going back to the baby. If it's a girl we could call it after my mum. It would be better having a girl, but don't suppose it matters. Whatever's going to happen will happen. There's nothing I can do to change things.

He rambles on for a while, repeating himself. Time will sort it out, and it's true what he's saying, but he's pissed and it could be the drink making him look on the bright side. I'm feeling the effects as well, trying hard to concentrate. After half an hour talking bollocks, we drink up and leave the old-timers snogging. The Ted's running his hand along the woman's legs, knickers out on show. It's a fucking disgrace. Makes me feel sick. It's horrible seeing grannies behaving the same as school kids. How they can call an old geezer like that a Teddy 'boy' I do not know. Least we have an excuse, can't handle our drink because we're young, allowed to make mistakes, but these two should know better. We head back, walking slowly, running through the lyrics of 'Anarchy In The UK', trying to work out what anarchy means. It takes us ages to reach the bridge over the canal, four shapes appearing out of thin air, spreading across the pavement. Gary Wells is at the front, a gold crucifix dangling from his left ear. Right away I know we're on for a kicking.

– You fucking wankers, he says, grabbing Smiles's collar and ripping the Sex Pistols badge off, punching Smiles hard in the face with the same fist.

– What's this then, boys? he asks, lifting the Queen's face up in the air, into the light coming off a street lamp, Smiles holding his nose, blood seeping through his fingers.

One of the others steps forward and thumps me in the face. I swing back but miss, too drunk to defend myself. All four of them jump in. We don't have a chance. They're bigger and older and better fighters, proper ruckers who love a knuckle same as we love music. We're halfway up the bridge and run forward, try to leg it, Smiles hitting the ground as Wells trips him over. I do my best to pull Smiles to his feet, but his head has gone floppy and next thing I'm on the floor as well, the kicks bouncing off me. I'm down for the count, brain spaced out, not feeling anything after the first few blows. The kicking goes on for a bit, then stops. Through the static I can hear laughing, Wells's voice the loudest, the only words I can make out.

– Come on then. One . . . two . . . three . . . four.

My arms and legs are being held out in the shape of a star and for a second I think of Jesus Christ nailed to the cross, but I'm not religious, never go to church, instead think of that exercise we do at school, and I'm moving back and forward, and on the fourth swing they let me go, and I hang in the air waiting for the pavement to smash into my back, but time freezes and I'm hovering, a real nutty feeling, and it's mental, my head and body floating, the clock stopped, and I don't know what's going on, doesn't make sense, drifting over the surface of the moon, between craters and rocks, my spine exploding as it finally hits the concrete, except the pain doesn't race into me, and I suppose one of the kicks has dented my brain, loosened the rockers, and I keep going, sink down into this gooey wet concrete, another set of roadworks railed off and signposted, dunce's caps and blinking bulbs, the non-stop pounding of drills cracking tarmac, tin hats searching for broken pipes and worn-out cable, laying foundations for a new row of houses, another terrace, more homes, more people, the concrete thin and slimy, sucking me down, ears popping as I keep sinking, down and down, the voice of Wells fading into the past.

– Fucking cunts.

It takes a few seconds to realise they've gone and chucked me off the bridge and into the canal, and it's funny at first, an easy way out, but I'm only glad till I try to breathe and the sludge comes flooding in through my nose. I open my mouth and half the canal chugs down my throat.

But there's no time to float around feeling sorry for myself because I have to sort this out right away, but don't know which way is up, there's no street lights or stars reaching into the slime, the canal full of rotten plants, face smothered in grease, back in my mum's belly knowing something has gone wrong, pressure in my head, like I'm going to die, and I spin around in the water trying to work out which way to pull, choking on the water, gagging on oil, my lungs heaving as they fill up, and realising there's no air starts me panicking, forces me to take a chance and dig into the water, stretching my arms out and pulling hard, forcing my head forward, bending my legs same as a frog, those primary-school lessons stuck in my brain, the canal full of long rubber arms that grab and pull me back, ropes curling around my legs, a noose round my neck, DMs heavy in the water, weighing me down, polished leather soaked, all that hard work pricing tins, don't want to end up drowned before I've lived my life, the water packed with drowned kids, dead babies, unborn lives, never had a chance, could've done anything, ears buzzing as the rope tightens, a rubber cord holding me back, thrashing around trying to escape, the end buried in my belly button. And I see a white dot in the distance, know that I'm swimming the right way, reaching out, finally blowing out of the water and sucking at the air, dipping back under, mouth open, swallowing more water, gagging, breathing, swimming to the side of the canal where I heave myself on to the bank, arms weak, coughing, spewing, boots full of water, clothes heavy, born all over again.

I lie on the ground and breathe deep, smell the grass and feel the warm air on my face. I look away from the gasworks and into the sky, see the stars billions of miles out in space, the darkness clean and fresh, a lot different to the canal, sucking into my throat to spit out the dirt inside me, spewing up all over the towpath. And it takes me a while before I think of Smiles and wonder why they didn't chuck him in as well, look up at the bridge. There's no one there, and a sharp pain shoots across my chest as I realise they threw him in as well. I stand up and look along the path, over the water. I call his name, but there's no answer. I try to undo my laces but they're stuck, so I jump in with my boots on, sink down and open my eyes, can't see a thing. I come up and swim around best I can, see a lump further along the canal, stuck in weeds. I swim over, panicking again, boots nailed to my feet, and Smiles is face down in the water, back arched, clothes slimy from rotten plants.

I turn Smiles over so his face is in the air, except there's no face, just a black outline, start pulling him towards the side of the canal. He's heavy, and I'm pissed, tired, fucked, can hardly keep us both up, water seeping into my mouth, dead brambles scratching my neck, and I get to the side, hanging on with one hand and trying to get him out with the other. I'm struggling, can feel myself getting weaker as two arms reach down from above and tug Smiles away. I look up and see the broken NHS specs of the Major, who spreads Smiles out on the ground and comes back for me, grabbing the back of my shirt and heaving me into the air.

– I've got someone phoning for an ambulance, he says.

The Major puts his ear to Smiles's face and starts giving him mouth-to-mouth, while I lean forward and cough up more water. The Major bangs Smiles's chest, where his heart should be, talks to himself, lowering an ear to Smiles's mouth several times, going through the routine, sits back and nods as Smiles starts puking.

– Thank fuck for that.

And I'm surprised to hear the Major swear.

He doesn't hang about either, bends down and lifts Smiles up, carries him as if he's a child, and I stumble after them, the pity I used to feel for the Major gone. I'm useless and he's in charge, my throat full of muck, the Major striding up the steps and back on to the bridge. He gently lays Smiles on the pavement and cradles his head in his hands.

– They deserve locking up, he says.

I sit down against the wall and stare at Smiles, his face bent and twisted, eyes shut, clothes black from the dirty water, dead leaves stuck all over. I look at the Major, clothes damp and glasses crooked on his nose. He's upset, I can see that, but he's saved Smiles's life and is in control.

– Where's the fucking ambulance, he says, jumping to his feet, but only after he's eased Smiles's head on to the pavement.

I see all his face now, and the Pistols badge is on his cheek. It takes me a few seconds to realise that Wells has bent the pin back and stabbed it in. I go over and pull it out, have to give it a tug. I put it in my pocket and search for the mark, but Smiles's face is too dirty. Can't believe they did that to him. Must be about an inch long as well. Stuck right in his gums, between his teeth maybe.

– If that man didn't dial 999 I'll be after him, the Major warns. I don't know if it's a criminal offence, but I'll nick him anyway. Every one of us has a duty to make sure justice is done.

I want to grin, but can't, the clang of an ambulance sounding in the distance, so I stand up instead, look down the road, and it's going to have a clear run, the bell getting louder, light flashing. At the same time a police car comes over the railway bridge, from the opposite direction.

– About time as well, the Major shouts. I don't call that an efficient response. Best not to say anything though. We're all doing our best. Pulling together against the criminal element, the mindless minority that threatens the fabric of society.

The car skids to a halt and two coppers jump out, white shirts and rolled-up sleeves. The ambulance passes on the other side of the railings, does a U-turn and comes back up the slope. Two more men run over.

– You the one who pulled him out, Michael? one of the coppers asks the Major.

Never knew his name was Michael. They know him, and seem friendly enough, don't treat him like a loony or anything.

– Alright, Michael? one of the ambulance men asks.

The police step back and the ambulance crew take over, peeling Smiles's eyelids back and using their radio, bringing a canister over and slipping a mask over his face. Next out is a stretcher, and they lift Smiles on, carry him to the ambulance.

– What happened, son? one of the coppers asks, the first time they've spoken to me.

I tell them some older boys threw us in the canal.

– Do you know who they were?

I say I don't. I'm not stupid. You don't grass people up.

– It was a youth called Gary Wells who led the attack, the Major says, taking charge. I recognised the other lads, but don't know their names. They attacked the younger boys, Joe Martin and Gary Dodds, punched and knocked them down, then kicked them while they were defenceless on the ground. They threw Martin in the canal, and tipped Dodds in afterwards. Wells was the ringleader, but the others are also responsible for their actions.

I wonder where the Major was standing.

– Thanks, Michael, the other copper says.

I tell them that the Major pulled Smiles out of the water. I wasn't strong enough to lift him up.

– Well done, Michael.

– I should've come down to the towpath right away. I didn't expect Dodds to stay under the water and walked to the top of the bridge to see them swim out. I didn't realise the boy was unconscious. The other lad got out, caught his breath, realised what had happened, and went back in. As soon as I saw Dodds face down I crossed the road and made my way along the path. I couldn't get there any sooner.

– You did well, says the same copper. It's not your fault. You're a hero. You both did your best.

They put Smiles in the ambulance, and I follow him.

– We'll be down in a bit to take a statement, says one of the policemen before I'm shut inside.

I sit in a corner of the ambulance as the two men work on Smiles, rubbing his skin and wrapping blankets around his body, one of them feeling his pulse. I just stare at his face and it's like I don't know him any more. All of a sudden he's this giant dummy, his body made of wax, the dirt in the canal smearing his clothes and face, all sorts of brown and green smudges. I look down at the floor, feel the scum inside me, millions of tiny green buds sticking to the walls of my lungs, slime in there mixing with the blood, oily canal water and too much lager. My fingers are red from where I was scratching at the bank, sharp rocks and brambles I suppose, ripe blackberry bushes. I suck my thumb. It's blood. And the ambulance is heavy with chemicals, the light bright, but still it stinks of death and decay, the men in here busy with Smiles, their faces serious. They check that the oxygen mask is still in place, the bell ringing as we race towards the hospital.

– What happened? one of them asks.

Just tell him we got beaten up and thrown in the water.

– Why did they do it?

I don't know what to say really, start choking and puke up over the floor. He reaches for another blanket.

– Put this around your shoulders, son. You'll be alright. You've swallowed water and it has to come back out. Don't worry if you make a mess. We'll mop it up easy enough. At least you're alive.

I wrap the blanket around me and he goes back to Smiles, who could be dead, the way he looks, but they'd have covered his head by now, same as in the films. He's going to die. I know Smiles is as good as dead, think about what the man said, why we got done like that, and it's just something that happens. I look through the glass and watch the road stretch out behind us, the gasworks the size of a toy now, canal buried away, out of sight. None of it seems real, the sound of the ambulance and the men in their uniforms, Smiles spewing, hair sticking up from the water, thick brown scum pumping out of his guts.

– Right, let's go, one of the nurses says when we reach Emergency. Follow us in. We'll take care of you. Your mate's going to be alright.

The next two weeks pass slowly. I catch the bus to work every day except Sunday, sit by the window wondering what's going to happen next, if Smiles is going to live or die, don't even bother looking in the windows for that blonde in the red stockings. When the bus turns on to the main road by the gasworks I make myself think about something else, don't look towards the canal. Smiles is in a coma. He never woke up when they got him to hospital. After the rush, seeing the nurses working on him in the ambulance, loading him on a trolley and running it deep into the building, swing doors slamming shut in my face, everything stops. The police come and ask me questions. A doctor takes me in a room and gives me an examination. Tony and his old man turn up, and I talk to them for a bit, tell them what happened, then the police give me a lift home. Smiles is the one in trouble. I'm lucky, the boy who got off, and until he lives or dies nobody really knows what to do.

I go back to the hospital next day, and Stalin sits me down and says the best way to get through the bad times is to keep busy, that's what he's found in life. He's been doing it for years, grabbing as much overtime as he can so he can blank out the nightmare of his wife cutting her wrists. The money comes in handy, of course it does, but really he wants to knacker himself out. He misses her like nothing else, and says if he didn't have the boys he'd probably do himself in as well. He thinks about her every day, talks to her in his head, runs over their life together and the things they had to look forward to, nothing is ever perfect, people make mistakes, but there's always better times around the corner. If you want them. He knows he's been hard on his sons and hopes he'll get a chance to put things right. Just because he's middle-aged doesn't mean he has the answers. I feel sorry for him, look at the floor as he talks. I see him differently now, try and feel what he must feel. It's the same with the Major. I don't think of him as a loony any more. Stalin says that if you find one woman in your life who you really love you've done well, but the woman he loved is dead and there'll never be anyone to take her place. It's the same with friends. If you have one or two real mates during your life, proper friends who'll always be there, then you're lucky.

Tony doesn't hang about, goes straight round Wells's house the day after with a baseball bat, but Wells and the others have been nicked and are tucked away in the cells. They're charged and released on bail, but first the old bill go round and tell Tony to behave himself, say they'll have him if he goes looking for revenge. They're watching him, and he tells me he's going to leave it for a while, till after the case comes up in court. But he's going to have them, specially Wells. When he's had a couple of days to think about things he realises he can't get himself nicked right now, not with Smiles sick, that's not going to help anyone. Him and his dad take turns sitting with Smiles, waiting for him to wake up, and they're close suddenly, same as a proper family, and it's obvious Tony is the strong one, the old man relying on him.

I take Stalin's advice and work my bollocks off down the orchard, keep away from the others and get stuck in filling boxes, don't waste time sitting in the sun enjoying the heat, watching a plane fly across the sky, stuffing my face with cherries. This is the real world now, and things have changed. When I get home at night I'm too tired to think. I go down the hospital every day, see Smiles in bed hooked up to a machine, tubes in his nose and mouth, eyelids swollen, lips bruised, cheeks puffed up same as the bruised apples on the farm, except the smell is different, clean and chemical, the smell of rotting fruit a lot better somehow. The nurses run around trying to cope, but take the time to stop and tell me he's going to be alright, that everyone has to keep their chin up and be positive. They don't forget my face.

Tony says the doctors are worried that if, they mean when, Smiles comes out of the coma, there might be lasting damage from him being under the water for so long and starved of air. They're talking about brain damage, but don't use those words. He's wrapped up tight and one day I see the doctor stick a needle in his arm, push the plunger when he finds a vein, emptying the liquid into Smiles's blood. There's nothing we can do, have to leave it to the professionals. If Tony and Stalin are there, I give it five minutes, show myself and get off home, don't want to be in the way. Otherwise I have a look at Smiles, drink a cup of tea and sit around, not knowing what to do. Stalin is a battered old man, puts his hand on my shoulder one day and says I'm a good boy. Whatever happens he won't forget how I tried to save his son. I don't know if he's right. Maybe I should've done better.

I don't go out at night, watch the telly with Mum and Dad, sit in my room listening to the radio, phone-in shows, rubbish really, and I suppose the people who call it don't have anyone to talk to so phone a stranger and share their secrets with the rest of the country. I don't play any records. Dave and Chris come round and we sit in my room sipping a bottle of vodka. Dave doesn't take the piss like he normally does.

Wells and the others are being done for attempted murder

and Major Tom is going to be the star witness. Dave reckons the Major will be looking forward to the case, and Chris tries to work out how long they'll get. One night I get off the bus and walk over to the Major's house to tell him thanks for pulling us out of the canal and saving our lives, but his mum won't let me see him, her face split by the chain as she hisses that the evidence mustn't be corrupted, witnesses should be left alone. I ask her to thank him for me and she smiles and says her boy's a good boy, one of the best, he'll always be special, her pride and joy.

If Smiles dies they'll probably get done for murder, and there's a politician on the telly one night saying hanging should be brought back for murder and terrorism. Smiles could die any second. I could've died. And revenge makes sense when you're there and know the truth, but at the same time, even though I hate Wells, I can't really believe they wanted to drown us. The man on the telly goes on and on, his face red, eyes popping, Dad's swearing at him, Mum saying to turn it over if he doesn't like the programme, why bother watching. The idea sticks in my head, same as a scratched single that hops back to the same line, repeating itself over and over. I can see the hangman fitting a noose around Wells's neck, same as in the Westerns, a quick kick of the legs and instant death. John Wayne rides off into the sunset. I don't think I'll ever forget what it felt like being stuck under the water, not knowing which way was up, the panic as I thought I was going to drown. I don't want the same thing to happen to anyone else, and that's what hanging would mean. Wells and the others were probably pissed and didn't think it through. Even if they were sober they must've thought we'd swim to the side and climb out.

I remember how Wells ripped the badge off Smiles and used the same hand to punch him. Smiles liked that badge, and the thing that gets me is that when he was on the ground knocked out Wells pulled the pin straight, leant down and pushed it into Smiles's skin. He had to think what he was doing and the hook fitting the pin to the badge was stuck in as well. That's worse than chucking us off the bridge. You sort of accept that getting a kicking late at night is part of life, and it was only that bloke asking why we got done that made me think about it, and all I could really come up with is that's the way things are, something that happens, but sticking the pin into his face isn't normal, same as Wells pulling a knife on Ali. Most blokes don't like that sort of thing, reckon carrying a knife is poofy, or for foreigners, fists and boots fair enough. Nobody should have to go around worrying about getting their heads kicked in for nothing. Not really.

The days pass, turn into weeks, and it sort of gets accepted that Smiles is in a coma and could be like that for months, even years. Maybe he'll stay in a coma for the rest of his life. I never thought of that at first, just saw life and death, a choice between the two, one or the other. I dream about the canal, wake up with a choking feeling, but I don't dip back in to the dreams and try to remember, let them fade, get up and run for the bus, make sure I beat the driver to the stop. I work hard and the money piles up. If Smiles recovers I'm going to buy him one of those flash record cases he always wanted, a professional job. You can get them mail order. Sometimes I think about him as a pensioner, stuck in a coma, or mental, and you get people like that, hidden away behind hospital walls. I remember how he used to go around selling those *Sunny Smiles* photos, collecting money for the orphans. Doesn't make much sense it happening to someone like that, a kid who wouldn't do anyone any harm, but there again, maybe it does.

It's a strange time, and I feel fit, speeding right up so the woman checking the boxes asks me what's the matter, wants to know if I'm on drugs. She's only half joking, and I tell her it's practice. Really, it's making the effort, and I push myself harder, get into a rhythm, stop daydreaming, stay up in the tree when Roy comes wandering past looking for someone to sit and have a smoke with, and I think about the strawberries but they mean working with other people and it's better here, where I don't have to speak to anyone, talking bollocks when I've got other things on my mind, wondering why it was me who got away. Suppose I feel guilty, but nobody says anything, know it's just me, except there was a minute or two when I only thought about myself, living in my own little world. It's something that nags away.

Then one day I come in after work and Mum says Stalin has been round and Smiles is awake and sitting up in bed. I can see him tomorrow if I want. This big weight slides off my shoulders. I eat quickly and have a wash, change my clothes, knock for the others, pass the good news on. It's Friday night and we're out for the first time since it happened. I've got a wad of pound notes in my pocket and buy Dave and Chris a drink in the pub, then a couple more, walk to the disco gobbing on the ground, trying to trip each other up, taking the piss, clicking our hands, snapping the fingers, Dave cracking his knuckles, a double-jointed wanker. We pay our money and go inside, buy cans and sip them standing by the wall, watch the girls dancing, and when the DJ starts playing his punk records it goes on longer than normal and it's obvious punk is taking over the world, smashing the discos and opening music up.

We're feeling good, know tonight is going to be the same as any other Friday night down here, more or less, things shifting around a bit, and that's not a bad thing either, we belong here, this is our world, and the thing is, at the end of the day, when it comes down to it, we're just three punk rockers, brick chuckers, lucky fuckers, fifteen-year-old boot boys with zero chance of a bunk-up even though we look the business with our stud earrings and cap-sleeved T-shirts, standing on the edge of the dance floor sucking cans of lager getting to love the horrible taste, eyes darting from one pair of bouncing tits to the next straining for an eyeful of anything worth a wank, and the Ramones whizz through 'Sheena Is A Punk Rocker', it wouldn't be Friday night without that one, and a few people start pogoing, taking the piss, things getting back to normal with Smiles on the mend, and he'll be wishing he was down here, knows the night off by heart but won't want to miss out, wishes he was standing with the lads, and the girls are looking good in their black pencil skirts and stockings, skinny bums and legs, C&A tops stained with rum and coke and halves of lager and black, balancing on high heels moving foot to foot so they don't snap an ankle, hanging around next to the bloke spinning records, and he's alright, like everyone's alright, he has to keep all sorts of people happy, Tracy Mercer up close with one of the Jeffersons, Soldier Barry back in Northern Ireland, out on patrol, wandering along a grim Belfast street waiting for a sniper to splatter his brains all over the pavement, nobody deserves that, Debbie dancing round her handbag with three other girls, talking to this boy who normally would be a wanker but tonight is just another kid doing what comes natural, and Debbie's alright as well, Tracy dressed up nice with a Jefferson hand drifting over her bum, tracing fingers along the outside of her leg, and she gets in closer, sucking at his tongue, Dave going to the bar and buying another three cans, adding lime for a change of taste, bored with straight lager, coming back and handing the drinks out, pointing at a redhead a few feet away, look at the fucking tits on that, Chris's eyes popping out of his head, and Johnny Rotten's out of the sleeve, the needle hitting 'Anarchy In The UK', and the whole place goes up, the music racing through me, and ten seconds into the song a big bundle starts as the bouncers and the Jeffersons clash on the dance floor, Tracy in the corner looking scared, on her own now, a couple of girls crying, and the DJ can't be bothered, lets the record run, and the Jeffersons have brought a crew with them tonight, carrying on from a few weeks back, and they're really sticking the boot in, a big gap appearing now, the bouncers backed up by some blokes they know, and the DJ realises the place is going to get badly wrecked if he's not careful, rips the needle over the vinyl, goes into Bowie's 'Life On Mars', shaking his head behind the turntable, and he's still got his sense of humour, isn't tempted by Elton John's boot boy classic 'Saturday Night's Alright For Fighting', and the aggro spreads towards the door, Micky Todd coming out of the shadows and cracking one of the brothers on the arm with his hammer, stepping back next to Delaney and Charlie May, and he's a silly boy, a couple of the Jefferson crew peeling off and giving the boys a pasting, and the bouncers move outside as the Jeffersons get all their boys together and leave, breaking the front windows as they go, and while all this is going on some pisshead is trying to tap Dave for 10p, it happens every week, regular as clockwork, there's always people taking the piss, boys a bit bigger and older than you looking for 10p to tide them over, that's how it is, they jump you on canal bridges and put the boot in, give you a kicking when you're not doing anyone any harm, because you're a punk rocker, a Paki, a pikey, a white boy, got hair that's too long or hair that's too short, drink in another pub, live in another street, it doesn't matter, and I just lean past Dave and tell the bloke to fuck off, never mind he's twenty or so, and surprise surprise he does just that, and there's flashing lights outside now, things calming down, and this is my life, this is England, and the DJ must be thinking the same thing because Bowie fades and 'God Save The Queen' pumps out, he knows he should play a love song, a brain-dead *Top Of The Pops* hit that'll knock everyone out, something mushy to keep us quiet, but he can't help it, sticks with the Pistols.

When the shit music finally starts, I tell Dave I'm going outside for a few minutes, for some fresh air, seeing as I'm sweating my bollocks off.

– Looks like Tracy Mercer's on her own, he shouts. Might walk over and give it a go.

I sit on the steps and watch the police talking to the bouncers and some other bloke, who must be in charge. The Jeffersons are long gone, and one of the bar staff is sweeping up broken glass. Debbie comes over and sits next to me.

– The music's not very good tonight.

I haven't seen her for a while. She's looking pretty.

– I heard about Smiles, she says. Do you think he'll be alright?

He's fine, heard a few hours ago, and she leans forward and kisses me. Her tongue darts out and before I know it she's got her hand down the front of my trousers. She tastes of rum, her mouth sweet, mixed with smoke. I look sideways but nobody's watching. We're in the corner here, light blocked out by a tin roof. Debbie's careful as well. Moves her hand slowly, tells me no when I try and slip my hand in between her legs.

– Someone will see, she says. Just let me wank you off.

There's not much I can say, and I suppose sitting there with your skirt up round your waist, legs wide open and knickers in your handbag is asking for trouble. I'm only a kid and can feel the spunk bubbling up, and all the tension is in there, groaning as I fill the front of my Y-fronts. Debbie smiles, well pleased with herself, watching my face like I'm something off a wildlife programme, and there's gallons of the stuff, can feel it soaking my trousers. It's got to be the best one ever. My brain is firing all over the place and I wish I had my own place so we could go there now and be together. But it doesn't work like that.

– Come on Joe, Dave shouts, and I jump forward and sit up. We're going down the van for some food.

– Hurry up, you wanker, Chris calls. I'm fucking starving.

'Hi Ho Silver Lining' starts playing, bouncers and coppers standing together by the door, laughing now. It's the last song, party music. They always play it to round off the night. Everyone will be coming out in a minute. I tell Debbie I'll walk her home if she wants, but she says no, she's come with her mates and can't leave without them. Girls have to stick together. She kisses me on the cheek, dips inside her bag and takes out a hanky, wipes her hand and goes inside. Usually you're wanking two or three times a day, really banging away every chance you get, sex on the brain every second of the day, but I haven't bothered for nearly a week and it's wet and messy down there, same as the last wet dream I had when I was twelve. Didn't used to be like this. When I was a kid everything was a lot easier. No girls to chase or records to buy. Everyone's at it as well, wanking their lives away, and any boy who says he isn't is talking out of his arse.

– I need some food, Chris says. I'm splashing out on a hot dog tonight. Special occasion. I'm doing it for Smiles.

We walk down the street, minding our own business, having a laugh, pushing each other off the pavement into the road. I stop for a piss, go in a corner and clean up the glue best I can, catch up with the others, Dave gobbing at me, a great big greeny landing on my right boot, a ten-eye DM smeared with snot. They need a clean, but he's not getting away with it, and I run after Dave, get him behind a car and rub it on his leg, and we end up on the ground, wrestling around in the dirt, going off the curb into the gutter. Neither of us is going to let the other one win, and even though we're only mucking about, it starts to get more serious, it's not a proper bundle but you can't let one of your mates take the piss, and we both know this and roll right into the road, with the oil slicks and fag ends, the concrete hot on my skin, and our grips get tighter, and it's going to turn nasty. I can smell the tarmac roasted nearby, inside some cones that Chris is busy kicking over as he goes, picking up a blinking light and lobbing it at us, the bulb smashing.

– Come on you two. Stop fucking about. How old are you? We'll get down the van first if we hurry, before the rest of them turn up. If we don't we'll have to wait ages.

It's a good reason to stop, equal with each other, and we dust ourselves down, brush the dirt off our clothes, and I look at my boots and they're dull from working in the orchard and not being cleaned. I'll polish them tomorrow. I'm going to have the day off, not bother going in, get the others and go down the hospital. We're sweating, and when Dave wipes the sweat off his face it smudges with dirt. I tell him, so he doesn't walk around looking like a prat, and we follow Chris, who's miles away now.

– Get your finger out, will you, Chris shouts, worried he's going to have to wait for his hot dog.

Chef is ready for us, leaning forward, his frilly apron and Noddy hat washed and ironed, the van spick and span. We have a hot dog each and a cup of tea, watch the onions sizzling away, sit on the wall stuffing our faces. Other people arrive and line up, and all of a sudden Chef is busy, rushing back and forwards, cracking jokes that nobody understands, the laughter ringing out. I watch him serve and he's a friendly bloke, can't see him chopping people up, even if it was a war. I don't know what sort of person does that, but I don't think he's one of them.

We hang around longer than normal, mainly because Smiles isn't with us. Tony and Stalin must be well happy tonight, even more than we are, and I wonder if the Major has heard about Smiles, think about going round to tell him, but it's late and his mum will only give me stick. I'll do it in the morning. I remember what Dave told his old girl and wonder if she's said anything more about that donkey porn. He laughs and starts telling Chris all about it, and I start counting, see how many seconds it takes for the skinny cunt to start creasing up.

We have a party for Smiles when he leaves hospital, two weeks after he comes out of his coma. Stalin goes to get him, and when Smiles comes in we're waiting in the living room, his auntie making us shout SURPRISE, the table covered with a pile of food. Stalin's made us do ourselves up in these paper hats he's kept from last Christmas, and Smiles laughs his head off when he sees us. It's not a brilliant party in the normal way, because Stalin sets it up, buys the grub and spends a bomb on his son's favourites, everything from jam tarts to Scotch eggs and a Fray Bentos steak-and-kidney pie, the crust cooked just right by this woman across the road, the ham-paste sandwiches stacked high. There's bowls of crisps and peanuts, and his auntie has made some butterfly cakes and brought them down on the train. It's the sort of spread that gets you going when you're six or seven, when you're more interested in chocolate than girls.

It's not the sort of party we're used to these days, sniffing around the one or two decent girls then making do with the giant tins of bitter, searching for a screwdriver and hammer, the usual aggro over what music to play, the girls running things because they love a dance and nobody wants them to leave, whoever's party it is preferring the soft option to getting the place turned over. It usually ends with everyone pissed and bored, the girls upstairs with the ponces who don't mind dancing to shit music and talking bollocks. It's always the ponces who do well with women. Then someone gets sick, or there's a bundle, or someone puts a window through. And the ponces stroll back in the room grinning ear to ear, go and pull out a can of lager they stashed earlier.

There's no supermarket bitter today, no Ramones singles or Clash albums, no Bowie or Mott The Hoople, not even a Woolworths compilation, but it doesn't matter, doesn't matter at all. It's the best party we've ever been to, and we're back to being six- and seven-year-olds, stuffing our faces, no cares in the world, not bothered that we look like a bunch of wallies in the paper hats, going back to the days when the only thing that mattered at a party was getting your share of fizzy drinks and crisps. Smiles is back from the brink, sipping lemonade and cutting the pie, Stalin fussing, treating his son like a king. I can remember being in this room when we were kids, before Smiles's mum died, and we played pass the parcel with her sitting on the same couch, Stalin doing the music, loving every second, same as he is now.

Stalin glides around the room, topping up our cups, chatting like he's our best mate when for years all you got out of him was a grunt and frown, tells us to call him Arthur. He's had a shock, another shock, and it's made him realise Smiles is important, that it's not just his dead wife who matters. I half expect him to make us sit in a circle and pull out a parcel, get the record player going, and Tony stands by the table with the paper plates in his hands, watching his dad, and Stalin goes over and puts his arm around Tony's shoulders to show him he's not forgotten. Tony goes bright red having his dad hug him, but at the same time I can see he's chuffed. Stalin's come out of his own coma, and that's what it was, like he said, feeling too much, making himself feel nothing. He was marching to work doing his duty, bringing home the bacon. His eyes are bright, shining inside his head, and he pushes Smiles's auntie over to meet us, a quiet woman who looks a lot like her sister.

Stalin's taken the day off work, and this is a first, seeing it's Saturday and he gets time and a half. He's a grafter, same as my old man, same as all the family men round here. You don't get anything if you don't work for it. And it's a new beginning, Stalin's invited everyone he can think of – family, friends, neighbours, passers-by, stray dogs. People have been stopping by to wish him and Tony well, people he didn't know because he was always walking around with his head down. I don't blame him, feel sorry for the man, after what he said and everything. Smiles is bubbling, the happiest I ever seen him. It isn't hard to forgive, specially family. You can't hold grudges for too long. Least I can't. After a while Smiles comes over and we tell him about last Friday and how the music is getting better down there, and soon as he's fit we'll have a good night out.

– We'll go up to London, Chris says. But I'm keeping away from all that foreign muck this time. Go see a band. I missed it last time, didn't I.

Still don't know the name of the band we saw. Me and Dave look at each other. Bad memories crowding out the good.

– We're going on holiday next week, Smiles says. Dad's rented a caravan. Tony's coming as well. It's where we went when we were kids. We'll go out when I get back.

It doesn't take him long to get tired and he goes for a sleep. The rest of us hang around, Chris loading his plate for the third time. After a while Stalin opens a bottle of champagne. He stands in the middle of the living room, easing the cork forward, fires it into the ceiling. He must've shaken the bottle because it sprays everywhere, but he doesn't care. It must've cost a bit, and the carpet's soaked, but Stalin just laughs. He knows the carpet's nothing special, when his boys spilt a drink it was just something to moan about. Tony opens another bottle, and we have some in plastic cups. I sip it and it tastes like shit, pour it into Dave's cup. I go upstairs for a piss and when I come out sit with Smiles on the top step, under the hatch leading into the loft.

– One of the nurses said Elvis died, he says.

He died last week. Mum was crying and playing his records all day. I know he got a lot of stick, the papers slagging him off for being fat, and the punks for being rich, but I always liked him. Elvis was the king. Can't be denied. You didn't have to be a Teddy boy to listen to Elvis. He was an ordinary bloke, a truck driver who loved his mum and lost his twin brother. He made a record for her and got rich, wanted to sit around eating peanut-butter-and-jam sandwiches when he got older. So they made jokes about him.

– It's a shame. Elvis was alright.

Elvis is right there in everyone's head, a big character who comes through the telly in all those films you watch even though most of them are shit. He's on the jukebox in pubs, and always gets a play. He was a person like anyone else, and I think of Mum playing 'Always On My Mind', telling me about his stillborn twin, how he always thought about his dead brother, and something like that is going to stay with you for the rest of your life. Don't care what anyone says.

– You know what, I don't even remember going in the canal, Smiles says. The last thing was getting the badge nicked off me, holding my nose and going down on the ground. Next thing I was waking up in hospital. Nothing else.

I take the badge out of my pocket and give it to him.

– No, you keep it. Dad said you saved my life. You have it.

The pin is bent and hard to open, but I get it on to my shirt.

– Dad's like he used to be, Smiles says, thinking to himself.

I tell him what he said, about working so he didn't have to think.

– Mum was in the bath right over there. Maybe it's even harder if you're older. She must've been very unhappy.

The bath is a couple of feet away, the door open.

– All her stuff is in there.

I look up at the loft.

– I'll go through it one day.

Stalin comes up the stairs for a piss, and I go back down, stay till people start drifting off, say thanks to Stalin and Tony, Smiles asleep, walk some of the way with the others. I leave them and go to the corner where I said I'd meet Debbie. I sit on a wall, kicking the bricks. She's late and I think about going home. She's probably forgot.

– Sorry I'm late, she says, and she's looking good, wearing her rock 'n' roll dress special for the Elvis memorial night down the social club.

We walk together, her arm in mine, and I tell her about Smiles and the food.

– I'll buy you a drink, she says, going to the bar when we get in.

Her dad's given her a fiver as a treat, so she can toast the king.

– Have lager if you want. Come on.

When she's been served I follow her to this table, realising that the racket coming from the bloke on the microphone is 'Jailhouse Rock', the only instrument a keyboard. I sit down and look around me, wonder what I've walked into.

– It was good about your mate, Katie says. I'm glad he didn't die.

I'm opposite her, and she's one of Debbie's best friends, a big girl who's got a low top on and a healthy pair of knockers, tight-fitting jeans that she somehow looks good in, and here I am stuck on a table with five Teddy boys listening to Elvis Presley songs that sound more like Des O'Connor. They're pissed and sad, and worse than that they're massive blokes in their twenties, the biggest the most harmless-looking, says his name's Stan and he comes from Langley. He's got NHS glasses he swears make him look like Buddy Holly. Dad's got a couple of Buddy Holly records and he was a skinny bloke while Stan is at least fifteen stone, nearer Elvis size than Buddy. The music is shit and when I look around there's a lot of other people down here, drinking, listening, and the thing is, the music might be bad but I'm not saying anything. They're talking to each other and I quickly raise my hand, take off the badge and shove it in my pocket.

– Joe's a punk, Debbie says.

It's like she's kicked me in the balls and there's nothing I can say. She doesn't mean anything by it, but every one of them stops drinking and looks at me, except for the bloke chatting up Katie, he's more interested in her tits.

– I got dragged down the King's Road by some of those cunts last Saturday, Stan says, leaning in so I can smell the light and bitter.

– Wankers stuck a chain round my neck and pulled me along in the gutter, gave me a kicking till the rest of the lads came out of the pub and sorted them out.

– I got one of them with this, another Ted says.

He opens his drape jacket and lifts a Bowie knife out of an inside pocket, holds it inside the fold so nobody else in the club gets a look. Must be seven or eight inches long, and I want to call him Davy Crockett and ask where he's dumped his beaver skins, but I don't. I might be a bit stupid sometimes, but I'm not brain-dead, so I nod and wait for him to bury it in my gut. Luckily the knife is still in the holder, and when I think about it I can't really see him stabbing me in front of all these people. He smiles and closes his coat.

– I got this toe-rag punk down in Brighton a month back, he says. Slashed him right across the cheek after he tried to stick a bottle in my face. I fucking hate those bastards. No offence, mate.

None taken. Whatever he thinks is fine by me. I'm shitting it, and even though I know he's talking about the fancy-dress punks rather than your everyday kid who likes the music, I wish I'd never bothered coming down here. Debbie asked me, and now she's getting chatted up by someone else. It seemed like something I should do, see Elvis out in style, but the music is mangled together so you can't hear the words. Sounds more like church music than rock 'n' roll. The slasher closes his jacket and offers me a fag as he shifts the subject and starts talking about the coons and wogs fucking up the nation, the way they go round tooled-up the whole time, selling dope and fucking white women. That's what really does his head in. He hates them shagging white birds. It's not natural and any girl who does that sort of thing is a fucking slag.

He's not bothered about me, and I suppose I'm just nervous after the canal. Stan heaves himself up and asks what I want to drink, a big round it's going to be hard to match, and he must read my mind.

– Don't worry. It's special tonight.

He goes to the bar and comes back with a tray full of drinks. Stella brings another one over and we sit in this little corner of the world raising our glasses to this good old boy from Mississippi, and I've gone from birth to death, from ham paste to lager. This is my first time back in the club since the night we went in the canal and I can see Henry Cooper over in the corner with his old woman, and there's loads of Teds down here, a few rockers with greased hair. Teds are the past, punk the future, but I drink to Elvis anyway, seeing as it's part of my history.

– I'm going to Graceland one day, Stan says. Elvis did his house up, every room different. One's done up as a jungle. He died young, but had a good life. He's done more than most people and he never lost his roots. He made a lot of money, but he was still a hillbilly.

Rock 'n' roll was rebel music, same as punk is today, except the difference is that the best punk has lyrics to go with the sound.

– He was just a good old boy.

He was. A good old boy. Mum and Dad should've come down, but there again, listening to the singer, maybe not.

– People slag him off for living it up, but what's he supposed to do with his money? If he wants to buy Cadillacs and swan around Memphis, why not? I wouldn't mind a Cadillac, pink with fins, except some little cunt would let the tyres down round here.

A Cortina would do me fine. That one we nicked and drove up to Camden would be perfect, the Cortina that belonged to that big ugly fucker standing at the bar drinking Guinness, the one stabbing at the window, the carpenter with his tool kit, and he turns and looks over, eyes zooming in on me. I lean forward and sip my drink.

– What would you do if you had a million pounds? Bet you'd buy yourself a big house, cars, drugs, girls, a Wurlitzer. I would.

I nod. Never thought about it really. I look at the bloke at the bar and he's checking his watch. I wonder if he's got his car back. He finishes his drink and leaves, and he's looked at me and nothing's happened. He doesn't remember. I don't need any more aggro, not right now.

– Come on, what would you do with a million quid? Stan asks.

It's hard to say. Can't think of much. I wouldn't mind a proper stereo. I'd buy all the records I can't afford. But it's a stupid question. It's never going to happen. A stereo would be fine. I'd give some to Mum and Dad, to my sister. I'm alright as I am. Wouldn't mind people leaving me alone, but if you had that much money it would probably be even worse, everyone tapping you for 10p the whole time, just to tide them over. Don't really know.

– You've got no ambition, mate, Stan laughs. No ambition. That's punks for you. Don't care about anything.

Debbie leans over and rubs my bollocks under the table. She smiles sweetly and licks her lips.

It's painful sitting down on the ground but I make it okay, pull the stem off a cherry and pop the red bullet in my mouth. It's nice and ripe, sweet and refreshing, the sun building up a thirst. It's a perfect cherry. Perfect day. Life is sweet, even if my back's sunburnt after two hours hunched over picking strawberries, bright red where the T-shirt rode up. Thought I'd give it a go before the holidays end and I go back to school, see if I could make more money, but they're harder work than cherries, the rows long and dusty, and you're right out in the sun. I did a box and took them over to the shed, and the farmer was there, showed me all these little nicks, bite marks from field mice. The rows are crowded, people chatting away as the sun beats down, and it's better getting lost in the orchard, an easy life under the branches, the cool corners and sweet smells, filling five or six easy boxes a day. I've given up now, gone back to the cherry trees where I belong.

It's mostly women picking the strawberries, tough old hags off the sites in Denham, Colnbrook, Burnham, scrap-metal witches who go door-to-door selling heather, chase you through the arcade going on about good and bad luck. Makes me laugh the amount of people who get scared when they have a curse put on them. These women fill their boxes fast, move quick, shifting down the line, scratching in the dirt, fingers hard, one of mine bleeding from a stone. Black hair sticks out of thin black scarves, long creases in outdoor faces. Their rings sparkle, don't seem to get dirty. Small boys and girls motor past me while their mums and grans take the piss. In Queensmere they'd be hassling me, but up close they're softer, nice people, and I can see how they trade on the reputation.

I don't care if I'm the slowest strawberry-picker in the world, don't mind if a seven-year-old pikey can piss all over me, don't give a fuck to be honest, because it's my first go and every job is a skill that has to be learnt. They've got a radio going, official voices rambling on about the state of the nation, law and order, sex and drugs, but I'm not listening, don't care about their arguments, everyone having a go at everyone else. It's quiet in the orchard, and I pick the stem off another cherry and split the skin with my teeth. This is the life, being left alone, doing your own thing, nobody around to give you grief. It's been a funny time. A lot has happened in the last few weeks. These things can get in your brain, mess up your head so you start worrying, and the only way round it is to take the piss, tell people you don't care.

– Alright, mush?

Roy comes and sits down. He pulls off one of his boots and takes out a stone, puts it back on, digs out his tobacco tin, opens the lid and starts rolling up. He concentrates hard so he gets it right. Part of him is carefree, easygoing, the other serious. The things he cares about he makes sure he does right. I don't really know him. Maybe I'm wrong. He lights up and sucks the smoke down, looks at me for the first time.

– I was down here last night and the farmer turned up. Almost caught me red-handed. Turned his lights on and I was standing right there in the beam, out in the open, but I was facing the other way and just ran straight ahead so he couldn't see my face. He chased me in the car, but I went in the trees and he had to stop. What does he think he's going to do if he catches me?

Don't know why Roy doesn't put a bag over the fence, same as I do with the cherries. Seems like a lot of bother wandering around in the dark for a few apples. I wouldn't come down here at night. No chance. Can't think of anything worse than being stuck in a wood at night.

– Apples are too big, and you'd get seen. Anyway, I was after more than a snack and had the car parked down the lane. He must've been sitting here for hours, hanging around in the dark. Can't see it's worth the effort. What does he think he's going to do?

Maybe he had his gun with him and was going to shoot Roy and bury him in the woods. Use his body to feed the land and give him more tasty cherries. Roy stops what he's doing and thinks about this for a while. I was only joking. His roll-up burns, ash building till he flicks it off.

– No, he wouldn't do that.

Goes back to his roll-up.

– You never know though.

We sit in the sun, not saying much, and Roy has done a lot in his life, a proper man of the world, while I'm just a kid starting out, without much to say. His life is exciting, a single man who moves around, and he's always going on about travelling, and every time I talk to him he wants to know what I'm going to do when I leave school. He keeps moving because he thinks that if you don't you end up with a stake in the system, get lumbered, same as a peasant in the olden days, who belonged to the lord of the manor. If you're moving, working day to day, cash in hand and outside the system, making the rules up as you go along, the government gets worried, can't keep tabs on you. He says that one day they'll get rid of the gypsies, have a crackdown on travelling people. There's changes coming, and he says as you get older you think about these things, but I shouldn't worry, I'm young with my whole life ahead of me. Right now he's quiet, but I'm playing old conversations in my head.

– Wouldn't you like to go on the road one day? he asks. See the world. Travel through France to the Mediterranean, go over to Ireland or up to Scotland, see the Highlands. You can stand in a field up there, keep still and in minutes it's full of rabbits, hundreds of them running around. You could join the merchant navy, go round the world on a tanker, get pissed and chase the girls in Rio instead of Slough.

I've never thought about going anywhere. I'm happy where I am. Wouldn't mind a week at the seaside, but I'm not interested in seeing the world. I'd miss home too much. Next year I'll leave school and find a job, and with some decent cash in my pocket things will pick up. I'll save and buy a car. There's pubs to drink in and bands to see. I can't wait. It's all here and I tell Roy that I won't ever go anywhere for more than a couple of weeks on holiday. I'm not interested. I'm happy. Simple as that.

– What about that plane up there, he says, pointing to a jet, so far up it's quiet, a silver speck of tinfoil. Don't you ever look at the aeroplanes and wonder where the people have been, where they're going?

It would be a laugh seeing what it's like flying, but that's about it really. I don't worry about the future. To me it's another record to look forward to, and I tell Roy no, I don't wonder about the big wide world. That's the truth. Life is good, and the worst thing that could ever happen has happened already. I tell him about Smiles and how we got a kicking, these older boys chucking us in the canal, how Smiles was in a coma and I was under the water thinking I was going to die, give him the whole story. It's already drifting into the past, so I tell the story in a different way, can't believe how quick things move on, and I have to force myself to tell him how it felt, and it's not that I've forgotten, I'll never forget, it's just that putting it into words is hard. It's not a big thing. I want him to know I'm not some sad case. I want to be my own person, do what I want, but I can do it right here.

– I thought something was up with you, he says, puffing away. A holiday will do your mate good. Nothing that bad's ever happened to me. I've been in punch-ups, stuff like that, but I've never nearly died, or had my best mate go in a coma. It's a big thing to happen to someone. Specially at your age.

When he's finished his smoke, Roy goes off, and I climb the ladder and start on the cherries. My back's baked and it's starting to tighten up and really hurt. I fill the box and take it to the shed, ask the woman to put it on the tab for tomorrow. It's starting to get dark earlier, and summer will be over soon. I've got another year at school and I can't wait to get out. I'll start looking for a Saturday job soon, but I've got nearly eighty pounds saved so don't have to rush. I'm sitting pretty. Doing well.

But if I get my finger out I'll beat the bus to the stop and wipe that grin off the driver's face, be home inside twenty minutes. Mum will have my tea ready, and I'll have a wash and put on some clean clothes, nick some of Dad's Brut, polish my boots and go and knock for Chris, meet Dave on the corner, keeping away from his mum. Tracy Mercer's having a party tonight and we'll have a drink before we go round, down the club probably, and this party should be stacked out with crumpet, I can see all these beauty queens lined up waiting for us to arrive. Tracy's alright, a friendly girl, and best of all she has some tasty mates. I'm taking some johnnies with me just in case. I don't want to get caught out like Smiles. Linda's phoned him and said she's had an abortion, so he's off the hook, but you have to be careful. Seems a shame in a way. And Tracy will let us play some records, I know she will. Smiles will be gutted he missed out, but he's probably having the time of his life with his dad and brother, a proper family living it up in Bournemouth, Arthur, Tony and Gary sitting on the pier eating doughnuts, playing the machines in the arcade. Things have worked out well. It's going to be a good night. I can't wait.

ASYLUM

Beijing, China
Autumn 1988

GARY DIED AT home, but it was no peaceful exit, no tearful farewell with his family gathered by a warm bed, united in grief, cherishing the happy memories, holding the boy's hand praying he's off to a better place, the ghost of his mum waiting in the shadows, spirit guides ready to calm his fear, some sort of spiritual affair. It was nothing like that. Nothing at all. Gary was on his own for a start, and he didn't gently slip away. He climbed into his dad's loft, pulled the ladder up behind him, tied one end of the rope he'd bought to a beam and the other around his neck, then jumped back through the hole. It took him time to die as well. The doctor told Tony there was nothing instant about this suicide. Problem was, Gary was too light, and the knot wasn't professional. He weighed less than nine stone and his neck didn't snap with the jolt. Instead of a quick death and painless release from the horror ripping through his brain, he hung over the stairs and slowly choked to death, twisting in circles as the rope cut into his throat, noose tightening as it squeezed the breath out of his body. The doctor could've lied, eased the pain and told Tony and his old man he didn't suffer, that he died in a split second, but no, he had to go and tell the truth, the whole truth, nothing but the truth. The doctor gave them all the grim details, really went into things, what the burn marks on his neck showed, the dried piss down Gary's legs and the shit filling his pants. He told them everything they didn't want to hear.

I'm sitting on the steps outside Beijing's main post office reading Tony's letter, the Queen's face on the stamp reminding me of an England I haven't seen for three years. I feel sick inside, read the letter again, stuff it back in the envelope, head down as the decent citizens click past, the military beat of

Communist China, big-time city living, big-face party members, the peasants stuck out in the paddy fields, locked away in stone compounds. England's a long way away right now, but I think of Gary, not England, Slough, anywhere, anyone else. Just his eyes bulging in the sockets, skin turning blue as he slowly chokes, blood vessels popping. I think of him getting kicked black and blue at closing time, unconscious on a dirty bridge crossing a dirty canal, flicks of moonlight skimming the steel pipes of the gasworks, catching the whites of his eyes, the outlines of rusty tanks, frogs croaking by the water, hiding in the undergrowth. I run a song through my head, can't help it, 'Down In The Tube Station At Midnight' by the Jam, talking about the smell of brown leather, except it was soulboys sorting us out that night, plimsolls not DMs. Stupid games you play when you're a kid. And that's all we were. Fifteen-year-old boys who thought we were grown-up. The splash of two kids hitting the water, sinking down, and one came back up for air, the other didn't.

Poor old Gary. He was in such a state by the end he couldn't even kill himself properly. I wish I knew what he was thinking when he did it, what was going through his brain as he set the thing up, decided life was shit and not worth living, that he didn't want to see what was going to happen next, just couldn't be bothered. He lost his curiosity and didn't care about the future. The doctor told Tony suicide isn't something that happens in a split second. Gary had to go out and buy the rope. Had to do his research and find the right shop. Get hold of a ladder and work out how he was going to arrange things. The length of the rope had to be right or he'd bang into the stairs and break his legs, paralyse himself and spend the rest of his life stuck in a wheelchair. I suppose nobody will ever know if he changed his mind while he was hanging there, if he had second thoughts and reached for a knife that didn't exist, wished he could cut himself down and give it another go, start all over again. I could never kill myself like that. It's another sort of madness.

Tony says Gary was hanging there for two weeks. I know it doesn't matter, not really, it was only the leftovers, skin and bones, but it seems worse than the actual dying somehow.

Nobody missed him till Tony and his dad came back off holiday. Two weeks in mid-air, stuck in limbo when he should've been in hospital. He felt alright on the unit. Drugged and safe. Tony reckons he was let out so the government could save money, Gary sent home to an empty house, something called care in the community. He was on his own, and I try to get inside his head, imagine his brain racing as the paranoia set in, ignoring the drugs that levelled things out, nobody there to spoon-feed him, the sound of taps in the bathroom and a picture of his mum dead in the bath, the voices coming back, eating into his soul, and I'm almost there for a few seconds, wash back out into a blank Chinese street. Tony doesn't blame the actual nurses, says they did their best and had to obey orders, and he knows what Gary was like, how the sickness changed him, how he learnt to lie and con people, manipulating them same as a politician.

I stand up and stuff the letter in my pocket, start walking back to the hotel. I don't see much of what's going on around me as I follow main roads, edges filled in with ink, racehorse blinkers, eyes dead ahead. I don't smell the smells or hear the sounds, don't see the faces or feel the bustle of busy lives, people laughing and arguing about the little things that are vital but right now seem like nothing. I know the way well enough to take a short cut, the streets here smaller, watching my step, eyes moving again, passing the hawkers and noodle-makers, the money-changers and chess players, ancient witches and new-born babies. Tarmac runs to stone as I cross a road and follow the pavement, broken slabs softening as I turn down an alleyway. Women wash clothes in bright plastic bowls and splash the earth with suds, soapy water quickly sinking away leaving dark patches of sweat, more memories, bloodstains, and the space is tight so I have to concentrate, the smell of charcoal and boiling vegetables stuck in a narrow corridor, planks of wood and patches of iron, voices darting out of glassless windows. I'm passing along a strip of life, all these connected generations I know nothing about, and I'll be gone in a couple of minutes, feel as if I'm trespassing, leave the alley and return to the bigger outside world with a gush of wind and the roar of a loaded bus flashing past my face. One second earlier and I'd be dead as well.

My head's throbbing and I feel like I've been on a session, pissing it up the wall. I walk faster, eyes down now, ignoring the yuan touts on the corner shouting hello-hello and quickly lowering their FEC exchange rate, past the youths crowding round one of the heavy pool tables that dot the street corners of China, in the countryside as well as the cities. Don't have a clue where these tables come from, how they end up in tiny dirt-track villages, and for a moment Gary's face fades as I think of Xiahe, how the green baize of the table was the only patch of colour in the Han section of the town, even the blue and green of those hardcore Mao uniforms washed out after years of cold water and Tibetan winds. They're good tables as well, with thick wooden legs and proper nets, better quality than the ones we play on at home. Males are the same everywhere, shooting pool on a street corner or in a bar, hanging around. I flash to Guilin, a grim town near Yangshou, in Guangxi Province, see the police on the steps of the train station, a line of ten teenage boys in front of them, two coppers to every kid, plaques around their necks, megaphone blaring, an officer behind a table denouncing the criminal element, proud police, humiliated boys, kids off to a prison camp, execution maybe. I push the picture away and Gary comes running back in, gasping for breath.

I'm staying in the concrete block up ahead, with its flashy entrance and dead lawn, the rest of the hotel a lot different to the front hall. It's obvious packaging, with a big mural of a smiling Chairman Mao, his rosy red cheeks beaming with sheer innocent joy, the look on the faces of the peasants around him reflecting the same pure happiness, showing how much they love their leader and system. The peasants are as chubby as Mao, a lot different to the people I've seen since I've been here. They say you never see a fat Chinaman because the food's so good, but you see them if they're party members. I've been to Tibet, seen how the Chinese treat the Tibetans, seen the difference between the skinny Han peasants in the countryside and the fat party members in Canton, Xian, Beijing. I've lined up with the card-holders and filed past Mao's embalmed body lying in state in Tiananmen Square, a glowing waxwork complexion and bloated face that keeps on smiling as trains ship the Guilin boys off to prison. They're the lucky ones, a sentence instead of a bullet in the head.

When I go into the reception area my feet echo on the stone floor, turning the heads of the girls on the desk. They're cocky as fuck and look down on me, forced into their jobs by the party but willing to go with the flow and sneer at non-party members, ready to accept their sniff of power, and they're racist too, see themselves as the chosen people. I've been in China for three months now and reckon I've learnt something about the place, had my easy views blown away by the reality of life in a dictatorship. Unless you see things first-hand you don't know, and then it's only a glimpse, the view of an outsider. People say they understand, but they don't. It's impossible. At least I'm more clued-up than when I arrived. Three months ago it was different, fresh off the night boat from Hong Kong and straight into a Canton dormitory, buying black-market yuan under a bridge from wannabe gangsters keen to make sure their customer was satisfied, something that jarred, wondering why these spivs were being so polite. And later I worked it out, realised they couldn't afford problems with the police. Chinese coppers don't muck about. It's the big time here.

Everyone in Canton was smiling, and coming into China from Hong Kong for the first time it made me feel easy, specially after the stories I'd heard, and everything seemed perfect till I walked into the animal market and saw every sort of creature tied and caged, waiting to be sold, dogs and cats along with the chickens, pigs, snakes, monkeys. Two men in suits were laughing as they took turns kicking a pregnant pig in the belly. I pushed them off and they thought I was mad. Their eyes glazed right over and they came back in, a crowd gathering, screaming at me. I walked off. There was a monkey in a bamboo cage, and the man with him had a cleaver, a sharp iron chopper to chop off his head. The monkey had the eyes of a child, something off a BBC programme except a million times stronger. The monkey was real and there was no escape. Under the surface there's all this anger bubbling away, and one day China is going to go up. It was my first glimpse in the market, and over the last three months I've seen it again and again. Don't know what's going to happen, but I can feel the tension.

I run up three flights of stairs and hurry past the room where I'm staying, just make it to the toilet. There's five cubicles, but I have to make do with a sink. Poison burns my throat. I gag and spew my guts up, the phlegm specked with chilli seeds and soy sauce. The seeds look like chicken skin, and I think of a white cockerel wandering around a hut in Yangshou, five tables and an open kitchen, the woman in charge grabbing the bird and slitting its throat. She kept talking with her friend and dropped the cock to the ground where it bled and kicked about in the dust, thrashing its claws and flapping pure white wings. The woman took a chopper and gently sliced spring onions and greens. The cockerel died slowly, the beating of his wings slowing down as his blood seeped into the dirt, leaving a damp stain, losing strength, life seeping away, the animal finally lying still. At the time I thought of Gary's mum cutting her wrists in the bath, how she must've died so slow, and I think of her son all these years later and the picture I have changes from a gently twisting suicide to a man panicking and struggling to break free, thrashing his legs as he tries to grab the banister with his feet, hands reaching to the knot but his fingers too weak to get under the fibre, Gary fighting for his life suddenly, now he's faced with the reality, knowing he has no chance, strength sapped through the years, one last flash of energy taking him back to the boy he was before he became a man, when we used to call him Smiles.

I turn the tap on and wash the seeds away, run my hands around the rim making sure they're all gone. Water does the job. I want to see my face but there's no mirror. It's something you realise after a while in Asia. The people don't bother with mirrors much. I've forgotten what I look like. I shave without a reflection, and know I must've changed. There's no plug so I turn the power up and scrub my face and hands, the blockage in the pipe backing up enough water for me to dip my face under the surface. I blow into the water and hold my breath, feel the skin close around my temples. It's cold and refreshing, and I open my eyes, the blinding flash of the porcelain giving way to a maze of cracks, each one with a depth that's confused by the water, a trip of canyons and craters. When I've finished I rinse the sink and dry my face on my shirt. My throat tingles but I don't feel sorry for myself. How can I after what's happened to Gary?

The dormitory's empty when I go in, and I'm glad, fists clenched, knuckles white. My head's buzzing, everything crowding in on me as I roll my sleeping bag out and stretch across the bed. The mattress stinks of bodies, the fabric soaked in the sweat of thousands of travellers. It doesn't matter. None of this matters. I don't bother wrapping my sweatshirt around the pillow to take away the smell of all those heads, the dead cells and old hair, bald men snoring, blonde girls tossing, every one of us slowly rotting, spines drilling into the bed, creating a dip down the centre. It doesn't matter. I look at the ceiling high above me, plaster peeling away, the pale skin of an old building, different shades of white, a gecko darting forward and stopping near the fan, just outside the reach of the switched-off propellers. There's two black blobs for eyes, and these are rock solid, specially compared to the yellow glow of a see-through body. There's no blood in there, and this little gecko stares straight back into me. He doesn't blink or move, the suckers on his feet giving him the edge as he hangs upside down, his breathing so deep and subtle there's no sign he's even alive. I stare at him, waiting for his eyes to roll, but he's not giving in.

I close my eyes and try to imagine the rope cutting into Gary's neck, how it must've hurt, the slow suffocation and flashbacks, his life whizzing past, the panic he must've felt when he realised there was no escape, no second chance, that he couldn't reach out and steady himself, cut the rope, make up for the mistake and come out a stronger person, go back to the past, to what he used to be. I can't help wondering if he thought about me as his life passed by, if he saw us how we were when we were younger, kicking a tennis ball around the playground, no cares in the world, least till his mum slashed her wrists. Then when we were older, looking at the girls but too afraid to go and talk to them, sitting for hours listening to David Bowie and Roxy Music albums in the winter, knocking around outside in the summer, saving up for the new records. The past is long gone and I don't usually look back. Gary wasn't thinking about the good old days either, just the present and maybe the future. Least that's what I imagine, but who knows. You just don't know. My eyes water and I do my best to think about something else. Poor old Smiles.

Smiles was a diamond, an innocent who was never going to grow up, least not the same as the rest of us, because this boy never had an ounce of spite in him, stayed open-minded against the odds, least till he got sick, but that was just the shell, the real Smiles could think further than black and white, wasn't stuck on one set of rules, shifted this way and that, making the best of things, the grin on his face hiding the horror of finding his mum in the bath, and Asia would've suited him, the contradictions less important in the likes of Hong Kong and Thailand, something you pick up day-to-day, China more materialistic, and thinking back I suppose our friendship was rooted in music, a shared interest, it was all we ever really talked about, and even now I can see Smiles coming into school with that first Clash album under his arm, 'Anarchy In The UK' tucked inside the sleeve, and when I got in that night I played them, hooked from the first drum roll of 'Janie Jones', my strongest memories of Smiles start from around this time, never mind I knew him since we were small, my snapshots stuck between 1977 and 1985, and I'm no good with dates, the exact order, and right now all I want to remember is the good times, the social side of things, words melting into the background, teenagers drunk on cider, snakebite, lager, filling up on the sulphate that was cheap and convenient, running off at the mouth, full of big ideas, speeding through our lives, out and about watching the best bands going, bouncing along to the Clash, Pistols, Damned, Vibrators, UK Subs, Dr Feelgood – the Jam, Buzzcocks, Ramones, Chelsea, Motorhead, Generation X – the Slits, Members, Lurkers, Stiff Little Fingers, Penetration – 999, X-Ray Spex, Elvis Costello, Sham 69 – the Boys, Adverts, Innocents, Siouxsie – the Rezillos, Undertones, Cortinas, Ian Dury, Public Image – the Ruts, Business, Exploited, Billy Bragg – the Rejects, Upstarts, Anti-Nowhere League, Cock Sparrer, Madness – the Specials, Beat, Selecter, Bad Manners – on and on, a long old roll-call, tons of groups, millions of memories, electric chords and electric soup, fizzy drink in plastic glasses, crushed cans and torn tickets, watered-down lager and hundred-per-cent-proof vodka, the thud of Doctor Martens and the flash of dayglo badges, the memories tangled up same as a ball of string that's been left under the sink, the threads frayed and knotted, soggy from leaking pipes, specked with paint, leading every which way, from the first groups to the second wave, the punk lyrics of 2 Tone and the stripped-down sound of Oi!, mohawk anarchist bands and punk poets, and even though they slagged each other off there was a common attitude, brilliant times, and there's me and Smiles down the front of the crowd pressed against the stage banging our fists on the boards, stuck inside Topper Headon's drum kit, ribs ready to splinter with the surge behind us, heart pounding and blood pumping, alive and angry and happy, knowing every single word off by heart, singing along, tuned in, lights picking out the dust, mingling with smoke, hundreds of people glued together, there's a glow in my head, crowding around dim-lit bars in the middle of winter, us in our donkey jackets and the girls in black leather, DJs out of sight spinning records, we did what we wanted, never dressed up to get in anywhere in my life, never will either, fuck them, and after three years away from England those punk years are right back in my mind, because this is what Smiles was all about, that was our link, and from this soggy tangle comes the night we went over to Uxbridge to see the Sex Pistols on their SPOTS tour, when they were travelling around undercover, skirting right-eous councils and militant preachers, and it was Smiles, Dave, Chris and me on top of a double decker sipping cans of lager wondering if the Pistols would really play, whether the plug would be pulled, and we had a drink in the Three Tuns opposite Uxbridge tube, the front bar full of dossers, smelly junkie girls and weedy greasers who fancied their chances seeing as we were a few years younger and they had the numbers, they came over and started spouting off about gob and safety pins, the same newspaper headlines that get people hurt in real life, and we fronted them up and they bottled out, snuck back to their corner, sat around scratching their scalps, picking at the lice, and we got cocky, started going on about rickets and the pox, how the plague was going to come back if they didn't have a bath soon, least till the landlord came round the bar and asked how old I was, next up Smiles, both of us saying eighteen when we were fifteen or sixteen, he was trying to put us in our place, and then it was Dave's turn and I knew what was going to happen, I could always read Dave's mind, he swore blind he was fifty-seven, then started arguing the toss so the landlord turned red, Dave going on about the time he spent in a German prisoner-of-war camp, how it kept him young, digging tunnels and building gliders, and we got turfed out with the greasers grinning as we went, so we went down the Printer's Devil and arrived a few minutes after some kid was axed in the back by this mob from Hayes, we still had a quick drink as the police questioned the bar staff and an ambulance took the boy to hospital, drank up and walked along the Uxbridge Road, past the Spitfire in the gates of the air-force base, found the sports hall where the Pistols were playing, everything busy now with the usual mix of herberts, and because this was Brunel University there was a lot of students, the sort who wouldn't normally go see a punk band, and Dave was going around with this meat hook in his coat at the time, we had to keep an eye on him, make sure he didn't hurt someone, he started giving these hairies an ear-bashing and was going in his pocket when I pulled him away, told him it was bullying, even if they were a few years older than us, they were from a different world, all Yes albums and lungs full of dope, acid trips and philosophy lectures, I was always rowing with Dave but we never had a proper set-to, not till we were grown-up and filled out, and then it was nasty, but I push this bad memory away and do my best to keep things positive, because we saw the Pistols and how many people can say that, it was pure luck we knew they were playing, a chance conversation the night before, and the Pistols were brilliant, didn't give a toss about anything, the hall was stacked and the Pistols had this bulb on stage, none of that progressive-rock shit, no expensive light shows for millionaires having a break from the country mansion, swimming-pool rebels saying fuck all, lost up their own arseholes, wankers who think spending thousands on illegal drugs means they're fighting the system, we hated all that, still do, the music pumped right up as I run 'Bodies' through my head, a song I haven't heard for years, dead babies, dead embryos, it's so sad right now, go to 'Seventeen', dead mummies and lazy sods, move on to 'Pretty Vacant', that's one of the great things about going home after you've been away, the chance to play your music, the soundtrack of your life, and Sid had taken over from Glen Matlock by now, poor old Sid, changing to the Exploited song 'Sid Vicious Was Innocent', a Wattie chant over Big John's guitar, and we missed the last bus to Slough, forced to nick a car to get back, and Chris was good at that sort of thing, training for the future, and Brunel had some decent bands over the years, the likes of Steel Pulse, the Ruts, Magazine, there were these punks who used to come over from Northolt and Ruislip, loads of miniature Sids, we got friendly with them, plus a load of kids from Uxbridge, West Drayton, Hayes, places like that, they were a hard little crew, and being a university the drink was cheap in the bar, a modern fleapit stuffed with hippy students, we used to take over one side of the bar, where the bogs and Space Invaders were, and they had the other, sometimes they tried to stop us getting in but there was a lot of us so they didn't have much chance, and it was easy being a punk, all you had to do was get rid of the flares and cut your hair, just live your life, we went with the times, and from where I was standing it was never about art students and fifty-pound haircuts, and while we laughed at some of the blokes playing at rock 'n' roll, the birds who dressed up were well appreciated, but mostly it was the same kids who went to football and ran around rioting in the bus station after school, who stood in the Shed and smashed up the trains coming back from Luton, the same hooligans who built that bonfire at Charlton and went in the Millwall end at Cold Blow Lane, that was all there was to it, stuffing Bowie's albums under the bed and letting the new music in, an education a million times better than what we got at school, and I can see Smiles laughing like a loony when we left, we all hated school, a waste of time, and I remember his face for a split second, know there's a better picture, something not quite right, look for another happy memory, fighting the inevitable, and later on Dave's mum and dad bought a caravan on a site outside Bournemouth, started going to the seaside every chance they got, and because Dave was the oldest he stayed at home and had the place to himself, he went once and said it stunk, couldn't get the smell out of his clothes, and with the house empty we started having these parties, there was fuck all to do locally, a disco here, a nightclub there, soon wrecked and closed down, funk all-nighters at the community centre, nothing for us lot, and the parties we went to stuck to the familiar sounds, shit off *Top Of The Pops* mingled with classic hits, everything laid on so the girls could dance, that's what I remember, had to keep the fanny happy, and we did something different, played punk all night, so there was a worse-than-usual shortage of girls, and Dave wanted some slow songs, love songs, reckoned there was no chance of getting off with a disco girl if all they could hear was Jimmy Pursey telling some sort he was breaking out of borstal to see her, or Paul Weller going on about a row down near Slough, but the rest of us had a go at Dave, why give in to prick-teasers, and I suppose he was a loyal mate seeing as it was his house and he could've done what he wanted, and the thing was, we got the best girls coming along, the ones who were into something different and dressed the part, there just wasn't very many of them, what we needed was a venue of our own, but this was Slough, a satellite town with a plague of soulboys coming through, but we had a laugh, till we played non-stop Ramones one night, and I suppose there was only two or three Ramones albums out at the time, we kept playing them back to back till in the middle of 'Go Mental' a punch-up started and the whole downstairs got smashed up, windows kicked in and the doors ripped off their hinges, something on top of the usual commotion, and next morning Dave had to sort out the mess, glass to replace, doors to fix, and it was lucky for him Smiles's brother was a carpenter and knew a glazier, and after that Dave was more careful, can't blame him, and it's funny what's in your head, right now everything shaded that bit darker so I have to force myself to think about the socialising, the drink and drugs and punk rock, that's what I remember most about Smiles, what I want to remember, and we got out and about, nobody can say we didn't have fun.

I get off my bed and go down to the basement, a four-bed room where two Poles have set up shop, experimenting with some free enterprise, selling tickets for the Trans-Siberian Express. They travel down to Budapest from their homes in Krakow, invest in a stack of tickets, go back up to Moscow and catch one of the trains east to Beijing. Here they sell the tickets on, adding a modest profit. These Poles aren't greedy either, and I buy my ticket for ninety dollars. Fifty quid for a six-day ride to Moscow, plus two days to Berlin, passing through Poland. My seat from Beijing to Moscow has even been reserved, and they can offer options from Moscow, on services to Budapest, Helsinki and Berlin. I choose Berlin, the fastest route back to England, but have to book a seat in Moscow. If they'd been raised in the West they'd be feeding me a long line of bullshit and charging ten times the starting price, adding tax for the Vaseline, but they grew up with Lech Walesa and Solidarity instead of Ronnie RayGun and the Iron Lady, have a more classy approach to business. They're almost embarrassed taking my cash, seem happy enough getting by, sitting on the pavement sipping tea in the daytime, drinking the cheap Chinese beer at night, spending long hours in their room listening to dodgy Bob Dylan bootlegs, playing cards and chess, waiting for a knock on the door, shifting their tickets at a steady rate. The ticket I buy is for the Russian train that goes via Manchuria, skirting Outer Mongolia. The Chinese service runs straight into Mongolia and passes through Ulan Bator, and is faster, but isn't leaving for another few days. It also means an extra visa, supposed to be the hardest to get. I want to leave right away. I've had enough.

There's two hundred dollars left after I buy the ticket, and I make sure the strap on my money belt is extra tight when I stuff my passport, notes and ticket down the front of my trousers. The Poles sell me roubles at six times the official exchange rate, making me a rich man. Gorbachev might be trying to ease things in the Soviet Union, but when I go to the consulate it takes three long hours arguing with an official before she finally gives me a transit visa. The Polish consulate is easier, and they stamp my passport without making me squirm. I was planning to go back to Hong Kong and do another six months in the bar I was working in before, but hearing about Gary changes everything. I get a bus back to the hotel, hanging on to the straps as it rolls across Beijing, squeezed in by bikes, arriving as night falls. There's this picture stuck in my head of Gary jumping around in the air, kicking against the banister, splitting his shins and breaking a foot, tearing the nails from his toes, a video nasty stuck on replay.

Everything is moving fast now. I have to get home and see the others, square things, back where I belong. For the first time in three years I'm homesick, feel like a traitor, someone who bottled out and ran away, abandoned everything for the easy option of a bar job and no responsibilities. I ignore the other people in the dormitory, take my soap and towel and go for a shower, stand under the cold water for ages scrubbing at the sickness, the pores of my skin shut, putting up barriers, protection, leaning back and opening my mouth, the water covered in film, a colourless slime that fills my mouth. I turn the tap off and watch the dregs spinning across the concrete, the froth of dirty soap and the stain of a rusty plughole. The towel is thin and frayed, sweat worn into the threads, and I pull it across my skin, rubbing away dead cells. I dress and go back to the dormitory, dump my bag under the bed and leave the hotel, pass the small group of Westerners sitting around admiring their rucksacks, a bunch of tarts comparing passport stamps and shit stories.

It's funny travelling, because you meet some good people, some real gems, but there's a lot of idiots who've never done an honest day's work in their lives. They're bumming around for a year or two after university, living off mummy and daddy, patronising the locals and preaching to other travellers, show no real respect for the culture of the country they're in, haggle over every penny with peasants struggling to afford a bowl of rice, swanning around playing at being down and out, more interested in drugs than the country they're in, a bunch of stuck-up lowlife. These soap-dodgers do my head in. There's no excuse, and the really dirty ones always have the poshest accents. When they get home they'll settle into their cushy jobs and that will be that, living off this CV for the rest of their lives. Never trust a hippy. China's not so bad, seeing as most of these people stick to easy places, Kathmandu and Bangkok for instance, but there's a few here.

But I'm not bothered about that right now, start walking.

Beijing is similar to the other Chinese cities I've been in, and the best time is in the evening, brilliant smells and sounds filling the streets, small fires shifting long silhouettes so it's easy to see why shadow puppets are so popular in the East. There's that Asian smell of burning wood and the Chinese scent of rice and noodles, thousands of pots of boiling water on the go, the sizzling of woks and quick snap of business. Down the back streets people smile, or at least when they see someone like me stroll past they smile, a foreigner, a novelty, and I look at these people, the old men and women who've been kicked back and forward all their lives, by the Japanese and Cheng Kai Sheck and Chairman Mao, and you'd think they'd be bitter and throwing rocks, but they're not. They're good people, the little people crushed and beaten by systems, dirt poor but with time to wave and say hello to a wanker like me, passing through, a rich man who can buy a bowl of food and drink ten bottles of beer if I want, then get on a bus and travel anywhere I want while they have to beg for papers to visit relatives in a different town.

I end up on one of the main streets and find a table, sit down and order a bottle of lager. Hundreds of tables line the sides of the street, heat coming off the fires as boys run around taking orders, filling up the chilli sauce and soy pots, adding to the heat coming off the road. Flip-flops click and a breeze blows. All these brand-new fridges are set back from the tables, engines purring softly, gleaming white machines packed with cold lager. And it's good stuff, between ten and twenty pence a pint, goes down a treat. It's hard to leave alone. Every night ends the same. Noodles and six or seven pints, all for around a pound. Sweat settles at the bottom of my spine, the breeze coming and going, and in my head Siberia is nothing but snowdrifts and blizzards, millions of slave labourers buried alive in Soviet gulags. I'll be off soon and drink quickly, the beer making me hungry, the bottle freezing cold in my hand. A boy brings me a bowl of noodles with wooden chopsticks, and I layer it with chilli and soy, mushrooms and greens over the noodles, wedge the bowl under my chin, shovel the food home.

Some of the people on the table talk to me, but I don't have a clue what they're saying. One or two pull the hair on my arms. Finally a doctor who speaks English sits next to me and asks where I come from, what's my name, the normal stuff. He works in a hospital. Tells me how much he earns and the state of medicine in his country, about the need to control the population. It's a strange thing, because it makes sense, the policy of each couple having one child, but when you sit down and work it out, it means that one day nobody will have relatives apart from their parents and grandparents. There will be no brothers or sisters, and if there's no brothers and sisters there'll be no cousins, nephews or nieces. Maybe that's part of the plan, to isolate people and get rid of family ties, make the party stronger than ever. These people have to watch themselves every second of every day. We talk for a while, and I think of the doctor at home telling Tony all these things about his brother, tell the man that my best mate has hung himself, rambling on about justice and fuck knows what else. I don't think he understands, but looks worried when my voice sounds angry.

I'm talking to myself really, more bottles brought over. He shakes my hand and pays for his food, walks into the crowd, his place taken by an old woman who smiles at me and orders off the boy, runs her leathery fingers over my arm, pulls the hairs and speaks to the other people, who laugh. They keep dipping into their bowls, and she strokes my face till her food arrives, entertaining the crowd. She eats quickly and leaves, and that's how the night goes, people sit down, have a laugh, eat quickly, then leg it. I keep going, soaking it all in, specially the beer, have nine bottles by the time things thin out and the boys start stacking tables.

I pay and leave, drunk and emotional, pictures flashing around in my head, tinted by the beer. I walk along empty streets, on my own as families settle down together, and I've been on my own a long time now, never really care, but tonight feels different, the letter hitting home. Drink can take you either way, and the alcohol lifts me up, makes me feel better as I pass under a row of trees. I smell the eucalyptus, then something more familiar, the strong flavour of home-brew, except it's coming out of a battered brick building. I stop and look down the alley, walls pitted with holes. There's an entrance without a door and windows without glass. Men sit outside, backs to the wall, pissed out of their skulls. I go over, look in the nearest window at a room packed with men in cotton shirts, no Mao uniforms in sight, a long counter selling beer in plastic containers. Fuck knows what it's all about, but when one of the men by the wall offers me a swig from his jug I take it, pour the drink down my throat, a rough taste with a kick, as if they haven't washed the petrol out first. He laughs and bangs his palm on the ground.

I sit against the wall and give one of the men some money to buy me a bottle. He goes inside and comes right back out. I sip the beer. It's nothing near the quality of the stuff I've been drinking. It's cheaper, and shows how poor the average Chinese is, when they have to drink this. I'm knackered and my head is all over the place. I can't speak a word of the language and I'm leaving tomorrow. I see Smiles in my head and want to black it out. My mood's swinging now and I know where I'm going to end up. There's nothing that can stop it, and even though I know I should do the right thing, I can't be bothered to stand up and walk away, the high turning into a low, racing downhill.

Tonight is going to end in tears, and there's that dark anger that comes along every so often, when what you want is to push things further, take the risk, like you've got to pay a penalty for a crime that's not even a crime really, just something you feel. I should've been smarter, realised what was happening, stayed in the canal and grabbed Smiles right away. Maybe I could've made a difference. I just don't know.

Six or seven Chinese come outside, pissed and larey, and I can see it coming, don't give a fuck to be honest. Looking forward to it in a way. They start asking questions, two of them sneering, one cocky fucker telling me to speak Chinese, speak Chinese, the only English he knows. He's swollen up on drink and patriotism, loves the party and Chairman Mao. I've heard this enough times, the Han seeing themselves as some sort of master race, the thousands of years of isolation, the symbol for a foreigner that puts someone like me next to a dog, the lowest of the low in their eyes. I think about how they treat the Tibetans and the people of Xinjiang, the non-party peasants. I see the market in Canton, how I walked away. There was nothing I could do about that monkey with the big eyes and too-small chain eating into his arm, raw meat where the fur had rubbed away and the metal cut into the skin. The living dead.

And I think of Smiles and how I went to the other side of the world for a job. He'd gone mad, was stuck in a psychiatric ward for the duration, living under the influence, drugged up to the eyeballs, trained doctors trying to keep the lid on the sickness, Smiles on another planet, going on about conspiracy theories and all sorts. I was working part-time in a pub, going nowhere, did what I had to do. I shouldn't have regrets, even Tony told me to grab the chance, but I still left Smiles to it, walked away, did what Norman Tebbit said and got on my bike. Did it big time. The last time I saw Smiles was three years ago and he was a shell of the boy I grew up with. When I told him I was going to Hong Kong he was glad, said he'd come over and see me. The border was tight and we'd be safe there from Hitler and Stalin, there was no love lost between them and Mao. And remembering him I see the monkey. There was no escape for Smiles.

So I feel guilty, and I'm pissed, and the fight just starts. Don't know how it goes off, but I'm up on my feet trading punches with Speak Chinese Speak Chinese and his mates, and I don't know if he's a Communist Party member or a Hong Konger, he's definitely a big shot, not your everyday peasant going along the ditches skewering frogs for tea, your factory worker burning his fingers on tank spares. Right now I don't care if he's the head of the secret police. Everyone's drunk so don't suppose they feel the punches too much, blood covering the end of his nose as I manage to connect. There's real hate in his eyes, and I've seen this around China, the spite seething under the surface, a country ruled by big-face and heavy-party discipline. They steam into me, screaming their heads off, and I'm down on the ground getting kicked along the street, on my hands and knees, not feeling the blows but numb in my back and legs. They keep going, and then it stops and they're gone. A couple of other men walk over and lift me up, dust me down.

Luckily this is a police state and nobody wants to hang around to answer questions. I've heard it's a major crime hitting a Chinese if you're a foreigner. I'm wobbly at first, but it's probably the drink. I get going, walk to the hotel, feel as if something bad has been beaten out of me. At least for now anyway. It's good I got done, otherwise I could've ended up in the cells. Those blokes had to come out winners. It must've been the same living under Hitler and Stalin. The uniforms had to win. Different level, of course, but the same idea. I think of the boys outside Guilin station on their way to prison and speed up, soon as I get back go in the shower room and wash the blood off my face, feel the bruises. I lie on my camp bed with the sweat and dead hair. Everyone is asleep, a man snoring at the other end of the room. I pull the pillow over my head.

I suppose I noticed Gary wasn't right early on but never thought about it properly. Change happens slowly and before you know what's happening there's no way back. People forget, accept and adapt to new ways. Smiles was different after he came out of his coma, didn't go around with the same grin on his face. He laughed at a joke, if something was funny, of course he did, he wasn't a basket case, but he didn't have that fixed smile any more. It was a few years after we were chucked in the canal that he really started turning, and a while after that when we stopped calling him Smiles. The name didn't fit now, but it wasn't like we sat down over a pint and made the decision. The establishment is obsessed with hierarchies, sees leaders and shit-stirrers lurking on street corners, outside agitators behind every riot and protest, but in everyday life things happen more naturally.

After Smiles came home from hospital life went on. Summer ended and we went back to school, wasted another year, and then suddenly we were leaving for ever, stuffing our books in a bin and setting fire to them. School did nothing for us. Punk was our education, the words reflecting our lives, tapping into the things we were seeing and thinking, the lyrics coming from people we respected, writing from the inside looking out instead of the usual outsider looking in. All we got at school was a worn-out needle stuck on battle dates and state politics, the heads of our lords and masters carefully drawn, their clothes brightly coloured, castle towers dwarfing the scum outside, grey peasants stuck in shacks outside the city wall, faceless serfs munching turnips. We knew where we were living, but that we had more colour and culture than the stuck-up twats poncing around inside. The fiction they gave us meant nothing, so boring and out of touch we actually believed the teachers who said we were thick because we couldn't stay interested long enough to understand what they were on about. There was nothing for us there, so we stuck with music, walked out of school laughing our heads off.

On the last day we got drunk and piled down the bus station for the traditional end-of-term punch-up, went out that night really happy to be moving on, punk right in the frame now with a lot more records released and new bands coming through. It was right there in the blood, and we were dressed different, the boot boy look faded by now, 'School's Out' getting the biggest cheer of the night. Next morning I woke up and realised that for the next fifty years I was going to be working five days a week. If I was lucky. I remember it clear as day, a bad hangover and this weird sadness that I was never going back to school. Mental really. I always hated it. But things were suddenly different. It was like I'd gone back to the beginning, the youngest kid in the playground, except now the pressure was really on.

First job I got was in this kitchen on the trading estate. I was the washer-up in a factory canteen, working ten till four, with an extra hour or two doing odd jobs, shifting boxes around and picking up litter in the car park. I loved that job. It was dirty work, hard graft with the trays and pots stacked up on one side smothered in grease and lard, layers of burnt food that split the Brillo Pads I used, but on the other side of the sink there was always enough room for an ice-cold pint of lager from the work's bar. The head chef was a fat bastard with this dog he brought in because it got lonely sitting at home, and he used to go around the kitchen fucking and cunting in front of the women, but he was alright, a good boss who didn't give the likes of me any stick. The two working chefs were a couple of hooligans in their twenties, butcher-coat boys in white aprons, and they treated me well. Everyone had a laugh, but the chefs took their work seriously. They kept an eye on me, made sure I always had a pint on the go, the smooth surface of the glass something from the adverts, a cold glow that kept me reaching over and pouring it down my throat. I was drinking five or six pints a day, and I reckon most of it was coming back out in sweat.

The sinks were always full and I needed boiling water to get rid of the dirt. It was scorching stuff that never ran out, so I was always hot, skin dripping, a long slog with the work piling up. It was one of those jobs that seem like they're never going to end, at least till two o'clock when I started catching up with the rush. It was the first time I'd really had to graft, and I was starting to wise up. Stacking shelves was easy compared to this, and picking cherries wasn't really working at all, a summer holiday with some pocket money thrown in. There was this real laugh-a-minute wind-up atmosphere, and when the last of the factory workers finished eating we went and sat at the long tables and had a feast. There was always food left over, and it was free. The chefs would have a drink as a reward for their day's work. The puddings were good and there was chips every day, as much as I wanted, along with the pies and sausages and cod, all the usual stuff. The bar was next door to the canteen so the chefs went in through the back, the drink subsidised, same as a social club, but the bloke who ran it let us help ourselves for nothing, one of the perks of the job. It was a good time.

I was part of the working population with all the benefits it brings, and stayed in the kitchen for a year before leaving. I'd lean over that sink and the steam would cover my face, and I'd watch white suds turn grey, the colour thickening and going black. I'd empty the sink and start again, the hot water sparking cheap industrial liquid, use one of the serving spoons to get a froth going. I blunted enough knives as well, scratching at the blocks of burnt food, digging in hard to find the silver lining below, knowing every day was the same, a real feeling of victory when the last pot was put away and the draining boards empty and rubbed down. All the time I was thinking of the money I was earning, singing along under my breath as the radio blared out Radio 1 hits, the soggy emotions of the DJs and their shit playlist, dipping into my own music, the Clash song 'Cheapskates', the line about being a washer-up and a scrubber-up, and that's what I was. There was the pride of earning as well. I felt good, felt fucking brilliant, saving for the mini van I bought for seventy-five quid when I turned seventeen.

It was the perfect car, with this long stick that made every gear change a juggling act, and a tank you could fill up for under four quid. Now, instead of nicking cars off people the same as us for a cheap run into London, or bunking the train into Paddington and legging it through the barriers, everyone would come round my house and cram in the back of the van. I'd put my foot down and we'd be in Camden or the West End inside half an hour. It was great having a car, gave us real freedom, and I suppose we felt like we could go anywhere we wanted, do anything. I put some old carpet in the back and had the cassette player going, Smiles playing DJ, Chris knocking off bottles of drink to get everyone going. Dave used to prop himself up in the corner watching his clothes for grease, a real tart, but playing the role a bit, winding us up. The girls were impressed by the van, a lesson I quickly learnt, that women prefer a bloke who's mobile. We were going to three or four gigs a week after we left school, everyone chipping in for petrol and me doing the driving. I didn't mind. I liked driving, putting my foot down and burning up other cars. It was good to be on the move instead of standing at bus stops in the pissing rain, a bunch of mugs waiting around for cancelled trains.

Smiles was dossing for ages after we left school, sitting at home listening to music. He was stuck on these reggae albums when he was indoors, Tony's mate Alfonso getting him interested in dub. He'd sit there for hours listening to all sorts of sounds, honking pigs and fuck knows what else, some mad noises only a nutter or genius could invent. I couldn't name the music, but it was the same as the stuff we heard when we went and saw punk bands. It was alright for Smiles in the summer, but when it started getting dark and cold he was bored, still didn't get himself down the job centre, didn't seem to want to work. And there was jobs around. This was Slough, and the trading estate meant you could usually find something. He said he didn't want to do a boring job like washing dishes, that he was going to get a proper trade, and this hacked me off because I couldn't believe it came out of his mouth. This wasn't the Smiles I knew. Dave asked him where he was getting these airs and graces, but he wasn't right yet, his head still stuck in the coma and its after-effects, so it didn't matter. It was just going to take time for things to get back to normal.

Thing was, Smiles didn't have any money, just what his old man and Tony were subbing him, and most of this went on the records he was buying, so we helped him out, bought tickets to see bands, a drink here and there. He wasn't sponging, tried to resist, but we told him he'd do the same for us, and he knew it was true. He was a giver, not a taker. He must've been getting money off the dole as well, but it's never enough to live on, never mind what these MPs and millionaire businessmen say from their country houses, sitting around swilling champagne, trying to justify their latest benefit cuts and redundancies. It's the same with Thatcher today, except now it's worse, with a righteous edge. We haven't gone forward at all, just rolled back, this swell of sewage softly running into the shore and gliding back out to sea, leaving the sand stained, cracked plastic and rusty tins stuck in the pebbles.

Dave was working in a clothes shop in the precinct, and it suited him fine, selling dodgy soulboy gear to the sort of dodgy soulboys we took the piss out of, and he was dressing well, got into the rude boy look of 2 Tone. Dave was looking to impress the girls with his fashion sense, and developed a talent for getting his leg over on a regular basis, while the rest of us were spending more time with the five-fingered widow than girls of our own age. He was knocking off gear at the shop, and later on started wearing some of it down the pub. I hated the labels game, seeing logos as a stamp of control like most punks. Chris, meanwhile, was soon out and about, robbing houses. He wanted me to go with him, but I didn't have it in me, didn't like the idea of going in someone's house, even if they were rich, more than that didn't fancy six months in borstal, marching up and down a parade ground in the freezing cold. I couldn't handle that. It would be the worst thing going being locked away. It's the biggest fear I've ever had.

Fair dues to Chris, though, because he wasn't turning over frail old grannies in their ground-floor council flats, or burgling working families in their mortgaged-to-the-hilt terrace castles. He was thieving from the big detached houses over in

Maidenhead and Taplow, out on the prowl in Alfonso's car till one night the Old Bill spot this black man in a half-decent motor and decide to give him a pull. The boys ended up in a ditch and had to leg it across the fields, heading towards Dorney, Chris knee-deep in cow shit with Alfonso and this other bloke, Clem, who'd started hanging around with us. After three hours getting cut up by barbed wire and brambles, then chased by a bull, or at least what they thought was a bull, it was probably a cow, or a calf, could've been a rabbit for all I know, Chris packed in the burglary, went back to petty crime, shoplifting and selling the clothes Dave was supplying.

Looking back, it's hard to put things in their proper place, but I remember leaving the factory, getting pissed at the sink and going to the pub at opening time. The chefs and a couple of girls who worked in the bar came along. The head chef turned up with his dog and bought me a pint. I talked to him for the first time socially. A nice bloke who wished me well. I was arseholed by nine, and went back with one of the girls. She was tall, over six foot, with long thin legs. She was a bit of a nympho as well, but I went and embarrassed myself, puked up over her couch. She didn't take it well, and I looked at those long legs and knew she was never going to wrap them round my face now. There I was, seventeen years old, kicked out on the street like a child, back to square one. Except I was moving on, another job lined up, starting Monday. The pay was better and it was half-eight to five. I was going to get some proper training. It was alright washing pots and pans, digging into the grime and striking silver, but I didn't want to do it for the rest of my life. The bloke who worked in the kitchens before me was there for eighteen years. Till he retired. Three months later he had a heart attack and died. It was time to move on.

I spent three and a half years at Manors, and then they made me redundant. They said it was because times were hard, but that wasn't the reason. The idea was I was going to do general duties and find something I was good at and they would train me. They dealt in electrical equipment, and I thought I might end up making parts, or become an electrician. But I floated along, never pushed myself, and when I tried to get something sorted out they let me go. It was an extra kick in the teeth. I never liked the place, the games the management played. There wasn't the same spirit as when I was in the kitchens, but I stuck with it because it seemed like the sensible thing to do. The money was better, and most people work to survive, make do, living for the weekends.

The union did its best to help me out, but it wasn't strong enough. The workers weren't united, and this was early eighties, when the unions were being murdered in the press and the bosses lining up to gang-bang organised labour. I didn't have a chance. Nobody was going to down tools and picket the gates, and the management knew they could do what they wanted. I didn't blame the other people there, it was a no-win situation. It was a small firm and the union just didn't have enough clout.

The country was in recession, unemployment high, so I went on the piss. There was doom and gloom everywhere. I'd started thinking seriously about politics, about the way big business and the ruling class affect us in everyday life. It wasn't enough to say it didn't matter. I suppose it was a natural progression from the music that helped form a lot of our views. It had nothing to do with Marx, Engels and the students in the SWP, more a question of basic fairness. It was obvious the Tories and Tory-controlled press were out to destroy the unity of ordinary working people, but it was mental the number of blokes I knew who were anti-union, ordinary men earning shit wages for long hours but who believed what they were being told. They took the piss out of the posh wankers on the telly, but still accepted what they said as the truth. This was southern England, and there wasn't the same tradition of trade unionism as in the North. Too many people were accepting dog-eat-dog logic, but more than that they felt that no matter what they did it wouldn't make any difference.

Chris had given up his thieving ways by now and was working for a builder's, Dave in the same shop he'd been in since leaving school, hoping he'd be made manager, which was on the cards. Both of them loved Thatcher and hated the unions, but really it was the students and posh wankers they saw running the Labour Party, people without a clue telling them how to behave, that ideology was more important than the rent.

The press talked a lot about muggers at the turn of the decade, and pushing the idea that the white man was being pissed on. The Falklands came and went, building up for the miners' strike of 1984, the collapse of the unions and Labour Party. There was the feeling people were being bought off in the South, as long queues formed for mortgages and tax cuts became more important than welfare.

After Manors I spent a few months on the dole, doing nothing for the first time in years, but I was soon broke and looking for work, found it in a pub. It was alright. I never really made enough to live properly, but ended up staying till I left for Hong Kong, drifting and drinking, listening to Smiles, watching him fall apart. I was in a rut and Hong Kong suited me. That was my working world, and it's easy to put in order, chunks of routine. The rest of it is harder. By the end I was rooted to the spot, going nowhere.

The train rolls through Manchuria, tall chimney outlines stacked against an orange sky, black rifles and burning nozzles at right angles to the land, furnaces filling the horizon, the ground flat and empty except for the shrubs and stubbed grass that could easily be barbed wire. I lean out of the window and feel the cold air wash my face, force my eyes shut. If there's such a thing as the edge of the world then this train is going to follow Columbus straight over the side. Sunsets look better when humans are involved, sticking concrete and steel in the postcard shot, messing up the perfect picture. I match the skyscrapers of Hong Kong with the Tibetan Himalayas, glass panels and towers of light topped by ice-white snowcaps. The scene outside has both, industry jarring with the rough spread of the grasslands, Red Army brick soldiers out on parade watching the Trans-Siberian Express rumble towards the Soviet border and a long old hike across Siberia to Russia and Europe.

The name Manchuria has this magic ring, impressions picked up from the telly when I was a kid, images I never knew I carried in my head, opium smokers and armour-plated warlords, sorcerers and horsemen, but from where I'm standing now it looks like another economic zone in the People's Republic,

more than a billion people being forced deeper into industriali-
sation, a totalitarian state where dissidents are buried away in
concentration camps and criminals shot in the head. Hong
Kong is more traditional Chinese in a lot of ways, in the back
alleys and side streets, away from the air-conditioned shops and
chilled expatriate bars, multinational banking centres and
electronics outlets. The communist regime has a new plan for
mainland China, while in among the trading blocks of Hong
Kong people stick to the old ways. I might've been in Asia for
three years now, but it's still special travelling through
Manchuria like this, Inner Mongolia in the north somewhere,
names in a geography book, places you never think you'll see. I
stay by the window for ages, back from the wind most of the
time, leaning into it for a while, back and forward, water oozing
from my eyes when the pressure builds, blowing the bad
memories away.

When night comes it's proper darkness, pure nothingness, a
solid wall of black, reflections cutting into the glass from behind
me. The Russian matron who runs the carriage squeezes past,
pushing me forward, her accent fresh off a spy film. This is her
carriage and I'm one of the people she's looking after. She
pinches my face hard with powerful fingers when I turn my
head, showing me I'm in safe hands. There's nothing to see
outside now, and the wind is colder, so I pull the panel up and
go back in the compartment I'm sharing with a German and his
Taiwanese girlfriend, the spoilt daughter of a gemstone merchant who plays on her looks, excited she's off to Munich.
Then there's this hippy in the corner, a superior expression
covering his ugly mug. Never trust a hippy. I nod anyway and
he blanks me, isn't going to lower himself. He's dolled up in a
Chairman Mao suit, the cap sitting on his rucksack. There's two
Mao choices on offer in China, green and blue, and he's chosen
the green combat look. He thinks he's the bollocks parading
around in peasant wear, and even though his passport says he's
Italian it's nothing to do with where he comes from. His
arrogance is international. I've seen enough of these wankers to
know what they're about. He'll be home soon, running
through his adventures, boasting for a couple of years before
signing on as a lawyer or banker.

I want to grab him round the throat and shake the cockiness out of his stuck-up head, nut him for fun, but instead I climb up to my bunk, lay flat out staring at the ceiling. I'm a lover not a fighter. That's what I say anyway, three or four times till I start believing it, even though I haven't had any sex since Hong Kong, not a sniff. Mind you, when you're dossing in dormitories trying to make the yuan stretch, you don't exactly meet the tastiest women. It's mostly hairies, but I've never fancied that sort. I agree with the equality view, of course I do, but I like punk girls. Nothing looks better than a peroxide blonde in a PVC miniskirt, high heels and fishnet stockings, thick black mascara over flashing eyes. The toffs say it's a tarty look, shows a lack of class, but out in the real world the porn actresses are long-haired dolly birds in thongs and perfect tans, the cocaine sniffers of Miami versus the snakebite drinkers of Britain. It's a way of thinking, that the mainstream is right no matter what it does, just as long as the trousers are expensive and the hair coiffured. Appearance over content. Same old story.

The carriage ceiling is four feet above my head and I stretch out to get comfortable. I'm on my own, hidden away in a quiet corner. Out of sight, out of mind. I fall in with the rhythm of the train, relaxing at last, taking time to form words, rhymes and songs, picking and choosing. I can make any words I want fit the sound of the train, a long line of piano rolls stretching all the way to the Urals and on to England. I get pulled in deeper but come back out and listen to the voices below. I'm tired, with a head full of pictures and stories. I don't understand the man and woman, talking in German. I sit up and pull my bag over, go through the cassettes wrapped in the towel, two-dollar bootlegs from a stall in Chungking Mansions. I plug in my headphones and click into Billy Bragg's *Talking With The Taxman About Poetry*, fast-forward to 'Ideology', the perfect song for China and its dictatorship of the proletariat, even though it's set in England. The busker guitar pulls me together, the English pronunciation he uses giving the music extra strength. I want to play 'Levi Stubbs' Tears', but it's too much of a tear-jerker, about a girl who's married before she's entitled to vote. I see the face of this girl I went out with when I was at school, and for a second I don't remember her name. She got married young. Debbie was her name. The jukebox in my head switches to the Specials' song 'Too Much Too Young'. I wonder what happened to her. Go back to 'Ideology'.

There's ten or so Westerners on the train, all in this carriage, sectioned, same as Smiles after we took him to hospital in Tony's car. I blank the memory of that trip, know it's there and I'll have to face it soon enough. The bunk is padded so it's going to be easier to sleep than on the Chinese trains, where the boards are rock hard and there's the non-stop gurgle of people digging into their throats and filling their mouths with spit, so by morning the floor's covered in slime. At six o'clock the lights snap on and propaganda screams from the speakers lining the train, the shrill screech of ideology. It was the same when I was in Xiahe, but the lectures went right through the day there, loudspeakers on top of the poles lining the main road, little more than a dirt track. The communists preach to a Xiahe mix of ethnic Muslims, whose roots go back to the Old Silk Route, native Tibetans, and Han who've been brought in by the government to change the racial make-up of the area. Nobody seemed to listen, but the voice was always there, a sharp noise in the background. The Han live at one end of Xiahe, by the dirt-patch bus station, in concrete boxes, the Muslims in the middle by the market, in older brick houses with wooden verandahs, the Tibetans at the other end of town past the monastery, in adobe houses with carved doors. Out on the grasslands, further along the valley, there's nomadic Tibetans who live in tents.

Xiahe is half a day's bus ride from Lanzhou, along rough roads and washed-out ravines, but it's a great place. I ended up with a room in a building where monks lived before the Cultural Revolution. In the morning women came in off the grasslands and sold yak's yoghurt for breakfast. When the men came into town they arrived on horseback, dressed in furs, once with this big bear-like dog. The local mutts mobbed up and had a go, but this nomad dog was a brawler and saw them off. Xiahe is a monastery town with a big temple, the remaining monks living in compounds that stretch from the river in the middle of the valley to the mountains. China's temples were battered during the Cultural Revolution, many of the monks murdered, but now the party sees a way of earning dollars, the hard currency it needs to industrialise, and charges an entrance fee.

I've run the arguments through my head, the way religion has been used to control people over the centuries, whether it's the Christian behave-yourself-and-you'll-go-to-heaven angle, or the Eastern everything-has-a-reason-so-don't-complain view, and I agree that religion has been used to crush people, keep them in their place as the leaders get richer, but Xiahe made me think. The Tibetan kids were always asking for pictures of the Dalai Lama, and they were better people than the materialists from the Han part of town. In China I've found out that communism is nothing romantic or radical, just another materialistic option to capitalism. Everyone wants to be top of the tree, and there's this lack of feeling, never seeing things through the other person's eyes. China's made me understand a lot of things.

One day I went down to the dirt road running along the valley. After walking for an hour a vintage truck appeared, and I thumbed a lift to the edge of grasslands that stretch right to the horizon. The land was covered in flowers and there was an old man with some beehives next to the road. There was also a hut where the truck dropped me off, and I sat outside with a cup of tea, watching ripples spread across the grass, patterns created by clouds shifting in the sky. The beekeeper lived in the hut with his wife, let me sit outside with a cup of jasmine tea, a warm breeze tickling my face, thousands of miles from anyone I knew. I felt good. Really peaceful. There was nothing to do, nowhere to go, and I sat there for hours, drinking tea till the same truck came back past and gave me a ride home. It was something to remember.

In the evenings I went to the centre of Xiahe, the nightlife two Muslim tea shops that also sold food, a forgotten corner of the world with loads of laughing characters, ancient Muslims with goatees, Tibetans, a few eccentric Han. It was mostly Tibetans, and they would sit staring at me, then someone would come over and pull the hairs on my arms. They don't have body hair and were interested, resting their rifles against the table as they tugged away. A Swede came in one day, with a beard and extra hairy arms, and the Muslim boy who ran the tables spoke to the Tibetans, then said he'd told them the Swede was a werewolf. The nomads believed this, and the boy told them the werewolf only changed if he was angry, so they should treat him well. The biggest Tibetan bought the werewolf a cup of tea. They sat watching for a long time, quiet and thoughtful. A few days later the Tibetans invited the werewolf to go into the hills with them, after more tea and a lot of watching. He stayed with their families, travelling on horseback. I saw him again on my last day in Xiahe. He was shivering and had lost weight. Don't know what was wrong with him, but he was sick. It was a hard life and even a werewolf struggles. He said they treated him well, but it was too hard for a European.

I stayed in Xiahe for two weeks, then took the bus back to Lanzhou, a rough ride with 4 a.m. kick-off, the sky packed full of stars, the most I've ever seen, bursts of meteors burning up as they hit the earth's atmosphere. From Lanzhou I went to Xining, got sick, and when I was well again spent three days trying to buy a train ticket to Beijing. The woman in the ticket office didn't like my face so gave me the 'mayo' treatment, which could've meant anything, that I was less than a dog, the train was full, whatever. She screamed at me, really bollocked me in front of everyone, her face turning red as if I'd pissed all over her bike. The angrier she got, the cooler I made myself. There was nothing I could do, and she was boiling right up. I realised there was another way to deal with these things, something I'd learnt in Hong Kong. I watched as she served other people. Most of the time she ignored me, but I was always there, lurking. She really enjoyed humiliating me, but I didn't crack, managed to stay calm, doing my own experiment. I hated her but never showed it, and this upset her more than anything. What was the point of her having power if I didn't respect it, and I realised that's what it's all about. I lay on my bed at night fighting my own anger, kept myself going imagining I had a gun and could walk up and blow her ugly face apart. I was the outsider, foreigner, subhuman. I went to the window five times before I found another ticket seller, and this woman sold me a ticket right off. If your face fits you're okay in a communist regime, the same as anywhere else I suppose.

My plan was to stay in Beijing for a few days, see the Great

Wall and the Forbidden City, then catch the train to Shanghai and take the cruise ship to Hong Kong. I was nearly broke, and had to find some work. The boat was supposed to be good value, with a swimming pool and half-decent cabins, an easy trip back to my job behind the bar and Sammy's room in Chungking Mansions. I would work six months and keep my head down, save hard and plan my next move. I didn't know what I was going to do once I'd saved enough, not really. Maybe I would've headed home, or gone somewhere else, tried the United States, the flights cheap from Hong Kong. I could get a job in a restaurant, cook burgers and open bottles. Listen to some of the new rap bands, the nearest thing to punk I've heard, NWA and Public Enemy cassettes from the market. There's plenty of punk bands in the US. That's probably what I would've done, but then I checked the post office and found Tony's letter. Smiles hanging himself made my decision for me.

Blowing out of China, the last few months crowd in, a chance to put everything in its proper place. And one of my worst times was Xining, another town on the Tibetan Plateau, again with a monastery but nowhere near the flavour of Xiahe. I was aiming for Lhasa, a two-day bus journey from Lanzhou, but the police shut the road. At times Lhasa is considered too sensitive for foreigners. I took a bus to Xining instead, a grim town with muddy roads and a depressed feel. I found a place to stay, more abandoned monk quarters with low ceilings and peeling red paint, musty rooms and sagging balconies. It was a dead place and the man running it said the corridors were haunted by the ghosts of monks murdered during the Cultural Revolution. The floors creaked and the corners were dark, but I never believed in ghosts. I got sick on the first night from some dodgy food, and spent a week soaking the lining of my sleeping bag in sweat, insides exploding early morning so I had to find a way through the maze of landings in the dark, to a toilet block outside the building, stuck on some waste ground. Built in the time of Confucius, order had broken down, but there was a light, a mystery when the main building didn't even have electricity.

This was sickness China-style, stuck in a stone block at three in the morning crouching over one of the twenty slats, a bare bulb hanging from the roof surrounded by thousands of insects, the mosquitoes biting my arse, arms, face, digging in through my clothes, sucking blood and moving on. There were some big fuckers hovering around the light, king-size moths and giant space insects I'd never seen before. Long antennae sticking out of their heads, flashing wings and stick legs. One little gang started dive-bombing me as I squatted down and the poison flooded out of me, waiting for the medicine to get in my gut and kill the amoebae. Worse than the flying squad were the dogs, a pack of five who came out of the night and lined up in front of me. There were no doors or walls in the block, just the slats, and these strays really took the piss, growling and barking their heads off, snarling and flashing their fangs. I didn't fancy rabies, but there wasn't much I could do as my insides spewed into the pit, head throbbing from dehydration, the mosquitoes biting and the dogs snarling, the biggest and meanest moving nearer so I could smell the meat on his breath. It was at times like this I wondered what the fuck I was doing on the other side of the world, why I wasn't at home sitting in front of the telly, half serious and half laughing.

And I probably wondered what I was doing rocking back and forward on the curb when I should've been standing in line with the others, waiting to see the Damned and Ruts when this mush hit the side of my head, a couple of hundred punks cracking up as I was sprayed with pigeon shit, and because I didn't know where to run I stayed where I was, looked up at this row of birds along a ledge of the town hall, saw their feathered arses hanging over the side China-style, a communal bog right above me, and I wasn't quick enough, got squirted again, just for good luck. Typical. And at least Smiles was laughing with the rest of them, bent double like he'd been stabbed in the gut, tears in his eyes, and I had to wait half an hour till the bouncers decided to let us in, Dave taking the piss, wouldn't let it go, and there's me doing my best with a hanky, finally washing it out of my hair when we got inside, a big sink of water in the bogs, but maybe it served me right, posing like that, trying to impress the girls. And the Ruts were one of the best bands around, we saw them all over the place, for some reason the Nashville sticking in my brain with a handful of NF raising their right arms in the air, a punch-up right there in front of the stage, and the Damned were originals, took no prisoners live, and there was a sort of a happy ending when this girl started chatting me up during 'New Rose', pissed out of her skull, Rat Scabies banging the drum for love and romance, said she recognised me from outside, sorry, couldn't help laughing when the pigeons shat on me, I probably smiled, glad she was happy, glad she fancied me, a local High Wycombe girl who lived a short walk away, up the hill. And she was with her mates who invited us back, real beauties done up in bondage straps and safety pins, we sat around playing records, drinking from a crate of lager, helping ourselves to the whizz on offer, but we were young and it was a mistake, kept us talking till morning when they kicked us out with hurt looks on their faces, said they had to get to work, and as we walked off it dawned on us they wanted sex, not chat, experienced girls two years older than us, and we shook our heads as the energy suddenly disappeared, knackered now, worn out, that's the sort of kids we were, useless, too pissed off to laugh at ourselves. And I skip to another time, another place, see us running down a grim maze of tunnels following the sound, a dark night in a dark part of London, a great night out with the Clash, Members, Misty and Aswad, and I would've felt good inside, skin tingling, ears buzzing from the sound system, legging it through the arches of Finsbury Park, the thunder of the Underground, thousands of tonnes of city on top of us, knowing this train might be the last one of the night and we'd have to sleep in the station if we missed it, Dave reaching the tube just in time, holding the doors for me, Smiles, Chris, Clem and some other bloke I can't remember, maybe two of them, letting the panels slip shut, rubber pressing together, lips kissing, and we were dying to give a mob of boneheads the finger same as in *The Warriors* but there was nobody there, just our imagination, and we laughed all the way back to King's Cross, over to Paddington, home to Slough. And there was always a band playing in those days, something going on, and I can see us running down from Chalk Farm and on to the High Road, police vans and police dogs, punks, skins, herberts, soulboys, the politics of the country played out on its dance floors, outside the venues, in chip shop doorways, late-night train stations. And we enjoyed ourselves, made the most of our youth, went up to Soho on a regular basis, in with the plastic-mac pervs, conmen, out-of-town football firms searching for a cheap clip joint and a traditional cockney pint, fat old brasses and skinny junky tarts, lost tourists, drug dealers, spivs, plus kids from every tribe going. If there was a load of us we took the train, if not I drove, this was later when I was out of school and working, on the piss, racing home after eight or nine pints, me at the controls feeling the power in the steering wheel, pushing the engine as far as it would go, windows foggy from the chips and kebabs, chow mein and saveloys, up and down the Westway, year after year, turning right for the West End, left for Camden Town, racing along the Chiswick flyover if we were going to Hammersmith. And there was nothing to do locally apart from drink, have a row, the only clubs soul-patrol efforts that soon got smashed up and shut down, so the van got us out and about with a minimum of hassle, Camden, Hammersmith and Soho the main places, Camden always lively with the Music Machine, Electric Ballroom, Roundhouse, Dingwalls and Dublin Castle, plus loads of good pubs, specially the Hawley Arms. Camden was the best night out, while Soho had the Marquee and the 100 Club on Oxford Street, Hammersmith with the Odeon, Palais and Clarendon, the Greyhound just down the road. Those were the main places for us lot, plus the Sir George Robey, Nashville Room, the Hope & Anchor, Aklam Hall, Lyceum, Moonlight Club, and so on, names I don't remember, never knew. And the van cost me seventy-five quid and did us proud, least till the night I wrote it off coming back into Slough, straight into a lamp-post in Langley at three in the morning, fresh off the motorway. I had Smiles in the passenger seat, and Dave, Chris and Clem stuffed in the back with their sweet-and-sour cartons. The van was a write-off and we legged it into the houses and worked our way home. I was so pissed I could hardly walk, but still sharp enough to know I didn't want to get done for drunk-driving, that the fine and ban would set me back. I stayed at Chris's till the next afternoon, then went home. The Old Bill came knocking, but I said the car must've been nicked and I didn't know anything because I was staying at a mate's house. I got a load of stick off Mum, but she wasn't exactly going to grass her own son up, and they couldn't prove anything, had to let it go. I got money on the insurance, but not enough, and it meant I'd lost a car and had to start saving. I wasn't earning enough to go out and buy another one so it was back to using the train, and we used to bunk it into Paddington, a quick ride then five tube stops to Oxford Circus, a quick pint at the end of Carnaby Street and into Soho for a drink in The Ship, or the pubs by the market, we saw some good bands at the Marquee on Wardour Street, the Vibrators, Chelsea, UK Subs always seemed to be playing there, backed up by groups you saw but never knew the name of, and every time Chelsea played 'Right To Work' at the end the stage was invaded, the number of people without jobs rising all the time, the flip side a song called 'The Loner', and Dave sat in The Ship one night and said I was turning into a loner myself. And he was right I suppose, but so what, and life went on, all lager and Space Invaders, the Marquee stank of this stuff I used to put down on the floor at work when I was sweeping the aisles of the warehouse, and everywhere you went you had to use plastic glasses, dipping your nose into the trough, and my training at work was slow, they made me do all the shit jobs, so I'd know the firm from top to bottom, and there was this bloke there who smoked dope as if he was a bong, so I wrapped this stuff up in tinfoil and sold it to him for a laugh. He was a poseur, as I thought, rolled it and puffed away behind the loading bay during a tea break, nodded his head wisely and agreed it was top-quality dope. And if we got up to Soho early enough we used to go round the sex shops, see what the women were spending their pennies on, there was always these stunners in little gangs checking the vibrators, didn't give us a second look, mostly older permed birds trying to spice up their lives, one or two nymphos as well I suppose, and seeing one of these full-grown women inspecting a ten-inch dildo was enough to scare you off sex for life. Punk girls were the ones who dressed in PVC and rubber, and I never saw them hanging around the sex shops. The clip joints always had them sitting on the door in leather miniskirts and cartoon purple hair, eyeing up the businessmen and tourists who kept the sex clubs going. And

we'd go see a peepshow, cheap screens with a woman stripping
and showing stretch marks, or bundle in the cubicles where you
paid 10p and all crammed in for a few minutes of some posh
bird in riding gear getting her arse caned by Colonel Bogey, and
all the time there'd be the poor dumb pikey farmhand who was
hung like a horse but wasn't getting his oats, peering through
the slats of the barn, his mistress bent forward over a bale of hay
as the sick old magistrate with the whip dealt out the sort of
punishment he wanted to inflict on the hooligans filling up his
court. And there was a lot of banter stuck in those booths, four
or five of us unable to move, the 10ps soon running out, and
we'd be telling the gypsy boy to step forward and service the
lady of the manor, you felt sorry for him, working in the
orchards for a pittance, shovelling shit and digging ditches in the
pouring rain, picking cherries and maggot-filled apples. But it
never happened, and it must've been funny seeing us crowding
in together. Those machines took us for a ride and after a pound
we'd give up, walk out pissed off, knew we'd been conned,
wishing the spud-churner had given the aristocracy a good
tonking. We hated the magistrate in his tweed jacket, a dirty old
man who got his fun tanning someone's arse, and we'd go in the
pub with the images in our heads, order four or five pints of
snakebite, if the pub would serve them, otherwise cider or lager,
eye up the girls. And I don't suppose we were handsome in
their eyes, most of the time they didn't want to know, suppose
we were a bunch of scruffy herberts when we were young. Me
and Smiles for sure, we hated labels and designer clothes, lived in
the same old gear, DMs and Harringtons, cap-sleeved T-shirts and
jumpers. For years we never bought jeans. I had a Crombie I got in
the market and I used to wear this in winter. It was a skinhead coat,
but I wasn't a skin, just a lot of the styles crossed over. And Dave
was a bit smarter, went rude boy and later on casual, Chris
everyday normal, and there was always something going on,
something to look forward to, I was always peering into the future,
even now lying flat out in the darkness, heading towards Siberia,
wondering what's up ahead, and I can't help humming along with
the Special AKA's 'You're Wondering Now', hear the saxophone
in the night, last one out shut off the light.

★

It's bright and crisp outside, but I stand back from the window, just in case, listen to the comrade running my carriage and keep out of sight as the train crawls towards the Soviet border. It would be faster to get out and walk, but only if you fancy a bullet in the head. The ground's covered in tufts of grass, two long swaying rows of barbed wire separating the China boys from the Soviet service crew, two chunky pigs strolling around in no-man's-land. The wood-and-pipe towers of the Chinese army lean into the wind, soldiers watching, fingers on the trigger. The Russian matron says they get nervous. She speaks good English, using her hands in sweeping motions, long bone fingers tipped with clipped, blunt nails. She's a hard worker, boiling water for the flasks she hands out, brewing tea in her cabin, looking after her passengers as we leave China behind, in control from the start. The train stops, stuck between two superpowers, time dragging, stopping dead.

We sit here for half an hour, the only sound the land breathing in and out, the crack of the brake being released echoing along the carriages. We finally arrive on the Soviet side, and the train stops again. Nothing happens. We're on the outskirts of a small town, and after another hour all these characters arrive and walk along the side of the carriages. They're wearing jeans and leather coats, hair greased back like rockers. They climb on the flat cargo trolleys next door and watch us through the windows. Matron says they're KGB, and there's police coming along the carriages checking papers. She says she hopes we haven't tried to smuggle currency in. The faces of the policemen are serious as they enter our compartment, picking and choosing the hippy. They search his bags. It takes a long time for them to go through the train. I think of the roubles stuffed in my pants and try to look innocent, but they're more interested in the hairy wearing the Mao costume. When it comes to border crossings and the smell of drugs and dodgy deals, it's always nice to have a hippy around to take the blame. Never trust a hippy. I wonder if they'll do a thorough search and call in special agent Andre Arseholovic, the specialist in rubber gloves, who'll make the hippy bend over and touch his toes as he checks for hidden herb.

Eventually the police finish and the train lurches forward,

stops again. A gang of men come forward to change the bogies to the Soviet gauge and we're ordered off. The carriages are unhooked and lifted into the air. I walk along the platform and go into the ticket hall, where I get a shock. Talk about time standing still, because now we're going backwards. This is time travel, never mind space. The people are white, most of them blond, fresh from the thirties. I thought they would be Oriental, Chinese, a mixture of Mongolians and one or two Cossacks. I could be in Saxony, or maybe even Slough before the war. It takes me a minute to realise that the white race circles the top half of the globe, that the clock on the wall is moving at a different speed, the ticking the loudest noise in the room.

I think of the Cold War propaganda I grew up with, atomic bombs and four-minute warnings, nuclear winters and radiation, endless doom and gloom, warheads loaded, coming our way soon. I see the faces here, and they're the ones with most to fear from the Soviet government, something they've got in common with the Chinese. They know how to behave, don't give anything away. Two more leather coats sit watching, one combing his quiff. I could be in 1930s Mississippi, but then when I go outside I know I'm in the Soviet Union, the wall opposite with a mural of a Russian soldier, sub-machine gun in his hands, a yellow star against a red sky. Nearby is a tank, with a small statue, names chiselled into brass. I follow the road for a bit, but there's nowhere to go. There's just this space stretching away from me, continuing on from Manchuria, all the way to the North Pole I suppose. There's concentration camps out there, where millions of people died, tortured for crimes they never committed. If nobody ever wrote it down, how would we know? It's the same with China. I saw nothing.

Once the bogies have been changed, we set off into the Soviet Union, a five-day run across Siberia to Moscow. I talk to the German while the hippy goes through his bag, muttering under his breath. I've got used to being on my own over the last few months, on the back of those three years working in Hong Kong. It was a good time, in its way. The chance to go overseas and work was there so I took it, rented a room on the eighth floor of Chungking Mansions, the owner of the hostel an old Tamil called Sammy. He spent most of his time sitting on a couch by the front door, chain-smoking as he waited for something to happen. I got to know him, a bald little man with smooth skin, who was a lot older than he looked. There was enough space for a bed and a chair in my room, and I ended up staying there the whole three years. It was dirt cheap, cheaper when I didn't move out after a few days. I lived out of my bag for the first year, till Sammy forgot how mean he was and bought a chest of drawers, a plywood effort that had been coated and lined with paper. If I went away, Sammy let me leave my stuff there for a week or two. It was all I wanted. I was always knocking the price down.

The best thing was the fan, a brand-new model that kept the air moving, chilling me nicely in my own little pressure cooker. There was no view from the window, just the dormitory and the kitchen of another hostel opposite, but the light got in, and I was happy. It gave me the freedom to leave the next day if I wanted. I wasn't going to put down any roots, living day-to-day. I was out on the piss when I wasn't working, or saving for a ticket to Manila, where I sat on the beach and baked, ate fresh fruit. Chungking was a death trap, a run-down fleapit, dirty and broken, everyone waiting for the fire that would probably wipe out hundreds of people. But it was a great place, full of chancers, Chinese and Indians, European drifters and an American deserter from Vietnam, an ancient German who Sammy reckoned was an SS man, everything going. It was like the whole world had ended up here, dossing on mattresses, each floor a maze of cheap hostels and indoor markets, whole sections serving the hottest, cheapest range of food I'd ever seen. There were Indians and Pakistanis, Bangladeshis and Sri Lankans cooking up curries, and I was eating Chinese and Vietnamese food every other day. At night I was working in the bar, serving drinks to a mixed group of mainly British, Aussie and Kiwi pissheads. Some of them were twats, the sort I'd never meet back in Slough, but there were a lot of good blokes there, men who'd seen a chance to do something different and grabbed it, one or two well educated men who didn't fit the arrogant stereotype and had broken free from the class system, spent the last twenty years travelling up and down the Far East.

But that was then and this is now, and I stand by the window for a long time as the train quickly settles back into its rhythm. Whoever thinks the world is overcrowded should come out here. There's grassland and forests running off to the skyline. There's no humans, and time passes till I go back into my compartment, lie on my bunk looking out at an angle, stay here for hours, get up and climb down again, go along to the bog, pissing on the tracks below, walking through the other carriages with their Russian, Chinese, Mongolian faces, men playing cards and sipping vodka. The buffet car is a cafe on wheels, hot and steamy, but without much food. There's borsch and chocolate, so I order borsch and chocolate. It costs me pennies and the borsch is good, thick and red from the beetroot, a dollop of cream curling out from the middle. Nobody talks to me. I don't know the language, and they keep to themselves, but it's okay. The vinyl is peeling off the tables, and the place is clean. There's no fry-ups, no steaming fresh tea and warm toast, the sort of food you miss when you're abroad, just Nescafé if I fancy a cup of coffee. I've stocked up on food, a bag of buns, dried tofu and a load of red-bean cakes, a tin of vegetables and packs of sesame crackers. I can't open the vegetables and only bought it because the picture looked good, a dark green plant with spikes.

I walk back down the train to my compartment, climb the steps again and spread out, wonder what Gary would've made of all this. I don't want to think about him too much, but still imagine what travelling through China and Siberia would've been like with him off his head, not depressed and asleep, hibernating through winter waiting for the sun to shine, spring pulling him out of the depths, watching the crocuses and daffodils sprouting in the park, the dossers on the benches rubbing their hands looking forward to summer. I imagine us lining up with the party members and Hong Kongers, stretching across the concrete quiet of Tiananmen Square, the Forbidden City on the far side with its dragons and cauldrons, me and Smiles standing in government lines, grinning, trying not to laugh at the serious faces of the police. Marching in small groups towards the mausoleum, up the steps and into the viewing room where Chairman Mao lies in state, Smiles opening his mouth and shouting out that the body is a fake, a waxwork forgery, where's the signature, because he's seen Mao in Slough, rehoused and working behind the counter in the Bamboo Garden, scribbling numbers on a pad. I see Smiles steaming past the soldiers and through the sacred rope, banging on the case, ordering king prawns in breadcrumbs, special fried rice and spare ribs. Taken out on to the steps and forced to his knees. A pistol pushed into the back of his head. Trigger squeezed. Brains on the concrete. Ruining the peaceful feel of Tiananmen Square. I blow the pictures out of my head, sleep for a while, wake up with the lights off, the train rolling along at the same speed as when we left the border.

I need a piss and watch my step in the dark, go down the corridor and into the toilet, stand over the tin bog, splash my face with water when I've finished. I go back out and see Matron standing by the door of her cabin, trying to open a bottle. She asks me to help and I unscrew the top without any problem. She asks if I'd like a drink, and I don't see why not, go and sit down just inside the entrance to her cabin, compartment, whatever it is, the place she lives and works and travels east and west across Siberia. There's a radio playing in the background, Russian love songs I suppose. She speaks good English and says she picked it up on the train, English the language of the world. She says her name is Rika, and I look at her properly. Her jacket is hanging behind the door and she's got a heater going. For the first time I see her as a woman. It's a surprise, but I'm not wondering now, know right away what could happen. Before, she was the commandant, someone in a uniform off the films, a lifetime of cold Eastern Bloc women with thick calves and weightlifter faces, but now she's Rika, with short blonde hair and nice legs.

We get talking and she, tells me about Moscow and her apartment, how she started working for the railways, the years in boring jobs, slowly moving up the ranks, the responsibility that comes with her position. It's taken her ten years to get here. I listen and watch her eyes, drink the vodka, feel a sharp burn on the back of my throat. I've never been much of a spirit drinker. She gulps hers back and refills our glasses. She says she's never off duty, but this is her quiet time. She reads my thoughts and says there are eyes everywhere. Everyone is watching everyone else. She leans over and pinches my cheek again. She's strong, laughs, and I can see she likes me. She sits back on her bunk and tells me how she loves the trip across Siberia, how it's different every season. In winter there's solid snow, the temperature a long way below freezing. In the spring everything is possible, and crossing the steppes she can never believe how the plants have managed to survive. Summer is warm and the windows stay open, while autumn is her saddest time, with the leaves changing colour, a time of death between the happiness of summer and the hard beauty of winter, everything dying and rotting away. I think of Smiles, know there's no more seasons for him, that he won't be coming back. She says she loves life and hates politics. There's a song in my head, a line I can't place. She wants to know if I understand what she means, and I nod and say I do, that she's explained things well. She gets angry suddenly and says she hates this time of year. Some people say autumn is beautiful, like spring, but to her it only represents death.

The drink doesn't seem to affect her, but after half an hour I'm struggling. Her mouth is bigger and redder than when I started, features stronger. But I like that. I love tough women, strong but feminine. There's no suntans out here, her skin white, same as a china sink but with none of the cracks. And she's telling me how she's been on holiday to the Crimea, sandy beaches and fresh air, small restaurants along the boulevard. I lean my head back and listen to her voice. I'm knackered. This vodka is proper paint-stripper, Russian moonshine. A while ago I was looking at Rika wondering if I was going to get my leg over, but that's not what it's about. There's more to her than that. It's in the face, bones, everything she says, sitting in the sun next to the Black Sea. She pours me more vodka, lifts her glass to her mouth and swallows it in one go. She leans forward and smiles, rubs my leg. She says she has to be careful, because if we're caught together she'll be in serious trouble. The police could make things very difficult for her. She could easily lose her job. That would be terrible for her, to be stuck in Moscow and not be able to move around.

There's this rumbling in my gut and I know I'm going to be sick. I haven't drunk a lot, not really, but this vodka is lethal. It's got a label, but is rough as fuck. Something to put in the engine of a clapped-out army truck in the middle of winter. Sex is the last thing on my mind right now. I stand up and tell Rika that I like her, but don't want to get her in trouble. She goes to say something, but I'm too quick, open the door and wave goodbye, pull it shut and stumble towards the bog, check she hasn't followed as I fall into the toilet. I lock myself in and kneel down, push the lever that opens the flap that lets the shit and piss splash over the land, a nice treat for the Cossacks who travel around on horses. Cossacks with swords and rifles. Cossacks with the wind in their faces. Cossacks on the brain. And I look into the mechanics of the Trans-Siberian Express and imagine I can see the tracks down below in the darkness, hundreds of slats of wood flashing past in time with the drumming of the wheels. Maybe I can. Maybe I can't. I jerk forward and puke my guts up, the second time in a few days, the worst sort of feeling, where nothing matters, just the pain in your throat.

I let the other bloke down, was just considering myself and never looked back, the sort of selfish thinking that mucks people up, something that's built into us and is exploited by the state, big business, our masters waiting as we sit pretty in the womb, least till the water breaks and the contractions begin, the struggle for survival starting with a flush of tears. None of it was planned, it was just the way things turned out. Instead of offering a helping hand I reached for the surface, struggled for life, instinct taking over. Survival was all that mattered, life too precious to give up on. I didn't want to die. Had to live and see what happened next, fulfil the potential. Not that I thought of it like that, went into things, there was none of that analysing and mind games, how could I think things through at that age, so I burst into the world and filled my lungs with air, let the oxygen race in and feed my brain, blood pumping, valves and muscles cranking up as my heart struggled to cope with the explosion of air down my throat, sucking in oxygen. I was greedy, the world turned upside down, hanging in the air, floating in space. I pulled myself out of the slime, eased back and enjoyed the peace, the worst behind me now, my back cushioned. The air was warm on my skin and I loved the taste of the oxygen, panic over as my heartbeat slowed down and became steady, settled into a rhythm, the best music going, hidden from what was going on behind me, not knowing or caring what the other person felt. We were close, as close, any two boys can be, but I never got in his brain and stayed there, lost touch and left him behind. I was glad to be alive, must've been happy, but don't remember exactly, my head fuzzy, mixed up and confused. There were no shapes in the darkness, just a vague glow of light in the distance, high above me, energy burning in outer space. I was young and none of it should've happened. It wasn't fair, just wasn't right, and that day stayed with me for the rest of my life. It's a simple rule, the law of cause and effect, something they understand out here, in Hong Kong, away from the big corporate skyscrapers, in China's country compounds, peasants versus the party. Back home we don't see this, just think about the short-term rewards, cut the cancer out and never wonder why it's there in the first place, why it keeps coming back. Everything that happens has a reason, and I should be able to turn that around and make it work for me, but I can't, not properly.

Once I realised that the boys who chucked me in the canal weren't coming down the steps for seconds I relaxed, tried to wipe the muck off my skin and clothes, got rid of some water and slowly began to see the stars, the light fixing and becoming brighter, billions of miles away, outlines forming in the darkness. It was a while before I remembered Smiles, half thought he was on the bridge. Then I realised they'd thrown him in as well. It made sense, and all this time Smiles was in the canal, stuck under the water same as me a minute ago, except I was still conscious and was able to struggle free, fought for survival and made it to the surface. He was tangled up, held down, unconscious when he went under, the next thing he remembered waking up in hospital. Later on I asked him what he saw when he was in the coma, if he had dreams, saw a white light, but there was no magic memory, no angels or spirits, no nothing. Just emptiness. And if I'd been clever I would've gone back down and searched in the darkness, found his arms and pulled him up to the surface, leant his head towards the sky and made him breathe.

Eight years later, in 1985, maybe I let him down again, but this time it was more planned, and it wasn't just me, seeing as it was his brother Tony driving the car back from Heathrow, conning him out of the hotel bar where he was sitting watching the planes coming in to land, off his head. And this is stuck in my brain, wondering if we let him down or did the right thing. We handed him to the authorities, but I push it away, don't want these memories crowding back in, fighting all the time but knowing I've got to work the thing through eventually. I'll do it when I get home. But Tony battered the engine while I sat in the back with Smiles steaming down the A4 past the lorries parked in the lay-bys, the long trails of grit from the nearby quarries, and I was trying to calm him down, nodding and dealing with the crazy thinking that touched anyone who got too close. We were busking it, not sure what to do with someone acting insane, so the ride seemed to go on for ever as Smiles looked right through me and saw things that weren't happening, while I kept playing the Adverts single 'Gary Gilmore's Eyes' through my head. I couldn't help it, madness crossing into humour so there were times I almost started laughing out loud, when he told me his stories, the things he saw at a local level, part of the broader picture, mixing state-of-the-nation politics with everyday life.

We took Smiles to the psychiatric unit where we passed the problem on, conned him because he had to admit himself voluntarily, he couldn't be sectioned seeing as he hadn't done anyone any harm, not till he left two days later and slashed his wrists outside the main gates. Then they sectioned him. For his own good. And it *was* for his own good. That's true. I know it's the truth and not a cop-out. I had to tell him a story, make up something that would persuade him the unit was a good place to be, get him through the doors where the doctors could sedate him, pump chemicals into his blood, slow him down and ease the voices in his head, the ranting of the dictators and concentration-camp screams. The boffins were waiting, men and women in wrinkled white coats, except they didn't act like boffins, more like human beings who cared about this man who was raving, tuned into another frequency.

And it's going to be a long trip back to England, five days

across Siberia and through the Urals to Europe, five days and all those years. It's a journey I've got to make, untangle the different threads, find some sort of peace after three years without any responsibilities, blanking the past and living day-to-day, five shirts and two pairs of trousers, underpants and socks. I have to believe that what I did was right, in the circumstances, helping Tony get Smiles into the unit like that. For three years he was in and out, till finally he sank as deep as he'd ever been, drugged and not speaking to anyone for months on end, a nothing life but better than being out on the streets, the psychosis turning him inside out.

Smiles was dead. The living dead. I never said it, hardly even thought it, but I knew. I went away to the other side of the world. The old Smiles was long gone, and I remember us lot down at the seaside, sitting on the seafront, suppose I was born again when I crawled out of the canal, out of the slime, croaking frogs and bundles of vegetation. And the other boy died, suffocated in the water so the oxygen didn't reach his brain. He was stillborn, no face and no name, floated face down in the industrial leftovers of the Grand Union Canal, his mother's love wrapped in there somewhere, stuck in the womb trying to claw out into the open, find the fresh air and feed the brain, a smack on a baby's bum and a gasp of life. Everything is jumbled together, confused, a mess of pictures, out of place and time, a fifteen-year-old boy sitting on a plastic chair in a hospital waiting room, sick in a toilet, puking my life away next to the canal, along the lines of a railway track.

And we used to call Smiles's old man Stalin, imagine that, and I'm sitting next to the drinks machine when Stalin comes in and asks me to tell him what happened again, one more time, he's been down Slough nick and buys me a cup of tea, says Wells reckons we were taking the piss, pointing to the GOD SAVE THE QUEEN badge, Wells doing his best to get the coppers and magistrates on his side, saying he read all about the Sex Pistols calling the Queen a moron in the paper so they lobbed us in the canal to cool down, never meant to harm us, never kicked us like that nutter Major Tom claims, who can believe a grown man who can't get a job and thinks he's Old Bill himself? That was going to be their defence, a badge that insulted the monarchy. Wells says he was being patriotic, standing up for England, for law and order.

I've still got the story he's talking about at home and read it when I get in. It says the Sex Pistols song 'God Save The Queen' calls the Queen a moron. This is wrong. I listen to the record again. Replay it five times to make sure I've got the words right. Rotten gets slashed and we end up half drowned. The song talks about the system, says it makes us morons, people like me and Smiles and those blokes who smacked us up on the bridge, then threw us into the canal, that it turns us into robots who do what we're told. Wells and his mug squad have proved the point, done as they're told, so who's to blame, the people in power you never get near, or the little people, the ones you see walking down the street? I was young, but knew the courts wouldn't believe a stupid story like that.

It doesn't take long to settle into a routine, the motion of the train calming things down, smoothing out the flashbacks, time to think rolling through big spreads of grassland that merge into hours of forest, millions of trees flooding down to the railway track, billions of fading leaves easing back to the horizon. We pass Baikal Lake and a couple of towns, smokestacks fuming, another step on from Manchuria, mental seeing industry in the middle of so much empty land. It takes ages to pass the lake, and I'm looking out for these places on my map, trying to get an idea of where we are in the bigger scheme, over a thousand miles of nothing between us and the top of Siberia. There's no centre to the world, just where you are at a certain time. Now and then we pass a village, the buildings made of wood, patterns painted into the eaves, nailed-together shacks that must be freezing cold in winter. These places aren't on the map. I wonder how these people ended up here, by choice or maybe descended from political prisoners, what they feel living so far away from the rest of the earth's population. I think about this a lot, the loneliness and the beauty. I don't take much notice of the others in here, do my own thing, say hello in the morning. That's enough.

There's not much to do except look out of the window and listen to the tapes in my bag. Sometimes I stand in the corridor, other times lie on my bunk or sit on the bottom next to the hippy, walk through the carriages to the buffet car. I eat and sleep, take my shirt off and wash under my arms, try and understand the German being spoken, feel the tension building between the man and woman. It's a good laugh mucking about with the music, trying to fit different songs to the scenery, but the protest music of Billy Bragg and Public Enemy belongs to cities and systems, a manmade environment where everyone's struggling for a slice of the pie. The anger is out of place, the sheer range of the land outside shrinking the lyrics till I give up and stuff them away. It's lonely out here. Easy to feel small and humble. The rhythm of the train takes over.

On our second day in Siberia we start to slow down. After all this time travelling at exactly the same speed, a tiny shift is like an emergency stop. I'm on my bunk and turn to look out of the window, climb down and go along the corridor. Rika is standing by the door telling anyone who'll listen that the train is going to stop for four minutes, and then it will leave. There will be no whistle and no warning. It will stop for exactly four minutes. Not a second longer. We can get off but mustn't wander away from the platform. The train will not wait under any circumstances. If we don't get back on the train we will be stuck in the middle of Siberia. Things will be hard for us. It will be days before the next train arrives, and that is a Chinese train. She says the words with disgust. The Russian train is much better. Worse than the Chinese service, anyone left behind will have problems with the police. Our visas will run out before we leave the Soviet Union. This could mean a heavy fine and even prison. The laws are very strict. We must stay close to the carriage and she will watch us. She smiles as I pass and I hope she didn't hear me being sick. I'm looking at Matron differently now, seeing her as woman instead of a cog in the great Soviet transport machine.

The train stops moving and people get off. I don't see anyone boarding, but there's a group of Russians waiting for us on the platform, big peasant women straight off the Second World War newsreels. And these Russians are poor women in thick coats, smiles showing off teeth drilled full of holes. They're all selling exactly the same food, boiled potatoes and the biggest gherkins

I've ever seen, heat rising into the cold air, this feast stuffed in paper. The gherkins make the wallies you get with your chips back home look like those miniatures they stick in hamburgers. I buy a healthy portion, the smell of chunky European food a change after the steamed noodles I've been living off. The women laugh, happy doing business, everyone selling out, tucking our roubles away. Their skin is burnt and tough, and they're no fools.

I keep watching the train as I walk up and down the platform, suddenly finding that my legs have tightened up, trying to stretch the muscles. Rika's nervous, standing on the steps of her carriage. I feel sorry for her, the look on her face a mixture of worry that we don't end up stranded, and the sort of fear I saw in China. She keeps checking her watch and calls out that the train is leaving in thirty seconds. I get back on and stand in the corridor looking into the houses and railway yards, bite into a potato, boiled just right. This is boring food, no spices and loads of starch, and it's perfect. I crunch into the gherkin and feel the tang of the juice. Beautiful. I watch everyone getting back on the train. Everyone except Mao and two of his cousins. I see the worry in Rika's face. Mao waits till the train starts moving, winding her up and showing how clever he thinks he is, the sort of thing you do when you're nine years old, jumping on the steps and strutting down the corridor. He tries to squeeze past without a please or thank-you and I lean into his face and tell him he's a cunt. He doesn't know the word, but understands the feeling. I want to smack him in the mouth, but pull back. This bloke gets right up my nose. I go back to the window. I'm a lover not a fighter. That's what I tell myself. Repeat it a couple of times, just to make sure.

That's life I suppose. You go to the other side of the world and things are never going to be perfect. A lot of wankers leave home to travel. You'd think it would only be the open-minded people, but it's not. The West ships its rich kids overseas for a break before they start their careers, and I've got this bloke down as a perfect example. Mao isn't a real hippy either. When we were teenagers going to see Sham and Madness play we hated hippies with a vengeance, saw them as part-timers with a headstart on telling us what to do, another fashion, but at least proper hippies had beliefs they lived by. Mao's just a fashion victim, arrogant despite his peasant pose. The train picks up speed and I stay by the glass as we pass a shunting yard full of steam trains, all these vintage engines in the middle of tons of twisted iron and stacked sleepers, a locomotive coming along another set of tracks, smoke curling out from its funnel, a hiss of steam smothering the wheels. It's a great moment, more time travel, and I stay here for a long time, these classics left behind as the Trans-Siberian settles into the same rhythm as before, and it's soothing, gets rid of the anger. The land's flat for a while, and the grassland returns, and then the silver birch takes over, a familiar pattern that puts me at ease.

I shouldn't have said anything to Mao. It was a silly thing to do, shows him he's getting to me. Going home means reviving old habits, remembering the snobs and posers, our class system looming in the distance, the break in the journey stirring things up. That was the best thing about Hong Kong, being an outsider who could live day to day, free from all that class bollocks, the media back-stabbing and political rows that got inside Smiles's head. In Hong Kong I was on my own, really free for the first time. It's all there waiting for me at the end of this trip and I push it away, go back to my bunk and tilt my head so I can see the world pass, more suspended animation. And this is how the rest of the day passes, and I fall asleep, rocked off by the train, don't wake till late, the only light coming from the corridor, peeping under the door, the window so dark it's as good as another wall, the blind left up. I have another guess what freedom means. Lots of different versions.

I stay where I am for a while, then leave the compartment. Don't know what time it is, but there's nobody about. I knock on Rika's door and she opens it right away. I feel the warm air and smell her perfume. The heater's on, radio playing, and looking past her shoulder I can see she's been lying on a green blanket, the shape of her body cut into it, the pillow with a dent in the middle. There's vodka mixed in with the perfume, but she isn't drunk. She's only wearing her pants and bra, stands to the side and tells me to come in, quickly closes the door. I don't have a chance to speak before we're kissing. She's a beauty and I can't believe I've been calling her Matron. Even the other night I didn't realise. It's the uniform.

Suddenly I'm sweating, and I don't know if it's the heat or because I'm nervous, trying to remember my last bit of sex, a woman in Hong Kong, both of us pissed and leaning over the balcony of her eleventh-floor flat, looking straight down, humid tropical air and a full moon. She was nice, with long black hair and a sister sleeping in the next room. But that was Hong Kong and this is Siberia. From a leftover of the British Empire to a modern-day dictatorship, firing squads and salt-mine exile, scorched earth and frozen wastes. A desolate land with nothing to offer. According to the propaganda. Just thousands of miles of swaying trees and clean air, a beautiful woman pulling me on to the bed and undoing my shirt. The room's warm, but she's warmer, friendly, and this is when you know you've cracked it, found the secret of life. When you're alone, thousands of miles from anyone who knows you, the pressures of life, old mates who end up on the end of a rope, fingers undoing your flies.

My brain's all over the place, pictures of Soviet gymnasts on the parallel bars, flat-chested kids twisting inside out, blowing the free world away. Maybe she's on steroids, but I don't think so somehow. Can't see any stubble or suspect muscle. And it isn't about sex, something different in her little hideaway, some sort of affection challenging the bad things that happen, the selling off of our democracy to media barons and big business, the more obvious dictatorship here in the Soviet Union, the dictatorship of the proletariat, the proles, thick knicker elastic you could turn into a catapult, firing stones at the KGB, spies and informers lurking in the shadows, scum of the earth. Rika's skin is soft and smooth, her uniform hanging on the back of the door hard and creased, the rub of a thick blanket, the voice of the storyteller on the radio, it's like I can tap into the fairy tale the woman's humming, werewolves roaming the steppes. And it's as if I'm hardly here, everything happening by itself until I'm on top of Rika, the cold glow of the window inches from my face.

Rika's head is knocking so I pull back, reach for a pillow. She smiles and says thank you very much. That I'm a gentleman. The famous English gentlemen she's heard about. I see my outline in the window, the pitch black of the outdoors forming a TV-quality picture of the top half of my body, so it looks like I'm all alone. I imagine a tired Cossack looking up from his fire as the train passes, catching a glimpse and opening his eyes wide, telling his horse that when it comes to love-making the British are in a league of their own. I smile at the thought, but Rika has shut her eyes and doesn't notice. I can feel her coming and move faster, try not to notice myself in the glass, because with Rika not in the reflection it looks like I'm servicing a mattress, and she's groaning, sweat pouring off us, I have to concentrate, work harder, just make it in time, blowing away some of the sadness. And out on the prairie that solitary Cossack spills his beans and nods his head, turns to leer at his pony as the Trans-Siberian disappears into the night and darkness returns, the deep loneliness of the land taking over, the horse tethered and nervous.

Rika sits in her chair while I lie on the bed. She smokes a cigarette and I sip the vodka she's poured. It brings back the other night, and I put the mug down. She talks, slower now, her voice quiet, taking over from the fairy story, radio switched off, telling me how her brother was sent to fight in Afghanistan and never came back. She hates the government for killing her brother. He was a year younger and is listed as missing, but she knows she'll never see him again. Sometimes she imagines he's been caught by the mujahedin and will return to Moscow one day, but then she thinks of the stories she's heard, how the Afghans torture prisoners for months before killing them. She hopes he died quickly. Her face is sad now. Two of his friends from the army came to see her family, told them how he went on patrol and was lost in the mountains. One of the men has killed himself since then, while the other's a drunk. She sees her brother's body on a plateau, the sun burning his skin and the vultures pecking into his brain, digging in through empty eye sockets, fighting over the meat of his memories, hundreds of screaming vultures flapping their wings, chipping at the bones, his skeleton broken and dusted in red earth, wind blowing the dirt away, a bleached skull on the surface of another planet, the landscape like something she's never seen in real life. There's tears in her eyes and I feel sorry for her, can see the picture she's describing. Everyone has their nightmares.

And she's a lovely woman stuck in a system, running back and forwards across a continent but fixed in one place, controlled. She starts getting dressed and reminds me she's taking a big chance, nervous suddenly, now the passion has gone. I want to stay here all night, but know she can't take the risk. She lowers her voice and tells me she hates communists, the politicians who sent her brother away, but she has to make the best of what she has. There is no escape. She can say nothing. Nobody she knows has ever cared about Afghanistan. She says I'm lucky to live in a free country. She admires Maggie Thatcher and Ronald Reagan, says they are on the side of the common people. She has obeyed the rules and done as she is told, and now she has a good job. She is trusted. She says I don't know how lucky I am, but not in those words. She wants to go to the West one day, so she can do anything she wants, have money and buy clothes, move freely, spend money on fine material. She holds the elastic knickers up in the air and laughs, smiling again. One day she'll go to New York and buy a negligee, romantic clothes from a romantic city. But I have to leave. She's sorry. She's scared, and I wonder if there really are professionals watching her out here, prowling the train, paid by the state, or whether it's more petty, her so-called comrades ready to grass her up for a pat on the back from their masters. Whatever the truth, I start getting dressed.

It was a few years after I wrote off the van that I bought another car, a Ford Granada, and this one had lots of room inside, an engine that could really shift, a bit more impressive than the mini. I splashed out on a decent cassette player as well, so I always had music going. We'd go for a ride when we were bored and fancied a change of scene, over to Uxbridge maybe, go see a band in Reading. Most of the time, when we couldn't be bothered drinking locally, we'd drive into London, all the usual places. The Granada didn't match up to the Yankees parked outside this pub we used by Heathrow, but that was the Hillingdon boys in their five-miles-to-the-gallon customised hot rods, against the grain for us lot, a bit too American, specially when England was going up in smoke, the riots in Brixton and Toxteth spreading into four or five nights of chaos across the country, out of the cities and into the provinces, till on the Friday night over twenty towns went up.

It was a shame that the political battles raging in England ended up ruining the punk scene. There'd always been trouble at gigs, but it got more and more political, till bands like Sham and the Specials were forced to shut down. These were hard times, with the media blowing things up and blaming the wrong people, promoters bottling out. The NF were wearing red laces in their DMs, while the British Movement preferred white, though most of them knew little about the actual politics, saw right-wing views as an answer to the middle-class Left. Jimmy Pursey was pissed on, by the NF at his gigs and a know-nothing media. He wouldn't shut the door on anyone, so was slagged off. It was the same with the Specials. The funny thing was, both were anti-racist, and if they were going to change anything they had to actually talk to the people concerned. The back-slapping tendency never understood this. Because the country was so tense in the late seventies and early eighties, there was some brilliant music coming out, everyone having a say, but in the end the media won and drove punk underground.

But that Granada did us proud. Saved our lives one night in Shepherd's Bush, chased by a mob who fancied cutting us up for fun. Just didn't like the way we dressed. I had a couple of dents to bang out next day, but we survived. Smiles made us listen to *Screaming Target* all the way down the Uxbridge Road, till Dave got angry and said he didn't want to listen to Big Youth going on about Zion when half that firm was black. Smiles made some crack about a combined Slough mob led by Adolf Hitler and Joseph Stalin that was a taster for later, but I never thought about it till this moment. I was still wired when I got in.

A while after I got the car, I drove us down to Dave's caravan for a week by the seaside. It was me, Dave, Smiles, Clem, a pile of sleeping bags and four crates of lager. Chris had given up thieving by now and become a copper. We never saw him much while he was Old Bill, till he saw the light and left. He let everyone down, became righteous same as if the police was a religion. Dave wasn't keen on the caravan, preferring the cheap Watney's in Majorca to a stroll down the pier and a stick of rock, but we talked him round. It was a cheap holiday. Clem was a good bloke, a gypsy lad who could drink and drink and never get pissed. He wouldn't touch spirits or speed, but could do twelve pints in a night and still be begging for another at closing time. He had a soft heart, but never backed down from a fight. He looked the part, at the same time a real gentleman with the girls, very easygoing with his mates. Twelve pints isn't a lie either. My top whack was ten, and that was pushing it, but Clem would stroll home and be up first thing, whistling with the sparrows. The sulphate had taken a back seat by now, and we were into getting pissed. The whizz was wearing us out, and it was getting boring. It was more lager now, a lot of pubs refusing to serve snakebite, people going mental on the stuff, and we'd gone off cider. Lager was taking control of the world. We weren't going to see so many bands, as punk dipped underground. The riot in Southall did nobody any favours, specially how it was reported by a gutless media, and a lot of the original bands were long gone.

It took us ages to get to the coast, and the caravan wasn't bad at all, musty, same as most caravans, with the heavy smell of gas Dave moaned about, but there was a new shower block with hot water, and a games room with a telly. When I was a kid we went to the seaside every year or two, and those holidays are some of my best memories. For your mum and dad it's cheaper than a hotel, and for kids it's more fun. We had fish and chips every night, sat outside the pub till closing time, stuffing crisps down our throats as we searched for the blue wraps holding the salt. Jilly used to swap hers and drove a hard bargain. Some Maltesers here, a handful of Smarties there. She knew I wanted the salt, and I'd empty the wrap and hold the grains in my hand, swirl them around the palm, rub salt into my tongue. During the day we sat on the beach, built sand castles and decorated them with home-country flags, ran into the freezing water shouting our heads off. Before teatime we'd go crabbing in the rocks, climb over barnacles and seaweed, the smell of the salty air packing into our noses, lungs, brains. When we found a pool Dad unwound the line from its block and me and Jilly took turns dropping the weight into the water. Ever so gently. We caught loads as well, put them in a bucket till we'd finished, counted how many were there then let them go, watched as they scuttled away. It made us feel good we were setting the crabs free. I remember that alright. And it rained a lot, our wet clothes clouding the windows of the caravan, mixing in with the gas, but they were good times. The best times.

Mum and Dad were happiest on holiday, and looking back it's easy to see why. They had a sniff of freedom, escaped the grind of work, sleep, work, sleep. The pressure was lifted for a week or two. You take things for granted when you're a kid, don't realise what puts that food on your plate, Dad knackered when he got home, sitting in front of the telly and getting wound up, but too tired to move. I never thought about things, had no cares, and that's what being a child is all about, the peace before the storm. When you're a kid you can't wait to grow up, and then when you're older you wish you could go back to being young again. And there was this dog that came to the pub we sat outside at night, a big seaside boozer with black-and-white photos of white-bearded fishermen with names from the Bible at the end of a concrete jetty, lobster pots and fishing nets stacked outside a row of tiny cottages, boats on the sand bank opposite, tilted on their sides, surrounded by worm shit, seagulls pecking at the decks. And the dog was a three-legged terrier Dad said was nineteen years old, he asked its owner when he went in to get a tray of drinks, the bar full of men and women, holiday-makers cheering up the locals, the flavour of the smoke and beer stuck in my memory, pipes we only ever smelt on holiday, another world when you're eight or nine. We looked out for that dog every night, and when we went home we hoped he'd be there again next time.

Dave's caravan was fine, rusty with a leak over the door where the metal had caved in, but it was a place to sleep and suited us fine. It's not like we wanted to stay in all day playing snakes and ladders. Dave was soon lording it, seeing as his old man was the rightful owner. He waved me and Smiles towards the shop to buy some tea bags and milk soon as we arrived, like we were his servants, and I asked him if this was how he bossed the Saturday kids around. We had a laugh, and he cocked his head. Everyone was in a good mood. We bought the supplies and stopped for a pint in the bar, sat outside with two ice-cold lagers, relaxing after the drive down, another sort of working-men's club that welcomed children, bingo for the women and an easy walk back for the blokes, plastic tables with umbrellas and a row of swings out back. We only used the bar a couple of times, we weren't family men, didn't fancy listening to country and western, and preferred younger company. We had a couple more pints before we went back. Clem had the deckchairs out and a line of milk bottles on a wall. There was a pile of stones next to him and he was lobbing them at the bottles. He was a good shot, cracking the Unigate returns one by one, the glass falling into a box he'd positioned below. Clem was no mindless hooligan. Dave was sitting next to him, staring into the distance like royalty, enjoying the pride of possession but pissed off we'd taken so long when he was dying for a cuppa. He was always like that. But it was good-natured. We were on holiday, our own out-on-parole tour.

We soon settled in and sussed out Bournemouth, found the best pubs to drink in, hanging around on the seafront during the day, stuffing our faces at dinner time, sleeping on the beach, maybe having a go on the slot machines before we went back to the site for a shower and a couple of hours' kip, then back into Bournemouth by seven for a night on the piss. It was a soulboy town to be honest, not exactly Brighton or Southend on a bank holiday with the skinheads and Glory Boy mods piling down from London, but it was fine, and there was a pub where the local punks and herberts hung out, with a decent jukebox and pool table, so we were happy. Dave was jumpy at first, couldn't relax, wanted to go to a club and show off his Tacchini, but he was on his own. Then he met a girl and got his leg over and that was him smiling again, seeing her two or three times during the holiday. The rest of us never had a sniff, and probably weren't too bothered either. It was a piss-up basically, and there was a venue that put on bands, low-key but good enough. There were a decent curry house for when the pubs shut, and a Chinese takeaway, except the food stunk up the caravan worse than the gas so Dave said next time we'd have to eat it outside in the dark. We had another one and he paid the price, spilling sauce all over a brand-new Lacoste he'd bought that afternoon. I didn't mind driving into town, the roads empty when we went back out to the caravan site. It's funny looking back on that week now. It was only five years ago, but seems like part of a different life.

It was just a week off work, the chance to do what we wanted, a sort of escape but different to being on your own, nothing like living on the other side of the world with no family or proper friends, the language around you foreign most of the time so you don't hear what's being said, getting away from the bitterness but also losing the humour, tucked away in your own little cave so you can do your own thing, nobody telling you to come on you miserable cunt let's get some beer down our throats. Nobody knows or cares who you are when you're in a strange town, so you're left alone. And these memories are all part of me, at the seaside with my family, my mates, the other sort of joy I had being on my own, closing out the voices. And I flashback to Clem getting his camera out one day saying he wants a photo of us outside the caravan, and we told him to fuck off and stop being soppy, but Dave still went and changed specially, so Clem got some bloke coming back from the showers to put down his soap and towel and catch the moment. We lined up and Dave told him to take a couple extra, just in case he was blinking and came out with his eyes shut. He wanted to look his best. And we all wanted the picture I suppose, just felt stupid asking, taking the piss out of each other, never really saying what we meant. Don't remember ever seeing the photo. And I start thinking about Dave and Clem, Chris as well, who missed out. It'll be good to have a pint with them, see how things stand. Maybe. Maybe not.

When we were kids, we used to cry when we had to go home, we wanted to stay on holiday for ever, and on our last day in Bournemouth I was sitting on a bench on the seafront with Smiles, a pint of lager in my belly tucking into a polystyrene plate of chips, probably with the usual watered-down ketchup you seem to get near the sea, a layer of salt on top, looking at the beach and watching the families on their leaking lilos, the burnt blubber of hundreds of men and women who didn't give a toss about appearances, knew there were more important things in life, laughing in the sun, and I was watching this girl with her two friends pass by, white T-shirts and black bikini bottoms, thinking it was a shame we had to go home, and it was as if Smiles read my mind, got inside my head, saw the world through my eyes for a few seconds, except I wasn't listening properly, concentrating on the wiggle of the girl's bum, catching her smile when she turned her head, and Smiles's voice jarred in my ear, turning hard so it shut out the laughter, killed the holiday atmosphere, the girl's smile gone with the swish of her head. I heard what he said now. Tried to laugh it off as he lowered his voice and hissed the words, about the evil and corruption that threatened us, the Devil's spawn, think of the Devil's 666, think of the band 999, the single 'Homicide', and his voice was like something from a TV seance, made me shiver. I looked at him and saw his face all mangled and twisted, as if it belonged to someone else. I couldn't look at him, just heard his voice, which became more soothing as he pulled me in. His story was funny in a way, but I knew now he was going mad.

Smiles was hacked off and had been meaning to tell me why, but had to be careful. There were spies everywhere. Agents looking and listening. We were safe on the front, with space around us. And two months ago he'd come out of the paper shop and spotted two pensioners across the road. Nothing strange in that, but when he got nearer to them he'd almost jumped out of his skin, shredded his skin like a snake in the desert crawling on its belly, legs chopped off, but it wasn't that, no, he had to get the facts right, so I'd understand him. He recognised one of the men, but couldn't put a name to the face, but then it was suddenly obvious. Here he was, Smiles, on an English street, staring at the unmistakable features of Adolf Hitler, the person responsible for the murder of millions of men, women and children, the leader of an evil regime that had built concentration camps and carried out genocide and vivisection. Smiles was stunned. He looked at the man next to the Führer and recognised the unmistakable features of Joseph Stalin, the person responsible for the murder of millions of men, women and children, the leader of an evil regime that banished people to the frozen wastes of Siberia and the gulag death camps. Smiles shuddered and I laughed. And Smiles leant right into my face so I could smell sour ketchup and told me not to be so fucking stupid. We had to stick together. His voice was cold, hissing again. He didn't understand how a democratic society could provide asylum for scum like this. One was right-wing and the other left-wing, but there was no difference. Even on race, Hitler and Stalin were not as far apart as some people seemed to think. It sounded like a funny story you'd tell down the pub, reflecting the Right–Left debate going on in the country at the time, being fought out in the punk, skin and herbert music venues, but it was the sound of Smiles's voice and the weird look on his face that showed me he really believed what he said.

He leant forward and told me how he'd waited till the dictators came out of the shop and followed them home. They were living together in a house nearby, and he'd been watching them ever since, both day and night, keeping out of sight best he could. He told me they were lovers and had been together since shortly after the war, losing themselves in the flood of refugees, burying their differences as they followed a new path of sadomasochism. Both closet homosexuals, the Führer and Uncle Joe were eager to corrupt Britain's youth, with violent sex and extremist politics. Both loved the feeling of power that controlling younger men gave them, and this bond was stronger than ideology. His face clouded over and he talked for another hour, mixing all this religious imagery with fascism, communism, power, sex. Smiles had been different the last few years, and come out with some funny things, but now he was well and truly on his way. For the first time ever I couldn't wait to leave the seaside and get back home.

The time passes. During the day I look out of the window at the endless forests and grasslands, occasional villages, one or two towns, eventually crossing the Urals and entering Europe. I sit in the compartment, stand in the corridor, eat borsch and chocolate in the buffet car, finish the food from China on my bunk. I stop listening to tapes, my brain slow and sedated, drugged on motion, the hum of steel wheels. At night, when everyone's asleep, I knock on Rika's door, sit and drink tea with her, keep away from the paint-stripper vodka, know it's only going to leave me with a hangover and sadness in the morning. I love the flow of her voice, not saying much, preferring to hear her talk, the murmur of radio fairy stories in the background, the warmth of her heater, everything blending in with the rhythm of the train. We have sex once more, the night before arriving in Moscow, when it turns cold and hard, like she's trying to kill any emotions. When we get to Moscow that's the end. She says this more than once, so I understand. There's nothing left in Moscow. No future. I know the watching eyes and whispering tongues are more than paranoia, that this is different to the nutty things Smiles came out with.

Back home, in my compartment, I ignore the cunt in the fancy dress, and Mao ignores me. We hate each other. There's nothing to say, and I wonder if I could get away with chucking him off the train. I'd do it late at night, wait for the Chinese dictator, the man responsible for the deaths of millions of men, women and children, to go for a lash, follow the mass murderer who unleashed the Cultural Revolution along the corridor, check Rika's door is shut, open one of the outside doors and toss the enemy of Tibet into the night when he comes back out. One bounce on the steppes and goodbye Mao. The idea starts to shape, and it cheers me up as I cross the world in a travelling library. The German and his girlfriend are either reading or sulking, and though we exchange a few words that's as far as it goes. Me and Mao are in the way, cramping their style. One day I come back from the buffet car early and open the door without knocking. Mao is down the other end of the corridor, near Rika, who thinks he's a fool wearing peasant gear when she'd kill for something expensive. I slide the door sideways and find that Himmler has got his woman bent over Mao's sleeping bag and is so busy knobbing her doggy-style that he doesn't notice me. When the cold air hits his arse he turns and I say sorry. He doesn't slow down or look embarrassed. I close the door.

Good luck to them. The Chairman is the one who's doing my head in. He deserves to be dumped in the middle of Siberia, the Urals, left to wander the prairies in Chinese army fatigues. Chances are he'd break his neck on touchdown, but there again he might survive, and then his troubles would really begin. I don't know how far the Cossacks roam, but when I first think of this we're still a long way from Moscow, and the tribesmen aren't going to be too pleased finding the Chinaman strolling around their plot, taking liberties, like he owns the gaff, taking the fucking piss. The idea of Mao getting chopped up by the Cossacks puts a smile on my face. I met a bloke in Canton, a teacher from Birmingham, who'd been to Xinjiang Province, rode his bike out of Hami and put his tent up miles from anywhere. He brewed some tea and was suddenly surrounded by a band of horsemen who he reckoned were Cossacks from Siberia. They didn't believe in borders, had a cup, then rode off again. Nice bloke. I put Mao in different situations, keep my brain working, trying to blank Smiles but drifting into his way of thinking, seeing dictators in my own carriage. The land is flat and hard, and when Mao comes towards me I can't help smiling. He doesn't know whether I'm taking the piss or being friendly, and this mucks his head right up.

The nights are sweet, except for the last bit of sex, Rika talking away, telling me her dreams. She doesn't mention her brother again, and as she talks I imagine him knocking on her door one day, telling his sister he went for a wander and crossed into Pakistan, ended up in Goa with the hippies, too stoned to move, couldn't be bothered with the tension and hassle at home, the pull of his culture finally too much, more important than his freedom. I think of different angles as she talks, dipping in and out, inventing happy endings. I see her brother as a deserter working his way along an anti-war underground, setting up shop in Hong Kong and living in Chungking Mansions, pouring lager for a living, settling into another way of life. It's all fantasy and dreams, the landscape and constant roll of the train drugging us, so much time to drift, words replaced by sound, Strummer, Lydon, Pursey, Paul Weller, Billy Bragg, Malcolm Owen, Nicky Tesco, Mensi, Micky Fitz, Terry Hall, Roddy Moreno, Chuck D, Ice Cube and all the rest of them buried away in my bag, stuck in cassettes, part of my luggage.

Rika wants to live in the USA one day, stop in Rome and Paris on the way. She isn't interested in England, a poor, industrial country where it always rains. She wants to eat ravioli in Rome, snails in Paris, Big Macs in New York. She wants to settle there and have lots of money. The tea is hot and her voice goes back inside the radio as I wonder what the welcome is going to be like when I get home. Three years is a long time, and I've changed, become less dogmatic, realised that rigid rules and opinions are just another flag to hide behind. Before I left I was angry, held grudges, so I got on my bike and only listened to tapes when I got in late at night, pissed. The words faded and the drums stopped beating. I bought cassettes in the market, bootlegs that I fed into the tinny Walkman, a tacky sound fizzing in my ears, a faint hum with words I knew off by heart but only really stirred me up when I was drunk and could pretend I wasn't in Hong Kong any more.

The night before Moscow there's scratch marks down my back, and I drink Rika's vodka, can almost feel bits of her nails stuck in me, poison pellets killing the romance. It's a way to deal with things, and I've got no choice in the matter, the state has the last word on everything. And I remember Smiles in hospital, living on the psychiatric ward scared to go outside in case he was zapped by Ronnie RayGun's Star Wars programme, in the television room listening to the endless slagging matches. I used to go see him twice a week, regular as clockwork, till it got so he didn't want to talk to me any more. He said I was wicked, that I couldn't be trusted, his paranoia increasing each day till he just wanted to shut the voices out, the doctors feeding him more drugs, knocking him out when they couldn't balance things in his brain. I'll never understand. Don't think anyone does. Whether if it's down to personal experience or chemicals. Tony was the only other person who visited on a regular basis. The old man looked in but couldn't handle it, and I reckon he felt guilty, remembered how he'd slapped Smiles around when he was young. Maybe he thought his fists were to blame, not the canal or his wife's suicide. Who knows? Not me. I'd be sitting on my own the first few months after Smiles went in, curtains drawn, and started feeling the strain, running through Smiles's talk, the insights he'd had. It was me and Tony who took him to the doctor's two years after that day on the bench in Bournemouth, but I can't think about that right now.

And on the last night I look at Rika and wonder what would happen if we were in England, if it's because there's no choice I feel so sad. When it's time to go I kiss her and she sees me out, cold and efficient. I climb into my bunk and listen to the sound of the train knowing it's going to stop tomorrow, and I wish we could keep going, round and round the world for the next ten years. The world is spinning and I don't want to get off. Things are going to harden up after this trip is over, when I get back to Slough and have to deal with all the things I've left behind. I try hard but can't get to sleep, pulled back to the psychiatric unit, to the day me and Tony took Smiles there from the airport. I push it away, think instead of how Wells and the others were let out on bail once Smiles was home and out of danger, how there was suddenly this doubt about what charges should be brought. The murder charge was obviously forgotten, but it was now a choice between attempted murder and assault.

There was a lull as summer ended and the dark started earlier. Nothing seemed to be happening, the Old Bill finally settling for assault and the case delayed. Tony was angry, trying to hold back, and I talked with him about it, knew he wanted to sort things out himself. He made a decision and Alfonso and this mate of Tony's, a bloke called Gerry, came round to pick him up. I made sure I was across the road when they arrived, said I was going as well. They told me I was a kid, this was men's business, told me to fuck off when I argued, I was too young, so I acted like a kid and sat on the bonnet of the car, said I was the one in the canal, none of them. They laughed and knew I was right, so I bundled in the back and sat next to Alfonso as Gerry drove slow, nervous in case we were stopped, except we hadn't done anything wrong. Alfonso was laughing and telling him to put his foot down, but in hindsight Gerry was a smart bloke and knew what he was doing. It didn't take long to reach Wells's house. He lived with his mum, but Tony had checked and knew she'd be at work. We parked across the road, the light fading.

I wasn't bothered about what was going to happen next, hadn't really thought about it. The house was on the end of a terrace, and this was handy because we could go in through the back. Gerry fancied himself as a part-time soldier, and was always down the Drill Hall, weekends away with the TA, said he'd done a recce on the place which cracked everyone up.

There were four blokes responsible, but the way Tony saw it, going on my evidence, the other three were mongs. Their time would come, but Wells was the boss. Right now he was our target, his reputation as a bully going in front of him, well-known for this sort of thing. Tony led the way, Gerry carrying a bag he pulled out of the boot last minute, me behind them with Alfonso at the back. We went down the side of the house, and because I wanted to be in on it Alfonso had to stay round the corner so I could use one of the balaclavas Gerry supplied. I felt like something off a war film, a commando blowing up a Nazi bridge, but it made sense if Wells couldn't identify us. We could see him watching the telly, and in the garden there was a load of wilting runner bean plants, threads curved around bamboo poles, same as Dad grew. Tony kicked the back door open and we piled in. Wells jumped up and Gerry stepped past me with a baseball bat he'd pulled out of the bag. One crack and Wells was down. Knocked out. I felt funny hearing the sound of the bat on his skull, but I was stupid, just a kid who thought it would be a couple of punches and a ticking off. Fuck knows what I was thinking.

Tony wanted his say, and rightly so, but Wells didn't even have the decency to stay awake and listen. It's funny looking back. We weren't hard men, just ordinary blokes looking for some justice. Alfonso was peering round the door and wanted to know what was going on. Tony told him Wells was knocked out and he laughed, said same thing happened when he nutted him in the station. Wells was defenceless and we could've done anything we wanted. Set him on fire, hung him, cut his bollocks off, kicked him black and blue. That wasn't what it was about though. Maybe we wanted an apology, but we never got one, not direct anyway. Gerry was different to us, with his TA training and holdall, whacked Wells on one of his knees with the bat so there was a crunch and Alfonso had to pull him away when he raised it up to have another go. Gerry shrugged his shoulders. Alfonso told us Wells wasn't moving and we panicked, quickly walked out of the house and across to the car, drove off. Wells didn't suffer any long-term injuries, even though his leg was busted and he had to wear a cast, and I was glad. Nothing was ever said about what happened in court, so at least he wasn't a grass.

When the case came up, me and Smiles had to give evidence. The defendants wore suits and looked different. They'd shaved and two of them were wearing glasses. The defence said we were under-age and causing a disturbance in the street, so drunk we could hardly stand up, breaking the licensing laws and singing 'God Save The Queen', a punk song by a band called the Sex Pistols, that insulted the monarchy. The magistrates frowned and the main one said we didn't look like punk rockers, a bit scruffy, but where was the purple hair and safety pins? Wells's brief smiled and said that Mr Dodds was wearing a badge on his collar, with the name of the song on it, and was pointing to it as he sang. The magistrates tutted and wrote something down. Wells's brief said there was an argument, but we had attacked the defendants and run off, stumbling into the canal. It was a joke defence and the case wasn't even going to crown court. The person I felt most sorry for was the Major. He was a good witness, polite and to the point. He was fair in what he said, but then the defence steamed in. We sat there as this stuck-up wanker ripped the Major to threads.

He asked the Major what he did for a living, why he didn't have a job, and was it true that he walked around the streets all day with a Joe 90 notebook, approaching children and talking to them. Wasn't it also true that he lived with his mother, didn't have a girlfriend, and one night had approached Mr Wells in the street. The Major pointed out that the accused had been drinking and had used the Lord's name in vain. A lot of people laughed, but not us. Wells's brief was the lowest of the low, kicking a man down on his luck worse than any thug. The magistrates were presented with the image of a sad, lonely man, almost certainly backward and maybe suspect when it came to kids, a nonce wandering the streets, inventing crimes and spying on people. The Major tried to defend himself, but had no chance. Respect to the Major though. He was humiliated but somehow maintained his dignity, whereas that solicitor never had any to lose. For the first time I saw that the Major had an inner strength, another step on from when he pulled us out of the canal. He saw and understood, people laughing at him as he moved through the shadows, accumulating information, watching the world with an intensity none of us could touch. Wells gave a moving speech, how he felt so bad about the boy going into a coma, but that he was innocent of assault. He really did seem sorry, and that's how I would've felt if I was in his place. He lied about how they attacked us, but I accepted he was sorry for the canal. After the not-guilty verdict the Major walked away before any of us could talk to him.

Tony wanted to have another dig at Wells, but things floated. Smiles wanted to move on, leave what had happened behind, while for me Wells honestly seemed to be sorry, and that made me see him as more human than before, specially as he was walking with a limp, fresh out of plaster. Even bullies don't want to kill children. They never thought what it meant chucking us in the canal, and everyone is basically good inside. Time passed and none of it seemed important any more. I went round the Major's a few times but his mum made excuses, said he was out, had the flu, anything so I couldn't talk to him. I saw him around, but he'd changed and didn't talk to children any more, kept to himself more than ever, walked off when I approached. A few years later I heard his mum died and he took over the tenancy. I hope things worked out for him, but I doubt it somehow. The world is full of victims.

I hear Mao get up for a piss, pull the door open and noisily slide it shut. I think about following him down the corridor and feeding him to the Cossacks, but it's not something I'd really do, and anyway, we're not far from Moscow now. It's bad enough the silly cunt is going to end up lying in state when he dies, embalmed and baking hot under the lights of a mausoleum, thousands of people filing past every day. Good luck to him, and I turn over and face the wall, trying to put things in order.

The authorities are the same all over the world, expect an answer right off, and in every detective film I've ever seen the interrogation light burns into the suspect and the police ask him where he was at half past nine on a Tuesday three weeks ago, when the victim's head was chopped off and the body hacked into tiny pieces, and I wish the man doing the sweating would stand up and grab the nearest copper round the throat, scream HOW DO I FUCKING KNOW? right in his face. That's the truth for most people, but instead there's a few seconds of thinking as the camera zooms in on a worried face, just long enough for the suspect to provide a perfect alibi, even knowing the exact time he was fifty miles from the crime scene with a married woman. It's all bollocks. I can't remember what happened yesterday, let alone five, six, seven years ago. Lots of things are forgotten, lost in the rinse. Life merges into itself, influences and events mashed together, everything part of everything else.

The kitchen I worked in after leaving school seems to have gone on for longer than the time I was at Manors, even though it was the other way round, and after Manors there was a factory for a while, I forgot that till right now, and then I worked as a barman. I can hardly remember the factory, just the heat of the building where I went for the boxes, and the cold when I went down the ramp and back out into the rain. But the pub sticks in my head. It was different to the bar in Hong Kong, more local and laid back. The kitchen and the pub, food and drink, being around people enjoying themselves. Manors was boredom pure and simple, something you believe you have to do, work for the future and forget the moment, falling into their system of thinking, the factory a lonely job moving between the different buildings. The pub was easy work, nothing like the pots and pans, with all that grease and grime in my skin. Pulling pints was fun, and the landlord was easygoing. I was honest with him and he let me get on with things.

To make a half-decent wage I ended up doing the day sessions and four or five nights a week. I was making tapes up and taking them in to play, and people who weren't normally interested in music liked hearing something different, and younger people started coming in specially, so the pub started making more money. I got to open up after a while, help myself to a drink after last orders, let Dave and some of the others have lates. I never took the piss, charged them even though they were always trying to ponce drinks. I drank for free, and it was an equal swap, perk of the job. I could've milked the situation, but the landlord trusted me and I wasn't going to throw it back in his face. Because I was working nights, I wasn't going out so much, and when I had some time off I'd stay in, or go local. From seeing bands on a regular basis, I was lucky to see two a month. My social life got stuck in the pub, which wasn't a problem, as it meant my work time was social as well. It was a gloomy time in England in general and for me in particular, the things Smiles was saying falling into place at the end of that week in Bournemouth. The personal and the social are connected, but with Smiles having a loose connection in his brain it was a lot more extreme. With Chris swinging from burglar to copper, and Smiles taking the Cold War to the outer limits and inventing a brand-new Hitler-Stalin pact, me and Dave were the only ones keeping a lid on things. Except when it came to how we dealt with each other.

We've always argued, as far back as I can remember, which is back to when our balls dropped, everything before that snapshots, mental pictures of kicking a football around in the sun and watching telly in the rain. I wouldn't be surprised if we were rucking in the playground at six years old, but I don't know. It's the way we've always been with each other and I don't know why. We get on each other's nerves, but lots of people get on your nerves in life and you don't waste time on them. When I was in the pub it got worse. He thought the sun shone out of Thatcher's arse, was doing well in the shop where he worked. He loved being in charge, as it meant he had less to do and could knock off more clothes than before. I was giving Dave stick, maybe because I was jealous of him doing so well, cash in his pocket and a smile on his face while I was working all hours just to get by, but more likely because he was lapping up the shit he was being fed by the press, while I'd been stitched up by Manors. He was narked I wouldn't give him free drinks. On top of this there was Smiles and the dictators, something I kept to myself, hoping it would go away. It got to the point where me and Dave couldn't sit down and have a drink without flaring up. Eventually it spilt over, but that was later.

Luckily I bought a stereo while I was still at Manors, and while it wasn't top of the range it was good enough, the best I'd ever had. I was buying all the music, listening to it in the morning before going in at ten, then when I got home, making tapes, mixing the punk of the late seventies with the punk of the early eighties. I had a pretty good record collection together and never minded how old a record was, playing the early stuff, which wasn't that old really, only a few years, just as long as it sounded good. Going to less gigs meant I was listening to the records as if they were new releases, going into the lyrics again, building pictures inside my head, appreciating things I'd missed. Suppose I was running too fast when I was a teenager and had slowed down, was able to appreciate the differences in the music. At first I could only listen to one sound, thought everything else was a sell-out. It was like with 2 Tone, thinking it was weedy because it was new, closing my eyes when really it was brilliant and carrying on the same ideas in a different form.

Some people get their ideas from books, but for us lot the likes of Rotten, Strummer, Pursey and Weller were the best writers, producing the sort of literature that dealt with our lives. They didn't need to fake anything, do any research, just wrote what was already festering inside them and connected with millions of other people who felt the same way. These people were the contemporary, everyday authors we've hardly ever had in England, writing about life through music because they never ght about doing it in book form, firmly outside the literary class and without the classical reference points. And that was what made these people so special, their reference points the same as ours, right there in our own lives, not thousands of miles and years away in ancient Greece.

I stayed at home after I left school. The money I earned meant I couldn't afford anywhere of my own, and it was easy enough there. Kids who leave home early either hate their mums and dads or go to college, but we all stayed where we were. It was fine with me. Dad sat in front of the telly when he got in from work, more and more angry as the eighties wore on. I'd sit with him sometimes and join in, understanding what he was going on about now, while Mum was always off doing something, telling him to turn the box off if it upset him so much. He couldn't, was addicted to the news, the endless arguments. I never thought about my mum and dad much, they were just there, fighting for their small victories in life, making the money stretch while I carried on doing my own thing. The only real problem living at home was if I wanted to take a girl home. It was difficult, specially when your mum and dad hardly ever went out at the same time. That's what I couldn't handle, being stuck indoors for the rest of my life, only going out to work. What's the point of watching someone you fancy turn into a relative? It's better to love and move on, take an exciting memory with you. Love and hate is all part of the same thing I reckon.

I had a few girlfriends over the years, but nothing stuck too long. They got fed up with me, or I got fed up with them. I was never looking to settle down. I always wanted my freedom, it's just the way you're built. Maybe I was waiting for Debbie Harry or Beki Bondage to stroll in the pub and pull me over the bar, drag me into a cab and take me away. The only way to do it is love at first sight, none of this long-term friendship bollocks. There has to be passion or you might as well be dead. That's what always got me about the smelly squatter punks who were really hippies, because you'd read one of their fanzines and they were analysing everything to death, done up like tramps when you knew most of them came from money, boasting about how the roof was leaking and how cold they were, killing any passion for life stone dead. If that's all punk ends up as, stud rebellion for a handful of wankers who think they're 'underground' or 'alternative' and wear Mao caps, then I'd rather be a fucking soulboy.

There was a bloke who came in the pub who wasn't into the music at all, but pointed out to me one night that there was a lot of women on the tapes, up front singing, and he was right. I pictured some of them I'd seen in the flesh – Pauline Murray, Siouxsie Sioux, Poly Styrene, Debbie and Beki, Pauline Black – plus bands like the Slits, Innocents, Bodysnatchers, and I'd never realised it was unusual for the harder music. It was true, there were women involved from the start, but without any big hippy feminist speeches or man-hating, and they weren't dolly birds in frilly dresses, or with their tits hanging out like on Page 3 of the *Sun*. It was natural and how we grew up, and you could read the papers and hear about weak women, but we never saw them. All the girls we met were sharp, and when we were kids they were into sex earlier than us, shagging older boys, so all that white-dress virgin stuff was bollocks as well.

Smiles was alright living with his old man for a few years after his coma, but then he started hating him, and once he'd told me about Stalin and Hitler he turned even harder, let the mask slip so I wondered how long he'd been thinking this way. I saw his dad trooping off to work, with every bit of strength he used to have drained away, probably still sorry for how he'd treated his boys and missing his wife. Smiles had his dad's nuts in a vice and was turning the screw. I felt sorry for him, told Smiles to give it a rest, that I know he got hit but there were reasons. Maybe I shouldn't have said what Stalin told me when Smiles was in a coma, but I did, wish I hadn't, because Smiles sneered in my face and told me to mind my own business. There were too many people getting involved in other people's lives, making notes and keeping files, telling them what to do and how to act, what to think, look at Hitler and Stalin, think of the men, women and children, all that torture and sex.

Smiles was different after Bournemouth. It was out in the open and I didn't know what to do. He used to come in the pub where I worked, and even though he sat in a corner nursing a drink I didn't want him there. He made me nervous, watching as I served people, asking me about the music I was choosing. I never kicked him out, and he didn't cause any problems, but I was on edge. When the light turned dim, he began staying in, his moods linked to the weather, as if he was hibernating. The clouds hung low and there was hardly any sun and Smiles was shut up in his house. I used to go round, but a lot of the time he wouldn't let me in, and when he did I couldn't get much sense out of him. I phoned Tony about what Smiles had been saying, but he'd moved away from here by now and only half believed me.

When I told Dave one night he started laughing, and it's sad to say but it was a good drink-up, getting pissed after closing time, playing pool in an empty pub with a tape going, talking about Hitler and Stalin. We were sitting there and I had 'Satellite', the flip side of 'Holidays In The Sun' on, and Dave said remember that time when we went in the North Bank with Tony and Billy, when Chelsea took the Arsenal end. We must've been pissed because we were really cracking up thinking back to the times when we were teenagers running through the Finsbury Park tunnels late at night shitting it in case we got mugged by blacks, carved up same as in the newspapers. Thing was, there was always some big-town snobbery towards anything that didn't fit in with the inner-city high-rise stereotype, yet there we were along with all these other Chelsea from outer London and the satellite towns piling into the North Bank and clearing the end. Even now I have to laugh at that one. Dave started going on about how Hitler and Stalin were going to put Slough on the map, if the papers ever found out how the council was paying for their keep. We had a laugh. Maybe it's just the fight we had before I left that's stuck in my head. Makes me almost look forward to seeing Dave again. We had a laugh at Smiles's expense and, even though he's dead, I can't help grinning in the darkness.

The train takes its time entering Moscow, the outskirts building up slowly, tenements growing in size and stature, majestic halls and concrete blocks, embankment walls rising at an angle to the track. My bag's packed and I'm standing in the corridor, watching Moscow grow, a shock after the space of the last few days. I look twice and laugh out loud. Someone's taken a tin of paint and written CHELSEA NORTH STAND in massive letters along the middle of the stone embankment. I can't believe what's in front of my eyes. This is the core of the Soviet Union, one of the world's hardest police states, and the locals are writing the names of English football mobs on their railway walls. It's mental. Barmy facing the same graffiti that was going around Slough ten years ago. I could be in any European city, but I'm not, I'm in Moscow, the heart of the Eastern Bloc, the power base of one of the world's superpowers, and the most feared security force in the world, the communist KGB, can't even stop the promotion of counter-revolutionary capitalist hooligan values.

The train cruises into the station, the crawling end of the trip an anti-climax after the almost constant motion since leaving Beijing. It's hard to believe the journey's over, Rika at the other end of the carriage waving to the railway workers lining the platform, a stranger now, back in uniform and acting out her official role. Everything she said is right, but I feel bad inside, and seeing as I've only known her a few days this doesn't make sense. Most blokes would love it, getting their end away and walking off with no after-effects, another sort of room service, but for some reason it's a choker. Don't know if I feel sorry for Rika, sorry for myself, or just sorry there's no choice. She keeps her head turned away and I wonder what she's thinking. We finish the last few yards of the ride hardly moving at all, the oversized architecture of Yaroslav Station rising above the carriages, dwarfing the train and everyone on board.

My legs feel funny once I've climbed down the steps and started walking down the platform, muscles stiff after six days on the train. I'm unsteady on my feet, but that's nothing compared to my head, feel as if I've been on those hippy drugs. My brain's spinning. As I pass the other door I turn to smile at Rika, but she turns her back. I leave her behind and lose the others, quickly melt into the mass of Russians heading towards the metro, looking around the station as I go, the ceiling arching high above us, built for giants. I can't work out the metro tickets and go on to the platform, a race against time to reach the main railway office and book a seat for Berlin. There's two Germans from the train nearby and when the metro pulls in we get on the same carriage. Once it moves a Russian comes over looking for things to buy. He's paying in dollars and wants jeans, Walkmen, trainers. I only have a Walkman, and it's a battered old machine that I want to keep. I ask him if he knows any good places to drink in Moscow, seeing as I'll be staying here tonight, but he's looking at the other two and moves on, buying a pair of Levis off the man. I concentrate on the map, checking station names, know that people are watching me. There's a mixture of ages, a wrinkled bulldog three seats away, a chest full of medals and a beret on his head. Nobody talks.

I get off at Belaruski, where the train to Berlin leaves, and the Russian with the Levis comes as well. He makes it ten steps before a man in a leather coat comes up from behind and jams his arm into his back. Two other men step forward and one hits him over the head with a cosh. There's a thud and he slumps forward. They're right in front of me and I tell the bloke with the cosh to leave him alone. It's obvious they're police, one of the others saying something in Russian and waving his hands. They frogmarch the bloke away. If that's what they do to someone over a pair of jeans, fuck knows what they do when one of their women sleeps with the enemy. I think of Guilin Station again, the boys with placards around their necks, megaphones and coshes, imagine the West European communists on their all-expenses-paid trips to China and the Soviet Union. There's nothing any individual can do, and yet that Russian came on the train looking for jeans knowing what could happen, and whoever hooked up a rope and swung down the embankment wall so they could paint some graffiti must've got their information from somewhere.

I find the ticket office for my train to Berlin. It's packed, families squatting on the marble floor, baggage wrapped and stacked in big piles. An official comes over and asks where I'm going. I tell him I have to get out of the country before my transit visa runs out. He's used to this, deals with the likes of me every time the Trans-Siberian arrives in Moscow. He puts me at the front of a long line of peasants. There's an argument and the official shouts at people who are angry about me pushing in. Don't blame them either. The official leaves and I stand at the head of the queue, feeling guilty, glad when he brings the two Germans over. There's an old woman who keeps going on, and the Germans talk to her. After a while the man tells me that these people are ethnic Germans shipped beyond the Urals when the war started, that they've lived in Russia for hundreds of years. Gorbachev is letting them return to Germany. She's laying curses on us right now, in a German dialect that goes back hundreds of years. He says it's amazing to hear her speak. She's praying the crows will come and peck out our eyes. She hopes that the worms will eat our flesh. She wants our souls to burn in hell. I look at her scowling face, and despite years of communist hatred for the Church, it's interesting to see that religion is still alive and well.

It takes three hours to get a seat allocated, never mind there's only two people in front of me. Three hours works wonders with the witch. By the end she's stroking my arm and feeding me apples. My train is tomorrow and I leave the station to look around. The hotels are expensive so I'll doss here tonight, stick my bag in a locker and get hold of a street map, walk outside and go back to the thirties again. An open lorry pulls up full of blond-haired blue-eyed troopers jumping to the ground and jogging past me into the station. The first thing I notice after the soldiers is that this might be the front of Belaruski, a major station, but there's hardly any shops or kiosks. The only shop I can see has a window filled with blocks of cheese. I'm hungry and go inside. It's packed with middle-aged women, except this lot don't have the happy faces of the gherkin girls in Siberia. Their features are tight and their lips sag, something you see in big Chinese cities. There's none of the Chinese hustle and bustle in here, just silence and some bread behind the counter. Bread and cheese will do me fine. I wait my turn and point when I get to the till, hold out my roubles. The Nazi serving gives me an ear-bashing in front of everyone. There's notepaper and pencils, and she's telling me to write something down. Maybe the food's rationed. Fuck knows. I point again and get another bollocking. Then I leave.

I walk towards Red Square, following the map. The streets are wide, with big pavements. It's cold out and the buildings lining the avenue are official-looking, but probably nice and warm. It's always hard to know how much is your conditioning when you go somewhere new, if you fit a place in with the image, but there's an edge to Moscow. Even if I got off the train and didn't know where I was, I'd feel the atmosphere. I keep walking and cross a road, the shriek of a whistle turning my head towards a policeman shouting and waving me back to the pavement. He keeps on till I'm back on the kerb. It's a fair old walk to Red Square, and I'm on the lookout for a shop where I can buy some food, but there's nothing. Anything will do. A bowl of borsch or a bar of chocolate. It doesn't matter. I'm not fussy.

I reach Red Square and see the Kremlin, picture Stalin on the balcony watching the Red Army march past, celebrating victory over Hitler. There's a thick column of people waiting to go in and see Lenin, who's lying in state. There's thousands of them, waiting patiently. St Basil's is right here as well, more impressive in real life. I lean on the barriers and let the experience soak in.

It's a funny feeling and makes me realise how much the Second World War and the Cold War politics that followed it have influenced my life. I've seen Mao, and it's a shame to miss out on Lenin, but the people aren't moving. I don't have enough time. After a while I walk over and go into St Basil's Cathederal, where the rooms are small and covered in drawings, proper little caves. It's a different country in here, old and Orthodox. I don't know much about this Russia.

When I leave it's colder, and I head for a block of buildings nearby that turns out to be a grand shopping arcade. There's lots of glass that keeps the weather out and lets the light in, the stone expensive and clean. The shops are packed with tinned fruit and preserves, whole rooms dedicated to fancy boxes of chocolate done up in bows, fine clothes and ethnic stalls for the tourists. Thing is, I don't see any tourists. It's warm though, and I walk around, taking my time. I've hardly spent anything yet, could've got away with changing ten dollars, a bundle of roubles burning away in my pocket. I can't change them back, seeing as they're black market, but there's nothing I want to buy here, apart from food. I get some chocolate and cakes, and keep walking. It's busy and I can't work the place out, suppose it's mostly party officials who come in here, same as the Friendship Stores in China. These are luxury goods in here, and have to be beyond the ordinary Russian.

I can't stay all day and go back to Red Square, sit down and eat my chocolate and cakes. When I've finished I walk around for a while, but there's not much happening, some sleet falling and melting. Time soon passes and the light starts to fade, so I head back up towards Belaruski, begin to notice the drunks, hear shouting and a bottle smashing in the gutter, don't take any notice of the three men coming my way. One of them punches me in the face and says something I don't understand. I turn and spread my hands out, head stinging, and worse than the pain is the surprise, being sober and knowing I'm on my own. They keep going as if nothing's happened, and I stand in the middle of the pavement wanting to follow but holding back. They disappear and I wipe blood from my nose, turn and keep going, looking for a bar or cafe to have a drink, a place to sit down.

Belaruski is home for me now, better than a street corner, and

I hang around the main hall watching a line of silent men and women twist back from a drinks machine that doesn't work. There must be a hundred people waiting for the bloke at the front, who's banging the panels. I can't work it out. They can see it doesn't work, but still they're waiting. It's the only machine in the station. Maybe they think it will work for them and not him. There's no laughing, no echoes in the dome. The silence is what gets me. People seem so crushed they can hardly speak. That's what I feel. And I sit around keeping warm till eight and go out again. There has to be something open by now. I walk for ages, groups of men sitting on seats drinking, and I don't know the places to go in Moscow. Some shout at me, then forget in seconds. Finally I see a bar, red light coming through a curtain. I look inside and a big man with a goatee steps forward. He shakes his head and waves me away, looks up and down the street, goes back inside.

I walk till my feet hurt, not used to so much exercise after the train. I want to get pissed, drink till morning and sleep it off tomorrow, but I can't find anywhere. Moscow is different to Beijing. I always felt safe in China, even when I was wandering around late at night, but here there's real violence in the shadows. Beijing is noisy and alive, but Moscow is dead. In China there was something going on that I couldn't see, but here it's much nearer. I'm alone, but hope I see the man who punched me. It's the same old bullying, the worst sort of person. I'm an easy target, with no defence and no comeback. I wonder what I'm doing here, wandering around Moscow at nearly ten o'clock, freezing my bollocks off. Then I think of Rika and wish things were different, that she'd asked me to come and stay with her. It's easy to see myself on the tenth floor of a granite block, looking over the twinkling lights of Moscow, a warm drink in my hand and a full-scale meal to eat, the central heating roaring away. And there I sit in my imagination, fresh out of the shower, dried and dusted, armpits in top condition, deodorant layered, the bristle covering my face shaved off, rolling the spirit back and forward in the glass, swilling it around my mouth and feeling it slide down my throat. This is Moscow and I should be doing something special, but instead I'm hungry and cold.

Back at the station I take my bag out of the locker and kip

down in the same hall where I got my reservation. This is where the sleepers are, a good two hundred of us on the floor, lights beating down, lit up and safe, the building and the body heat raising the temperature. Every half an hour men in long leather coats come and look around, smoke a fag and talk quietly with each other, and it's sad to say, but it feels good having the Moscow Old Bill as babysitters. I go to sleep wondering what would happen if the KGB packed it in, decided to let the comradeship of the people run things. The whole place would go up I reckon.

I'm not religious, never went to church as a kid, don't believe or not believe in God, but after being in China, and going on what I've seen of the Soviet Union, the problem with communism is that there's no deep feeling of unity. A war can do it for a while, and the revolution was a class war, but now that's gone communism is just a materialistic doctrine, with rules, regulations and officials to be obeyed. There's no spiritual side. Religion must've done it in the old days, provided the comradeship, but all they've got now is the daily grind. They say communism is the opposite to capitalism, but it's more of a complement. They're both rooted in science, the argument about who should get the rewards.

This journey is an education for me, and I run these ideas through my head until I fall asleep, getting the sort of rest you always end up with when you're travelling, whether you're in a station or on a train, waking up ten times to feel my money belt and make sure my passport and ticket are still there, on guard the whole time. I toss and turn and every time I wake up I think I'm somewhere else, in Chungking Mansions, Slough, back on the Trans-Siberian. It takes a few seconds to sort myself out, get comfortable, hold on to the piss in my bladder looking forward to morning when the bogs will be unlocked and I can have a wash, leave Moscow and go home.

Smiles had dropped out and tuned in and used to come round to share the news, his eyes drilling into me as he explained how the air was alive with messages, how he'd cracked the code and was tapping into the dark secrets of the state, the long-term aims of our controllers. The Falklands War had been and gone and the right-wing press was running the country, the Tories sharp enough to see that the worker's dream was more ambitious than a condescending nod from an Oxbridge-trained intelligentsia. People wanted to buy their council houses, to get a mortgage and buy a home on a new estate, away from the dirt and decay, keep more of the money they earned and see the petty dictators on the local council kicked in the head. The Tories were experts at simple slogans, repeated the same short messages again and again, firing the points home while the left-wing committees and chattering tendencies told us Britain was shit and, by definition, we were shit. The Labour Party disappeared up its own arsehole, student cells squabbling over procedure while the Tory press fed people a long line of shit, exploiting the usual targets, saying that millions were going to single mothers, battered wives, lesbians, refugees, heroin addicts and sun-drenched holidays for vicious teenage criminals. When I left in 1985, the same old scapegoats I'd heard about all my life were still in the spotlight, people on their own with no way of defending themselves. On a bigger scale, the state targeted the miners and eventually crushed organised opposition. The coal strike dragged on, television channels shooting their footage from behind police lines, giving the official view, the union leadership painted as bitter men who wanted the Soviets to take control of Britain. When it came to party politics, the country was split, the South mainly Tory, most of the rest of the country Labour. It was divide-and-rule tactics, based on a turnaround in class. Labour was seen in the South as posh ideologues running the ordinary person into the ground, while the Tories were presented as the hard grafters working people respect. In the South, Labour was talking with the same plum in its mouth as the Tories. The North is rooted in heavy industry and has a Labour tradition, but in the South the post-war sprawl of London and the change to light industry has made people more isolated. Labour's biggest mistake was the way it ran down patriotism. They let the Tories decide what being patriotic meant. If you tell people their culture is shit how can you expect them to vote for you? I was never someone to wave a flag, but could see the Tory view of patriotism was a lie, that pride in your country meant pride in your culture. For me, it was the people I knew and the place I lived, the music I listened to and the way I behaved. Thing is, too many people in the Labour Party were outside the everyday culture.

Britain was in chaos, and from the mid-seventies to mid-eighties it was all-change, and with everything confused and turning bitter Smiles cracked up. His brain was melting as he listened to the arguments and lies, and, while everybody was affected, Smiles couldn't cope. One day the phone rang and he was on the other end of the line. He was excited, told me he'd heard the Clash single 'White Man In Hammersmith Palais' on the radio this morning, and wanted to know if I remembered the line where it says that if Adolf Hitler flew in today they, the government, would send a limousine anyway, never mind what he'd done during the war? Of course I knew the line, 'White Man' one of the greatest singles ever released. And didn't I think it was strange that the radio, which only ever played shit and ignored proper music, should choose today to play the song? I didn't see why, and he sighed on the other end of the line.

This was Gary talking, and he told me how he'd been walking along on the road behind the sorting office that same morning and a limo had passed by. The windows were tinted black so he couldn't see in, but it was heading towards Heathrow. This proved that it wasn't just two old dictators conning the council with false identity papers, leaving their gas-and-electricity-included box unticked so they could claim an extra six quid on their housing benefit, but a conspiracy that went even deeper, straight to the heart of government. He said I had to admit that it was true what the song said, we'd joked about it in the past. He asked when had I ever seen a limousine in Slough, and I hadn't, that was true. It was also true that if Hitler really was alive, living the life of Riley in South America, or been deep-frozen and reanimated by a mad scientist, and if he was jetting into Heathrow, then I couldn't see them rolling out a Black Maria to pick him up. The authorities would send a car. A limousine, or maybe a Rolls. But I kept my mouth shut and waited for the next instalment.

Gary started shouting down the phone at me, angry like I'd never heard him before, telling me that this was the big time and something that couldn't be ignored. He screamed at me to wake up, that the government were rubbing our noses in it, taking the piss. It was bad enough Hitler and Stalin were living on benefits, love on the dole in a council house that could've gone to a needy family, and this was in Slough, a town that still voted Labour. It was bad enough how the state had allowed two mass murderers to assume new identities and escape justice, but now they were even picking them up in high-class luxury automobiles – while he was forced to catch two buses to get to the airport. Because that's where he was. He was at the airport waiting for the Führer's plane to land. And when he touched down, Gary would be ready. He was going out on the runway as Hitler crossed the tarmac, before he reached customs and entered the country, and that way Gary couldn't get done for murder. He had a knife and was going to kill Hitler.

I told Gary he was talking shit, that he was a sick man and needed help. I was trying the direct approach now, but when he started shouting down the phone again I knew it wasn't going to work. I had to think fast, and tried to reason with him. Hitler couldn't be arriving at Heathrow if he was already here in Slough, shacked up with Stalin. What did he think, that the Führer had been over to Spain on holiday, two weeks swanning around Benidorm getting a suntan, pissing it up on San Miguel, chasing the girls. Hitler was too old for that, and Smiles had told me himself that Hitler and Stalin were a couple of poofs, two ageing sadomasochists who didn't let their political views or something as minor as a world war get in the way of a good torture session. It didn't make sense. Did he think Hitler was strolling along the promenade in San Antonio in his Union Jack shorts and string vest, dancing all night to Shalamar and Shakatak? That wasn't the Führer's style. Smiles knew he preferred Skrewdriver. If he was a shirt-lifter, then he'd book into a sleazy hotel on the coast somewhere with Uncle Joe, resting on his Zimmer frame as he gave the red dictator's arse a pummelling. I could hear Smiles laughing and told him to ignore the messages he was getting. He had to get out of there and catch a bus home. Or better still, tell me where he was so I could come and get him. There was silence for a few seconds as he thought about things. I heard him laugh some more, as he ran the image of Adolf Hitler and Joe Stalin on the seafront at Bournemouth, the rock breaking their teeth, wind howling in off the Channel, a long way from the world supremacy they'd dreamt of as young men. But then Smiles stopped laughing and said he had to go. He was in a hotel waiting for the flight to arrive. He couldn't tell me which one in case the phones were tapped. If he died on the runway, in the engines of a jumbo, he wanted me to tell everyone that he'd done his best.

Gary was off his head, the words flowing like he was on some serious whizz, speeding right over the edge into this paranoid world where he saw conspiracies and secret plans in everything around him, tapping into colours and following imaginary trails through Slough, up and down the terraces and over the train tracks, reading the posters in Queensmere and breaking secret codes, making connections where connections didn't exist. He came out with some mental stuff, and the worst thing was that sometimes it made sense, or made you laugh. He'd watch my face and grin, but inside he was serious. He hadn't done anyone any harm, so there was no way you could force him to see a doctor. He was clever enough to tell me things when we were alone. Other times he was quiet, kept the mad stuff to himself. There'd be things he said that I wondered about, whether there was some truth in there or if it was just rubbish. Ideas spread so I suppose insanity can spread as well.

I phoned Tony and he came round right away, gunned the engine as we crossed Slough and took the A4 through Colnbrook. We raced down the wider road lined with parked lorries, gravel pits and long-distance cafes, makeshift car parks jammed with containers, rubble lining the ditches, stones and mud covering the road, spitting up and scratching the paint, pebbles stuck in the wheel sounding like the big end was going, the thunder of jets coming in to land. We were passing through a long-distance world of half-sleep and burgers, tired men catching some shut-eye before they collected their loads from the airport. The lay-bys were full of deep mud tracks, rubbish filling the nettles and grass. We were in a hurry, Tony following the white line down the middle of the road, cars and lorries coming the other way shifting left, a cabbie keeping his nerve and flashing his lights. For a few seconds I thought Tony was

going to wipe us out, but then they both veered left just in time.
I looked at Tony and he was panicking, seeing the madness in
his mum spreading through the family. It was an illness, the
same as cancer, except it was mental and not physical, mixed up
with ideas of right and wrong, good and evil. None of us knew
what to do, how to deal with it.

If Smiles was in a hotel, and stayed there, we had a chance of
finding him, but we had to guess right. We checked the first
hotel and Tony went over to the phones and got hold of a
Yellow Pages, called them one by one. He gave a description and
was lucky fourth go. The woman on the other end could see
Smiles in the bar, watching the planes coming in to land with a
drink in his hand. We drove over, parked and went in the foyer.
The clientele was all well-heeled tourists and businessmen,
piped muzak and rubber plants. We got a couple of looks, like
we'd come to fix the bogs and should've come in the back way,
but it didn't matter. We didn't want Smiles to see us and do a
runner, stood by the door of the bar plotting our next move. He
turned suddenly and spotted us, waved us over. He was good as
gold, talked about the jumbos and Boeings coming in to land,
and how he wouldn't mind flying on Concorde one day. It was
easy getting him to drink up and come with us. It was like he'd
forgotten about Hitler and the limousine. There was no
problem, no punch-up, and I sat in the back of the car with
Smiles so he joked and said Tony should have a uniform if he
was going to be a chauffeur. He was unpredictable, and you
never knew what was coming next.

Once we were on the move he started drawing this picture
for me in a notebook he had, arrows pointing up and down the
page towards boxes he'd marked HEAVEN and HELL. It was
black ink on white paper, so in triangles he'd written
YELLOW, RED, BLUE, GREEN. I didn't know what it
meant. Maybe it didn't mean anything. He held his hand over
his mouth and whispered that there were bugs everywhere and
we were being tracked, but if you knew the magic word you
could turn things around and hear the voices passing through us,
tap into the airwaves, and he asked me again why the sick cases,
the perverts and mass murderers, were being protected by
Thatcher, rehoused and allowed to live normal lives, by the end

his voice loud so Tony could hear. Smiles tried to pull me in, said I could hear the truth if I wanted, if I listened hard enough and did as he told me. It was a bad time, that ride to the hospital, walking around trying to find someone who would section him, talking to a doctor who explained the situation, going back out to the car where the two brothers were sitting and persuading Smiles to come inside. And we spent three hours talking to him till he agreed to admit himself.

All Smiles's madness comes back to me as I try and get comfortable on the floor of the station, the man next to me snoring, dreaming of a new life in the West. And my journey will be over soon, reliving the trip from the airport to the psychiatric unit. We did what we thought was best. I was just his mate, didn't see any other answer. When Smiles hurt himself they sectioned him, but up till then it was his choice. We thought he'd be better off with professionals. They tried different drugs, worked on the chemical levels in his brain. The doctors were honest people, and when I went back to visit him in the months that followed we'd sit in the television room of a run-down NHS building, a one-storey, wartime building, and he'd come out with some real gems, putting me to shame. Nothing was changing, but at least he was being supervised.

Smiles said he was a free spirit and superior to the people around him, that he'd sunk to the lowest depths and reached the highest heights. We sat in a corner of the room with the evening news on and Thatcher was inside the set, her face lit up by studio lights, and I looked at Smiles and started whistling the tune of a Fun Boy Three song, 'The Lunatics Have Taken Over The Asylum', and he laughed, clicked back from this story of Mao running the chippy, repeated the words under his breath, tapping his hands on the arms of his chair. In front of us a middle-aged woman and teenage boy played ping-pong, and he switched to the Clash's 'What's My Name' – 'I tried to join a ping-pong club, sign on the door said ALL FULL UP, I got nicked for fighting in the road, the judge didn't even know, what's my name' – and he got angry suddenly, said that was the worst insult, when people didn't even know your fucking name. And he asked if I remembered being chucked in the canal, and it was because we were punks without names, cartoons in a *Sun* headline. Just like Gotcha, where the same paper trivialised the death of hundreds of Argentinians. He shuddered, music forgotten, told me to imagine those men stuck down below as the ship went down. He gobbed at the face on the screen. He knew what was going on. And that's why we handed him over to the doctors.

The Moscow-to-Warsaw train takes some finding, but it's half empty and I get a compartment to myself, spend the day watching Russia slowly pass by, stopping and starting, a lot different to the smooth ride from Beijing. At night I spread out on the top bunk. There's no buffet car and I can't stop thinking about food, hardly sleep even though I'm knackered after last night. People come in and sit down, talk and have a smoke, leave before morning. I wake up early, rain bucketing down outside, and we stop again, the land green and flat, topped by low grey clouds, the horizon a skinny yellow plaster stuck on for decoration. Cool condensation fights the heavy smell of sweat and ash. A local train stops next to us, going the other way. It's packed, and everyone stares at me, a hundred pairs of eyes examining the outsider. I stick out my tongue. A boy says something and points. People laugh. An old man waves. I do a monkey impression, tickling my armpits and jumping up and down. Monkey in a zoo. More people laugh and a woman with red hair winks. Their train moves on while mine stays still for an hour. The ticket collector says we're in Lithuania when I ask, and the fascists and communists probably fought over these fields. I want to say this is the middle of nowhere, but that's too easy. Everywhere is somewhere. All those people on that other train have families, friends, work, history, culture. Before the border I walk along the train and find an old woman waiting to get off, stuff the roubles in her hand and hold my finger in front of my mouth. No point wasting good notes.

The Russians and Poles take turns checking my ticket, passport, visas at the Polish border. In Warsaw the city spreads out around open platforms, the buildings post-war, the Poles caught between the bullies of the Left and Right, East and West. I go out to the front of the station looking for something to eat. The street is quiet and there's no food, and anyway, I don't have any Polish money. I have to catch the train or my visa will be out of date, and it's a wasted opportunity, the chance to have a look at Warsaw, a city I watched burn as a kid on the telly, pictures from the ghetto, Treblinka bodies piled high, grinning skulls that gave me nightmares, the Jews, gypsies, others. I walk along a tunnel, walls clean and disinfected, and when these three figures block out the tiny prick of light at the other end I understand why there's no broken bottles or graffiti. Three policemen march my way, more like paramilitaries as they swing their arms, jaws sticking out, eyes straight ahead, long legs doing a communist version of the Nazi goose-step. There's no recognition, just the thud of jackboots from three machines. I press against the wall of the tunnel so I don't get trampled to death, watch them disappear round the bend. I walk back to the platform and sit on a bench, suck deep on the cold air, wait for the tracks to hum. It's very quiet here. Maybe it's Sunday.

The Berlin train is busy, but I find a corner at the end of a carriage, try and sleep till the East German border when the Poles and Germans have another go at my documents. People get off so I sit in a compartment as police patrol the corridor. I'm wide awake as we enter East Berlin, the building blocks of the city grey squares on a black sky, some sort of a ghost town with dim street lights the only colour, the train slowing, stopping, and I find a metro to Friedrichstrasse, stand on the platform at midnight, play 'Gates Of The West' off the Clash's 'Cost Of Living' EP. Have to laugh. Kiddie games. Waiting on the platform tired, dirty, hungry, thirsty, sad, happy, don't care about the police watching me, pistols in their holsters. There's tension in the air, and the people around me are nervous, know this is the end, the beginning, hope they don't get stopped before they reach the West.

The train to West Berlin is a tinny effort held together with tacks. It rattles along the platform where everyone is crowded together in a small patch, the rest of the station empty. The train stops and the door stays shut. The driver waits for the official nod. People sweat, eyes darting, wondering what the delay is, if something has gone wrong, and when the doors open everyone rushes forward, jams inside. I stand by the doors on the opposite side, and after a few more minutes we're shut in and the train jolts forward, bumping as it goes, wheels screaming as steel connects. The tracks really howl as well, but at least it smothers the clank of the carriages, and I shut the sounds out and press my face into the glass so I can see the stone of the East, buildings that are clearer now, tenements rooted in darkness, the flicker of a light, matchsticks flashing, ghosts from the war, this side of Berlin dark and powerful. Light catches my eyes and makes me turn towards the West, and it's a strange thing to say, but West Berlin is actually glowing, as if it's on fire, thousands of incendiaries lighting up the sky, and even though it's beautiful, the East of the city has this extra dignity, cold but solid, and I realise how calm most communist cities are at night, from China to East Berlin. Everyone stretches to see West Berlin, and I've got the best position as the train reaches the Berlin Wall and starts crossing, the track suspended above no-man's-land which is lit up by spotlights, control towers lining the walls, extra soldiers along the Eastern side, a big dog on a chain sitting down and looking at the train, the light so bright it dazzles me, the earth in no-man's-land almost yellow, and if a spider moved it would be seen. I can understand why the people on here are so nervous. It's science fiction, a divided city and continent. Seeing the Berlin Wall like this will stay in my head for ever.

We leave the Berlin Wall behind and enter a funfair where this is the only ride, a blaze of colour and light, millions of bulbs buzzing out of control, and I feel excited and let down at the same time, because this might be the free world but the technology and gadgets belong to big business, everything connected with advertising, and I'm trying to get my head around it, stunned after months in countries where there's no such thing, where the vegetables are bent out of shape and meat, when you see it, isn't lined with cellophane. I'm in a capitalist wonderland that pisses all over Hong Kong. It's cheap but beautiful, empty but cheerful, stupid but clever, a big show of wealth and possessions. I look back and forward, East to West, and wonder if the Wall will ever be knocked down, who's going to win. Can't see it ever coming down somehow. At least not in my lifetime.

I change the rest of my money at Bahnhof Zoo, and a man at

the hostel stall sends me outside and round the side of the station, to a door in a brick wall. The hostel is dark, but an American lets me in and explains the rules. I sign my name and pay for a bed. It's not cheap, some sort of Christian mission, and my head is tripping all over the place as I follow him into a massive room that was probably built for storage, two pine tables in the middle with burning candles and incense. He leads me to an arch, the space filled with a mattress, pillow and blanket, a curtain on a rail for privacy. Shapes line the tables, some of the people with their hands together, praying, others upright, arms folded, one white-haired man with his head in his hands. A woman stares at the white flame of a candle, behind her Jesus nailed to a crucifix. I ask the man who they are, and he whispers refugees from the East. I nod and he disappears. All I need now is Count Dracula to turn up. But the incense smells good, and there's an atmosphere. I can't work it out. If it's good or bad.

The most important thing is that I've got a bed for the night. Now I need some food. It's gone one o'clock and the only place I can find that's open is McDonald's. Can't believe it. I never go in the place at home, but there's nowhere else. So inside an hour of coming back into Western Europe for the first time in three years I'm sitting in McDonald's with two cartons of reheated chips, an apple pie and a large Coke. Piped music plays. The streets are quiet, but lit up. Advertising covers everything. Seven youths with skinhead crops come in and order, sit at a table digging into their food. I think they're French soldiers. They're too busy stuffing their faces to say much, mellow music and bright yellow walls doing my head in. I'm in a plastic world eating plastic food, counting the adverts, all the colours of the rainbow trapped in the neon signs, millions of dollars spent on nothing, the glamorous faces of blonde models and tanned sportsmen, the emphasis on American youth, clear skin, designer clothes. And I can hear the disco soundtrack.

Back in the hostel my bed is warm and comfortable, and I close everything out when I pull the curtain shut. It's the first real deep rest I've had since China, the best since Hong Kong, and I sleep till nearly midday when the cleaner wakes me up.

The shower is even better, my first for over a week, the first proper hot water I've washed in since I left England. When I pick my clothes up I realise how bad they stink. I shave my face and look in the mirror. I've lost weight and my eyes are almost popping out they're so bright. I sort out the train to London, then walk around, see the Berlin Wall at street level, have a roll in a cafe, a slow beer in a bar, catch my train at half-eleven and doze till we reach the Hoek next day. I nick some chocolates for Mum and Dad in the ferry's duty-free, broke now, thirty dollars to my name after the ticket. They always used to have a box of chocolates for their end-of-the-week treat. I travel up to London from Harwich and round to Paddington on the tube, sit on the platform waiting for the Slough train to come up on the board. Chewing gum sticks to my leg. I work it off and move over. Three youths jog past in a selection of labels, trainers flashing. I'm coming home with less than twenty pounds to my name, but it doesn't matter. Part of me is excited. I'm going home. The words sink in.

I think of all the times we bunked the milk train back to Slough, early Sunday morning after a night on the piss. Some poor sod would have to come down the carriages checking tickets and there'd be us lot pissed, speeding, larey. They didn't want any trouble, and if they asked us for our tickets we'd say we didn't have any money, just couldn't pay. And what were they going to do? Everyone on those trains was pissed, travelling for nothing, making up for British Rail overcharging on the way in. But they were ordinary men and it couldn't have been much fun, stuck with a load of cocky kids effing and blinding their way across West London. And I remember this old Sikh who got lumbered one night, how he was bound by the rules and had to do it right. I felt sorry for the bloke because he kept going on and on till Dave grabbed him round the neck, still wouldn't let it go, and I told Dave to leave it out, he was just an old codger. We squared up and the Sikh told us to get off at the next stop or he'd have the police on us, but the next station was Slough and that was fine. It was the fact he was an old boy that made it bad, and I knew he'd been embarrassed, and on top probably thought it was because he was a Sikh, except it wasn't the reason, none of us was like that, it was just him acting bossy when he should've known the score and moved on.

My train comes up and I get on, polystyrene cartons and plastic cups covering the seats, red tabloid banners spread over the floor, the bare tits of a teenage blonde and an article on voluntary castration for rapists, the familiar smells of the carriage, last week's piss and today's coffee dregs, the face of Margaret Thatcher smiling up at me, an article about something called the poll tax. Dust is ground into the seats and it must be a while since the windows were cleaned, but this is England and these are the proper sights and flavours, and as we pull away and gather speed I watch the tangle of tracks and cables, which are quickly replaced by sturdy red-brick homes, the houses newer once we've gone through Hanwell, the blocks fading, textile factories and haulage yards taking over, lining the track as we pass Southall and Langley, the street lights dimmer and less crowded, more shadows and space, breeze blocks instead of red brick, the lighter cheap bricks of the new estates, and it's after ten now, my reflection in the glass again, Siberia a long way away, Rika gone, and when I look at myself I see a worn-out man with a bag full of smelly clothes and empty pockets. I lean back and close my eyes, listen to the roar of the engine dying as we coast into Slough, open them in time to see the gasworks on my right, the canal out of sight down below the tanks and pipes, the Grand Union forgotten, railways faster and more efficient. Modern life is all about speed and expansion, never-ending growth, production for production's sake. Or so they say. Plastic makes perfect. Never mind the quality. The fairy lights of hundreds of houses filter through the dust and into the train. I stand by the door and wait till we stop, get off and walk along the platform, climb the steps and pass along the wooden corridor, the white panels we used to spray, our words long gone, and I lift my head and see ANARCHY IN THE UK in fresh black paint, straight ahead.

There's nobody on the gate, so this saves me going back along Platform 1 and up the embankment like when we were kids. I can leave through the ticket hall and pretend I've moved up in the world. I stand in front of the station for a few seconds, by the photo booth. It's a strange feeling, coming back after so long, and my brain clanks as it gets into gear, taps into a hidden bank recognising things I never thought I'd taken in. There's three taxis opposite me, the smell of petrol and the concrete of the multi-storey car park, a low sky and dark clouds. I turn right and walk up the slope next to the tracks, cross the bridge as a customised Sierra bumps over the ridge, engine shouting as the driver accelerates, a long silver aerial bent back from the bonnet, stretching to the boot, one of those electricity tapes flowing behind, a double set of brake lights in the rear window. I walk with my eyes wide open, one minute happy to be back, the next sad, all the time appreciating what I can see. Before long I'm standing in front of the house I grew up in, the familiar flash of the television in the front room. This is my home but seems much smaller than I remember, the terrace like any other terrace, nothing obvious in the bricks and glass of the houses. I lose my nerve suddenly. Inside it will be warm and friendly, a place where I don't have to worry. At least I hope so.

I ring the bell and wait. I ring again. I stand here for a couple of minutes before I remember. The bell was broken when I left and it hasn't been mended. But that's not important, means only people who know the secret get let indoors. I knock hard and look through the frosted glass, hear the living-room door creak, like it's always creaked, since I don't know when. It only needs a couple of drops of oil in the hinge, but who cares. It doesn't matter. Just doesn't matter. I can see Mum's outline coming to the door, moving slowly, a woman past fifty now, taking her time wondering who's come knocking this late, Bible-bashers or locked-out neighbours, a drunk who's chosen the wrong house. She undoes the bolt and peers over the chain, stands for a few seconds trying to make out my face, and then she realises and jumps back, like she's seen a ghost. Her hair is grey and she looks a lot older than when I left. She shouts and fumbles with the chain, pulls the door open and hugs me, starts to cry.

Dave and Chris lift their glasses, knock them against my raised pint as we toast the memory of Gary Dodds, better known as Smiles, a kid we knew from the infants, a teenage punk rocker lobbed in the canal by four soulboy tarts stirred up by the great British press, a mental case who believed what the voices told him, dropped out and tuned in, a scruffy herbert who gave up on life and topped himself. He was a happy-go-lucky kid who went round flogging *Sunny Smiles* pictures because he felt sorry for kids who didn't have mums and dads and had to live in a home. He was a decent bloke who had the knack of feeling what the other person felt. He had a good heart. Wouldn't hurt a fly. Used to trap them under a cup and take them out before his old man grabbed the spray.

Dave and Chris are toasting Smiles for my benefit, a slow-motion replay. They've been to the funeral, gone on a bender and wrecked the nearest parade of shops, doing the windows with bricks out of a skip, from the launderette down to the chippy. They ended up in the back of a police van and appeared in court first thing next morning. They were bound over by a sympathetic magistrate, but have a hefty bill to pay. A grand apiece. There's not much to say and I wonder why I've bothered, travelled halfway across the globe to sit in a near-empty pub pouring fizzy drink down my throat, the bleep of a slot-machine gambler and the clink of an alky the only background noise. Last time I saw Dave we weren't saying much either, just kicking lumps out of each other in the street, outside the Grapes at closing time.

Tony's nowhere to be seen, and old man Dodds is staying with Smiles's auntie in Southall. I've been past the house. Stopped and stared on my way to the pub, waiting for some movement. There was nothing but blank reflections off the street lights, solid net curtains and jammed levers. I felt the decay, day and night feeding through the glass of the front door, skeleton rays not quite catching the dangling legs of a dead man, the dust building up. I stood there for five long minutes before going to the end of the houses, past the smashed-up phone box and down along the back alley, hopped over the wire fence and ran to the kitchen door, scared in case someone saw me and phoned the Old Bill. I pressed my hands on the glass and peered inside, the draining board empty of plates, the only things on the table a plastic bowl, rags and a big tin of Vim.

The window broke easy enough and I reached in to open the door, went through the kitchen and down the hall, stopping at the bottom of the stairs. Don't know why, but I had to see the exact spot where Smiles died. There was no point turning the light on, yellow street lamps coming in from his bedroom. The landing was small and bright, as if something was burning in the corner. The walls were bare, and when I think back I can't remember ever seeing pictures in that house, and it's worse now, the last bit of life sucked away. It was always a house where men lived. You felt it soon as you went in, the dust and sour air, a house that was neat but never clean, no photos on the windowsills, knick-knacks on the electric fire, washing on the couch waiting to be ironed. It was a shell, ever since Mrs Dodds slit her wrists. Maybe I was out of order breaking in like that, but I couldn't stop myself. I'll get some putty and a pane of glass first thing, go round and mend the window. No one will ever know.

I stood in the hall for a few minutes, finally went up the stairs to the landing and stopped under the loft, the hatch back in place, and this was where Smiles killed himself. I don't believe in ghosts, but something bad happened there and this terror came from nowhere, the sort of mental thinking that belongs in horror films. My legs were frozen and I was shitting it. Really cacking myself. Never known anything like it. There was a cold silence, and I passed Smiles on the stairs and raced back to his mum, for a second feeling what it was like for Smiles living down the landing from where his mum killed herself. Why didn't they move? I saw myself sitting in a bath where my mum died, billions of cells ground into the pores of the tub. There's nothing in that house but sadness, the drip of a tap and a plughole blocked with the long hair of a depressed woman. Smiles didn't want to die in water, same as his mum, and I felt the motion of a train crossing Siberia, the rhythm of running water, left the house as fast as I could, jogged to the pub where there's light and warmth, Dave drumming his fingers over the table, lifting a hand and running it along the collar of his shirt. His eyes move left and right, brain working out the right words to say. I wish he'd get on with it.

– Me and Chris have been talking, he says, leaning forward, with a serious look on his face.

I nod and lift the glass to my mouth. Dave's in control.

– I know Smiles hung himself, and he's a silly cunt for doing that, bang out of order for what he's done to his family and friends. He's wasted his life and everyone is unhappy. It's down to him what he does, I know that, we all know that's the way the world is, it's survival of the fittest and we're responsible for our actions, but listen, there's more to it than some loony stringing himself up from the beams. Don't you think so?

I nod again and Dave's manner eases. Something flickers, the friendship we used to have. However much you try and be your own person, pull out of the crowd and go your own way, you're always getting invited back. There's safety in numbers, a common enemy the easiest way to unite people. Chris moves forward in his chair. Dave is almost smiling, the first time tonight. We used to smile all the time, when we were kids. We didn't bother about the serious stuff, only saw ourselves and what we were going to do next, the music we were listening to and the pubs we were drinking in, the bands we were watching, the girls we were going to fall in love with one day and the girls we were going to knob in the next few hours. The bare essentials.

– He was different before he went in the canal, Chris says. He was, wasn't he? I'm not making it up. After he came out of the coma nothing was ever the same. It changed him. He was damaged.

I nod, slower this time. I know all this and reach for my glass. Pour half the drink down. They're not telling me anything new. I've had time to work it out in my head. Years away, free from the pressures of life, buried away in a Chungking room, knocking around Hong Kong, no responsibilities weighing me down, breaking away from the propaganda and hatred. It's easy to see where this is going. But I've had a long train trip to get used to the idea of Smiles's death, days with nothing to do except look out of the window, letting the facts sink in and the truth come out. I know my part in all this. It's straight in my head. I listen to Dave.

– He goes on about Hitler and that other cunt, talking a load of shit that used to fuck me right off, ends up in the nut house, and then he goes and builds his own fucking gallows. Now everyone else thinks it was just Smiles being sick, a fucking loony who wasn't really alive, but it's not that easy. The way we see things is that he was murdered. As good as, anyway. That slag Wells who chucked you both off the bridge is guilty. Murder or manslaughter, take your pick, it doesn't matter. Thing is, he was older than you two, and there was four of them as well. It could've been you who got stuck under the water and ended up brain-damaged. Think about it.

I don't disagree, can't argue with the logic, except that there's a lot of different reasons why things happen. They've forgotten what happened to Smiles when he was a kid, how he came home from school one day looking forward to some food, calls for his mum and she's not there, goes upstairs and finds her sitting in the bath with no clothes on and no blood in her veins. What does that do to an eight-year-old? But I don't say anything. I've just come back after three years away and to them I'm the bloke who turned his back. I'm on the outside and have to watch what I say, work my way back in and earn the right to have an opinion. I can't start preaching fresh off the train. They don't say anything, probably haven't thought about this, but I know the feeling's there, in me more than them probably. Our differences are forgotten, but could flare up any second. Smiles has brought us together. I know what they're working towards, building up the story.

– Same again? Dave asks.

I smile and make the most of the break.

– Good boy.

He goes to the bar and takes his time.

Chris is concentrated and takes over, moving around on his seat and lowering his voice.

– That Wells needs sorting out for what he did.

He looks left and right.

– I know he got a slap off Tony and had one of his legs broke, but it's not enough. He's killed our mate and got away with it too easy. Just walked off laughing.

You do stupid things when you're pissed, when you're young. If you got hold of Wells and asked him if he meant me or Smiles to end up stuck under the water, for Smiles to go into a coma and get brain-damaged, fucked up, whatever happened to him, he'd say no. Anyone would say no. You have to think what finding his mum in the bath did, the hidings Smiles got off his old man. Does it matter who's to blame? Smiles is dead and that's the end of it. You have to be reasonable, see things from every angle. Revenge isn't an answer.

Except Dave and Chris aren't in the mood to be reasonable. I haven't been part of this for three long years and it's hard now. I worked in the bar, got pissed, knobbed a few girls, went up to Taiwan and Japan, did the same there, over to Manila and out into the countryside, through the rice terraces and down to the beach, sat in the sun and had the massage girls rub coconut oil into my back. Most of the time I kept to myself, the hours I spent with other people social. In one way this is a bad dream, but in another there's this big shot of commitment, the feeling of belonging that comes when you're sucked back into your own community.

I'm part of the brickwork now, not some drifter passing through, getting pissed on cheap Chinese lager, the big shot showing big face at a communal table, flashing my money around as I order more noodles. Back home I'm another face in the crowd, sitting in a pub, having a pint. I think of the bars in Hong Kong, the dark shades and dim lights, the drying sweat of these one-night-stopover Europeans lining the bar, ogling the young girls in hot pants, these financiers and businessmen on their way to the whorehouses of the Philippines.

Here things are different. It's in this pub, in the pint of lager resting in my hand. This is my culture, my world, and certain things are expected. Wells can pull us together. I see this easy enough. It makes us feel good inside, being part of a group, even if the group's small and isolated. Everyone's got a bit of the martyr in them. The Left hates the Right and the Right hates the Left, and they both hate the anarchists, who say they don't have any leaders or flags but are proud that they've got a name.

– Here you go. A decent English pint. Get that down your throat.

Dave puts the lager in front of me. I sip the drink, enjoying the effects of the alcohol. I can feel myself getting pulled in. The comradeship you feel when you're together, the warmth of the pub, the drink that makes you do the sort of things you regret in the morning, when you wake up with a black eye or in the cells. The prisons are packed with blokes who had one drink too many, got carried away.

– So we're going to sort Wells out once and for all. We're going through his front door and kill the cunt. Or at least cripple him. What do you think about that?

And what can I say. It's the drink talking, and it doesn't make any sense. Smiles wasn't like that, he wouldn't want blood on his hands. Even if they want to do the bloke you can't steam straight into his home. They'll end up inside. Institutionalised same as Smiles. I've got too much guilt to go round battering people. I need time to settle in again. Smiles died years ago. I nod but don't say much, dodge the issue, go with the flow and let the lager simmer, stay till closing time when Dave starts stirring Chris up. We leave the pub and Chris climbs into his car, Dave's voice ringing out in the night air.

– I'm going to break his kneecaps. Do a proper job on him.

He's talking bollocks, his anger mixed with sadness, needs to make sense of something that doesn't make any sense at all. Chris sits behind the wheel as Dave holds the back door open. I look at the seat, the chance to get in, drive a mile or two down the road, pull Wells out of his front door and kick him to death. It's tempting, it really is, and I'm pissed, but still strong enough to say no. And I'm tired, only got home last night. If they're going to do Wells they should wait till they're sober. Fuck all that. It's a mug's game. They have to be honest. Say it could've happened to anyone, that maybe it was the old man, or his family history, something in his genes. It's easy to go with the flow. Jump in with your mates and find an enemy. It'd feel good, till tomorrow, and it won't bring Smiles back. That's the important thing. Smiles wouldn't want us running around hurting people. He wasn't a fighter. I tell Dave to let it go, it's all in the past now.

– You're a shitter, Dave sneers. A fucking shitter.

I know I'm not scared. It's just not right. I turn to walk away.

– You're a bottle merchant, turning your back on your mates and fucking off to the other side of the world.

I swing round so I'm a foot from the cunt's face, pull my arm back, fist clenched by my waist, ready to curl the knuckles into his face. One punch and his nose is broken and his shirt stained.

I ease back and Dave takes a swing. I move sideways and he carries past, kick his legs away so he goes down. The hate bubbles up, but I control myself. It's hard to be honest, but I come through alright, turn and walk off. I can hear Dave as I go, mouthing off like he's always done, ranting and raving. I'm better off on my own, making my own decisions. Always have been and always will. I feel good, coming out a winner.

I stop for some chips, the anger bubbling away as I wait for them to come out of the fryer. A couple argue over fish cakes or cod. They're drunk and confused, start laughing at themselves when the drink clears and they see the answer. The bloke serving reaches for one fish cake and one strip of cod. The woman leans her head on the man's shouder. I go to the door and look down the street. It starts to rain and puddles quickly form. When my chips are ready I shake salt over the vinegar, go out into the rain and walk home. The chips taste like shit, but I eat them anyway. Dave's a mug, but fuck him. Chris can fuck off as well. Fuck all these cunts who can't move on. That's the end of us three as far as I'm concerned. They're people I used to know, and now they're in the past. I'm a grown man with no job and no money, but what I do have is a fresh start. I don't need those two. We've got nothing in common these days. Nothing at all.

DAYGLO

Slough, England
Spring 2000

Sitting pretty

I BANG ON the pub window as I pass, Dave and Chris turning and taking a second to register, grinning back, Dave sticking up a single finger US-style, the bulldog two squeezed out. I go in and filter through the Friday night drinkers, a mass of shaved skulls and bleached blondes, running across the ages eighteen to forty-five, older grey-haired men stuck in the corner by the game machines. Dave leans forward and tries to smack my head as I pass, but I'm too quick and swerve left, leave the silly cunt flapping air as he tilts off balance and nearly tips over. Tricky's grumbling away in the background, going on about standing in government lines, and I reckon I know what he means. His voice fills every corner of the pub, merging with the laughter, the deep thud of life away from the glossy advertising posters, free from the sugary lies of those party-political soundbites. I get served straight away, a non-Irish pint of Guinness poured in one go, the white cream backing up the glass, black base slowly rising, turning solid.

I'm gagging for a drink but wait till it settles, sip an inch of milk off the top. Beautiful. Nothing compares on a Friday night. Could be lager, could be stout. Doesn't matter. I turn around and find myself face to face with Micky Todd, a well-respected member of our local free-enterprise culture, a man who samples his product before selling, thereby ensuring he supplies the best gear, eyes sharp, mind alert. He wonders if I got hold of those tickets we discussed, and I smile my best smile, dip in a pocket and pull out a plum, a long brown envelope with four seats for next month's heavyweight bout at Wembley. Micky kisses the tickets, mentions gold dust and peels off the fifties. He thanks me for the friendly price and efficient service, taps me on the shoulder and says that if there's anything he can do, anything at all, just let him know. Cheeky cunt. A businessman by any other name, he likes to play the gangster, and I'm not going to stand here and tell him he's a tart, that I remember when he was a snotty-nosed little hooligan in cherry-red DMs and a cap-sleeve T-shirt, a cocky herbert running around bashing people up with a hammer. I'm attached to my kneecaps for a start, and anyway, there's worse around.

It's better dealing with people you know, earning a modest profit and keeping things tight, specially with the likes of Micky Todd who, with his brothers, runs a local security firm, at the same time dealing a selection of Class A drugs around the M25, in the boom towns and sprawl of Outer London and the Thames Valley, where the population is young and larey and looking for an edge, proving that only the fittest survive. After a brief chat he goes off to the bogs for a toot, and I take another inch off my drink, continue towards Dave and Chris. Two kids see their chance and step forward, all acne and one-colour tattoos. I pop their money in an outside pocket without counting the notes, pass them their blow and ask what they think of the track. They ease up and grin, say Tricky is one evil fucker, that he leaves the opposition standing. They fade away as I step forward, transferring the cash to an inside pocket where it'll stay safe and sound.

– Fuck me, it's Al Capone, Dave shouts, turning a couple of heads.

He's got his arms wrapped around these two women who grin but don't laugh, and they've got friendly faces and fit bodies, done up for their end-of-the-week drink, shopping-mall fashion and pale faces shown up by Dave's tan and slicked-back hair, easygoing girls who want to love and be loved, not worry about the bigger issues clouding the horizon. I gulp my drink as Dave holds court, follow the easy flow of his humour, deflecting the needle and not letting him slip under my skin, the same game we've played since the day we met. Those late-night rows and broken bones are in the past, the battle more cunning these days, twice as deadly, a sign of the times. His energy carries him along and I watch as he races past at a hundred miles an hour and bangs his head into the nearest wall, pick him up and dust down his Stone Island. It's obvious he's been at the charlie.

– Seriously, girls, this is an old mate of mine, one of the best blokes you'll ever meet. He's a bit serious, bit of a wanker to be honest, the sort of man who sits around brooding when he should be out and about, a miserable cunt who needs to smile and leave all that state-of-the-nation bollocks to the professionals. Our betters know best.

The one with the short hair tells Dave not to be so rude. He apologises and wonders if she's related to royalty, on day release from Windsor Castle maybe, on her way to Balmoral for tea with the Queen, stopping off for a quick drink with the plebs. He goes to pull her close, but she shakes off the arm wrapped around her back in one easy move. She sways her body, and I love the easy balance, the way she escapes without Dave seeing what's happening, trying to keep things friendly but at the same time making her point. She's wearing a half-cut top under a PVC jacket, faded jeans that are loose around her legs. She's a looker alright. Razor green eyes and tough features. She's a bruiser who can look after herself, her lips thick and full of blood.

– My mate here, the one drinking the Paddy water, has got his own little record empire, haven't you?

Dave doesn't stop, keeps on going, banging away.

– This woman was saying there's a lot of shit music around, and then you come strolling in.

Chris raises his eyes into his head, Dave gearing up for one of his coke-fuelled rants. Chris keeps quiet. Prefers the easy life. Sticking to the straight and narrow.

– While the rest of us are out doing a nine-to-five, this bloke is sniffing around in people's lofts, standing in church halls dealing with dodgy men in plastic macs, selling them scratched wax. Don't know how he survives. Don't understand it at all. Must be something more to it.

You don't need a lot to live if you're a single man. You don't have to have all the new gadgets. But Dave's brain is racing, tongue sprinting to catch up. Walk into a pub sober and the last thing you need is someone done up like a clothes horse running off at the mouth, giving you grief in front of people you've never met before. I want to thump Dave and knock him out, but I don't do that sort of thing.

– I call him Punch, he's such an ugly cunt. The rest of us are happy enough going down Rocket's to pull a pig, happy to fuck some old boiler in the car park, but he won't come in because you have to wear a shirt and trousers. Says the music's shit. What kind of cunt is that?

– You know what, says the short-haired bird, her face red, blood boiling. You're no oil painting yourself. He's not ugly either. You should have a look in the mirror.

Her jaw shifts forward and for a moment I think she's going to smack Dave, and I look at the smooth skin of a flat belly, the clenched fist. Get a compliment like that, a stranger telling everyone that you're not as ugly as you thought, and you're laughing. Well away. Can't let Dave take the piss in front of strangers though, so I lean forward and slip a finger inside the logo of his Stone Island top, tell him it's Mr Punch to the sort of greaseball who spends half his life under a sunlamp and soaks his hair in engine oil. I give the label a tug and he wobbles, eyes fixed on the buttons, the stretch of white thread, pounds and pence.

– Leave it out, he blinks, trying to set things in their rightful place. Okay. Mr Punch. Come on, leave it. I was only joking.

There's days you have to let the opposition think they're winning, go with the flow but stay staunch inside and bide your time, but there's times when you have to make a stand. Dave's face is frozen. He knows I'll give the label a good pull, and even though it's buttoned on I could do a lot of damage. Stone Island costs a packet and it's the sort of designer gear Dave creams himself over. He loves his clothes more than life itself. You name it, this boy has the lot, expensive at half the price.

– Come on, Joe. Where's your sense of humour? I was only mucking about. It's this charlie, it's blowing my fucking head off. My throat feels like it's caked in sand. Feel like I've been licking a camel's arse. Micky should be charging extra for this, but don't tell him.

It's not nice having your life stretched out on the rack, and just as bad for him being put in his place. I laugh along with the others and sip my drink. He's been caning it recently, jamming the coke up his nose like he believes all that anthrax-in-a-suitcase propaganda, doom-and-gloom end-of-the-world prophecies, a glut bringing the price down so ordinary folk can get in on the act, taking it away from the inner London elite in their three-storey Georgian mansions and Victorian loft conversions, shifting it along the great arterial roads to the London country sprawl surrounding the capital. This is where you find the people, in the low-lying landscape of the satellite towns, the new-brick estates filling in the connecting villages and junctions, lining the trunk roads, the pubs full of eager young men and women tuning into satellite football, a St George Cross behind the bar, a free-for-all paradise where the property is cheap and there's a chance to get ahead.

Dave is out on the piss seven nights a week, parading his labels in some sort of ponce routine, milking appearances. I look in through his shining eyes and spy the holes in his brain, a yellow block of rubber cheese pocked with craters, edged by mould, field mice nibbling at the edges. I look out of the pub window and see how he's parked his car up on the pavement, black bodywork gleaming as the sun sinks, aerodynamic curves still dripping after a run through Khan's Deluxe Car Wash, a line of white suds on the front bumper, begging some kid to run a key down the side. Dave's doing alright for himself in a local sort of way, steaming along at a hundred miles an hour, system firing, but he's bogged down with his HP stack system, a big pile of easy-listening CDs, stickers still in place, stuck in the trap but on time with his car repayments. Most people live on tick, but Dave pushes things to the limit. If he wants to put on a show that's his choice, but I don't want to see the bloke buried so deep he'll never get out again. It's the oldest trick going, the financial institutions following the company-store tradition, building up a debt that can never be repaid.

– What sort of music do you listen to then? the bird with razor-sharp eyes, who's called Sarah, asks, moving over so she's next to me, the faint touch of her tits on my arm.

Dave turns his attention to the other woman, her bleached hair a bit longer, a single stud in her ear. Chris is happy sipping his pint, raising his eyes when Dave isn't looking. Chris is a happily married man. He's a dad, a diamond, a man who likes a drink and a bite to eat. I fill her in.

– You're right about vinyl, she says. You can feel the music better.

It's the way she rolls the words around her mouth, the smell of her perfume. I know I'm in. Dave knows it as well.

– Forget Al Capone, now he's Richard Branson.

The blonde next to him must be out of it, because she laughs and leans against his chest. It's the drugs talking. We're always taking the piss out of each other, but now he's going public.

– Piss off, you, Sarah says to Dave, only half joking. You're getting on my nerves. It was you who started on about music.

Dave turns back to the other woman.

– Sorry, he mumbles. It's this gear. Blinding stuff, but I don't know if I'm coming or going. Anyway, who are you telling to piss off, you cheeky mare.

– Wanker.

Chris checks his watch and says he's off home for his dinner, hungry after trying to sell computer parts around the West Country's trading estates. He hates the job, but gets a car, a small basic wage and commission. It's a cut-throat business, full of chancers, but he's doing okay. People trust him. First he was a robber, then he was a copper, swinging from one extreme to the other, and one day he just upped and left the Old Bill, said he'd had enough of dealing with scum, that the sick cases, the rapists, child molesters and wife batterers were making him look at people differently. He was seeing the worst of human nature and it was doing his head in. From now on all his attention was going on Carol and the kids. He's a different person these days, real middle-of-the-road honest. Chris is the perfect husband. He says there's no way you can keep order in this country, so why bother trying? He wants an easy life.

– Come on, have another one, Dave tells him. You're hungry, aren't you? It's that time of night. Get a cheese roll to tide you over.

There's a glass cabinet stuffed with rolls, cheese-and-tomato and ham-and-lettuce. They're thick and tempting, lined with mustard and sliced onions. Chris loves that cabinet same as Dave loves his clothes. For Chris it's taste, for Dave it's the look, and I suppose for me it's still music. This bloke eats and eats, stays thin as a rake. Dave says it's because he's got Aids, but it's how he's built, something in his genes.

– One more, then I'm off, Chris smiles, and he knows it's Friday night and he'll be in here till closing, just as long as he gets some grub down his throat.

What he usually does is give Carol a ring and say he'll bring home a treat, spare ribs and egg-fried rice from the Chinese, cod and chips if she's in the mood for something more traditional. Or he could give Chapatti Express a call and order her a chicken tikka, grab a vindaloo for himself. The moped service crew deliver quick, the pop of their machines and the trail of curry fumes part of the late-night landscape.

– I'll give the missus a ring, pick up a Chinese on the way home. She won't mind. She likes me staying out. If she wants some chips and a pie, I'll get her that. Whatever she wants. She likes the peace and quiet. Says I should go out more, but I like staying in and watching the telly. I'm tired when I get home and just want to do nothing, specially after I've been driving around all day, trying to con these brain-dead cunts into buying my gear. I could phone for a curry. A vindaloo would do the trick.

Chris loves spicy food. He takes out his mobile and does the business. Snaps it shut with a grin, licking his lips and draining the dregs of his pint.

– My round. Who fancies a roll?

We shake our heads and he goes to the bar. I wait until he gets served and follow him over. The landlord is pouring, and I pick up on the music again, Paul Weller's voice coming through loud and clear. Weller has stayed true to his Woking roots and talks a lot about keeping that DIY ethic going even when he's successful. It gives people a boost when someone like that stays honest. Too many people sell out. Take the shilling and say they've grown out of their ideals. The boys next to us are younger and would never have seen the Jam, don't know what they missed.

– So the meet's all set up on the mobiles, and Chelsea have got a good firm of three hundred. They take the local service into the city centre and steam straight into the named boozer.

Somehow the Old Bill have got wind of it and are recording everything from across the road.

– How did they know that?

– Maybe they had a scanner, or there's a grass, I don't know. You can imagine they aren't exactly pleased, and the Leicester firm haven't even shown up, as per fucking usual. The pub's empty.

– Northern tarts. Least they can't get nicked if there's no one there, can they?

– True.

Chris orders my Guinness and the two blokes nearest to him look at the tap. Some of the boys round here don't like Irish beer, never mind that Slough has plenty of Irish blood.

– Fuck me, look at the arse on that.

I follow their eyes to a nice-looking girl in tight jeans.

– I'd give that a good service, I can tell you. Pump a couple of gallons of bunty up it any day of the week.

– What, a Paki? You're fucking joking, aren't you.

– Don't care if it's a fucking Scot. I'd do it no problem.

– Suppose so. Did you see that bird Ferret was with last week. Fuck me, what an old grinder. He knobbed it as well. That Ferret fucks anything that moves. Anything in a skirt, and that includes the Scots Guards.

– So what, says this bloke from the background.

– So what? You should be ashamed of yourself. Monster mash she was. Pure fucking monster.

– Come on you cunt, stop grumbling and buy us a drink.

– Same again?

– Yeah.

– Go on.

– Put a top on mine, will you.

– She wasn't that bad, was she?

– I didn't think so. Comes from Langley. Nice girl as it happens. Works at the airport.

– Sounds alright.

– She is. Come on, you mouthy cunt. You getting served or what?

– Hold on.

Chris's paying for his drinks now and I lean in and grab three pint glasses. One of the blokes next to us recognises Chris.

– Alright mate? I didn't see you there.

– I'm alright. Didn't see you either. I'd have got you a drink.

– I'm in a round.

I go back to Dave and the girls, pass the drinks round, the two women talking, Dave placing his glass on the nearest ledge. Chris shakes his head, says he went over to Antwerp for the weekend once with that Ferret and the lanky bloke going on about Pakis. Dave asks if anyone fancies a toot and Chris shakes his head, says he needs a good night's sleep, he's taking the kids out to buy some football boots first thing. He looks out of the window and down the street, waiting for one of the women to include him in their conversation, probably thinking about his vindaloo. Sarah slips me a casual smile. She's a looker alright.

– Come on, Dave says, when we've finished our drinks.

I follow him into the bogs. We go in the cubicle and he chops up the powder with his credit card, cutting us each a line, moulding coke in the same flamboyant manner as the kebab-shop boys carving their meat loaf. Dave makes me laugh. There's a fair bit left in the wrap, and the thick gold ring on his middle finger and choice of drug doesn't exactly go with the line of shit down the back of the bowl. I drop the seat and pull the flusher, tell Dave it puts me off.

– You fucking gay boy, he laughs.

He leans forward.

– Did you know, he says, after he's filled his nose, that the bloke who invented the toilet bowl was called Matthew Crapper.

I laugh, help myself, feeling the effect at the back of my throat. He wasn't joking about this charlie. It's good gear. Shows he's been building up some resistance if he can hammer this stuff all night.

– Straight up. His name was Crapper and that's why they say you're going for a crap when you're going for a shit. Funny, isn't it. What comes first? The real name or the nickname?

This bonehead in a bright YSL button-down gives us a look when we open the door and come out, rocking back from the wall where he's been resting his skull in snot, mullered by half-eight, and I know he's wondering whether to whip his knob away and have a dig. It takes a few seconds for the truth to work its way through the lager clouding his brain.

– Wondered what you were doing in there, he laughs, eyeing the silver foil. Mind you, there's no queers round this way, is there? Wouldn't raise their heads in Slough, the dirty bastards.

– The government's got another gay rights law going through Parliament next week, Dave says, opening the door and standing back so I can get past.

– They're not lowering the age of consent again, are they? the bloke asks, looking worried.

– No, it's nothing like that, Dave says, shaking his head sadly. They're making it compulsory now.

The door drifts shut and I can hear nervous laughter from inside the toilet.

– What do you want? Dave asks.

He leans in and orders.

– That bird fancies you.

He could be right. He slows down and relaxes properly for the first time tonight.

– Do you want some crisps?

I shake my head, carry the drinks over to the window and line them up on the ledge, see Chris has his wallet out and is passing around pictures of Carol and the kids, playing happy families when he's out with his mates. Dave stares at two teenagers sniffing round his car. He bangs on the window and they walk off. I laugh out loud, feel the charlie work its way in, start going on about all the new music worth listening to, running on for ages as I concentrate on the bones in the girl's face, pressing against her skin.

It's a short ride to Sarah's flat off the A4, past the Three Tuns but before the trading estate, and we travel in silence listening to a programme on the radio, the skinhead driver tuned into a bombing raid, cheering the boys on as the fascists take a pounding, the big Union Jack logo of Estuary Cars plastered all over the window next to me. The path to Sarah's front door is dark and I slip, try to disguise it, give up and tell her I'm pissed. We climb the stairs to the second floor, a new four-storey block with carpet in the hall and walls that shake when I close the front door too hard. There's a fresh smell of paint and plaster inside, the rooms clean and bright under bare light bulbs, big windows picking up our reflections. Sarah goes into the kitchen and brings back a bottle of vodka. I don't fancy another drink, but take the glass she pours to be sociable. Haven't drunk vodka for donkey's years. Can't remember the last time. She goes for a wee and I walk over to the window and look outside, at an empty street and swaying tree, branch fingers shifting shape under a street light. Sarah comes back and we sit on the couch talking, having a laugh at Dave's expense.

– That bloke loves his clothes, she says. I gave him some peanuts and one bounced down his front. For a minute I thought he was going to start crying. He was that scared it was going to leave a stain. It probably will, but I told him it would wash out, just to shut him up. No woman likes to see a grown man cry.

Dave's always been like that. I've known him a long time, since we were little. He's alright.

– He loves you, Sarah says. I can see he loves you like family. He takes the piss, and you let him wind you up too easy, it's in your face, but if you needed him he would be right there to help you out.

Don't know if that's true. Never thought about it really.

– Me and my sister are the same. We're always rowing. Once we never talked to each other for over a year, all because of something stupid that I can't even remember now. But we're close, would do anything for each other. She's always there when the crunch comes. That Dave is more of a brother than a mate.

He's not my brother. My brother died years ago. Smiles hung himself from the rafters, up in the loft near his mum's old clothes. Except Smiles wasn't my brother either. He was my best mate. He was a simple kid, an honest boy who went mental. No, my brother died when I was born. He was my twin. I lived and he died. I never met him, but grew with him in the same womb. They say you can be hypnotised and taken back to when you were an embryo, but I don't believe that, and it would be too hard even if it was true. I was the first one out, and my brother was left behind. He was stillborn. Never cried out and breathed the fresh air. You can't change things, but I've never been able to work out why I lived and he died. It's not fair, and I don't believe in fate.

Dave's not my brother.

– You know what I mean. He reckons himself, that's all. Least that's how he acts. The big mouths are usually covering up how shy they really are. It's the quiet ones you have to watch. Acting cocky like that turns a woman off, but he's harmless. My husband was quiet as a mouse, and he was out shagging everything that moved. One day he walked out and joined the navy. Haven't seen him since.

It's a shame. Women get a rough ride. I sit back and wait for the story to come.

– It was nearly four years ago now. We were happy for a while, then everything went wrong. It was money really. Trying to get by, both of us working. Life just got boring and he was off. At least I've got Jimmy. He's the best thing that's ever happened in my life. The sad part is he never sees his dad.

I feel bad for Sarah and her son.

– Colin was a good-looking man, a real charmer, but once he was married and had a kid, he gave up. Everything was too much trouble. He felt trapped. Like that was it for the rest of his life.

Doesn't matter what age they are, women always want to fill you in on their past. It's a different way of thinking. I try not to look back too much. What's done is done. You've got to go forward. It's more exciting, seeing what's round the corner. But I can understand not wanting to get cornered, stuck with someone for the rest of your life, nailed into the system, your whole life controlled by bankers as you graft to pay off the mortgage and credit cards. It's a decision you have to make. Don't commit and you don't hurt anyone else. On your own, there's nobody to blame for your mistakes. That's the way I see things. That's my choice.

– I just hope Jimmy will be alright. You worry about them getting into trouble. Lots of boys go off the rails when they haven't got their dad around. Don't know what it is.

You need a role model. Doesn't help when the politicians cut the benefits for single parents. Makes the kid's life even harder.

– Jimmy's in school now, so at least I can get out and work. You go mad stuck indoors, worrying about money all the time.

There's this sound in the background, and it's getting louder and faster. At first I think it's someone's music in another flat, echoing along the pipes, but it doesn't sound right. I try and place the beat. Then I wonder if Sarah's CD player has been left on, or maybe it's the tuner stuck on a garage track, but again it doesn't sound right. It takes a while, but finally I work out that the noise is coming from next door. Sarah's face has gone red. It's not music at all, more like her neighbours on the job. She lifts her glass and empties it in one go.

– Sorry about the noise, she laughs. Don't know what they get up to in there. There's screams and all sorts sometimes. Anything could be happening on the other side of that wall and you'd never know. Did you ever see that film about a man with X-ray vision? He could see through walls and everything. He knew what was going on in his block of flats, but at night he couldn't stop seeing things, because he was looking through his lids. He was looking right out into space. Seeing further and further. In the end he was seeing heaven and hell. Imagine that. It's better not to know sometimes. It's a good film. You should see it.

The sound winds down and stops, and I tell her I wouldn't mind getting the film out on video.

– You won't find it in Blockbuster. It was on the telly years ago. It always stuck in my head, X-ray vision driving you round the bend.

It would upset Dave, mean his clothes weren't worth having, and she goes on about this for a while, then she says she knows someone I know. I shrug my shoulders and ask her who. Says I got off with this girl at a party years back, tells me the year and everything. Can hardly remember what happened yesterday let alone years ago. I've always been like that. It's a mug's game, living in the past.

– Don't you even remember what this girl looked like? And she seems narked for some reason. She had short blonde hair.

Something stirs, brain clicking as she keeps talking, and I don't hear her for a while, finally tuning back in.

– She's a lovely girl, you'd like her if you saw her again.

It slowly dawns that Sarah's talking about herself, and the more she goes on the more I'm sure. Just can't remember. We couldn't have had it off. It's not like I'm some stud who doesn't remember his sex. I know it's her.

– We had a kiss and a cuddle, she says. We were pissed. You don't remember, do you?

Don't have a clue. I lean over for another drink. Sarah pours it nice and slow, doesn't seem phased with me acting like a cunt. If I can't remember a face like hers I'm in serious trouble. It'll come to me in the end. Hope so anyway. It's an insult for her, and I feel like a wanker.

– Never mind, she says, going and sitting in a chair opposite. I remember. You were fresh out of prison.

She puts on a pretend pout and I lean back, watch this cat stroll into the room. He stops dead when he sees me. His eyes catch the light so it looks as if there's nothing inside his head, and I think of Dave earlier, in the pub, his brain rotting from the charlie, big holes in yellow chunks of cheese, tongue lashing. The cat stands still for a few seconds, then struts across the room. He reaches out these long legs and digs some wicked-looking claws into a chair leg, drags back, pulling threads out. He walks over to Sarah and jumps straight on to her lap, purring as her fingers run over his fur, his nose buried between her legs. This is his patch, and he's showing me who's king.

I get up and go for a piss, and I'm trying not to splash water when Sarah flashes back into my head. I don't see her face, just a bedroom at a party and another girl walking in to puk p over a pile of coats. When I go back in the front room I ask about her mate, pretend I was having her on, that I knew all the time. She opens up now, laughs as she lifts Claws down to the ground, comes over and sits next to me. The cat looks pissed off about this and goes to a chair, a thin piece of superstore furniture, digs his nails into a soft arm, reaching for wood under the fabric. Sarah lobs a cushion at him and he trots off.

Nobody wants to be forgotten. It's the worst insult. I've carried her in my head for years, and it's not nice thinking that all the faces I've seen in my life are filed away, waiting to rear up. It makes me feel good that I came up with the memory and reach for her hand. We start kissing. I look over her shoulder and see the cat lifts its tail in the corner. She stands up and I spin her round so she won't notice him having a piss, don't want to spoil things.

Sarah dips into the bathroom for some rubbers and we go into her bedroom. She tucks them in the waist of her jeans and tells me to come on. I hate these things like nothing else. Never used one till I was well into my twenties, after I'd come back from Hong Kong and everyone was going on about this sexual disease that could kill you. Things were more relaxed in the old days. We fall on the bed, undressing, the silent patter of paws on the carpet next to us, the sound of my shirt ripping in the background.

Sarah sleeps curled up, but I'm wide awake, look at the clock and see it's nearly four. I'm not complaining, feel happy enough. You get better as you get older, and I haven't reached my prime yet, doing okay with money in my pocket and some sort of freedom. The Labour Party used to slag off the self-employed and tax them to the hilt, driving anyone who wanted to stand outside the system out of business. I used to believe in Labour politics, but there's no Labour Party these days, just a bunch of yuppies mincing around Islington and Notting Hill, the sort of areas that used to have flavour when we were teenagers but have been gutted and gentrified by the sort of scum that leeches off other people's culture.

I'm doing alright, sitting pretty, make a living buying and selling second-hand records and the occasional tickets, DJing, plus selling a bit of home-grown ganja to people I know. Doing the record fairs and mail order sees me alright, while Satellite Sounds, which I run with this bloke Alfonso and a young lad called Charlie Parish, can bring in three or four hundred in a good month. The tickets and blow are handy top-ups. I don't have a big rent or mortgage to pay, so if I can pull in a grand a month, that's two-fifty a week for bills, food and socialising, most of it tax-free. Can't see how anyone needs to spend more than that in a week. The biggest expense is accommodation, and I bought a derelict flat seven years ago, did it up off my own back, paid it off double quick.

Satellite Sounds is a laugh, and I shift a lot of records that way, hand-to-hand and through the flyers that key people into the mail-order business. Distribution is a problem, but if you can crack it yourself, you've taken control and hold on to profits that would otherwise be milked by middlemen. It's all about keeping some control of your life, deciding how you spend your time, and we generally play the sort of places where the people live, areas trendy DJs don't bother with, the likes of Slough, Hayes, West Drayton, Bracknell, Woking, Camberley, Feltham, Reading, and so on. Sometimes we take a ride on the M25, north to Rickmansworth and Watford, south to Croydon and Epsom. Parish knows a local football firm who'll run the door when the place is dodgy but paying enough for us to afford them, but mostly they're easygoing nights, not too professional if I'm honest. We're making money from our favourite music. We're pulling in a cross-section of people as well, dipping into a bubbling pot of men and women, boys and girls who want to listen to something a bit better than the normal greatest hits of the local pub disco, but don't want to spend a fortune going into the West End just so they can stand next to the trendies, students and tourists, listening to weedy dance music that's just disco under another name.

The cat jumps on the bottom of the bed. I click my fingers and he comes over. He's careful, but once I tickle his head he lies down and purrs. I used to hate cats, before Hong Kong. It was after I'd done my back in lugging crates around the bar where I worked that I got a different view on them. The doctor told me to see an osteopath, and instead of a slim beauty queen rubbing oil into my muscles, cracking the joints in the neck and spine, head buried in a firm bosom, I got this bloke who was a dead ringer for a boxer, and not a very good one either, with a bashed-up face and puffy eyes. It wasn't cheap, but he knew what he was doing and got me standing straight, told me to sort out my spine. He asked if I'd been in an accident, jolted myself, and the only thing I could think of was a couple of kickings when I was younger, otherwise nothing. That and smashing up my first car. He told me to try t'ai chi, as this would help my back. I took his advice, and learnt the short form, took it on another stage and got interested in the martial arts. I got hold of some books and sat in my room at Sammy's with the fan spinning and a bottle of iodine-treated water on the floor, reading up on the different options before choosing karate. Sammy put me in touch with this bloke in Chungking Mansions, and he started teaching me the basics.

John Ho was a mad character, an opium addict with a taste for cold Heineken, and I had lessons with him twice a week in a hall three floors below Sammy's. He let me go in and practise when it was empty as well. Didn't ask for a penny, just that I gave the floor a sweep after. The ceiling needed a paint and the walls were peeling, but Ho had got down on his hands and knees and polished the floorboards till they shined. Don't know if he owned the room or had a lease, but he loved those slats of wood. He taught me that karate is a passive art, a lot different to the Bruce Lee films. It's about turning the other person's anger to your own ends, conserving strength and letting an opponent wear himself out, picking your moment. The way Ho explained it, this made a lot of sense. It got me thinking, and I stopped drinking so much for a while, did some training and went over to the Philippines for a couple of weeks, later on along the North-East Asian coast on small-time smuggling runs that let me see Seoul, Taipei and Tokyo.

Ho told me to watch the next cat I saw. They sleep most of the day, but can hear a whisper and are awake right away, sharp and alert. He told me that the secret was getting out of the Good–Bad, Left–Right way of thinking, that if you really want to think for yourself you can't hide behind any group, have to break away from the set rules. He was right when he said people take themselves too seriously. All of this tied in with punk, which had a lot to say but was forever taking the piss out of itself, moving on and breaking its own rules, always one step ahead, mutating and carrying on regardless. It was the same piss-taking humour as the *Carry On* films we watched and the saucy postcards we sent from the seaside. When the Pistols did that gig in Finsbury Park a few years ago, people said they were going against their ideals by playing together again, but for the Pistols it was perfect. They wanted a pay day, and if people were prepared to fork out twenty-five quid to see them taking the piss, then whose fault was that?

Ho couldn't have weighed more than nine stone, and he was at least sixty, but he was a hard bastard. How he smoked his pipe and drank three bottles of Heineken as a warm-up, then chased me across the boards I'll never know. He was half-Chinese, half-British, his dad a civil servant who'd got a Chinese girl in the club and done a runner. Ho didn't give a toss, or at least he said he didn't. Deep down he must've cared, but was standing firm, and he'd taken his mother's Chinese name. He didn't believe in sympathy, for himself or anyone else. His wife was a chubby woman, but pretty, thirty years younger. Ho was a bit of a boy away from the karate and philosophy, and not just with his opium and Heineken. He had a couple of rooms with his wife down the corridor from the hall, and sometimes he used to invite me in to listen to his Bob Marley tapes, recordings he got in one of Chungking's markets. Ho said he liked Marley because his dad was British as well. I did the karate for a while but wasn't disciplined enough, started drinking again and stopped practising, went to China where I heard about Smiles and headed back to England.

I knew the basics when I got back, but it wasn't till over a year later, after I got done for assault outside the Grapes and ended up doing six months, that I thought about karate again. It was self-defence, or at least helping someone who was getting the shit kicked out of him, but coppers don't listen. Prison was shit, the set-up bad enough, but the real killer was the loss of freedom. It was a nightmare for me. Most of the blokes inside were fine, each with a story to tell and a life they were missing, but it was the boredom that did my head in, knowing I couldn't move around, another sort of claustrophobia. Going to the corner shop and buying a paper was suddenly important. There was no space inside. It's something in me. I thought I was going to crack up, sentenced by the sort of scum I always hated. Prison was another lesson, and an old boy passed me some blow, which calmed things down. I started reading up on karate again, ordering books from the library, thought things through and made a proper plan for when I was released. I was never a hard man, wasn't interested in getting a reputation for myself, kept my nose clean, used the gym and kept away from the harder drugs on offer. I turned things round. There was no way I was going to beat the system banged up, so I played the game and went with the flow, but it didn't mean giving in, just another approach. I remembered what Ho taught me, and things came together, I found this determination I'd never had before.

When I was released, the first part of my plan was to sort out a place to live. I was never a thief, but there was a job nicking off a big firm, a major pharmaceutical company who'd been done for cruelty to animals. This made them fair game as far as I was concerned, and I came away with eleven grand. It was simple robbery, no violence, and it was a one-off. Enough to put a deposit on a flat nobody wanted and start doing it up. I got into the karate as well, went into it properly, applying John Ho's standards to the more brutal classes on offer. I moved through the gradings and got my black belt. I was an unskilled man, and after thinking about what I could do for a living for months, the answer popped up one week before I left prison. It was so obvious I couldn't believe I didn't think of it years ago. The thing I knew most about was music, mainly punk, so all I had to do was put this knowledge to use. And that's what I did.

My brain's still racing as I leave Sarah's flat and stroll into a brilliant Saturday morning, her phone number in my pocket and a big smile on my face. Life is sweet, it really is, don't care what anyone says, the only downer the sick tug of a stout-charlie-vodka cocktail swilling around my gut, worse than a Chapatti Express special, their off-the-menu pharl with twice the strength of a vindaloo, the sort of food that turns the lining of your gut into the inside of a heavily oiled balti dish. I need something to soak up the drink and wet the tonsils, my left nostril numb and a trickle of blood down my shirt. Sarah's gone and pushed me out before her mum brings Jimmy home, and it's a good job too, because I don't fancy standing in the hall with three generations giving me the once over, the old girl checking to see my flies are done up. Can see her lifting cushions and pillows, finding a used rubber under the bed. I'm better off out of it.

I cross the road and go in a paper shop, buy a bar of fruit-

and-nut and a carton of milk off an old geezer listening to a cricket match on his radio, drink the milk leaning on the railings outside, watch the world go by, except the traffic lights are blinking stop-go-stop-go at an empty road, yellow cones on their side next to a hole in the tarmac. The roof of a factory I worked in as a kid peeks over the buildings, and the community centre is on the other side of the bridge, and I laugh thinking how pissed I was with Dave one time, when he conned me into going to an all-nighter, a horrible fucking jazz-funk disco, and I asked for my money back but was soon getting slapped up in the air by three massive bouncers in dicky bows. Ended up with six stitches in my head, but at least I didn't have to listen to their shitty music all night. It's half-eight and the rush hasn't started yet, and soon Chris will be rolling past with his family, heading for the superstores and their seven-days-a-week bargain shopping. And I'm in the clear, on the move, breathing cool refreshing air as the chocolate and milk ease the pain in my gut. I'll call Sarah next week. See if she'll come out, go for a drink or something. I head home, thinking about her as I walk. She's alright.

I have a wash when I get in, put on some clean clothes and skin up, the coke still lingering from last night, grains itching away, wedged in between the soft sponge of my brain and the hard skull bone. Drugs mess my head up first thing, so during the week I keep off the drink simmering on tap, never mind the charlie Dave's shoving up his hooter like there's a shortage looming. I try and save the serious socialising for Friday and Saturday nights, a slow session with the old man and brother-in-law Sunday dinner time. Dave calls me the Lone Ranger, and maybe he's right, but I work for myself and have to stick to a routine otherwise nothing gets done. Micky Todd's shifting some powerful gear alright, and it shows how the flow of goods has picked up, trade routes dipping into the new towns, one-man labs and small businesses flourishing in the back streets of an England the cameras never record. I make some coffee and sit down on the couch, light up.

Everything's available these days, all you need is the money to take part, and if you're skint the financial institutions are ready with a long line of credit that'll stretch to your dying day, gagging to sign you up. People are sucked in and spend their whole life working to pay off the interest. The coffee is smooth and slips down a treat, the grass strong, home-grown and free. It pisses all over that oily Moroccan muck. I pull the nearest box of albums over and take Asian Dub Foundation's *Rafi's Revenge* over to the record player, turn on the amp and gently spin the Rega turntable, flick the switch. I place the LP on the mat, ease the arm across so it's a quarter of an inch over the record, lower the needle on to the vinyl and wait for the speakers to boom. It's the small things that make life worthwhile. It took me years to get this system and I love every click and whiff of the separates, the delay and small pop of electricity connecting. I turn the volume down, stretch out on the couch and enjoy life, this feeling of well-being that's hard to explain taking over. I've been lucky in life, living in the South where there's always been work, my crunch years coming during punk which shaped my thinking, the family and friends I've had. I'm a lucky man and not afraid to admit the fact. One of the best tracks on the album is 'Culture Move'. Sums things up to a T.

When we were kids we smoked a bit of blow, but it was mostly speed we were into, along with the drink, the cider and lager, the snakebite mixture that a lot of pubs stopped selling because of the trouble it caused. Whizz was cheap and easily had, and fitted the speed of the music we were listening to. Coke was a posh person's drug in those days, something for the trendy wankers in London, the rich kids who didn't have to work for a living. Some of the punk bands started doing coke, and we used to slag them off, saw it as more of a sell-out than when they tried to experiment and move their music in a different direction. Dope was a hippy drug and we slagged it off non-stop. We used to go around spraying NEVER TRUST A HIPPY on subway walls, even though I don't remember seeing any locally, but we hated them because they were always telling us how to live. They went to university and didn't work, and we knew they would end up in all the plum jobs. And they did. You see them on the telly now, in their country mansions, running multi-million-pound businesses. Hippies meant dope and student lectures. Full stop. But my six months inside made me appreciate the herb and helped me handle the sentence.

I think about what Sarah was saying, how she reckoned me and Dave are close. Never really thought about it before, and we've always argued, smacked each other up on occasion, but maybe she's got a point. It can take an outside view to get to the truth sometimes. When I was inside it was Dave who came down and saw me the most. He visited four or five times, but always said he was on his way to the family estate, the rusting caravan outside Bournemouth, and happened to be passing, but thinking about it now it was just an excuse. I wonder if his dad still has the caravan. Last I heard the roof had caved in, and the site was being sold, a computer warehouse planned, the grass concreted over for a giant car park. The phone rings and I reach over, punch a button and wait for the handset to find a channel.

– You got home then? Dave says. Thought you'd still be round that sort's place giving her a second portion. I was going to leave you a message while I remembered.

I tell him I've just got in. I reach for the amp's remote and turn the volume right down.

– She's alright, isn't she?

She is, and I ask him if he's at home, tell him I'm having a smoke and he can come round if he wants. I feel good about Dave right now, the drug doing its job, and I'm remembering how when he came to visit me he used to bring music magazines and books, even went round and recorded some of my records for me, so I could listen to them on the Walkman, put 'Rotting On Remand' right up front. Mind you, he was the reason I got done, after he picked a fight outside the Grapes and came out second best, on the ground with this bloke using his head for football practice. I helped Dave and ended up inside. And prison was the first time I really took any of that slower reggae and dub seriously. If you're banged up, you don't want fast music getting you excited, so I started smoking and listening to more mellow stuff. It was always there in our youth, floating around in the background. There was no need for words in prison, I just wanted to keep my head down and get out. There was nothing left to say. It had all been said and nobody took any notice. Just like Britain today.

– I would do, he says, but I'm round Sharon's. You know, Sarah's mate. She's down between my legs right now, giving me a blow job, running her tongue round the back of my helmet, licking my balls, and any second now I'm going to give her a mouthful of bunty, find out if the girl spits or swallows.

The muffled sound of a woman's voice says something, then more clearly tells him to shut up. Dave screams down the phone and I move it away from my ear. Doesn't take a rocket scientist to tell me she's just bit his knob. He tells her to let go, that he was only joking. She tells him to say she's not sucking him off.

– I was only joking, he tells me. Sharon's in the kitchen rustling up some bacon and eggs. I can't think straight. My cock's rock solid from that gear and this girl fucking loves it.

He screams again, louder this time, and I can hear her voice saying that's it, he can finish off himself. A door slams somewhere.

– No sense of humour.

I wait patiently, trying not to laugh.

– You still there?

I tell him he should leave off the charlie. It's going to do his head in and wipe him out money-wise.

– You sound like my fucking ex, he says. I didn't phone up for drug counselling, just to see if you're coming out later? It's Baresi's birthday and he's got a stripper lined up for tonight.

Baresi's a wanker. His old man always used to stitch us up with his ice creams when we were little, give us half a flake in our 99s. Baresi Junior took over, and probably goes around turning kids over same as his dad, who got his name off the Italian hatchet man. I tell Dave we've got some work in Hillingdon. He can come along if he wants, bundle in the back of the van and help us unload.

– What's the occasion?

It's a benefit for this skinhead who died of cancer, me with the punk and Alfonso with the ska, Charlie coming along for the ride and to help set up.

– Fuck off will you, he says, spluttering. Don't fancy that at all, spending my Saturday night in a pub full of miserable cunts sitting around thinking about death. I'll go and see the stripper. Baresi might be a cunt, but it's local and he's got this girl who's going to do some extras.

The line starts cracking and covers Dave's voice.

– Better get going. I need to have a chat with that Sharon. Do some sweet-talking.

The phone goes dead and I make some sandwiches, eat them on the couch and drift off to sleep, the click of the record-player arm gentle in the background, a steady rumble across the windows from the motorway traffic. It's a good sleep, and when I wake up at six I'm raring to go, a busy night ahead. I phone for a cab and realise I didn't turn the receiver off properly, so Dave won't have been able to make a call all day. Estuary Cars arrives on the dot, the driver a chatty bloke with a number one crop and two photos pinned on his mirror, twin boys sitting with Father Christmas and a blonde girl with a teddy bear, all three kids beaming sunny smiles, the happiness oozing out. The twins are identical, which means they come from the same egg, and it's all out there waiting for them, the future packed with possibilities, just hope nothing goes wrong, and for a second I lose control and sink into a dark pool of melting fat, my stillborn brother shoved into a furnace, his brittle bones and blind eyes incinerated in a council oven so I'll never know if we looked the same, if we were from the same egg. But there's no point brooding over what might've been, and I pull myself back into the open.

The driver stops outside Alfonso's house and I pay, go up the path and knock on his door. All the lights are turned off. There's no answer. I try a few more times and peer through the window, notice Parish hasn't arrived yet with the van and my singles. I wonder if I'm late, but I'm sure they said seven. Maybe it was last night. No, definitely Saturday. Maybe Alfonso's won the Lottery and fucked off somewhere exotic. Except no one you know ever gets lucky like that, least nobody I know. I walk down the side of the house and lift myself on to the gate, undo the latch and go round the back. There's a note on the door – TONIGHT CANCELLED. GONE TO SEE BARESI'S STRIPPER. PAY YOUR PHONE BILL. He's guessed I'd come round here, seeing as he sits in the back room with his speakers blaring half the time, and I start walking back, but it's Saturday night and I decide to go and see him in the pub, find out what happened. Seems like the whole of Slough is going to be down there tonight, and I start wondering what sort of extras the girl is going to do. It's not hard to guess.

I walk along and pass the pizza place we used to go in. Have to laugh, spying the manager through his new glass front. There's one of those all-you-can-eat salad bars that try to be like the Americans but never pull it off because English-run companies are too fucking mean, give you one helping, charge a fortune, and then act as if they're being generous. We started going in there after the pub, when we didn't fancy a curry or wanted something cheaper, worked out a good way to wind up the tart running the place. First you have to get them to fill up the red beans, rice and tomatoes, because they let those run down. Then you build from the sides. Celery gives you the cross beams, then cucumber builds a wall, makes the poxy little bowls three times as deep. Then you stuff the food on top till it's overflowing. It's the principle. I hate all that petty thinking, taking you for a mug. Someone decided to cut the celery sticks shorter so we couldn't use them as beams, but we were too smart. Used the spring onions instead. Next time the onions were an inch long. They thought they'd won, and there was no point going in there again, the smug wanker running the place prancing around like Saddam himself. I left it a couple of weeks and bricked their windows instead.

I walk past the window of the pub and spot Dave talking with a couple of blokes we know, move through the ranks of shaved heads, no women in sight except for the barmaids who are getting treated with extra-special respect seeing as in an hour or two everyone will be steaming into the hall out back to shout at the stripper. Alfonso's standing at the bar with Parish and Billy Clement, and Clement adds a pint of lager to the round he's buying, passes it over soon as it's been poured. He wraps his arm around my shoulder and gives me a kiss on the cheek, asks me where I've been, hasn't seen me for a while, checking his change and quizzing the girl who's short-changed him a fiver. She gets worried, eases up when she sees his easy manner.

– They phoned at six o'clock to cancel, Alfonso says. Cheeky cunts. Couldn't really charge them seeing as it was going to be a benefit for cancer research. Could've let us know earlier, though. They said sorry and all that, but it's not the point. What do you think? We're in this together. You reckon I should put my foot down and get the cash off them?

Me and Charlie shake our heads.

— Don't worry about it, Charlie says. It can't be helped. How can you charge a cancer benefit for cancelling.

— That's what I thought.

I sip my drink and nod my head. I'm lagging suddenly, and this is my first pint. I'm glad tonight's been cancelled in a way. It's that charlie keeping me up all night. It's knackered me out. You've got to be in the right mood to make the music work.

— Only got up an hour ago, Dave says, looking at me. Couldn't resist tonight then? That Belinda is a right old dog. She did a show down here a couple of years ago and had two blokes up there onstage, both ends at the same time. She's a smackhead, and takes it like a trouper.

He stuffs her card in my top pocket. There's Beautiful Belinda cards scattered all over the pub, a picture of a good-looking half-caste bird on the flip side. I'll have a pint then piss off. Some strippers do a good show, but birds like this Belinda are just sad cases. I don't like all that. Someone's daughter, sister, mum. Doing their best to get by. It's just ordinary people fucking each other over, but I don't say anything to Dave who's off his nut again. He just needs a top-up, and I can see Alfonso eyeballing Dave. Get a black bird onstage and there's a current that comes through from some of the lads.

— Baresi's is a fucking muppet. He just wants to get the woman up because she's black.

— Don't think it's that, Dave says, genuine, looking a bit wary now, seeing Alfonso's narked. I mean, her manager's black as well.

— You don't think black people stitch up their own kind? Do us a favour.

— Baresi's a mug, Charlie agrees. He got done for flashing some girl when we were kids.

Never heard that one before. I look over at him. He's cocky, and when his old man used to do us on the 99s young Baresi took the piss, even though he was little compared to us, so in the end he got the same name as his dad. His coat's slung over the back of a chair, mobile phone out in the open, on a table.

– Honest he did, Charlie says.

Halfway through my pint I go for a piss and grab the phone as I pass. The bog's empty and I take the card out of my pocket, phone the Beautiful Belinda and get a man's voice, tell him that due to unforeseen circumstances tonight has been cancelled. He tenses up and says there's no refund if we cancel, and I tell him no problem. Belinda's off the hook, and when I go down the corridor leading back into the pub, I jam his mobile behind a pipe, leave it on so if he uses another phone he won't be able to get through. He's going to have a nice bill to pay, and no single-mum-junky-half-caste to fuck. I go back to the others and get a round in. Must be sixty blokes down here now. I sit back and wait for things to kick off.

– You're happy all of a sudden, Dave says. Here you go, have some of this.

I shake my head, while Charlie, Clem and a couple of others have a go at the coke. Alfonso stands out of the circle, chatting with someone I don't know. I tell Charlie about the big record fair coming up.

– Come on, Dave says. Have a dab, you tart.

Not interested.

– What time's the stripper get here? Charlie asks.

We get stuck in at the bar, and after a slow start I'm building up, the old thirst returning, the excitement in the pub growing, and I can see Baresi checking his watch, wondering why Belinda's late. He looks for his phone, then borrows someone else's. Soon he's red in the face, his brothers and cousins around him, getting wound up. People start drifting off, moving on to other pubs. Alfonso has a big smile on his face, and none of us seem too disappointed.

– That's two no-shows tonight, Charlie points out.

Baresi's mullered, and has to be helped from the pub. Some kid walks up and punches him in the mouth, runs off into the night.

I heard he got onstage once and pissed over this girl who was down on her knees trying to get a hard-on out of him for a blow job. Poor girl was humiliated right there in front of fifty blokes, worse than having to suck him off. The bloke minding her couldn't do much. Thing is, you can't always point the finger at the rich cunts in power, have to take some responsibility yourself. You can make allowances for a while, and then you have to be honest and sort yourself out. I think of Sarah.

– It was worth coming down to see Baresi's face, Dave says. I reckon that's the only sex he gets, standing up on a stage.

When the pub shuts I walk along with Dave, and we stop for some food. The chip shop's busy and there's these youths in front of us, giving the man behind the counter a load of mouth. Everyone gets served and ends up outside. Don't know how it starts, but I've put my chips on an electrics box and square up to one of them. He thinks he's the business, except I knock him down with a textbook punch. His mates pile in, but me and Dave have the experience and we're more filled out than these skinny little shits. There's only two of us, though, and seven or eight of them. Dave grabs one around the neck and drills his head into the wall. Another bloke comes in and Dave dips down the front of his joggers and into the pouch he carries his wallet and charlie in, pulls out a knife. I'm surprised, but not as much as the wanker in front of him, who backs off as the blade flashes past his face, two inches from his nose. There's a bang as a car hits the pavement, Parish, Clement and two others from the pub jumping out. The chip-shop boys leg it, including the one I've smacked. The owner of the chippy comes out and says the Old Bill are on their way, sorry, he thought we were going to get done. We'd better not hang around. We hear the siren and start walking, Parish loading up and driving away.

We get lost in the narrow little roads behind the high street. Nobody is going to track us down here, everyone long gone, the whole thing quickly forgotten. We sit down on a wall to eat our fish and chips, and it takes me a while to ask Dave what he's doing going around with a knife. Wouldn't have thought it was his style.

– You've got to look after yourself, he says, stuffing fish in his mouth. You can't be too careful these days.

The batter falls into his chips, and he's left with a long strip of skin hanging through his fingers, white flakes of cod stuck to the lining. Dave sounds a bit paranoid to me. He sucks the skin down and licks his lips.

Loud and proud

THERE'S THE SOFT crunch of chicken bones under the tyres as I pull away from the kerb, the snap of brittle ribs under bargain retreads, and usually I'd kick them down the drain except it's gone ten o'clock and I've got to be in Swindon by eleven. The sewers must be stewing with hormones, the Colonel's secret recipe mixing in with the pill's own special ingredients, cooking up a treat. The motorway's clear and I put my foot down, the stink of the sewage works on my left, bones so weak they'll turn to slush before they even arrive. Intensive farmers and their corporate pay masters are the scum of the earth. Never mind the dope dealers and bank robbers, the duckers and divers and juvenile joyriders, those are the ones who need sorting out. Tonight the Kentucky's going to get its windows bricked, a good way to ease the tension and put something back into the community. I reach over and get hold of a tape, shove it in the cassette player to block out the stuck-up cow on the radio running on about football hooligans. Anything's better than the wah-wah bleat of the media elite.

One day this motorway will be lined with concrete, the Thames Valley a solid block of houses and trading estates, new housing estates fed by service-station mini-markets and warehouse superstores, a spread of car parks and shopping malls, multiplex cinemas and fast-food strips. In the old days there were city walls around the ruler's towers, and now there's the M25. We're working to the American model, extending the highways and cutting down on public transport, spreading out, more and more people flushed out of London by the rich. There's probably more white Londoners outside the M25 than there is in London proper, from Margate to Milton Keynes, Southend to Reading. Life is being stripped down to the bone, another sort of factory farming, but wherever there's people life blooms. This is something the scum in control don't understand. They pontificate from a distance, tell us we've got no culture, that we're brain-dead, standing in line, hands on the shoulders of the person in front, tapping our feet to a mindless single note, out of our heads on E numbers. They don't have a clue.

Big business runs the show more than ever these days, and the politics I was raised with are long gone. That dream of a job for life and a place in the greater scheme of things has been blitzed, the asset-stripping years leaving a stack of bones rotting in the gutter outside my flat. Job security is a thing of the past, those doing well mortgaged to the hilt, credit cards struggling to handle the debts of a catalogue life, clothes to buy and bills to pay, and these are the lucky ones, strugglers washed over the edge. There's less difference between the parties than ever before, New Labour prancing around the gentrified areas of London with their Tory cousins, messing up the likes of Islington, Camden, Battersea, Clapham with their poxy theme bars and restaurants. Change is more cunning and manipulative, while the wahs running the show flash their wealth and power around same as ever.

The ordinary person is isolated, told they've never had it so good, and too many of us bend over and touch our toes as the Establishment's best-dressed nonce applies lubricant and gently slips in, fucks us on the sly, moves on to the next starry-eyed punter. We get this inflated sense of our place in society, accept the state's values, believe we're better than our neighbour, that we're a social class up the ladder with an extra tenner in our pockets and a house that belongs to a bank instead of the council. It's classic divide-and-rule tactics. Britain is a post-industrial society, but the image of the common people is stuck in grainy black-and-white footage, a dusty column of Jarrow marchers and the coal-dust face of a Yorkshire miner, pre-war East London ragamuffins and shoeless Somerset peasants nailed to the back of a plough. Heavy industry has been and gone, the green fields of England soaked in insecticide. Protesters travel by coach and the pits have been flooded. The East End has moved out to Essex and the peasants are all tuning into digital TV.

Scabs have been renamed strike-busters by the media, and the People's House has passed a law that lets the judges control union funds.

Cities have spilt into the countryside, but the lecturers are stuck in the sixties, explaining how half the population is stuffed inside a single Birmingham high-rise. Your everyday man and woman is described in terms of failure, whether it's the Left slagging off the boring conformity of the masses who want to improve their lot, love and be loved, or the Right busy highlighting the anti-social behaviour of a minority. Regional accents are presented as quirks, media whores dropping their Ts as they play at being cockneys when the cockneys are all speaking Bengali and the white boys are out in the shires listening to Underworld and Orbital. Society has changed and the pressures shifted. The Left and Right lecture us from their period homes, the same old professional class that has always controlled this country, without an original idea between them. Our masters wander around public parks sucking off strangers, hang from the rafters with plastic bags over their heads, lurk in slave dungeons with clips on their nipples, at the same time coining it Left, Right and Centre, telling us all about morality and thrift.

I slow down for the lorries taking up all three lanes, an old banger on the inside, middle-distance forty-footer in the centre, a refrigerator steaming down the outside. This National Express coach gets right up my arse, a cheap ride to Cardiff. Don't know what he wants me to do. There's nowhere to go except the central reservation, and the tape rolls through the Business album *The Truth, The Whole Truth, And Nothing But The Truth*, 18-Wheeler's 12-inch 'Crabs' tagged on the end, good travel music, and the lorry in front takes its frozen chickens into the central lane while the coach stays wedged behind me as I overtake, so I bang the brakes for a laugh and he backs right off, cut inside and slow down in front of the lorry, give him a go as well. The coach moves forward and I indicate right, move over a foot to shit the bloke up, give the driver a wanker sign when he finally gets his nerve back and passes. He points to his head and frowns, moves on. Fucking tart. The lorry with the frozen meat is on the inside lane now, so I go over and slow down again, hit the brakes for the death-camp driver who flashes his lights. Then I accelerate away.

Funny thing is, the destruction of organised opposition has created a new problem for the authorities, something that's a lot harder to police. The masses are more isolated and powerless, drugged and misled, but the flip side is a nation of lone rangers, freelancers following the US model, serial killers and one-off dissenters, nutters and idealists going about their business on their own. Organisations are easily policed and calm people down. Abide by the rules and everything is filtered through a structure that soaks up the original anger and gets rid of the power to change things. There's strength in numbers, but a lone gunman is more dangerous, the sniper who picks off his targets and never gets caught. Every organisation, doesn't matter what, ends up with the same professional clique in control, whether it's quangos or elected committees. If someone gets through the wringer with their beliefs intact, they're called a maverick and sidelined, an old-fashioned eccentric who's crucified then patronised when they're cut down, loved now they're no longer a threat.

If I got sacked by Manors now, I wouldn't go running to a union. It's a waste of time. Information is controlled by business interests and the trendy Left fucked things up for all of us, gave the tabloids a free hand. If I was working for a firm these days, was promised a trade and let go, same as Manors did when I was younger, I'd go along early morning and hook up a hose, flood the warehouse and walk round the company fleet splashing anti-freeze over the bodywork of every single twenty-grand tax dodge. They used me for cheap labour and what they did affected my life. Then I'd go home to bed with the alarm bells ringing, thousands of pounds' worth of damage nicking into their profits. It's easy and there's little risk getting caught. It's personal, eases the tension so you don't go round taking things out on some bloke down the pub who catches your eye, and that's exactly what I did with Manors, went and set the record straight, it just took me a long time to work it all out. It wasn't about revenge, more a question of justice.

Have to smile thinking back five years, climbing over the mesh fence done up in a plastic Mickey Mouse mask for the security cameras, a blue boiler suit, feeling like a twat but needing to sort something out that had been nagging away for ages. The managers there treated me like shit, tried to fuck up my life. I was lucky because things worked out, but a lot of people don't get the breaks and never recover. They say it's only business, being professional, nothing personal, but that's bollocks. It was a calculated decision. Once I'd been on the rampage around Manors I never thought about the company or what they'd done again. It was sorted out once and for all. Before, I tried to pretend it didn't matter, but it did, kept cropping up every few years, like I'd bottled out. Life is in there spinning around in your head, every little thing that happens, from cradle to grave.

Junction 15 is where I get off, go back under the motorway and follow the road into Swindon, do a couple of turns, and this bloke Barry lives on the outskirts on a quiet estate of twenty-year-old houses. There's ancient stone circles and White Horse carvings nearby that have lasted thousands of years, but the slates on his house need mending and the pavements are all cracked. I spot the pub, turn into the right street, count down to number 23, park and go up the path. He opens the door just as I'm reaching to ring the door bell.

– You found it alright then?

I go in and he sits me down in the front room, goes in the kitchen to make a cup of tea, a woman in there fussing with a packet of biscuits. There's a sign out front saying the house has been sold, and the only thing in the living room apart from the couch, chairs and electric fire are these plastic boxes loaded with vinyl. I always get excited at a time like this, a kid who's rubbed the lamp and found a genie, been invited into Aladdin's Cave but doesn't know what he's going to find.

– Here you go, he says, the woman closing the door behind him, the soft murmur of her voice in the background as she talks to herself, or more likely into a phone.

– They've been stacked under the stairs for years, but I want to unload them quickly. You can have the lot for two hundred quid, like I said on the phone. Have a look. They're in good nick. I always looked after my records. It's a bargain.

I have a flick through the albums, and he's got loads of punk and 2 Tone, some older ska and British reggae, a bit of soul. It's a good price, too good, and that's without the singles. I pull a box over and flick through a parade of picture sleeves. Most will fetch four or five pounds each, some of them a lot more. The Cortinas single 'Defiant Pose' would be worth near enough a tenner, and that's right next to Combat 84's 'Rapist', which is worth a lot more. I take some of the 45s out of their sleeves and check the vinyl for scratches, do the same with the LPs. Most are near enough mint.

– I live in New York now and was renting this place out, but the tenants have moved out so I decided to sell up. I used to think I'd come back one day, but I won't. I've been clearing everything out and thought about taking the records with me, but it was part of my youth and I don't listen to much music these days. It would cost a fortune shipping them, and I prefer CDs anyway. They're easier to handle. Two hundred's a fair price. What do you think?

It's not fair at all, and I tell him he could get a lot more if he sat down and drew up a list, put an advert in *Record Collector*. Suppose I'm a mug saying this, it's not exactly good business, but it wouldn't be right not to. The sleazy fuckers who go round clearing dead people's houses, paying pennies for stuff they know is valuable, are cashing in on the dignity of a family who doesn't want to argue over money. I'd rather be straight.

– Can't be bothered with all that, mate, listing them and trying to sell each one off its own back, work out what they're worth on their own, worrying if I'm going to get ripped off. It would take years and I'm flying out next week. That's your job. Two hundred quid and they're yours. Someone else phoned up, so if you don't want them . . .

I'm not complaining, just want to be honest about things. Some of the Oi records are worth a bomb on vinyl, and it's funny how the Oi bands got so much stick at the time, but now collectors are paying top dollar. I'll have to check up on some of the albums, work out the prices. I pull out an envelope and open it up, count the twenties into his hand. We toast the deal with our mugs. I ask him how he ended up in New York.

– I went abroad ten years ago, when I lost my job, worked in a bar in Majorca for a bit, then signed up on a boat to Florida, worked my way up the East Coast and arrived in New York. I found a job and ended up marrying a local girl. I'm half-owner of a little pizza restaurant now, none of your fast-food shit either. I got divorced last year, but I'm an American citizen so I can stay. It's a good life.

I tell him I worked in a bar in Hong Kong for a few years. It was alright, but I came home again and stayed.

– Couldn't do it, he says, leaning forward. Couldn't come back to this place after being in New York. You can make good money over there and have a better standard of living. New York's exciting, the original rock 'n' roll town. This country's all washed up, been taken over by queers and yuppies. It's petty over here. Small-time thinking.

I bring him back to the records, wonder how he built up such a big record collection when he was young. I could never afford to buy half the records I wanted. I buy more new records today than when I was fifteen or sixteen, and music was my life then. He doesn't sound like he comes from money, with a West Country twang, so he must have an angle.

– My brother worked in a record shop in town, and I used to go down there and help myself. He even ordered records in special and fiddled the books.

He's laughing now as he remembers good times, and it's one of those lucky breaks in life you just can't beat. Everyone dreams of having a big brother or sister who works in a record shop. Money was always short in those days. It wasn't till I was at work that I started seeing bands on a regular basis.

– I was well into it when I was younger, but I'm not bothered now. Used to go see loads of bands. I saw the Clash in Bristol and Millwall played Rovers that day, and Millwall turned up outside and chased us all over. They were great days. I come back now and wonder if it's the same country. It's lost its guts. You watch a band on telly and they're either dancing around to disco or knobheads dressed up in sixties gear.

His eyes glaze over, and maybe he's starting to regret moving. He's wrong anyway. There's some good music around, but these are drugged, sedated times, so it's all to do with sound. There's very few people writing socially-relevant lyrics these days. The Right won the political war in Britain and we ended

263

up with acid house. Instead of writing about big business, war, the police, prison, jobs, violence, racism, education, health care, housing and all the rest of it, any words that do filter through focus on Es, love and the right to dance. When we were kids there were two sides. Now there's just the one. The same things are happening, but now nothing much is said. Different times I suppose.

– You should get yourself over to New York.

Punk is big in the US right now, but I don't suppose Barry's noticed. I sit with him for a while, having a laugh, leave two hours after I arrive. I drive back feeling bad he's sold the records, but glad he's sold them to me. Must be a hundred albums and two hundred singles. I'll have a good look when I get in. It's a brilliant day's work.

If things had turned out different I might have ended up the same as Barry, living the rest of my life abroad. If Smiles hadn't died and I'd gone back to Hong Kong, maybe I'd have met a girl and got married, headed for the States and settled in New York, opened a bar, had Barry working in the kitchen. It's like seeing another version of myself. I never believed all that bollocks about punk starting in New York, part of a cunning plan by that genius Malcolm McLaren, the view of your average kid a lot different to that of the establishment, the fashion victims and vested interests who see punk as nothing more than a safety pin and art-school bin liner. My punk was anti-fashion, boot-boy music with lyrics about everyday life. Dr Feelgood and Slade are more important to my view of punk than Iggy Pop and the New York Dolls.

Nobody's going to deny the Ramones were right up there with the Pistols, Damned and Clash, and I can remember hearing 'Sheena Is A Punk Rocker' for the first time, standing on the edge of the dance floor waiting for my balls to drop, making a can of lager last three hours, and my skin tingles same as it did then, and I got to see the Ramones a few times over the years, the GABBA GABBA HEY sign summing things up, how punk was sussed but had a sense of humour, taking the piss out of itself. Punk is about my life, and there's millions of stories, whether it's someone from Finsbury Park, Ladbroke Grove, Hersham, Swindon, Slough, Leeds, a Midlands village or a

Welsh valley, Belfast or a seaside town in Scotland. To me, American punk is the Ramones, Dead Kennedys, Black Flag, Minor Threat, Nirvana, Fugazi, Rancid, stuff like that. Hip hop is another line of punk, and the Beastie Boys saw it from the off, same as the Clash. And that's the thing to remember, punk is just a label. Means everything and nothing.

I start thinking about Hong Kong, the spark in Barry's eyes as he was talking about New York. It's the freedom you get as an outsider, but at the same time you're always scratching the surface, a passer-by looking in. There's no perfect answer, life's full of contradictions, and that's why the party political system is fucked, because if you go with one brand name you have to accept everything they say. More important are the actual issues, and there's no way the ordinary man and woman has a say in this country. Everyone knows it as well. Doesn't mean you have to drop out and live off other working people, the trustafarians and student classes pretending they're poor, living in squats for a few years before they set up in business. That's the problem, the alternatives sewn up by another load of wahs, the same blood as the Tories and New Labour. So everyone's given up.

The traffic slows down near Junction 10, and I'm crawling past the Woking turn-off, two girls in a Mini smiling as they pass. They're not bad-looking and I nearly smash into the back of a Jag. That bloke from Swindon is stuck in my head, and he's wrong what he was saying, because it's just the fashion industry's control of music that means decent bands are denied access to an audience. There's new stuff coming through that can't get played, and the originals are still producing. Nobody ignores what an author says because they're over twenty-five, yet the best writers in this country have been doing it through music for years, it's just business takes over and they're marginalised. It's this shit idea of fashion over content.

The traffic slows right down and I go through the bag of tapes, grab Billy Bragg's *Mermaid Avenue*, put it in the slot and rewind as the two girls smile, move on again, slow-motion bumper cars, and I'm tempted to put my foot down and smash the back off the Jag, but don't. There's a museum in New York dedicated to Woody Guthrie, and Billy Bragg went over and fitted tunes to lyrics Woody never wrote music for, and it's like all these things keeping coming around. When I was eighteen or so I bought the 101'ers single 'Keys To Your Heart/Five Star Rock 'N' Roll Petrol' on the back of the Clash, because Strummer used to be in the 101'ers. He was called Woody on the label, after Woody Guthrie, so I went out and bought one of his albums. Then I read about his life, how he was a child on the streets during the Depression and travelled on the boxcars, became America's greatest folk singer. He died in New York, from the same disease that killed his mum. It's good music. Part of a tradition. Wouldn't mind going over to New York see that one day. That would be worth a visit.

Charlie comes knocking at half five and we tuck the flight cases in the back of the van, jam them behind the driver's seat wrapped in blankets so they don't get scratched, flat cardboard boxes covering the floor, doing our best to protect the cases from the grease and dirt, and they're the proper job, full flight cases with stucco alloy finishes for the 7- and 12-inch singles, black-vynide semi-flight for the LPs, each one fitted with heavy-duty steel corners, lift-off hinges, catches and angle trim, go back for the Technics 720s, the hip-hopper's wheels of steel, classic decks first used more than twenty-five years ago and never bettered, at least in this price range, and it's all down to the direct-drive, strobe-monitored turntables, lovely, and we wrap another blanket around the decks, make sure they're wedged in tight and won't get knocked about, every bit of gear has its place in this transit, and the three of us put five hundred quid in each to buy the van, the company motor, and Charlie pays the road tax and insurance, gets it through the MOT seeing as he uses it for his regular job during the day, and I sit in the back to make sure nothing comes loose as Charlie drives over to Alfonso's, reverses up the drive, getting as near the garage as he can, Alfonso coming out and banging on the panel right by my head so it rattles my brain, undoes the professional locks that turn a battered breeze-block garage into the Bank of England, well beyond the abilities of your casual robber, the passing stray with nothing better to do than thieve a jar of screws and some worn-down sandpaper, and we strap the speakers to the walls of the van, the back-up deck and amp next, a chest full of cables and peripherals that mean nothing to me, Charlie's the technician round here, then Alfonso's records, and he's the worst one of the lot, loves those discs more than his woman, locks up, and we're on the move, a quick ride to Feltham joining the M4 at Slough Central, three junctions to Heston, down along the dual carriageway and on to the Great West Road, and we're playing in this stone building that must be a hundred years old but looks as if it goes back to Saxon times, the walls bleak and pocked like something off a Cornish moor waiting for the Devon boys to follow up the grapeshot and pile in through a reinforced, anti-squatter door, but the two blokes who've hired us have a cheap lease on the place, which is still boarded up, and they're going to turn it into some sort of local venue, put a recording studio in when they have the cash, one day in the future, big dreams we all have, running your own set-up, controlling the means of production, and they're local lads so it's a good idea, something for the community instead of a massive profit, and being in Feltham means it's not going to get the trendies coming down and lowering the tone, there's none of that bollocks in outer London, and we're five minutes from the train station tucked down a side street with a primary school on one side and some tired old council offices further along, a small centre for single parents down the side, the rest of the street residential, kids shouting and adults talking, these are the areas we usually play, pulling in a crowd that's got nothing to do with fashion, a range of ages, people with zero facilities who are gagging for some music and aren't into any specialist scene or dress code, the usual British look of short hair for the men and blonde dye for the women, and we get all sorts, one crowd can be different to the next, we can switch things around, and another bonus with these venues is we don't have to be all professional and come up with flashing lights and videos, set up screens and pump ice around, it's easy come, easy go, in and out, seems to work okay, start-up costs are low with none of that dressing-up wank and stroppy bouncers, and with the big flashy places you get the dance floor packed with wankers of every description because money and pose is what it's all about, but for us it's a hobby, something we love doing, we have a chat with the men with the lease, one of them knows

Charlie, and they help us unload and set up, and sometimes we get to play a more professional venue, there's a few around that are okay, you can never generalise, have to give everything a go, stay open-minded, it's different music but the same honesty, and once we're done me and Charlie go for a wander while Alfonso stays behind and impresses the others with the size of the spliff he's rolling, a big chunky bonfire effort, we go up to the main road, past the lorries stuck on the bridge by the station to a low-rise shopping centre, chunks of concrete smoothing out the wind, the usual outer London bulk-selling supermarkets and a new pub on the corner, windows covered in pound-a-pint promotions, hand-drawn cards for the twenty or so lone drinkers scattered around the bar, and Queensmere pisses all over the shops round here, pride in your town, pride in your arcade, specially now it's been refitted, and we go in the Wimpy and have a cup of tea, watch the men and women pass heads down against the wind, traffic backing up for the roadworks, the thump of drills, go back to the venue as the sun starts sinking, muck around with some records, put on Cock Sparrer's 'England Belongs To Me', then Black Grape's 'England's Irie', line up the records and test the turntables, and I'm up front getting in there with the words, then Charlie does his set, and finally Alfonso comes in and slows everything down, because by this time the crowd will be lagging, feeling emotional, that's the plan anyway, depends on what sort of people we get in and how they're feeling and when we open at nine there's a rush of punters to the bar in the corner, and some of the walls have been painted, others left bare, and I'm off and running with punk from the seventies, eighties and nineties, the different influences of different times, a couple of rap records thrown in for good measure, polishing off with some 2 Tone, ending with Madness, and I'll make sixty quid for a couple of hours' work which can't be bad, cash in hand, and the music goes down well, specially the classics, all the older chaps singing along to 'Hersham Boys', 'Babylon's Burning', 'Harry May', 'Sound Of The Suburbs', 'One Step Beyond', 'Eton Rifles', the kids who were hardly born when some of these singles were first released right into it as well, I see it every time, it's in their blood, punk the high point of rebel music in this country, before the meltdown began, never had a bad response yet, it's part of our tradition, and looking around there's always girls who stand nearby giving you the eye, some of them young, others grown-up and filled out, there's some real crackers in here tonight, short cotton skirts and bare legs, loose yellow material wrapping curved bums and legs, sipping fizzy drinks and bottles of lager, and there's four blokes standing nearby who obviously know they're the bollocks in their Fila, Nike, Reebok, probably think I'm a cunt, I've done it myself, and you have to laugh, seeing things through someone else's eyes, can't complain, I'm just looking after the work of other people, not afraid to look back and forward, working over the same themes, and that's what life is really, and though we loved music when we were kids we never seriously thought about having a band and standing on a stage, up above the audience, but this is different, you play the music and stay in the background, and it's all about timing and feeling what's right and wrong and even if some people say there's a formula I don't see it, hot and sweaty now, making sure every record goes straight back in its sleeve, words banging out of the speakers, people singing along, angry words and smiling faces, that's what it's all about, make your point but never take yourself too seriously, demolish serious culture, pumping things up, and a month ago me and Charlie played this pub in West Drayton packed with seventeen- and eighteen-year-olds, a larey bunch of kids who weren't interested in reggae, a night off for Alfonso, and as soon as I played 'Anarchy In The UK' the whole place went up, the bouncers steaming in to sort things out, and then it kicked off again and I stopped the record, played 'Life On Mars' for old time's sake, had to smile, and when it comes to music there should be no sell-by dates, that's the best thing about sampling and mixing, reinventing and recreating, everything connects, and in everyday life our history is sold cheap, dismissed, doesn't matter if it's popular music or any other area of social history, and in a place like this it doesn't matter if the 7-inch vinyl I'm lining up is twenty years old or something more recent, and when Charlie takes over it will be another wordless version, machines taking over the world, it's all part of the culture move, and it's turning into a good night with Charlie raring to go, and I hand over, go and have a drink,

lost in the crowd, out of sight and out of mind, except for Sarah
who comes steaming in with a mate, didn't expect to see her,
it's a surprise but I'm not complaining, I told her to come along
if she wanted except I never thought she would, just met the
woman, and she's looking good in PVC trousers and a small
top, can feel my knob twitching, and she's sweating, her face
covered in water, powerful perfume, the smell of drink and
drugs and football thugs all around us, the mascara thick about
her eyes, perfect, Charlie boy going straight in and speeding
things up, stripping the music down to the bone getting rid of
the vocals, right to the nitty-gritty, and things go in circles so
one day the words will matter again, one step back and two
steps forward, that's the way of the world, nothing ever stands
still and the only thing that's certain in this life is that everything
changes, an endless cycle, and there's no perfect world waiting,
moving forward in time doesn't mean we get better, in my short
life I've seen some things get better, others worse, and Sarah and
her mate are out of their trees, Sarah's babbling away with this
look she carries in her razor eyes, talking into my ear, can't
understand her with the music turned right up, smell the fags
and drink, I love that smell on a woman, and she's introducing
me to her friend who says hello then goes and starts talking to
someone, and I'm left drinking lager from a can, no pipes set up
yet, and the rest of the night I spend with Sarah, speeding into
the distance not knowing what the fuck's coming out of my
mouth, going on, like you do, and now the music's slowing
down and Alfonso's shaking the speakers with the Soul Sisters'
'Wreck A Buddy', his timing's just right with people lagging,
dirty words to a dirty song, some slow dances, and I'm leaning
against the wall tapping my foot on the bricks, the crowd
thinning and disappearing, leaving us to stack our gear and load
the van, taking the cases outside, Sarah's friend long gone, lives
local and is walking home with her sister, Sarah gives us a hand,
doesn't mind getting her hands dirty, and we're standing in the
street with the van full of all this vinyl and equipment, a quiet
street and a beautiful sky, millions of stars twinkling, Sarah
pointing at the moon, ears ringing from the music, coming
outside makes you appreciate the simple things, this is what it's
all about, good music and good company, no nutters looking to

glass someone, now and then there's a problem but most people don't piss in their own lift, it's not the sort of night where a mob of blokes turns up for a row, or just to get their leg over, it's different to that, people know the kind of music that's coming their way and show an interest, most of the time anyway, and we stand around having a chat with the blokes running the place and it's a shame tonight has to end, and we're on the move, rolling through the empty streets of West London, on to the M4, the motorway perfect this time of night, a long empty strip of black tarmac that the beams dig into, Charlie snapping the brights on as we pass under the M25 and hit the freeway-style lanes leading into Langley, passing over the hump to Slough Central, the surface bumpier as we slide off the slip road, and I'm sitting in the back with Sarah rubbing my bollocks, every now and then Alfonso leaning over trying to make himself heard over the music, Charlie playing his Outcaste compilation, the mix of tablas, digital beats and the clank of a dodgy exhaust drowning him out, I move her hand away, and we get round to Alfonso's, the air fresh and cool after the stink of oil ground into the van, I help the others unload the gear, leave my records in Alfonso's living room, walk round to Sarah's, everything dead and shut up like there's a curfew on, a police car passing and slowing down, seeing it's a man and a woman, speeding up again, and when we get in she starts going on about phoning Chapatti Express, till she hears what I'm saying, it shuts at half-eleven, and she's got me going so I can almost smell the fumes, makes me some toast instead as I sit on the couch playing with the telly's remote, flicking channels, and she's got the lot this girl, terrestrial, satellite and cable channels loaded and firing, a black mesh dish outside her kitchen window catching the cartoons, all the old favourites, anything to keep the kid quiet, and I chug past the cheap imported films, endless newsflashes and current affairs programmes that say nothing, programmers more interested in filling airtime and attracting sponsors than quality, creating stories out of nothing, lines of American game shows, poor whites and blacks battering their nearest and dearest, German and Scandinavian cookery, every sport ever invented, and I'm into a cathode-ray tirade of law-and-order good-versus-bad moralising by brain-dead careerists with no guts, no humour, no nothing, the screen sucks me in and I see the face of one of my betters feeding the same old line to the nation, channels clogged with shit, and it's the same old mantra, SINGLE MUMS, SINGLE MUMS, never mind their kids, these fuckers love it, hanging from the rafters and preaching to the masses, it makes me sick, the same old shit I've been hearing all my life, and the thing is they never go away, just put on different masks, and I turn the telly off, tempted to kick the front of the screen in, look up and see Sarah standing at the door with a plate piled with toast, and it's like I've died and gone to heaven, sit down and eat, drink the mug of tea she's made, sitting opposite smiling as she pops pieces of bread in her mouth, crossing and uncrossing her legs, she could be a model, if the models weren't being sold as skinny under-age junkies battered by their pimps, and when I've finished eating we talk for a while, till she stands in front of me and reaches for my hands, pulls me up and leads me into the bedroom where we stand kissing for a while, undressing, and then she's turning round and leaning forward with her hands resting on the dressing table, this cheap effort that looks like it'll fall down any minute, artificial grain glued to plywood, the mirror huge, too big for the dressing table, and the curtains are thin and the sun is starting to rise, must've been talking for ages, and we're covered in this orange light, I feel sorry for the people who have to get up at the crack of dawn and go into work, the shelf-stackers and forklift drivers, the bartenders on their way home and the dads getting in early for some overtime, all of them hidden from the sun, building tin pyramids and sweeping floors, the repetitive production-line jobs, Sarah wiggling her bum in the air as I move forward, and I'm looking around for the rubbers, spot them over the other side of the bed, slip one on quickly, slide in watching the knobs of her backbone and curve of her hips, and when I see myself in the mirror I start laughing, can't help myself, this scruffy herbert who needs a shave, the faded old LOUD PROUD & PUNK T-shirt I've still got on, I was wearing it under my shirt, using it as a vest, and I start creasing up so Sarah looks into the mirror, her face is red, she wants to know what I'm laughing at, thinks it's her, that I'm taking the piss or something, and I say it's nothing, but it's the sort of thing that creases me up, like when you watch a film and a ragged old actor is busy shagging a classy woman forty years younger than him, it doesn't make any sense, no sense at all, Sarah reaching down and grabbing my balls, giving them a hard squeeze that stops me laughing, and it's me I'm laughing at, not her, just taking the piss out of myself, the pale white skin of an English new-town, the hair I cut with my razor, shaving it number two before I left, and I must stink as well, need a wash, get rid of the sweat and drink, and I have to get this together, shut up and go over to the decks set up in the back of my brain, nick into Parish's selection, try and get into the mechanical rhythm of electronic sex, and maybe it's the wrong thing right now, but I'm cracking up inside, so what, no words to worry about, and you have to let yourself go sometimes, put lyrics on a back burner, concentrate on the business in hand, and I'm in the groove, looking down at the rubber doing its job, and it's the new breed of condom built to go through the rougher types of sex, and I look up at the mirror again, see this rag-and-bone man in action, make faces in the mirror, just can't help it, crack a smile and show my teeth, and Sarah comes, moves forward, says it's hurting now, and I pull out hoping for some hand relief but get an earful instead, she thinks I'm taking the piss, but I'm not, it's this sort of relief or something, and I try to explain, that it's just being happy, and when you're happy you can have a joke, and I tell her what I was laughing at, and she smiles and says the T-shirt needs a wash, I need a shave, there's no problem, a tough woman who can look after herself, and this is what it's all about, it doesn't get much better than this, good music, good mates, good money, and a good girl offering up some good loving, she sits me down and finishes me off, I reckon I could be falling in love for the first time in my life as she goes into the bathroom and starts running the bath, and I sit on the bed for a few minutes, go over to the window and look out at the empty street, no people in the world right now, and I stay here for a few minutes thinking, then go and see what she's doing, find her in the kitchen dressed in a fluffy dressing gown and Mickey Mouse slippers, boiling the kettle up for another cup of tea.

★

I suppose it's all about reproduction at the end of the day, the constant throb of life and death, seeds that have to be planted, coaxed and cared for in the warm belly of Mother Nature, and I spot Dad in the distance as I come off the main road, a white dot of hair moving through the bamboo canes and rusty mesh of the allotments. Mum comes out of the shed and the old man turns and nods, goes over to her and disappears inside. My brain is nice and level, one of those mellow moods that come after a good week, life motoring along nice and steady, a beautiful woman on the go and money in my pocket. This is how things should be, the days rolling into each other, no aggravation, and it's when things are at their best that the clouds gather, building up for a storm, so I laugh and tell myself to take care.

I squeeze in next to Al's van, ALBERTO PLUMBING covering the panels. Albert's a middle-aged bloke with a wobbling beer gut and hacking cough from the hundred fags he smokes every single day. There's nothing Latin about him, but he's a tradesman and did a cheap job for me when I was doing the flat up, reckons the O on the end of his name helps pull in extra business. Says it's the women who run most homes, make the decisions that really matter, and when they read the name Alberto they think of a good-looking Italian. Seems like it would work the other way round to me, their husbands flicking through the *Yellow Pages* and spotting the Latin name, rubbing the bloke off their list as they imagine a Baresi-type greaseball. Albert says the woman always has the final say, and when he turns up the blokes are so glad he's not a smooth talker with his eye on the woman's panties that he's given the job. It's the old double bluff. Sounds like a load of bollocks to me, but it keeps him happy, tending the allotment next to Dad's.

I go in through the gates, Mum coughing as she mucks about with a flask, the same dirty cough as Albert. She's addicted to the worst drug going, never mind Ecstasy. She's tried, but can't give it up. And I never really thought about my mum and dad when I was a kid, they were just there, living their lives, stuck in a rut, making every penny count, raising their kids and happy to sit in front of the telly five or six hours a night. It wasn't till the old man was laid off and unplugged himself from the telly that I saw things as they were, the choices people make to raise a family, the sacrifices, and the simple truth is that if you look after your own nobody's ever going to go without. It makes me laugh the number of big-time moralists preaching about helping others, but never bother with those nearest to them, where they could actually do some good. Too much theory and not enough action, just want to be seen in a good light.

Spring is the best time of year, life stirring again, women coming out of hibernation, everything possible. The old man's down here every day, Mum when she can. This is his paradise, and he comes a couple of times a week during the winter to turn the soil, so the frost can get in and break it up ready for planting. We had his sprouts at Christmas, and he was that proud he'd grown them himself, didn't have to go buy them. Winter means nothing to Dad, he's just waiting for the light to come back so he can get outside. He doesn't bother with the telly much these days. I used to think he was a mug sitting there on the couch, a mental patient in hospital letting the doctors inject him with whatever they fancied, the waves of trivia doing their best to melt his brain. But like he says, if you're working all day, and doing overtime, then when you get in you're too knackered to do anything else.

– Alright, son? Dad says, leaning on his fork.

I nod and sit down in one of the deckchairs he nicked off the beach in Selsey last year. Mum's got a flask of tea on the go and pours me a cup. It's a tiny patch of countryside here, and when I was a kid I used to go cherry-picking in the summer, a couple of miles down the road. There was a bloke there who went nicking apples at night, a gypsy who travelled all over, but since the new-age travellers came along things have changed, the old sites shut down and the original travellers squeezed out. It's a good memory and I understand why Dad comes down here. Fair dues to the man. That bloke from Swindon ended up in New York, and I wonder where that apple-picker is right now. I try to remember his name, but it's gone. I don't see many fields these days, stuck in town, but that's okay, my choice. I ask Mum if she remembers when I went cherry-picking, when I was a kid.

– You used to come home with stains over all your clothes, where you'd been climbing trees, she says, smiling.

And I look at her face that's showing the years, imagine the tar lining her lungs, eyes starting to go misty, and I want to grab her and tell her not to get old, that she should stand up and live for ever. I look at Dad and want to do the same, do the impossible.

– We should grow some cherries, love.

Dad raises his eyes and sits down in the other deckchair.

– It's hard enough growing the normal stuff. We'd have to put netting to stop the birds eating the lot.

Over by the road a radio is turned up, a love song I couldn't name. Somebody's favourite ballad. Dad's face tightens, but he lets it go, looking at the Major in the far corner of the allotment, clematis curling through the chicken wire he's set up for some sort of bean or pea. The Major keeps to himself, an easy life since his old dear died and he took over the house, went to work on the trains and then got a decent redundancy with privatisation. He bought the house and is doing alright. He has no family or expensive habits, least I don't think so. Don't know a lot about him to be honest. He keeps himself to himself. Thatcher served the Major well.

– We'd be dead before the trees grow and start fruiting, Dad says. Stick to the crops you know, and you won't go far wrong. Leeks, rhubarb, spinach, beetroot, spuds. Can't fail there.

– Carrots as well, dear.

– Carrots aren't easy, Dad says, frowning. The sand we got off that skip last year thinned out the soil and we had a bumper crop. We were lucky. We need more sand. Hope we get some tomatoes this year. That would be nice. It's the enzymes under the skin. Good for your gut.

– Two or three days a week without chips would be better, Mum says, leaning forward and laughing, coughing, taking the piss out of Dad who sits there like a big Buddha.

I do some digging for the old man, whose back is playing up, big chunky worms sliding through the prongs of the fork, and when I'm done I have another mug of tea, the sun high in the sky heating the sweat covering my skin, stirring things up under the surface, warming the earth. When the traffic on the main road fades, we could be in a garden in the country. It's nice and peaceful, mostly pensioners and the unemployed during the day, people with time on their hands, refusing to sit at home rotting away, fighting back and choosing another option, doing it for themselves in a forgotten world of rusty wire and splintered wood, the plastic Coke bottles stripped of their advertising and used as cloches, old windows for cold frames and concrete-splattered planks, vines budding from dead wood, lining the tilting sheds and stringed coconut shells, daffodils bursting out all over, saved from the council tip.

The Major's digging a fork into his compost heap, stabbing the blades into a pile of rotting weeds. A police car pulls up and this copper gets out, calls over to him. I wonder what he's been doing. The copper goes to the boot of his car and pulls out three bin bags. The Major walks through the gate and up to the car, and after a quick nod carries the bags back to his plot. The car leaves and the Major goes back to work, transferring the manure to his compost heap, pumped-up riot-control horse shit that'll kick things off big time. He used to be the local nutter, patrolling the streets and nicking people for spitting on the pavement, and thinking back I suppose it was all fluid when we were kids. Lots of gobbing and too much wanking. I can remember the Major standing in court getting the piss ripped out of him, labelled a nonce who hung around schoolkids. I never saw him that way. He was just a bit slow, and because he was out and about all day everybody knew his face. Now he's rarely seen, except down here on his allotment. I try and talk to him sometimes, but he doesn't want to know.

The allotments are on the edge of town, a pub down the road pulling in the punters every Friday dinner time with regular strippers, a straightforward boozer's pub with straightforward girls, none of that Beautiful Belinda live sex. One of the two petrol stations has been boarded up, bullet-proof glass replaced with plywood. Weeds have already started sprouting on the forecourt and it's mental the way billions of seeds and insects lurk in the cracks, biding their time, ready to take over. There was a plague of slugs last year and most vegetables were wiped out, but it didn't matter too much, the allotments an excuse to get out in the fresh air, though it can obviously help money-wise. I've brought Dad the special-offer seeds he asked me to pick up in Woolies, runner beans and radishes, and every penny counts, the likes of spinach expensive in the supermarket, available most of the year if he grows his own leaf beet.

When the veg sprouts the insects come out of nowhere and start nibbling, slugs firming up under every brick and plank. Dad has got hold of an old sink and dug it into the ground, plugged it with Polyfilla, built a pond from scrap, the allotments a tribute to a DIY culture that grew up during the war and continued through the hard times that followed. This has filtered down. These people were recycling plastic, paper, glass, metal, wood, long before the council thought to stick bins in the Homebase car park. There were a couple of frogs down here last year, but even they couldn't eat all the slugs, and he's already got frogspawn in the pond, and is hoping some water boatmen and newts will follow.

– You got any energy left? Dad asks. That patch over there needs digging. If you fancy it.

I stay till six, then stop round Chris's house on my way home, leaving my shoes by his front door but still dripping mud on the carpet. He's sitting on the couch marking off his Lottery numbers, the kids arguing over their tea, sitting at the table tucking into cheese pizzas and chips, and Chris isn't phased, knows his time will come, that magic moment when the balls come out right and he can retire. I tell him he's got more chance playing bingo with his mum.

– Fuck off, he says, under his breath.

Carol brings in a plate with a slice of pizza and some beans she's heated up. I balance it on my knees, get Darren to bring the salt over. He's a quiet kid, ketchup down the front of his England shirt smudging the three lions, makes it look as if they've been chewing up Germans. Carol sits down and grabs the remote off Chris's lap. She clicks over and turns the volume down, beautiful people giggling, lining up a blind date.

– I'm starving, Chris says. Is there any pizza left?

– Joe's just finished it. You must have a dodgy thyroid. Like Mum had, when she lost all that weight.

She turns to me and shrugs.

– He never stops eating. Don't know what's wrong with him.

When we were kids we said he had a tapeworm, because there weren't many Chinese takeaways around and they always said that if you ordered spare ribs you'd end up with a massive worm gobbling up your foot, swelling and taking over, except we never bought spare ribs because they were too expensive, the real jewel on Mao's menu. Now Dave's usual joke is that Chris has been going up to London on the sly and has caught Aids off an MP. I tell Carol that it's in his genes, part of his DNA, built into him from the beginning.

– I suppose so. Just wish he'd put a bit more meat on his bones.

– Not an ounce of fat there, Chris laughs, standing up, looking at the telly. Dear oh dear, that girl's going to get a fright when they move the screen.

The boy on the programme is done up in some seriously flashy clothes.

– Fucking ponce, Chris says.

Carol slaps his legs.

– Not in front of the kids.

Darren turns round grinning, while I get stuck into the beans and pizza, have a can with Chris when the kids go to bed and Carol has a bath. He's sitting in these Bugs Bunny slippers he got for his birthday and I ask him who's the ponce now, think of Sarah in her Mickey Mouse slippers early morning, the sun coming through her kitchen window. He smiles and nods, and I should be getting home, have to sort those records out, a long job that has to be done if I'm going to sell them. I leave Chris's at half nine, get indoors and pour out a nice cold can of lager, flick through my albums and pull out Massive Attack's *Blue Lines*, take it over to the record player.

I sit down and get stuck in, and even though the records are taking time to sort out it was a good buy. Old sleeves have to be replaced and plastic covers added, but more important is the actual vinyl, and I go through checking for scratches, cleaning it up with my magic solution. Records I fancy and don't already have I keep for myself, and if a picture cover's in better shape than one of mine, I swap it around, but I have most of the stuff already. The quality of the picture covers varies. Some are alright, others ragged. There's a big fair coming up in Victoria and I'll take this lot along, with the stock I've already got. First I'll put them on the Internet. Last year I topped three hundred pounds at Victoria, and reckon I could do better this time. There's enough teenagers looking for the original music, not to mention the older faces. Vinyl's more of a specialist medium than CDs, so records pull in the serious people. CDs have to be deciphered and translated, whereas with vinyl the sound goes straight up the needle and out through the speakers. It's warmer, and DJs choose it every time, right across the board.

Machinery can only go so far, and while CDs might be perfect for classical music, this is all about rough edges and a feeling you can never get from a computer. Nobody's going to better the Sun Studios sessions with Elvis, Carl Perkins, Jerry Lee Lewis and the rest of them. The equipment was simple, but meant the feel wasn't lost in the machine. You could spend a fortune and never get near the feeling of the legendary Jamaican producers. It's the feeling that counts, and this goes for the new music as well. DJing is an art, and I'm just a spinner, but I'll stand there and watch Charlie mixing up sounds and that's a massive skill in itself. Anyone who gets stuck in a time warp and misses all the innovations, the scratching, sampling and mixing is losing out.

The Slaughter & The Dogs single 'Where Have All The Boot Boys Gone' is getting a spring clean as I mumble that I'm right here, go on to 'The Call Up', a Clash 7-inch, taken off the *Sandinista* album. I never really appreciated this LP when it was first released, a triple sold for the price of a single album, and I put it on when *Blue Lines* ends, and it's obvious the Clash were ahead of their time. I play all six sides, move the needle back to 'The Equalizer', do the same for 'Crooked Beat' and 'One More Time', Mikey Dread right there on the talkover. 'The Call Up' reminds me of a train trip I made across Siberia, all the way from Beijing to Moscow, not long before the massacre in Tiananmen Square and the collapse of the Soviet Union, and around the same time the Berlin Wall was demolished as well. Those years away gave me a glimpse of the world, taught me some truths, made me realise that this is a moderate country at heart, showed what racism and communism are like close up. The seventies and eighties were lively times. We grew up with

Europe divided and the threat of nuclear war. Vietnam filled the screens and the Second World War and Holocaust were right there in our heads. Kids we knew were getting shot in Ulster, and there was a constant battle between the state and unions, riots around the country and on the terraces, constant battles and opinions. So the music was angry and hasn't been matched since.

I line the singles up, thinking about when we used to go up to Camden and how it's changed, become a tourist spot, full of professionals and students, the boozers we used to drink in gutted and turned into trendy bars. I've been to the record market there a couple of times, been all over the place, and you get some loonies going around the fairs, blokes who have to own every pressing ever released. They start off with their favourite music, then move on to something else. It takes over their lives. They'll go everywhere looking for a particular release, building up the suspense, and when they find it, it's like they've had sex with a beautiful woman. You get all sorts. It's not just your Clapham Junction trainspotter, overweight and underloved, but a mixture of introverts and extroverts, the sort who want to pocket the records and move on, or the flamboyant ones who stick around talking about pressing plants and obscure groups who were shit but because the print run was so low have made records that top the price charts. I mostly do the big fairs, mail order easier, but I get to see places like Morecambe, Bradford, Leicester, and I've been over to the continent a few times. It's a good life. I've been lucky.

As well as the straightforward collectors, there's the music lovers, people who get into every note and lyric. People want to build up back catalogues, match the new music with older material, find the influences and fit the whole thing together. I get people who dress in motorbike jackets and suits, a lot of kids who mix records and concentrate on the electronics, but want to know about the Sex Pistols and Special AKA. It takes all sorts, and I suppose I could go into other areas, get into more types of music, but I concentrate on twenty years of punk, 2 Tone, plus the reggae and ska I know. Punk is my speciality, from the seventies to the modern day. I'll sell the soul stuff as a bundle. Move it on. Don't want to waste my time trying to work out prices. Nirvana's *Nevermind* is in with the albums, and it's out of time with the rest of the records. Maybe he bought it on a trip home, or it belonged to one of his tenants. *Nevermind* and *Never Mind The Bollocks*, plus *Never Mind The Ballots*. Nirvana kicked off another flood of punk in the US. I've got all their records.

When Kurt Cobain blew his brains out the papers chalked it up as a rock 'n' roll suicide, dismissed the man and concentrated on their idea of drug addiction as some sort of romantic rebellion, dismissing depression as creative misery, while the righteous put it down to self-indulgence. So the face of an ordinary man who loved music and could write a tune and lyrics ends up on a glossy poster, same as poor old Sid Vicious, a teenage kid who was exploited by big business, his self-mutilation touted as more rock 'n' roll chic. I read in a paper that Sid was gang-raped in a New York prison, after he was charged with killing Nancy Spungeon. It was a casual sentence in a newspaper article. Don't even know if it's true. Maybe some people think he deserved it, seeing as he spat into the crowd, sliced up his arms, and had a spiky haircut. Probably they reckon he deserved the heroin he shot into his veins when he died.

I wonder how many people know Sid's real name was John, that he was a boy when he replaced Glen Matlock in the Sex Pistols. Look at his face in the photos, before he joined the band and learnt the cartoon snarl, and he's soft, a child. Someone older should've helped him out. You look at McLaren and Westwood, swanning around twenty years later, and it doesn't seem right. They were part of the Establishment while the band members were just ordinary kids, the whole fashion parade and avant-garde as much a part of the system as the House of Lords. They're all the same, obsessed with empty statements, living in a fantasy world, chasing fame and fortune, acting out the system's idea of rebellion, as if dressing up is hard. We used to call the bloke Stupid Sid, because everyone knew the score, that he was being conned, used by business interests, the sort of scum we hated. It wasn't meant in a bad way though, just that we could see he was being stitched up.

It's a crying shame that a human being is remembered as a

cartoon character on a poster, the good looks and Elvis sneer milked by faceless businessmen, promoted as a plastic cut-out who OD'd in New York City, their dumb idea of a rock 'n' roll town, a glitzy arcade of smackheads and platinum records. I play the Clash single 'City Of The Dead' in my brain, see a Disneyland city full of dead musicians, Janis Joplin and Jimi Hendrix on the run from Sid, Kurt and Malcolm Owen, a battered Ford Cortina bumper-to-bumper with a chrome-plated Cadillac, Owen pressing the accelerator and banging into the back of the Cadillac, denting the fins, scratching pink enamel, Sid riding shotgun as Kurt leans out of the back window and levels a pistol at the longhairs, calls them a couple of goddam hippies, Marilyn grabbing James Dean's bollocks as he pumps her in a penthouse filling station, watching the plebs down below, Johnny & The Self Abusers on hand with the johnnies, that Stewart Home song 'Necrophilia' pounding through a city broken into musical barrios, the ring of a police car chasing the Cortina. I pick up the phone and turn down the music, listen to Sarah's voice, sit talking as the deck spins round, record finished, and I talk to her for a long time, don't hang up till nearly an hour later, arrange to go round and see her next week.

Version

My head's buzzing as I leave Sarah's flat and stroll into a misty Saturday morning, a big smile on my face. Life is sweet, it really is, don't care what anyone says, the only downer this Chapatti special bubbling away in my gut, an off-the-menu pharl, twice the spice of a vindaloo, meaner than a jalfrezi, worse than any stout-coke-vodka mix. I need something to ease the pressure, chilli simmering under my skin, oozing through the pores. My knob's numb and there's a trickle of spunk down the front of my jeans. Sarah wanted me to stay and meet her little boy, but I pushed myself to get out before her old dear brought him back.

I cross the road to the paper shop, buy a carton of milk off a bloke who's talking into a phone, says his old man's gone on holiday to Great Yarmouth, and I drink the carton outside watching the fog swirl around the lights, traffic picking up, lights blinking stop-go-stop-go, dented cones on their side, tarmac cracked. The morning rush has started and I look out for Chris who'll be rolling past with the family, his kids pumped up for a trip to paradise, off to the loaded racks of the superstores. And I'm in the clear, on the move, milk mingling with the pharl, doing its best to turn it into a korma, least in my brain anyway, it's all about psychological warfare, and I head off past the factory where I worked as a teenager, sweating my bollocks off in the foundry, trying to get the forklift up the ramp, fucking murder, metal filings itching my scalp, boils on my arms, the walls of the buildings vague outlines in the fog, ghosts that spring up out of nowhere pulling me back, and I can laugh it off now, doing well, moving on, slip back and wonder about the men and women, boys and girls working in the factory now, some kid fresh out of school scrubbing at grease, looking forward to the end of the week when he can have a pint with his mates, a couple of Es and lots of music, the throbbing beat of life going on and on, an endless creative circle.

The air is fresh, cool mist swirling around me, thicker away from the main road, and Sarah's a diamond, a lovely woman full of soul. A bloke in a Muslim cap hurries past, on his way to some Saturday overtime, sandwich box tucked under his arm, and I wonder how many times I've done the same thing. We work hard for a few extra pounds, think we're doing well if we can save a couple of hundred quid, and in the meantime the captains of industry are spending a year's wages on a holiday. I cross the street and walk past the cemetery, houses broken apart by the mist, showing off a window here, a brick wall there. I feel the oxygen in my lungs, nicely chilled, mist rumbling along the pavement, look over the cemetery wall at a big concrete cross, fog hanging above the grass, and I shiver from the cold, my legs going rubbery and brain cracking open as I'm sucked into some sort of horror show. I stop walking and look into the graveyard. Stand and stare. I don't believe in ghosts, must be tripping, my tea spiked, the sun trying to break in through the fog creating the sort of vision that belongs to mushrooms, acid, peyote, religion, mental illness.

Smiles is standing thirty feet away from me next to his grave. He turns and a white cloud covers his body for a few seconds, drifts away, and now he's kneeling next to the headstone. He leans forward and rubs at the inscription with a piece of cloth, cleaning his own memorial. I'm panicking inside, scared of the flashback, cross the road and sit on a bench dedicated to someone knocked down by a bus in 1985, the brass plaque worn down by the elements, a yellow stain covering the name, the wood soggy and lined with moss. I keep my eyes on the graveyard. Smiles is still rubbing the stone, digging dirt out of the letters, and I sort my thinking out, know that it has to be a trick of the light. The council must be funding a cleaning programme, paying this bloke time and a half for working early Saturday morning, fighting off his hangover. It's just that he looks like an old mate of mine, one of those coincidences in life, if you believe in chance, and I don't, so it must be in my head, looking at the factory and seeing myself on the forklift, shifting back in time. I don't know.

The ghost stands and turns, drifts towards the gate and gets lost in the fog, body melting into the clouds, vanishing, and it's like I've seen a miracle, know that there's a spirit world now, that ghosts really exist, get this feeling inside me, confidence maybe. I lean forward and shake my head, look up again and see Smiles come through the gate, under the little porch with its own bigger plaque, columns of names from the First and Second World Wars, and I wonder if they include the soldiers who died in Northern Ireland and the Falklands. There was a bloke we knew called Barry Fisher who died in the South Atlantic. He was in the papers and everything. And I watch the shape turn towards me and come down the road, stare into the face as it gets bigger, the hallucination sticking and the body rock solid. I'm waiting for voices to start inside my head, radio messages and a television set that only shows one single gold-plated skull.

The mist lifts and the face is huge, glowing, there's no mistake now, the body alive, breathing, moving. Smiles is marching towards me, crossing the road, ten feet away. I call his name, and it's not Smiles, it's Gary coming down the road, Gary Dodds, an early-eighties version, must be twenty-one or twenty-two years old. There's no smile, and the face is bent out of shape. I call his name again, and he looks over not sure what to do, peers at me as if he's forgotten, a puzzled look on his face, stops and tries to work things out, needs time to remember who I am, and he's got lighter hair than I remember, and maybe I'm face to face with a test-tube baby, Frankenstein getting hold of Smiles's DNA and building a monster. I'm tired. Emotional. Head clanging. Caving in. The world crashing down.

– I look like my dad, do I? he says at last.

I nod because there's nothing else to do. I don't understand, move over so he can sit on the bench. He leans forward with his elbows on his knees, same as me, funny bones digging into the thin fabric of tracksuit bottoms, Nike trainers resting on the pavement, worn-out soles flat on the paving stones, a hole in the toe of his right foot. The fog is fading fast and I can see more clearly, my mind doing one of those trampoline tricks where a charged-up athlete flips right over and comes out on their feet. I forget about spirits rising from the dead, ignore the hypodermics and loaded test tubes, start acting reasonable. Look blank.

– My name's Luke, the boy says, his head turned towards me, short hair and a gold tooth in the front of his mouth.

– My dad was called Gary Dodds. You must've known him because you called me Gary. I didn't realise I looked so much like him. Mum never told me that.

Yes, I knew Gary Dodds. He was my best mate, from the age of six or seven, something like that. It doesn't make sense. He looks like Gary alright, but how could he have a son? I'm struggling for something to say, don't know where to start, what questions to ask. I do my best.

– My mum got pregnant when she was fifteen and went to live with her auntie. Mum's in Brighton now and that's where I'm going next. She told me where Dad's grave is a couple of years ago, but I never came down till last night. I left my job yesterday, and was on the platform at Ealing Broadway, waiting to go to Paddington, when the announcer called out the Slough train, so I crossed over and came down here. I'd had a drink. It was nine o'clock and I slept on this bench till morning.

I've only been to the grave once, after I came home from working in Hong Kong. Haven't been since. It's just a headstone, a stone oblong, and it did my head in to be honest, imagining the body under the earth, rotting away. I saw all sorts of things. Parched skin and a skeleton. No worms or maggots. Just slow decay. It's better sticking a baby in the ovens. Try and cut it off once and for all. Do your best to look ahead. But each to their own, and if Luke had to clean the stone I don't suppose it's getting visited very much. I feel everything flooding back, can feel the spice in my gut, need a drink, a pint of Guinness and a triple whisky, a plate of food, something to concentrate on, a knife and fork in my hands, a glass to lift, anything but sitting on this bench with the smell of wet moss and wood, the smell of the past. The pubs aren't open yet so I ask Luke if he wants to go for a cup of tea, sit in a cafe and have a proper chat.

– I could murder some breakfast, he says. I haven't eaten since yesterday morning.

It's a five-minute walk to the nearest cafe. We order and sit down. Luke pongs, needs a bath and some clean clothes, dumps his bag under a table, eyes moving side to side, clocking the men with their faces buried in newspapers, filling up on the latest scandal, more concerned with the back pages than the front. For the first time in my life I feel old. I'm not, haven't reached my prime yet, but the breath is squeezed tight in my chest. It's a shock being pulled back and forced to dig up memories. The cafe's not that busy, the bloke who runs the place going around collecting empty plates, most of them wiped so clean they look like they don't need a wash. And I'm doing my best to stay calm, choose the right words from the swirl crashing around inside my head.

I don't want to scare the boy off, try to handle all this mad-scientist footage that's flashing up, concentration-camp experiments and mad-cow economics, genetically-modified human beings where all the emotion and individualism has been erased, clone culture, multinational-sponsored boffins stripping life bare as they fiddle with our chromosomes and DNA, corporations kitting out the dissection chambers, the synthetic beat of a computer-generated world. The Nazis had the same idea. They talked about it, while today it's done in secret. But if I talk same as I'm thinking then the boy will be up and out the door, look at me the same way we used to look at Smiles when he was running off at the mouth, talking about communist and fascist dictators, the council's housing policy. So I keep quiet and Smiles sits opposite me staring at the table, lifting his head as he sips his tea, face lit up by the light blaring in through the glass, the fog suddenly gone. Close up there's differences, the shape of his head and the look of his skin, lots of things you never know you see, but are buried inside somewhere. He's his dad's boy alright, but I don't see how. And then something clicks.

– I've been working in Ealing for a year. Computers. It's the sort of thing you can teach yourself. You have to get on a machine to start, find a manual, but once you've got the basics you're off. It's easy to bullshit your way in somewhere. People who've been to university get straight in the door, so you have to tell them you've been as well, then you're in and it's up to you. If you can do the work you're away, and there's money to be made. Computers are where the cash is. You've got to get in there and grab your share, take what's yours. Doesn't matter how good you are at something, it's getting in the door that counts, squeezing past the interviews. Those cunts are so dozy they don't check the references, and all you've got to do is have someone on the other end of a phone, or give an address where you can do a letterhead. You've got to use the system. I didn't work this out till I was a teenager. It's a shame, because I caused a lot of grief when I was a kid, mostly my own fault.

Luke doesn't smile the same as Gary, but he's positive, upbeat, even if there's sadness in his eyes, the black bags of someone knackered after a night dossing on a bench, the visit to the graveyard knocking him out. If he's working he shouldn't be sleeping rough, freezing his bollocks off when he could be in the warm. He might catch pneumonia. Should've paid for a bed and breakfast.

– It was spur of the moment, like I said. Don't know why I decided to come down here. It's only a fifteen-minute ride from Ealing Broadway, and I've thought about it enough times, but always put it off, said it wasn't going to change anything. I'm glad now. It's sad, a real choker, but there you go.

It's true what he says about working the system, and it took a lot longer for me to figure that one out, but you can only go so far. People used to bang their heads against walls and pile in full-frontal, say exactly what they thought, and that's the way things were, and it was more honest, you knew what people stood for, but sometimes you have to use a bit of nous, if you really want to win. Problem is, some people are so fucking cunning they've given up thinking altogether, while the rest of them, the scum really milking the system for every penny, never had any guts in the first place, the original yes-men.

I wonder about his mum. She'll be worried if he was supposed to be in Brighton last night. I try and think of her name, but can't remember. Feel guilty and think of Sarah, how I never remembered her name either.

– I phoned Mum last night from the station. Didn't say I was here, just that I had a few things to sort out. I'm going to live in the hotel where she works. There's a spare room in the attic that never gets used. It's on the sixth floor and I'm going to paint the walls and do it up.

David Bowie's 'Sound And Vision' plays in my head, an

electric blue room where Luke can live. Fucking hell. Wonder where that came from.

– The bloke who runs the place is sweet, Luke continues. He says I can stay there for nothing if I teach him how to use a computer. He's doing it as a favour for Mum really. She's a good worker. There's a window that looks out over the sea, and you can climb on to a flat bit of roof and see all the way over to France. You don't hear the cars down below either. It's like I'm up in the clouds, on a mountain or something, and no one can touch me. I'm going to bury myself away and make my own music. I'll have to get a proper computer, and the money won't last long, but I can get a job in the bar, or in a pub, to keep me ticking over.

I ask him what he listens to.

– Everything from Kraftwerk and Brian Eno to Headrillaz and Goldie.

Maybe he knows the *Low* album, that song 'Sound And Vision'.

– Blue, blue, electric blue.

He's laughing now. We're both laughing.

– The bloke who runs the hotel, Ron's his name, he's always been good to me. Him and Mum are just friends. Suppose he's the nearest I ever had to a dad. It's a shame my old man didn't live, that they didn't stay together. It would've been good to have had a proper family. Mum put me in care when I was small. Anyway . . .

Our food arrives and there's a bucketful of tears behind his eyes, so I look at my plate, pretend I don't notice, get stuck in. I give him a minute, swearing at the salt shaker, moaning about how it always gets clogged up, the mark of a good cafe the condition of the salt shaker, the attention to detail that keeps the salt flowing, time ticking. I stick my fork in the holes, dig the knife in deep, chipping plastic, this rotten feeling in me as I think of this kid, any kid, stuck in a home, my brother stillborn, Mum and Dad never gave him a name, they should've given him a name, imagine Sarah's boy asking her where his dad is and she has to say she doesn't know, he could be anywhere, and I think of the teenagers standing outside a Chinese railway station, plaques around their necks, condemned to hard labour, maybe death. And what I really want to do is drill my fist into someone's face and break their nose, splinter the bone into their brain, pay someone back for the unfairness and bad things people do to each other. Life doesn't have to be like this. If people worked together instead of pulling in different directions we could have it all. Someone has to pay the price, but nobody wants to take the blame. It shifts around, moved on to the next institution. The anger rises, but I control it, let it go, clear the holes and give my food a nice healthy layer.

– Fucking hell, Luke laughs, you like your salt, don't you.

I nod and grin, pleased he's smiling. I tell him his dad was seriously into music, same as him. We were punks when we were young.

– With Mohican haircuts and safety pins through your nose? Going around begging and sniffing glue in doorways?

It was nothing like that. It was about the music and most people couldn't afford to dress up, and that beggar act is a con. Punk was about ordinary kids. It was anti-fashion, yet the fashion journalists and university lecturers who have made a mint trying to intellectualise the subject have concentrated on the management end of things, the bands they were ligging with instead of the people, the masses, the social climate at the time when it all kicked off. Punk was anti-fashion.

– I've got a punk CD somewhere. Greatest hits.

I enjoy the flavour of the tinned tomatoes, juice soaking a slice of toast. So what's he's going to do now? Visiting a grave is fair enough, but what next? Is that all there is, a headstone and a message, then back out on the first train to Paddington?

– I'll have a walk round and see where Dad grew up. Get a feel of the place. When I was in the home I used to think about having a mum and dad. Used to lie awake at night and wonder what it was like, and I used to try and imagine how my mum and dad would be. I drew pictures of them, mostly faces off the telly, or out of books, and when I went back to Mum I found out that she was a beautiful woman, a beautiful girl who was let down when she was a kid. Mum never had a photo of Dad. I don't know what he looks like. You don't have a picture, do you?

I shake my head. It's not the sort of thing you do in everyday life. People take photos when they're away from the routine. On holiday escaping the daily grind, a quick taste of paradise. Walking down the promenade eating sugary doughnuts and drinking tea, going to the funfair and playing crazy golf, donkey rides on the sand and chips twice a day. No, we never went around taking photos of each other, probably never had a camera till we were in our twenties. Can't exactly see us standing in a pub on Friday night posing for a snapshot, or at the Electric Ballroom saying cheese. Wish we had in a way, but I've never bothered, not even when I was on the train crossing Siberia, at work in Hong Kong, travelling around China. I'd like to give Luke a photo of his dad. I could see if Tony's got anything. He's bound to have a picture. He's living in Langley I think. Haven't seen him for years. Don't have a clue where old man Dodds is, except that he moved out two months after Smiles died and was staying with Smiles's auntie till he sorted things out. I heard he'd gone down to the coast, but Tony never talked about him much after he left. He could be dead for all I know. They're Luke's uncle and grandad. Never thought of that. He probably doesn't know about them, so I start to fill him in, get excited thinking about it, how it'll pick everyone up.

– I'm not bothered about them, he says, an edge in his voice. I know who they are, but don't want to make a fuss. This is about my dad.

Doesn't seem right somehow, but I let it go for now and decide to try again later, wonder what he's going to do in Brighton.

– Computers is how I make my money, but I want to use them and make music. They've opened things up. You can do what you want and don't need a studio. Do it all yourself. You don't have to waste time fucking around trying to persuade people to see things your way.

I tell him there's a bloke I know called Charlie Parish who's into all that. There's three of us play records together. I take care of the punk, past and present, while Alfonso deals with the reggae side of things. I tell Luke he takes after his dad, never mind the looks. Luke's eyes open and he seems embarrassed, but really I think he's chuffed. He looks like Gary but the longer

I look at him, the more differences I see. We have another tea, keep talking till they're finished.

– I'll pay mine, he says, when we get up to leave, but I tell him it's my treat.

He insists, and I respect him for it.

Down at the end of the road we stop and Luke says he's going to walk around and see what's what. He's got the addresses of his mum and dad's houses. I tell him that if he wants somewhere to sleep tonight he can crash out on my couch. He nods and says he might. Doesn't know yet. I go into the bookies across the road, write down my address, phone number, draw a map. I hurry back over and give it to him. He nods. Thinking about something else. Says thanks again and walks off in the opposite direction.

It doesn't take me long to get home. I boot a KFC box across the lay-by, bones tinkling on the ground, sit on the couch and wait, the room quiet except for the rattle of the windows and the hum of traffic on the motorway. Downstairs, pipes yawn and stretch, vibrating up into my kitchen, dying down again. There's lots of things I should've asked Luke and I hope I haven't missed my chance. Everything's falling around me, and all I can do is sit on my own and hope I get a second chance.

Luke stays two days and I give him the guided tour, show him the sights, the market with its special blend of pet-shop seed and butcher's livers, the racks of polyester shirts and plastic toys, the stall selling old rockabilly records. We go through a spruced-up Queensmere lined with jewellers and shoe shops, computer chainstores and high-street fashion, come out by the ten-screen multiplex and Virgin Megastore touting US blockbusters and US gangsta rap, do a circle past Smith's and end up at the top of the high street with the fun pubs and burger bars on the crossroads. The traffic lights aren't working and buses block the way. Drills pound and grit flies. People flood past, young and excited, don't notice the granny in her sari pushing a baby along, the three pocked-faced men with their bent cans of lager. Behind the market there's a maze of houses, car parks and building work, a hospital that keeps the babies coming, while up on the high street everything's been scrubbed, like one of those Western towns in the middle of the prairies, where the shopfronts are spotless and look just like a film set.

We sit in a cafe with two mugs of tea, look out of the window for half an hour, drink up and get the car. It doesn't want to start, and I've got the choke right out, accelerator on the floor, listening to the turn of the engine, knowing either the battery is going to run down or I'll flood it, the little niggles of life, the starter motor finally catching. I show Luke the houses and factories, the warehouses and supermarkets, depots and superstores. I don't know what to do next. He doesn't want to go find his grandad and uncle, flares right up when I mention them. I don't understand, but don't go on about it. If Smiles's genes are in his face, then the same DNA boosts his manner. He's a happy bloke, but now he goes quiet on me. There's questions he needs to ask, things I want to know. Like why he ended up in care. But where do you start? Don't have a clue. And I suppose there's not much to see really, no famous sites or classic architecture, just everyday life, same as most places. Luckily I'm carrying a special-offer trowel to give the old man, tell Luke we have got to go over to the allotments. He'll get the boy talking. He's got the experience. Father figure, I suppose.

– What do you do for a job? Luke asks, as we drive over.

I tell him I work for myself, that I love music but prefer the words, the social lyrics that have been sidelined these days. Songs can give you the answers books rarely deliver, dip into your life and make you laugh, draw out things you already know but can't put into words yourself. I go for content over style. I think about it and I suppose I sell things. Music and myself. Tell him I'm a capitalist, think properly and say I do what I want. I'm my own boss, sell and play records, make enough to live on and keep my time for myself. I don't mention the tickets and dope.

– Suppose we're the same in a way, he laughs, easing up now.

Maybe he is, a thinner version, hasn't filled out yet, like he could snap in half.

– I want to make a living out of music, but prefer sound myself. I wondered why you had all those boxes of records stacked everywhere.

I get ready to argue the toss about sounds and lyrics, but the music he's into has a harder edge than all that disco/house bollocks, a tougher home-made sound for a soft commercial era, and it's another time now, everything melted down and sanitised, following the American pattern. Even though the logic is plain, that the fighting between the mods, rockers, skinheads, Pakistanis, suedeheads, Hell's Angels, boot boys, greasers, Teds, punks, soulboys, rockabillies, rude boys, casuals and every other shade of herbert going, was just ordinary people fighting among themselves, it's right there inside me. We roll past the Slough Town football ground and I'm humming along to the Business classic 'Smash The Discos'. I fucking hate disco. Just can't help it. Must be something in the blood.

I don't have a clue how much Luke knows about his dad, except that he topped himself. I wonder if he knows why. The memory makes me jolt, and there must be people in that house right now, having some evil dreams, two suicides in one building, a few feet from each other. Mind you, I don't really know why Smiles hung himself either. It was one of four possibles. Tipped over finding his mum in the bath, which makes sense, but then why the delay, and when you look back it explained the *Sunny Smiles* photos, the loneliness he must've felt. Could've been something in his make-up, a self-destruct gene waiting to take over, which seeing how his old girl went the same way, makes sense as well. Third, the punches he used to take off his dad, but I don't go for that really. Lots of people get smacked about and don't string themselves up. Fourth, getting stuck under the water damaged his brain, or triggered something else that was already there. The doctors said he was okay when he left hospital, but he was never the same.

Like everything in life, I suppose it was a mixture of influences. I let things run, wait for Luke to ask or say something. Can't do better than that. I park up and we go in through the gates. I tell Luke to wait a minute, so I can warn my dad, seeing as he knew Smiles as a boy. I go and explain things, wave Luke over.

– Fucking hell, is all Dad can manage, before he shifts out of neutral, and then he's sweet as a nut.

We sit in the deckchairs and share Dad's flask, the smell of the leeks he's pulled hanging in the air. He gives Luke a tour of the spinach and rhubarb, the broccoli he's trying to grow, having another try after last year when the slugs steamed in mob-handed. The pictures on the packets show glossy blue buds and thick stems, but without gallons of insecticide it's hard going. The old man doesn't get wound up, takes things nice and easy, doesn't see the point in chemicals. He's taking Luke in his stride, now he's used to the likeness, and it's as if nothing can surprise him these days. It's experience that does the trick.

– He was a good boy, is all I can hear from the other side of the allotment, when Dad takes Luke on a tour.

There's an ant hill next to the lavender, a butterfly sitting on the flowers, massive red-and-white wings strapped to its back. And I watch Dad leading Luke around, doing his best not to stare at Smiles's face. He shows Luke a mouse run along the back of the rhubarb, the pea seeds he put down long gone. He doesn't drown the ants or try to poison the mice. Suppose he's content. That's what it is. The responsibility has been lifted, any ambition to get rich a non-starter, no chance, so he's done his best and now he's unplugged from the bullshit and lies, gone his own way. He realises it's not worth bothering with the media and politicians, who only exist to wind people up. This confidence has swelled in him. He's not rich in terms of money, but rich because he's got family, friends, food, drink, a roof, his health, knows his neighbours. Those are the essentials.

– You're set up here, Luke says, when he's sitting down again, making the effort, even if he's bored.

Instead of going down the pub I've brought him to meet my old man. They seem to get on well enough.

– It's not bad, Dad admits, with that twinkle in his eye he gets when he knows someone's humouring him. Could be worse.

The Major stops and stares over, the top half of his body at an angle to the bottom as he concentrates. I wave him over but he turns away, lifting straw into the compost heap. He loves that heap, and as the weather gets warmer it'll start cooking. He looks back over and I wonder if he sees Smiles same as I did.

– I tell you what, Dad says. The Major's on the warpath. I took him some spinach and I've never heard him talk so much the whole time I've known him. Says he's not putting up with what happened last year, the way the slugs ate everything. Says it's war and he's going to wipe them out, even if he has to come down and sleep in the shed, go out on night patrol. These kids went round breaking stuff last summer, and he kipped out, borrowed a mobile phone so he could dial 999 and get the TSG down. It was Kenny's boy and some of his mates, and the Major caught them. Called up Ken. You know what Kenny's like. Those kids won't be back in a hurry.

– No, it's the slugs I feel sorry for. He had his table out and was standing there slicing them up, great big juicy slugs with feelers, four or five strokes with a clasp knife. They were oozing. There was a stack of body parts and he stuck them in the compost. Said flesh is as good as plants. If it's cut up right it'll boil down and produce something healthy.

The Major must've turned nasty torturing something living like that, even if they are slugs.

– They were dead, Dad says. He kills them with pellets first, and was slicing them up so they'd rot faster. Least I think he killed them first. He said he did. I hope so anyway. He must do, don't you think so?

Luke looks over at the Major, the man's back to us as he digs into his compost heap.

– He must do.

It isn't nice, imagining a mad grin on the Major's face and a cold butcher's knife, but he's never been mental like that. If he says the slugs were dead I believe him. I want to tell Luke about the canal, because he doesn't seem to know, tell him it was the Major who was on the path and probably saved both our lives. I couldn't get out of the water and he pulled us out. He went to court and did what he thought was right, but got ripped apart by the defence. So far we haven't gone into things too much. Maybe Luke has important questions to ask, maybe not. I have to decide what to tell him. There's no point going over things that are best forgotten.

– It doesn't matter if the slugs are already dead, Dad says. That's what the Major told me. He said that if slugs have souls then they're long gone, and he can't be sentimental with the price of food these days. Started going on about the extra penny they've put on a tin of butter beans. Said it was natural justice, survival of the fittest. What does it matter if the slug's already dead, and he's right.

I thought something similar when I read Tony's letter in China, almost felt as bad about Smiles hanging over the stairs for two weeks as I did about him dying. I push it out of my head and Luke will never hear that from me. I change the subject but walk straight into an ambush, Luke grinning as Dad unwinds and starts amusing him at my expense, telling him what me and Smiles were like when we were kids, and it's as if his memories come from a different life.

– These two were mad about guns and soldiers when they were little, he says. They were always playing war, shooting each other, throwing hand grenades, cutting each other's throats.

It was all the stuff on the telly. *The World At War* was on every Sunday, before *The Big Match*. Dad would be down the pub, mum cooking dinner, Jilly off somewhere, and I'd be sitting there in front of the box watching the Germans pound Stalingrad, or the Luftwaffe bombing London, or the D-Day landings. Then I'd go straight into *The Big Match*, YOU'RE GONNA GET YOUR FUCKING HEADS KICKED IN and HELLO HELLO, CHELSEA AGGRO filling in where the bombers left off, hoping Dad would have an extra pint and Mum would be late with the food, so I could watch the Third and Fourth Division games. We always sat down and had dinner on Sunday, and Dad would be there in his vest during summer, stuffing the potatoes down. He loved soaking his bread in the gravy after, and we all used to have a go, watching it ooze through, turning white bread into brown. It's no surprise we were into war films and soldiers.

– Later on they got interested in music. They loved Alvin Stardust and Showaddywaddy. Then there was Mud and Gary Glitter, before they started listening to David Bowie. They both had stupid haircuts. Spiky on top and long on the sides. They had these cheap brothel creepers when they were twelve. Bootlace ties for a while. Remember the flat cap?

I do now, and nod. Must've looked a right state, with the DMs and sleeveless jean jacket, patches of bleach on the denim, the badges and razor-blade necklace that was made of plastic and cost pennies from one of the shops on the high street. There was a craze for flat caps, and I bought one with my shelf-filling money. Didn't last long. Old working-men's caps your grandad wore. Both of them are laughing hard.

– They used to wear all these rings on their fingers, hair down to their collars, a couple of right old scruffs. Me and your mum used to have a good laugh, but that was nothing on your sister. She had those tartan trousers up to her knee. Remember?

He goes on like this for ages. I lean back in the chair and close my eyes, let them enjoy themselves, drift away and imagine I'm round Sarah's house. Wouldn't mind going and seeing her, but I've got to stick with Luke and show him around. Look after the bloke. I think of her boy Jimmy. Maybe I should buy him a toy or something.

– Seriously though, Dad's voice is calm at last, your dad was a good boy, one of the best. I saw him grow up, and he was always good-natured, would do anything for anyone.

After an hour having my life opened up for Luke, it starts to rain. We get going, leave Dad who wants to wait and see if it stops. He stands in the door of the shed and I wonder what to do next, have an idea. It's a five-minute drive to Slough Town's ground, and they're playing Hayes today. Luke fancies it, and we go in the social club and have a drink, sit in a corner nursing our pints as the rain spreads across the glass, eating our cheese rolls. Three generations sit at the next table, on the piss, and we only have the one pint, things easier now. Dad's done the business. We go and stand down the side of the pitch, under the roof.

– I used to go see QPR play when I was working in Ealing, Luke says. I was renting a room in Acton, so it wasn't far.

The crowd isn't bad, and Hayes have brought a load with them. I tell Luke how Millwall played here in the FA Cup, and I came with his dad. We were standing behind one of the goals, and Millwall came straight across the pitch at the Slough boys, chased some of the kids up trees. One of our mates, Billy Clement, got bricked outside the social club. Slough had a go back but this was Millwall after all. I tell him how the ground used to be over the other side of Slough and double as a greyhound stadium. There's a Co-op there now. When Chelsea won the Cup Winners Cup in 1971 they played Slough right after they came back from Athens. Eleven thousand turned up, and Dad took me and his dad along. We were little boys and the crowd seemed huge. Dave came as well. You wouldn't get that now. Money fucks up everything it touches.

We don't bother going in the social club after, end up in a pub just off the high street. We sit in the corner, me with a pint of Guinness, Luke with lager. I should buy him some food, but a drink seems better.

– You remember Mum, don't you. Linda Wilson?

I tell him yes, that she was a nice girl, even though I don't really, just a glimpse at a party. She could've told Smiles she'd had the kid instead of lying to him, saying she'd had an abortion when she hadn't. It might've helped as well, given him something more personal to think about. Maybe she was going to tell him later, but heard things had gone pear-shaped, but I don't see how she could. We didn't even know he was going off his head ourselves, and we were his mates. Maybe she wanted to keep things simple, didn't want him around. I try to remember what Smiles said, what he thought about her having an abortion, but it's too long ago now. Things are hazy, memories lost, and suddenly there's another truth coming along and taking over from the old truth. At first this does my head in, but then it makes me laugh. Nothing is solid. History is another invention, same as the microchip.

– It wasn't Mum's fault she put me in care, you know. She was a kid when she got pregnant. Her mum and dad gave her a lot of grief, traditional Catholics more worried about what the priest would say than their child and grandson. She stayed with her auntie for a while, till I was born, then ran away and ended up squatting in Finsbury Park. She gave me up a year later, so I'd be looked after properly. It was the money. She was young and didn't have any. Later on she moved to Brighton, found a job in a hotel, tried to get me back, but it took her time to convince them that me living with her was better than being alone in an orphanage, the thick cunts. She got me back when I was nine. If she was a problem child, I was worse, a proper little hooligan nicking cars and joyriding, getting in fights because I was unhappy, ram-raiding shops so she didn't know what to do with me. Eight fucking years in care. But she never gave me away again.

I look away.

– She found a job in one of the big hotels on the seafront, like I said. It was hard for her and I caused a lot of trouble. When you're in a home you want attention. You're on your own, with nobody to love you, and I played up so no one would adopt me, and when I was back with Mum I kept on. But it worked out alright in the end. Least I wasn't killed, like her God-loving parents wanted. They bow down for Christ but don't mind an abortion to keep up appearances. They're fucking rubbish. Ron was good to me, always seemed to understand. It's only when you get older you realise what's going on, why you do the things you do.

He picks up my pint glass and goes to the bar. I look at him standing there and try to think what it must've been like, and it's the worst sort of irony, seeing how we nicknamed Gary after the *Sunny Smiles* photos he went around selling, how he felt sorry for babies given up when they were born, without a family, stuck in an institution. Maybe he was seeing into the future, turning time on its head somehow, or maybe it was because of his mum killing herself in the bath. It's mental that his own son ends up in the same sort of place, a face in a book full of baby mugshots. Maybe Luke's face was in one of those books. He comes back and I sit and watch the head of my pint tighten up.

– Cheers, and he raises his glass, seems alright.

It's a quiet boozer this, tucked out of sight, the sort of place you can settle in and have a long, relaxing session. Quality beer and enough room to breathe, no packed bar and tinny house music. Time to think.

– Fuck them anyway, Luke says. If people don't like you, then why should you worry about them? I don't believe all that stuff about letting people off the hook, forgiving and forgetting. It's fine to forget, but why bother forgiving. Fuck them. Mum's staunch as far as her mum and dad go. Never mind anyway.

There's an edge there, the result of being on his own, and it shows what being alone really means, a different story when you don't have a choice in the matter. He eyes up two girls who come in the pub, order and then sit in the opposite corner. A soul singer croons in the background. People come and go.

– You should visit us in Brighton. See if Mum recognises you. They must have record fairs down there worth going to, and there's got to be somewhere you could DJ.

We're quiet for a while.

– Thing is, you learn quickly when you're on your own. You get treated different when you're in care. It was shit, but I learnt a lot. I could blame Mum, I suppose, but I don't. Just wouldn't want it to happen to anyone else. You get through the bad things earlier, causing trouble and that, and at least Mum came back for me. That doesn't happen to a lot of kids and it lasts them their whole lives. They could be fifty or sixty years old and still wondering what went wrong, why they were given up. You have to sort it out. I think back, can't pretend I don't. If I had nobody it would be much worse, and I was always putting off coming down here because there's nothing I can do to make things alright with Dad. I'll never know him, and he never even knew I existed. Imagine that. Never knew my name or what I looked like.

I lift my glass and wonder about the women through the years, the one-night stands, the girls you never see again. For some reason I think of this Russian woman I got off with once. She was called Rika and ran my carriage on the Trans-Siberian Express. She was beautiful, but it was never going anywhere. She might've ended up pregnant and I'd never know. I remember she wanted to leave Russia and go live in New York. Maybe she'll end up with that bloke from Swindon, and he'll meet a son I never knew I had. I know it's not going to happen like that, I'm just thinking about what Luke's saying.

– You have all these dreams when you're a kid, and the thing is they can come true if you want. You come out of care either strong or weak, and I came out strong. My gran and dad killed themselves, but I've got my mum's blood in me. She's strong as well. It was just she was young and there was nobody to help her. She was under pressure, no support, nowhere to live, no money. Simple as that.

Luke's sharp, much more together than I was at his age. It depends how you look at things, whether you blame the priests and politicians, or the people who believe what they're told. It has to be a bit of both really, but the thing is you're always going to blame someone at a local level, because it's easier and the others are out of range. I think about the blokes who chucked us off the bridge and how they believed what they read in the papers. Who's to blame? Again, both of them, but the journalists walk away whistling. There's no comeback. Wells and the others got off as well, while I never went after them because I honestly believe they were sorry for what happened. But it's in the past and I don't say anything about it to Luke. There's no point.

Luke sees posters for a fair and wants to go, says he never went when he was a kid. He seems a bit old to be lording it in a bumper car, larging it in the house of horrors, but he's serious, dead keen, and seeing as he's off tomorrow I go with him. The organs are rolling when we arrive, pumping out choirboy chimes that roar up and merge with the latest chart-toppers, teenybopper anthems and a free-enterprise version of girl power. Thick insulated cable stretches behind the stalls, the steady hum of an industrial generator backing up the screeching vocals. Stroppy kids hang around the dodgems, doing their best to look hard as love songs blare out, gypsy boys eyeing up the girls as a gang of cocky young hooligans eyeball the gypsies, who casually shift their gaze and eyeball a dressed-up Asian mob. Only the gypsies are out of school and you have to laugh, specially remembering what we must've looked like when we were young, doing the same thing, posing at the fairground, all bovver boots and clicking hands.

A little girl passes us and bumps into the fortune teller's sign, Sheri charging five pounds a session, drops her goldfish on the ground, and it's bad luck all the way as the bag splits and the water vanishes, the fish gasping for air, sucking plastic into its face and flapping its tail. The girl screams and her dad steps forward, picks the goldfish up and pulls the plastic off. He takes it back to the stall with his daughter jumping up to see what's happening. The gills pulse and the tail speeds up as the fish panics, suffocating on fresh air laced with candyfloss, and maybe it's having flashbacks, seeing more than Sheri in her deluxe caravan with its freshly-painted Romany trimmings. The girl on the stall drops the fish in a bowl where it floats for a few seconds, another fish sniffing its scales, and in seconds they're swimming in circles together, charging back up. The stallholder gives the girl another fish and she wipes her tears away, shows off her gums in a big toothy smile, her old man ruffling blonde hair, glad he doesn't have to try and explain what death means, all that stuff about heaven and hell he hasn't worked out for himself.

– That was a lucky escape, Luke says, moving on, excited same as a child, wanting everything at the same time.

Fairs always seemed expensive when we were kids, and going with Mum and Dad, me and Jilly were allowed two goes on the stalls and two rides, one extra if we really played up. Most of the time we were walking around listening to the sounds and watching the lights, smelling the smells, letting the atmosphere flood over us and take control, the rough edges I found later at punk gigs and football matches, all the fun of the carnival. And all the time Dad must've been digging deep. No one wants to let their kids down, even if it's a struggle, pushing themselves and trying to do the right thing. Luke's a big kid going around the stalls, the same con as an amusement arcade, and me and his dad used to spend a bomb shoving pennies in the slot, specially when we were at the seaside, waiting for the copper mountain to come tumbling down. Luke has a couple of goes on the rifle range, loading up and popping off shots, tries the darts, thinks about the goldfish but decides he doesn't need a pet, ends up on the coconut shy where he wins a plastic gun. He sticks it in his belt and walks around like Jesse James himself, a top gunslinger.

– Just need some water and I'll be off on the rampage.

We have a go on the big wheel and the machine cranks up, a spinning time capsule that lifts us into the evening sky which is dark and cold, the lights stretching out around us, the motorway on our left, a line of flickering red and solid white, Windsor Castle in the distance, a dark block of stone on the horizon, the Queen in her counting house and the squaddies in their garrison, counting out her gold as they polish up their leather brogues for a night on the piss, same as the stallholders juggling silver and copper, touting for business, and we begin to pick up speed, a small wiry man at the controls, and everything starts melting together, thousands of light bulbs losing their power, the smell of hot dogs and hamburgers brushed away by the breeze, the motion of the machine blurring shapes, little kids holding on to the hands of their mums and dads scared in case they get lost in the crowd, drop their goldfish, excited by the noise and sound, adults scared in case the paedophiles shift off the front pages and steal their babies, carry them away same as gypsies were supposed to do in the old days, and this machine is in top-notch condition, moving faster now so the fine points of the stalls, caravans, cars, trucks, people are lost, and the reds and greens, blues and yellows, oranges and lemons turn to a swaying wash of white light, and each time we pass the man at the controls his face melts a little bit more till there's nothing left, just a smear of wax, and the images crash in on themselves as the wind chaps our faces, styles fading, leaving the same old essentials of life, and nothing's changed that much, Smiles next to me shouting his head off, and the big wheel is in a better state than when we were kids and it broke down, the slow-motion replay speeded up, and everything is faster and more fused these days, the hard edges have been blunted yet there's a sharpness in here somewhere, the big wheel a high-tech helter-skelter ride, mashing up our brains along the way, and I turn sideways and see Smiles's skull straining the flesh, bone pushing against the surface, high in the sky with popping eyes, keeping away from water, and the screams of the girls in front cut through the air, bring me back as the sickness simmers in my gut holding on now as the speed of the machine blows any thoughts away, waiting for the ride to end, Smiles shouting something next to me, laughing, the machine peaking, billions of snazzy camera angles and special effects, photos taught to lie, airbrushing the past and future, two-second time spans for children's television, technology taking control, appearance over content, glitzy lights and easy convenience, nothing but profit, profit, profit, the slick workings of the machine, designer lives and designer politics, and our time is up, the wheel slowing down, a queue of eager people waiting, the bulbs forming up and the man's face falling back together, Luke laughing as we stop and wait our turn, the music clear and the smells sharp, looking at stalls, caravans, cars, lorries, people, the hum of the generators, moving forward, loading and unloading, the bar released as we get off and a happy couple take our place.

– I wouldn't mind going on that again, Luke says, thinking. I've always wanted to have a ride on the big wheel.

He can go on his own next time. I see Sarah standing by a stall, teddy bears and plastic jars of sweets stuck on square wooden blocks. She's on her own, lobbing hoops and missing the prizes. I wink at Luke and go up behind her, grab her round the waist and lift her into the air. She screams and tries to turn round. I let her go.

– Fucking hell, she says.

Laughs when she sees it's me.

– You said fuck, this kid pipes up, a little boy standing in front of her so I couldn't see him. Don't say that word.

Sarah's gone red in the face.

– This is Jimmy. My son.

The kid leans against his mum, shy, wearing an England shirt and trainers with these monsters on the side. I think of Chris's boy Darren who wears the same shirt, knows his language as well, both with their heads shaved, number two crops in a skinhead nation. The Undertones song 'Jimmy Jimmy' flashes into my head, but this Jimmy is okay, there won't be any ambulances for Sarah's little boy.

– Say hello to Joe.

He squirms into her legs.

– Go on, say hello.

– Hello.

He's shy and looks up at his mum. I introduce Luke.

– Hello, Luke. Say hello to Luke.

– Hello, Luke. Mum, I want to have another go on the hoops.

– I told you one. It costs too much. We're going home in a minute. I told you when we came in so don't argue or you won't come again. If you're good I'll buy you some chips.

This is when it's nice to have money in your pocket. I pay for the kid to have another go, try and get in with him while I can. I give him a hand with the hoops and win a bottle of sweets. We walk over to the counter and buy some chips. I ask the bloke serving to fill the salt properly. We stand out of the way, chatting about nothing special. Seeing Sarah with her boy is strange, but it only adds to her. Makes her stronger. The kid doesn't say much, concentrates on his food. We leave together, me and Luke stopping for a drink, Sarah off home with Jimmy.

The pub's busy, but not packed, and I order two pints of lager, sit with Luke in a corner and tell him how me and his dad got stuck on top of the big wheel, how Smiles was swinging back and forward in the chair, trying to scare me. It seems like yesterday. Everyone says that, but it's true.

– You had a laugh anyway, Luke says, emptying his pint.

It's true, we did have a laugh together. Before things went wrong, but I keep that to myself. No point raking up bad memories. Part of me wants to go into it, but the sensible thing is to talk about the future, so I ask what Brighton's like these days. Haven't been for years, and I tell him how me and Smiles went down and slept in a boat on the beach, and I bet it's a lot different to the days when the mods and rockers went on the rampage, the skinhead beanos when we were kids. I talk and he drinks.

– You're a bit slow, he says at last, taking the piss now. What do you want? Same again?

Luke goes to the bar, and I glance around the pub, passing the time, jump when I spot Dave sitting on a bar stool talking to Micky Todd, who gets up and leaves. Dave turns and looks straight at me as if he's picked up on a radar message. He orders himself a drink, cutting across Luke who's next up. I see Luke shake his head at the pissed cunt with the slicked-back hair, Made In Slough tints, lets it go like you do when you're on your first pint of the night and the other bloke's mullered.

– Didn't see you come in, Dave says, sitting down next to me.

He's out of his tree, and his nose is going to blow up one of these days, the tubes worn down by the amount of charlie he's sticking up there. Can't say anything to the man when he's in this state, just have to grin and bear it. It's Sunday night and Dave's roasting.

– Thing is, Dave says, all these cunts think they're the bollocks when it comes to anything that might be a bit naughty, and what I reckon is so fucking what. I mean, you look at that bird serving behind the bar. Nice tits, big smile, but the whole time she's creaming a nice profit on the price of a pint, and she's eyeballing me when I'm buying something off Micky to tide me over. It's three pence more for a pint of lager in here compared to down the road. That does my fucking head in.

Dave's well pissed, rambling off in different directions. His hand is bandaged up, and he's keeping it under the table. Too much wanking.

– Cheeky cunt, he laughs. There's nothing wrong with my hand.

He's looking sheepish, never mind the bluff.

– He got carved up, says this bloke Mo, who stops on his way out. Carved up and stitched up.

– Other way round, says his mate. Stitched up and carved up.

– Stitched up, carved up, stitched up again.

They laugh and I sit still, doing my best to look blank. Mo leans forward as Dave eyes up a couple of teenage girls passing by the window, long stick-insect legs clicking down the road, a layer of china-white skin coating brittle bones. They can't be more than fifteen, and Dave shrugs when he turns back.

– He got stitched up buying drugs off this Paki in Reading, Mo says. Then he got carved up. He drove back and went down Wexham Park, where he was stitched up by a local nurse from Bangladesh.

I look at Dave. He's wearing another Stone Island top, different colour and style. Don't know how he does it. I ask Dave who it was, if the man used a knife or a razor.

– Don't worry about all that. It was a flick knife. He's been watching too many films.

– Fucking Pakis, selling drugs and working in the hospital. They're everywhere.

If I was buying a round I'd sink a mouthful of gob in the head of Mo's pint. Nurses are important, part of a welfare system mugs like Mo would close down if they had the chance, so they could have an extra five pence in their wage packet. The bloke's a cunt.

– It was nothing, Dave says. I was pissed, that's all, and I started mouthing off. Too much whizz mixed with the drink, too much coke. It was my own fault. I only had two stitches. It looks worse than it is.

– Thought you said eleven, Mo says. Eleven fucking stitches off some smelly Paki.

Mo and his mate leave, laughing. Dave looks out of the window and watches them go.

– Wankers.

We sit quietly sipping our drinks, looking into the street. I ask him if he remembers when this pub was called the Grapes, before they gutted it and put in a big screen.

– That's right, he laughs, sitting back in his seat. We had a punch-up outside in the street. We ended up rolling around in the gutter like a couple of tarts. Chris stepped in and sorted us out. What was it about?

Fuck knows. I knocked Dave out when we were back on our feet. He forgets that. I walked off, next stop Hong Kong. Probably wasn't about anything in particular, just a feeling, settling old scores. Least he doesn't remember me knocking him out.

– You knocked me out, he says. You always had a good right hook. Mo was right about the stitches as well. Eleven of the fuckers. They'll leave a scar. My hand's killing me.

I made up for it when I came back, helped him out on that same patch of concrete and did six months. I tell Dave I'll go down to Reading with him if he wants to sort the bloke out. It's out of order using a knife like that. Dave's not a shitter or anything, but he's no nutter either.

– It doesn't matter. I was giving the bloke too much verbal at the time. You're right what you said that time, when we were pissed and wanted to smack up that geezer who lobbed you and Smiles in the canal, right after you came home. Revenge is for mugs, specially if they never really meant it. Mind you, the bloke who cut me wasn't worried about all that. Fresh off the train from Russia and we had a row. How long was it till we had a drink? Didn't talk to each other for a long time.

It was six months more or less. Something like that. Six-month sentences everywhere you look.

Luke comes over and Dave shifts, hardly noticing till Luke places a drink in front of me and sits down. Dave's in trouble, a mixture of drink and drugs, prescription now as well as recreational, head floating outside his body, except it's no hippy trip this, just another night down the pub. He's got to sort himself out, but if I try and talk to him he doesn't want to know. He's floating in and out, making sense, talking shit.

– Thing is, I didn't go tooled up. That was a mistake. It was you giving me looks after that barney outside the chip shop that made me leave the knife at home. I thought I was paranoid, like you said, but I was right all the time. There's always some cunt after you. I won't be making the same mistake again.

And Dave's rabbiting away, at the same time sneaking a look at Luke who's got his pint glass wedged in his mouth. Something's ticking away in Dave's nut, but he's too far gone. He shakes his head.

– I've got to go home, he says. I've had enough.

He looks at Luke.

– Don't I know you from somewhere, mate?

– Don't think so, Luke answers.

– You look familiar, that's all.

Dave leans over and whispers in my ear, nice and loud so Luke can hear, his volume control gone.

– Who is he?

I catch Luke's eye and know he doesn't want the hassle, tell Dave he's a mate of Charlie Parish.

– Parish? Who the fuck's Charlie Parish?

He knows who Parish is, he's drunk with him enough times, maybe doesn't know his second name so I fill him in and he nods again, makes a big deal of shaking Luke's hand. He goes quiet and gets up to leave, his pint still half full.

– I'm off home.

When he reaches the door he stops and looks back, frowns, wanders off into the night. Dave's confused, and Luke's face is going to spin around in his head. I wonder if he'll remember any of this tomorrow.

– He's a bit of a state, Luke laughs.

I tell him that was Dave Barrows, punk, rude boy, soulboy and casual, who loved his clothes when the rest of us didn't give a toss, but came along anyway, what we used to call a part-timer. But if I'm honest, Dave has all the same angles as the rest of us, knows the music and shares the feeling, it was just that when push came to shove he was more interested in getting his leg over. He's alright. Dave's a good bloke.

– You ready for another?

Luke hurries back to the bar with the fiver I give him, seeing as it's my round. He's either got a thirst on or he's a pisshead. And I look at the barmaid and she's flat-chested, so I don't know what Dave was going on about. Funny thing is, we've argued since the day we met, kicked lumps out of each other a few times, but I'm worried about the bloke. It's a funny thing to admit, and maybe Sarah's opened my eyes. She's got a point. Maybe the people you fight with are the ones you're closest to, otherwise you wouldn't bother. Sarah's in my head a lot now, and she's the sort I should be keeping away from, with her kid and everything.

– That barmaid's flat as a pancake, Luke says. Nice arse though.

We sit drinking till closing time, Luke lagging after his third pint, a quick start then runs out of stamina early doors. We get home with five minutes to spare, and Luke's visit has to be polished off in the proper way. I'm quickly on the phone and the usual soothing voice is waiting, full of understanding and a willingness to help, the same face I've never seen, chiselled old features and misty brown eyes. When this man is in a good mood, with time on his hands, he loves a joke, enjoys some friendly banter with his callers, but now it's late and he wants to get off home. Can't blame him either. He's polite but firm, listens and reads back what I've said, adds a tub of lime pickle, takes my address and says the boy will be here inside half an hour. I put the phone down and imagine him at the end of the Chapatti kitchen, keeping tabs on the lads working in hot conditions, the chefs lording it like chefs do, treating the washer-up to a pint of lager from the pub across the road. I can see the kid stuck over a sink, scratching at the balti dishes, trying to get rid of the grime.

– Tell me about the canal, Luke says. Mum said you and Dad were chucked in a canal and he ended up in a coma. She went to her auntie's when he was in hospital and never saw him again.

We're both pissed, and because he's leaving tomorrow I tell him how we got beaten up by this bloke Gary Wells and three others. I tell him how Smiles was face down in the water, how some people blamed his suicide on that. There were other things that could've affected him. He nods. Smiles told Linda a lot about his life, and it's strange as he didn't really know her, but maybe he found it easier talking about those things to a girl. Suppose we all need that at the end of the day.

– Mum says Dad used to get slapped about by his grandad. That's why I never want to see him. She thinks that really upset him, with his mum dead and everything. Life just went wrong for him, finding the body and then getting beaten up like that.

It's true. Smiles didn't have much luck.

– That was bad enough, and then one day his brother tells him the reason their mum cut her wrists was because the old man was shagging a woman he'd known before they were married, in their bed as well, on and off for a couple of years. Imagine that. The old cunt was doing the dirty on her, and then when she tops herself he takes it out on his sons. Fucking cunt. My uncle should've kept his mouth shut as well. Dad didn't need to know. There's some things you should keep to yourself.

I never knew that, and it takes a while for the shock to wear off. I listen to Luke talk until the bell rings. I open the front door and take the plastic bag, put it down on the carpet in the living room, get some plates, spoons, knives, forks from the kitchen. Luke's quiet as I open the lids, peel them off the cartons and spread the food out. I get stuck into my pharl, the sort of heat that melts your mouth, makes your nose run, burns all the badness away. Luke has a Madras. I'm tired and go to bed when we're finished, my head spinning trying to get to grips with what he's said, leave him sitting on the couch watching a Jerry Springer show, sex-change couples battering each other for a screaming audience, poor blacks and white trash chanting JERRY JERRY JERRY. Some old bollocks like that. I think of Stalin and maybe I should've guessed what happened, that there had to be something more to it, try to imagine the guilt he must've felt.

Against the grain

THERE'S A MILLION different truths, and I reckon Luke's got one of the best versions going. His face is bruised, but he seems alright. That shouldn't have happened. He should've stayed home instead of going out early morning, stirring up trouble. The anger firms up in my knuckles and what's happened to him is wrong, right down the line. It's out of order. Bang out of order. But I'm keeping quiet, least till he's left. And Luke's got his whole life ahead of him, a cheap room and a sea view, his mum nearby, dreams to chase. He swings his bag as we cross the high street and go into the arcade, rockets exploding inside computer shops, kids bunking off school, roaming the racks, and we leave the warm glow of the shops behind, the pad of rubber soles on subway steps, the click of a teenager's high heels in this long grim tunnel with the tiny dot of light at the far end, conversation dipping as our words are punched back from the sort of grimy walls you normally find in a train-station bog, the stink of old piss and sweat swamping the disinfectant, the babble of police radios fading as the biggest boy in a crew of crop-skulled wannabes fizzes up a can of Coke and sprays the runt. The kid shrugs and tries to smile, walks taller. One of the boys. Fitting in.

We swing through new perspex doors and keep going past the ramp leading into the bus station, the smell of trapped fumes making my eyes water, some loony on the prowl with a bottle of ammonia, bright hip-hop graffiti and markers covering the tiles, blazing colours showing off cartoon characters, flashy designs without a message, a long hike to the end of the tunnel, that prick of light growing and turning into a beam as we get nearer the exit, a big punch of energy when we come into daylight. We keep going to the train station, past the taxi rank packed with Estuary skins, engines revving as a train glides in, heading west. I buy Luke a one-way ticket to Paddington and push his hand away from the glass when he pulls out a tenner, CCTV digging into a friendly row over which one of us is going to pay the fare. The girl behind the glass looks up from her computer screen and clocks Luke, surprised by the bruises, deep patches of red and black, the tape in the camera and film in her head recording his battered face.

We cross the bridge and wait on the Paddington platform. The monitor says the next train is due in four minutes, blinks, shuts down. And after talking so much over the last couple of days we wait for the train in silence. It would sound empty going on about the weather, or the trip ahead, even the look on the girl's face. I check the bruises and Luke's right eye has swelled up so much he can hardly see out of it. It makes me sick seeing him like this, but I keep a lid on things, want to wave him off, make sure he's safe and sound, out of harm's way. There's no point making a fuss. CCTV keeps on ticking, indexing two men on a platform, rocking foot to foot as they stare down the line, a friendly Big Brother making sure one man sees his friend off in safety, the easy flow of everyday life, time recorded, the routine of a normal existence, every curve of our faces burnt into the memory banks.

– Thanks for letting me stay, Luke says.

I nod and tell him it was a pleasure. It was an honour to meet him. He's always welcome, and I hope he comes back one day. He should come and stay at Christmas. We'll go round the house I grew up in and he can eat Dad's sprouts. My sister and brother-in-law are always there, plus their three kids and dog. Christmas is a good time. It doesn't have anything to do with religion, it's just a chance for people to be together.

– I might do that, he says.

Maybe he will, maybe he won't. Can't force him. Christmas is a time for family, and it couldn't have been much fun stuck in care. Mind you, he's got his mum now, and he should be with her.

– I'm glad I came and saw where Dad lived. It was a mystery before. I used to think all sorts when I was growing up, specially at night lying awake in bed, putting Dad in films off the telly. I look like him, don't I? I wish I had a photo. Least I saw where he lived anyway. Dad was lucky to have a friend like you.

It's the best compliment he could give me and means a lot. I look at the ground and say thanks. I lived, Smiles died. It could've been the other way round. I lived and my twin brother died. There was nothing I could do about him, but I've spent my whole life wondering why. If I was quicker, maybe Smiles would be alive today. Luke doesn't know how much I've thought about that night over the years. I don't know if he's right about Smiles being lucky, but it's a nice thing for him to say. I did my best.

– I'm not just saying it.

We both look away for a second. I've tried to give him the good memories, done my best to show Luke what Smiles was like before he got sick, going back to when we were little boys in primary school. Maybe Smiles was dead when the Major pulled him out of the canal, the rest of his life twilight years where he went through the motions. I've tried to cut out the dark frames, except for last night when I was pissed. That was a mistake, but overall I think I did alright. I should've kept my mouth shut last night.

There's no point making things worse, adding another layer to the years of loneliness, the tragedy of suicide. Luke is going to think he missed out on the chance to grow up knowing his dad, and that can't be changed, so it won't do him any good hearing how Smiles used to go on about dictators living in the community, the mass murderers lurking in the corner shop, shoplifting cartons of milk. He's had enough bad luck for one lifetime.

The tracks ping and Luke's train is on its way. The sound firms up and becomes more steady, the rumble of carriages taking over, the engine reaching the platform, stopping, doors swinging open.

– Thanks.

We shake hands. His grip is firm and we're both emotional. We control ourselves and he gets on, slams the door and pulls the window down. He leans out and smiles. This is the modern world and soon he'll be plugged into his Walkman, the sounds of Britain pumping into his brain, the clanks and blips of the machine. I look along the platform and an old man blows a whistle, the light catching the backdrop just right turning it into a scene off an Indian film, breeze blocks lining one side of the tracks, the light dimming as I look further along to the dirty bricks of the bridge. The train sucks in air and starts moving.

– Good luck, Luke shouts. Good luck, Joe.

I laugh and wave, wonder why he thinks I need luck, watch the train pull away from the platform. Smiles leans out with a big grin on his face, old beyond his years, as if he knows something about me I don't know myself, feeling what the other person feels, Smiles in a jean jacket with the sleeves ripped off, bleach worked into the denim, and I know his Martens will be polished up special for the trip into London, satellite boys on the prowl. Luke in his sweatshirt and trainers, a kid moving on.

The train picks up speed and shrinks into the tracks, flashing under the bridge and vanishing. I stand on the empty platform as the sound in the rails fades, imagine Smiles shooting into the distance leaving crumpled tin cans and sweet wrappers flapping behind, the dead hair of thousands of people passing through, dead hair in the bath, blocking the plughole, just passing through and going nowhere. I think of that stuck-up cunt John Betjeman and his poem asking German bombs to come and fall on Slough, saying it's not fit for humans now, and what did that wanker know, sitting in first class, cruising through and passing judgement, slagging off thousands of ordinary lives. Fucking cunt. Places like Slough get caned by these self-appointed experts, one of thousands of places where the social commentators never stop, flashing past in a train or on the motorway. It takes time for things to grow, for a culture to sink roots and flower, same as in America. Over the years life has spread out, the local markets and pubs as well as the houses, roads, depots, shops, jobs. Betjeman rolled on through and didn't even bother to get off. He sums up the condescending attitude of this country's Establishment, who look at the housing they've forced people into and turn up their noses. Everyone and everywhere has a culture, and if someone can't see it then it's because they can't be bothered. The best thing about life is that there's always something new coming through.

Fuck them.

Luke's gone and that's the end of Smiles. I push it away and look on the bright side, the sun shining along the tracks, catching broken glass, the sparkle of diamonds and the smell of tea cooking in the kiosk. I walk up to the bus station. It's the best sort of day, spring getting ready to turn into summer, something to look forward to, running through the music I'll play next week, a big night in Slough, just me playing punk. I go into the back of the station and there's a *Yellow Pages* advert up on the wall, a twenty-foot-high frog with green skin and a red trim, massive eyes popping from his prehistoric head. The railings are the same ones where I got mugged as a kid, the felt-pen graffiti long gone and painted red, emulsion flaking, and this dark corner brings back memories. Lessons in swimming pool learning the breaststroke, told to move our legs same as a frog. Me and Dave standing against these railings early evening getting robbed by older boys. They took our money and that was it, end of story. Must've been thirteen. There were no punches or kicks, just a simple handover of coins. Stairs lead to the car park where a woman was raped, and I remember when it was brand new and we went in with our spraycans. There's the bog I ran in one day after a bad curry the night before, washed through by the snakebite we used to drink. And the bins are on rollers these days, the same old squashed chewing gum, spit and smell of sweat in this little corner of my life, never mind the flashy advert, the magic of a computer design. And I let my legs do the walking. Piss off into the precinct and come out the other side.

There's always something stirring in your head, and it's as if you always think best when the moment's gone. But it's not too late. It's never too late.

Billy Clement runs a shop back off the high street, where there's a few older houses, everything on a lower level behind the concrete slabs and sheets of glass, tiny pubs forgotten except by a handful of men who keep them going, the old twang lingering over pumps that serve Director's, everything pushed on by expansion, progress, competition. Clem operates down these streets, coins it as well, hundreds of lone rangers coming to him for their spares, the self-employed men driving around in their vans, the plumbers, carpenters, electricians, couriers, rat killers, mini-cab drivers working hard for a better life, men who want to get ahead and do their own repairs. Clem is the supplier for these people. Everything from pliers and fuses to starter motors and heavy-duty batteries.

I go inside and Clem's behind the counter watching the news, another righteous man in a suit going on about transport, drugs, crime, fuck knows what. It doesn't mean anything right now, it's just sound, static, fuzzy feedback spat up and spewed back out under a different label.

– Alright Joe? Clem asks. What are you doing in here?

He turns the telly off and leans on the counter. I'm looking for a photo and ask him if he remembers when we went and stayed in Dave's caravan that time.

– Yeah, I remember. It was a good laugh, wasn't it? What made you think of that?

Clem had some pictures. Maybe he's still got them.

– I suppose so. There's a box upstairs in the cupboard. I could dig them out. What do you want them for?

Doesn't have to be a reason, just something that comes into your head and you have to sort it out, and it would be good if they were there, if I could look in the box and get some copies made.

– What, now?

He's an easygoing bloke old Clem. Real gentleman. And I've been there with coppers giving him grief, and when he deals with officials there's always an edge, like they expect his fist to connect any second. It's a shame. He's a diamond. Honest as they come. He can handle himself, but is a gent, isn't interested in bullying people. He'll do anything for you, and most of the time won't ask why. So I go upstairs into his flat and he pulls out a big box of photos, makes me a cup of tea.

– You okay?

I'm fine. Clem nods. Goes downstairs, back to work. Leaves me to get on with it. Clem's life is in this box, his family and friends, Clem as a baby with his mum, dad, gran, grandad, uncles and aunties. He's got lots of uncles and aunties, old-time gypsy characters in gumboots, and there's Clem as a boy, a youth, Clem on holiday with his mates, in Bournemouth. And there we are standing next to Dave's caravan, grinning, whizzing, laughing our heads off, and all these years later it looks more like a tin shack than a caravan. Clem's at the end of the row wearing a dodgy-looking tash. Then there's Dave, decked out in a shirt with a label I can't make out, really beaming like this is the happiest day of his life, and Smiles is next, a straight shot that catches him fine but gives nothing away, and last is muggins, a real scruffy bastard with a can in my hand. There's another picture, but it's more or less the same. I wonder who took the photo. I take the first one and show Clem.

– Fucking hell, he says. What a bunch of mangy-looking herberts. Least we are anyway. Dave looks smart enough. What do I look like? And you, you cunt. Fuck me. Talk about drug-crazed. Look at your eyes.

My eyes are blazing away. Must be the light.

– Don't lose it, Clem says, as I leave and head for the photo shop.

I pay extra for the one-hour service, sit outside on a bench with three old gits chewing their gums. There's nothing for them to do except sit and watch the world pass by, and now I'm with them, watching the girl in the shop move around, working this big white machine. I talk to the man next to me, and he's alright, served in Malaysia, in the jungle, fighting in the tropical heat, and now he's stuck on a bench in a new town, concrete taking over from forest. Coca-Cola rules the world. Coca-Cola, Kentucky Fried Chicken, McDonald's, Levi Strauss, Sky TV, Disney. The bin next to us is overflowing with polystyrene cups and cartons, chocolate milkshake dripping through a Pizza Hut straw, a small pool of brown muck on the pavement, packet wrappers and frozen chips, another run of Coke, McDonald's, KFC.

– Nice arse on that, the old boy says.

I follow his eyes and he's right. Very nice. The spirit lives on.

– I could fuck that all day long. If I was young, like you.

When the photo's ready I take the original back to Clem, borrow an envelope and write out Luke's address. Clem's looking at me a bit funny, trying to work out what's going on. I tell him not to worry, it's a surprise for someone. I tell him he's a good bloke. One of the best.

– What's the matter with you? Something's up. You been on the piss?

I walk to the post office and stand in line, buy a stamp and put the envelope in the box. Luke will be chuffed with the photo. It was sitting there in my head all the time. Don't know why I didn't think of it before. I go home, stop and buy some chips and a couple of pickled onions. When I get in I lock the front door, heat up a tin of beans and dump them on a plate with the chips and onions, go in the living room and put the food on the carpet for a minute. When the M4 is busy the windows rattle, the non-stop throb of traffic piling through, crossing the big banks of the motorway, metal flecks on the flyover, the smell of petrol heavy in the air during the busy times. I flick through the past and pick out the Sex Pistols single 'God Save The Queen', ease it out of the picture sleeve, protected by a plastic cover, place this 7-inch classic on the mat and drop the Rega needle into position, adjust the amp, let the words come steaming through the B&W speakers. I love it. If this stereo was a woman I'd marry it tomorrow. A dream come true.

I eat my food, wonder where Luke is now, ease back as everything comes crashing in, glad the door's shut and I'm indoors. The record runs through and nobody cares about the lyrics today. The press that made such a song and dance about 'God Save The Queen' is the same press that routinely slags the royal family off today. The press that put the Tories in power backs New Labour. Everything has changed, and nothing has changed. Not really. And Luke is getting further away, into Paddington and around to Victoria, a fast train to Brighton and a life by the sea. The letter will be sorted, stamped and follow him down. He'll be pleased. I know he will.

I turn the telly on and the volume down low, don't bother with another record, there's nothing left to say, eat my beans and chips, crunch into the onions, fill my fork up, wash it down with a can of lager from the fridge, the same old faces pushing into the screen, coming back to haunt me, self-appointed moral guardians lurking in the circuits, microchip men and women with lots of opinions and zero knowledge, so many versions of the same song, and the way we look at time is a con, it goes in circles, everything is always there, dipping in and out of focus, the basics never change, and the man filling the screen has this big boiled head that turns gold as I watch, the needle clicking on the back of the turntable, and the news shows bright explosions and figures in grey suits, the picture flickering as the face of the man inside the television set takes control, interviewing guests, lobbyists and professional opinion-formers spouting the same old lies, the familiar beat of their voices right here in my head, I know it all off by heart, shifting to urban decay and mindless violence, the steady whine of SINGLE PARENTS, SINGLE PARENTS in the background, the so-called immorality of single mums raising their kids best they can, and it's this scum that forces people to make decisions, aborting kids they'd like to keep, putting them in orphanages, making the benefits nice and low, that same old law-and-order mentality that keeps banging away in the background, the same trendy hypocrites who never get tired, just keep going, year in, year out, mutating into another group, the same faces, different clothes, rosettes, we get it all the time, see the headlines, hear the speeches, and I don't care about the crime wave filling the cells, the mindless hooligans, the white boys smashing up pubs, the black boys raiding shops – the scroungers and do-gooders – the muggers, pimps, drug dealers – the decent majority of law-abiding citizens – the rule of law – the social order – the best police force in world – the best legal system, medicine, education, army, democracy – best of everything – best sounds, pubs, curries, girls, football hooligans, drugs – specially the drugs – epidemic proportions – the call for hanging, flogging, stocks – the death penalty for child molesters – terrorists – young offenders taking the piss – life far too easy inside – far too hard for our rulers – it isn't like the old days – the good old days – *Blue Peter* and Gary Glitter – eco-warriors and anarchists threaten the very fabric of society – ravers, ecstasy, repetitive beats – sound systems – everyone taking drugs, taking the piss – road protesters and neo-Nazis – too much sex, too many skivers, too much freedom – too young, too old – unmarried mothers, unwanted babies – socialism tried and failed – the kids today – never had it so good – never had it so tough – and on it goes – on and on.

*

They say home is where the heart is, and I suppose it's true. I hope Luke settles down, finds a place he can really call his own. Maybe he'll end up serving lager in Hong Kong or pizzas in New York. Sounds romantic, but it would be a lonely way to spend the rest of his life. He's a good boy and doesn't deserve what's happened. You can't escape your roots, whether it's the place you grow up in, the music you listen to, the pubs you drink in, the girls you love, everything that happens along the way. It's not hard to work out, and at least he's got a chance. You try and do your best in life, treat people how you want to be treated yourself, show respect and expect it in return. Most people learn this as they grow up, so it doesn't matter if they talk to themselves or go out on night patrol, get abducted by aliens or believe in miracle births, just as long as they don't strut around thinking they're the only person who matters. It's something the wahs never learn, and that's why they're so arrogant and everyone hates them. They've got no manners. No humility. If everyone understood what the other person was thinking, felt what they're feeling, life would be easy. It's a truth, more important than the state's endless laws and regulations, passed by the rich for the rich. Thatcher said there was no such thing as society, but she was wrong. It's just looser and more easygoing than she thought, doesn't run on snobbery and political correctness. Most people get on with things. Make mistakes and try to learn from the experience. Do unto others . . .

– Come on, you tight cunt, it's your fucking round, Dave shouts, a foot away from me.

My right eardrum's ringing so I give the bloke a hug to shut him up, pucker my lips so he backs off mumbling about gay boys taking over the world, never mind the government and media. I stare at his Stone Island logo, take out a tenner and lean over the bar, hold the note at an angle, sharp crease slicing though Her Majesty's face. The barman knows the pecking order, everyone taking their turn, polite and friendly, getting on. Tricky's grumbling away in the background, going on about standing in government lines again, his voice filling every corner, merging with the laughter, the deep thud of life away from the glossy advertising posters, free from the sugary lies of those party-political soundbites. The lager's off, so the barman's mate goes off to change the barrel. He does me three pints of Guinness and a bottle of Mule, as the bloke he's serving decides to hang on for the lager. Chris and Clem are fine with Guinness, and Dave is struggling anyway, so the Mule will give him a kickstart without the same volume as a pint. I let my drink settle, the thick white cream backing up the glass, black base rising, turning solid. Beautiful.

– So Alfonso's on the job, Dave says, going back to his story. He's almost there, with Lizzy spread out under him, legs up in the air, knees pressing into his chest, groaning like a trouper, sweat covering her body and soaking the sheets, gasping for more, when the dog starts barking his fucking head off. The mutt's going mental, scratching at the door and digging in the carpet, needs to get out of the room sharpish.

Dave pauses for breath, the Mule filling the gap. Talk about gay boys. He should forget the drama and get on with his story. He stares at me and Clem butts in.

– What's the dog doing locked in with Alfonso and Lizzy when they're on the job?

It's a fair point and needs to be answered. Dave frowns. Sucks at his bottle. Lowers it to his waist as he weighs up his reply.

– I don't fucking know, do I? I wasn't in there as well. What do you think? Alfonso's servicing Lizzy on the bed while I'm entertaining Mutley over in the corner. Do us a favour. Do you think I was rimming the dog or something?

– Fuck off, will you, Clem says.

The picture of Dave servicing Mutley gets stuck in Clem's head. He looks like he's going to flush his drink back up. It's not nice, not nice at all.

– It's Augustus, Chris says.

– What?

– The dog's not called Mutley. It's called Augustus.

– Augustus?

– Alfonso's dog is called Augustus. After some Jamaican geezer.

Dave sighs. Hangs his head. He's showing us he wants to give up, can't be bothered wasting his breath when we keep on interrupting him, putting him off his stride and breaking the rhythm. I tell Chris it must be Augustus Pablo. Melodica player. Alfonso was going on about him the other day, leant me an album he produced, *King Tubby Meets Rockers Uptown*. Lots of it sounds familiar, and we probably heard it enough times when we were kids, just never knew the name.

– He gave me *Rockers Meet King Tubby In A Firehouse*, says Charlie Parish, arriving on the scene. It's too slow for me. I prefer speed. No fucking about. No fucking words and no slowing down.

– You'll learn, says Chris, sipping his pint.

– So this fat bloke meets the rockers uptown and they meet again in a firehouse? Dave asks. Why don't they go down the pub like any normal cunt instead of hanging around with the fire brigade?

– Because they live in Jamaica, Chris says, laughing into his drink.

– You telling me they don't drink in Jamaica? What about the Red Stripe? The rum? Nice bit of Navy warms you up nicely.

– I'm not saying they don't drink, it's just a different way of doing things, and it's where they mixed their music. It wasn't a social.

Dave nods. Tries to remember what he's talking about.

– He probably wanted to go for a walk, Clem says. Needed a shit or a piss. He's not going to do it in the room while his master's banging the mistress. Animals have standards. They're a lot better behaved than humans most of the time.

Dave looks at Clem. Looks at Chris. Looks at me. Finally looks at Micky Todd who's squeezing past with a grin on his face, charlie in his pocket. Dave watches him disappear into the bogs and knows he's going straight in the cubicle. Thinks about something, then shakes his head slowly. Makes the effort.

– So, Dave continues, Alfonso's busy with Lizzy and the dog won't stop barking and then she says maybe someone's trying to break in, tenses up so he thinks his knob is stuck in a vice. You know what she's like.

– What do you mean? Clem asks, licking the froth off his lip. Lizzy seems alright to me.

– She is. Lovely girl. But she gets nervous. Highly strung.

Anyway, the dog keeps barking and Lizzy's going on at him, so Alfonso pulls out and fucks off downstairs to have a look. He pads through the house and into the kitchen, and hears voices outside. He peeps out the window and there's these two toe-rags trying to undo the locks on his garage.

People don't like having their property nicked. Specially when it's something that's cost them hours of hard work. Alfonso built the speakers himself, and it takes time to get the balance right.

– So what happened? Clem asks.

– He goes in the kitchen, grabs a carving knife and steams out of the house. Soon as they see him they're off, shitting it. They're just kids and don't expect to see a six-foot-six black man flashing a knife and a hard-on. It's their worst nightmare come true, thought they were going to get stabbed twice over. They do a runner and Alfonso's left standing in the road stark-bollock naked when a car comes round the corner and lights him up like a Christmas tree. It screeches to a halt, does a U-turn, and shoots off the other way.

Micky Todd comes back out of the bogs, smiling, chatting to people he knows, looking pleased with himself, like he's one of the royal family out pressing flesh, filling up on cucumber sandwiches instead of coke, thinks he's at a garden party full of lords and ladies instead of a pub packed with dodgy geezers.

– How do you know all this? Chris asks after a while. When did Alfonso tell you?

– He never told me. I heard the story off this Sharon bird, who knows Lizzy.

And there was me thinking Dave was in the room, under the bed, sitting in the corner stroking the dog. Clem's thinking the same way.

– You fucking plum.

Dave laughs, more relaxed tonight, giving the charlie a miss. He's had the stitches taken out of his hand and shows me the scar. Didn't want to earlier, but now he's had a drink it's out of his pocket and on display. Getting done like that has made him sit up and take notice of what I was saying. He has to watch himself. The scar crosses his life line and I tell him he should keep away from fortune tellers.

– My whole hand aches, he says. There's a lot of nerves been cut. The doctor says I've got to take it easy. Imagine slicing me up over something like that. Micky's sending a firm over to Reading. I told him to leave it, that it was my fault and up to me to sort out, but you know what he's like. Said it was bad for his reputation.

I tell him what Dad was saying about the Major, how he went over and there was all these slugs lined up on his work table, and the Major was cutting them up for his compost heap. I can almost see the slime oozing out of their pimply bodies, feelers twitching from the pain.

– I always said he was a psycho. You never believed me.

The slugs were dead. It makes a difference. It's only meat. People get more upset by mutilation than the actual death. We all do it. You think anyone who carves up the dead has to be mental, but really, it doesn't matter.

– You're right, I suppose, it doesn't make any difference, but it's not nice, is it? It's not exactly normal. You've got to be a headcase to go round chopping up dead bodies.

We're quiet for a bit, thinking about the madmen who come in the night and cause chaos, move on before the sun rises, and it's the same as when there's a riot and the Old Bill blame outsiders. It's an easy way out, pinning the blame on an unseen enemy so you don't have to look too close to home.

Dave nods, looks at the empty glasses and presses into the bar, orders when his turn comes, and I suppose I did alright by Luke, gave him a place to sleep and showed him round. It was long enough. There's only so much you can say. And I said too much, when I was pissed and should've kept my mouth shut, telling him about Wells, so Luke only goes and looks him up in the phone book when I'm asleep, calls Estuary Cars and goes round his house. He knocks on Wells's door and wakes him up. Luke's half-cut and wants to talk to him, except there's nothing to say. Wells laughs in the kid's face. Knocks him down and kicks him in the head. Says he chucked some punk in the canal, so fucking what? Heard he topped himself and reckons it's a good job too. Steams in and gives the kid a pasting. Kicks the shit out of him.

– You want lager or Guinness?

What sort of man does and says those sorts of things about someone who's killed himself? Everyone should be humble now and then. Learn from past mistakes.

– Can you hear me? What's the matter with you? Do you want lager or Guinness?

The Guinness is going down a treat.

– Cheer up, will you.

Claret and his mates come in the pub. They don't like it round here, reckon Slough should be renamed Paki Town and twinned with Calcutta, most of them from the surrounding towns and villages. Claret is handy with a knife, part of a new generation of football hooligans who'd rather have a toe-to-toe halfway across London than bother with the game. Even Micky Todd treats him with caution, waves the bloke over.

– Todd's sending Claret down to sort those blokes out, the ones who cut me up, Dave says. He won't let me go. Says I'm a liability, the amount of charlie I've been doing. Still, I've got a handle on things now.

I hope so. It's alright for rich people who get addicted, but if you don't have the money to either feed your habit or go in a clinic and sort things out with the help of professionals, same as these pop and sports stars, then you don't stand a chance.

– It's a load of bollocks, Clem says, turning his back on Todd and the others. Don't understand this fighting bollocks.

He sips his pint, and Charlie leans over, starts talking to this girl he knows, big hoops through her eyebrow.

– Do you remember that holiday we had at the seaside? Clem asks Dave. When we stayed in your caravan.

Dave nods and laughs.

– Didn't get much sleep either, and it wasn't the shagging keeping me awake, because there wasn't any. It was you snoring.

Clem smiles. He's thinking about the photo I borrowed off him. I try and think of something to take him off the subject, don't want Dave and Chris wondering what I was doing. Charlie steps back in, the girl blowing him out, saves my life.

– We're going over to Ibiza in the summer, he says. Never mind caravans in Bognor. What do you want to stay in a caravan when you can go to Ibiza?

– Bournemouth, Dave says. We don't have it any more. It rusted away. And it was Bournemouth, not Bognor.

– Bournemouth, Bognor, what's the difference.

Dave smiles.

– You should come over to Ibiza, Charlie says to me.

I tell him no, I don't fancy it, all that sun, wine and disco house shit driving me mad, brain-dead music pushing me over the side. If I go on holiday I prefer a bank holiday at the seaside, a week in Amsterdam or Berlin, a few days in Dublin pissing it up, catching the EuroStar over to Paris when there's a decent band on, buying a cheap flight to Stockholm or Oslo and staying in a youth hostel for a week, dipping into the scene over there, a week in Lisbon or Barcelona. But I don't say anything, don't want to start an argument. It's different tastes, and when I was younger I'd have taken the piss something rotten, because that's what we did, and I used to give Dave a lot of stick when him and Chris went off to Spain for two weeks dancing with Donna Summer, just so they could get their end away, and they did the same with me. They're welcome to their resorts. Mind you, if they played some decent music I'd think about it, but if I spend big money going anywhere it'll be New York. But I'm not bothered about that right now. I've got other things planned. Bigger fish to fry.

– I could do with some sun, Dave says, turning to Chris. What about you?

– We're booked up. Two weeks in Cornwall. Can't wait. The kids wanted to go to Disneyland, but we can't afford it. Maybe next year.

There's always next year. Things to look forward to. New music, places, ways of doing things. I put my hand in my pocket and feel the toilet paper wrapped tight, the strip of harder tape.

– You'll be off with that Sarah bird, Dave says to me. It's love, mate, fucking love. It's in your eyes.

I haven't known her long. Can't think about things like that right now, and anyway, I'd never settle down and live with someone. Death on wheels. No offence, Chris.

– None taken, he says, grinning.

It was funny meeting Sarah's boy Jimmy like that, at the fair. I thought it would put me off her, but it doesn't, makes me see her as stronger than ever. I've always liked strong women. Some blokes go for looks pure and simple, something out of an advert, but it's the personality with me. She's a good girl.

– Did you hear about Baresi? Dave asks.

Everyone shakes their heads.

– You know the other night, when he was supposed to have that stripper coming down to suck him off onstage?

– The Beautiful Belinda.

– From Barbados?

– Brixton more like. Well, someone called her up on Baresi's mobile and told her not to show, then left it on. His phone was on for four days till the cleaner found it by the bog door. It's going to cost him a fortune.

We all laugh. Couldn't have happened to a nicer bloke. Well, it could, but he deserves everything he gets.

– I'm starving, Chris says.

– Have a roll.

So Chris has a roll and we do what we always do, stay till closing time, have a laugh, feeling good together, and I'm measuring my drink, not going overboard. One or two people can control a session, by either drinking fast or going slow, and with Dave struggling it's not hard to come out of the pub fairly sober.

– See you, boys.

I walk some of the way with Dave. We go in the chip shop and the bloke behind the counter nods when he sees us. Don't know why he's being so friendly, then I remember the other night when we came in pissed, the punch-up with those muppets. We buy some chips and walk down the road, sit on a wall stuffing our faces. A police car steams past, its light flashing, faces staring straight ahead, gagging for some action. We eat slowly. I've forgotten to put salt on the chips and I have to force them down. I've got other things on my mind, gearing up for the night's work. The KFC and McDonald's windows are safe tonight, and Manors is out of the picture. Sarah's face flashes in my head. Tonight's a special night. I finish first and lob the wrapper into a rubbish bin. It's a good shot. But I'm still hungry. Should've bought something to go with the chips, and I could go back to the chippy but can't put this off any longer. I fancy a samosa now I'm thinking about it, some spice, an onion bhaji or something, push the images away, tell Dave that it's been scientifically proved that cocaine is worse than wanking, really does make you go blind as he lobs his paper and misses. I tell him I'm off. I'll talk to him later.

– Where you going? Dave asks. Your place is the other way.

I tell him I'm going for a wander.

– Where you off to? Come on, Joe. What's the matter with you? You've been acting funny all night. What's happened?

I'm fine, but he's got to go home.

– I'll come with you. Something's wrong. I know you.

I turn round and square up to him, tell him to fuck off and leave me alone. He stops and stands on the corner looking confused. It's for his own good. He watches me go and I turn the corner. Take my time walking through the streets, eventually find the house I want and plot up across the road. Stand in the shadows. I watch Wells in his living room. He's on his own, just back from the pub, or been watching a video maybe. I can see right through the house, the living room going from front to back. He comes over to the window and looks out, pulls the curtains. The rest of the house is dark. I can't believe he gave Luke a pasting like that, slapped him up in the air and kicked him down the path next to the house. But what really gets me, worse than this, is that he doesn't even know Smiles's name. He almost killed the bloke, almost killed me, and there was me thinking it was an accident, believed all that stuff he said in court, kids going too far, can't sleep at night, feels so bad about what happened. I did my best to think how the other bloke was thinking, but the thing is, I was putting my thoughts in his head. If that was me I'd be cut up about it for the rest of my life. He doesn't call Luke's dad Smiles, or Gary, or even Dodds, just labels him 'some fucking punk'. That's what really gets me.

I reach in my pocket and feel the badge wrapped in toilet paper, held together with Sellotape. I walk across the road, face down, feeling like something out of an old black-and-white B-movie, the assassin who comes in the night, faceless, collar up, except I don't have a collar, and this is personal, doing my best to keep the anger under control. I ring the doorbell and wait. I haven't set eyes on the bloke for years, and he's got the same sneer on his face, a pile of change in his hand which goes flying as I move forward and catch him in the face so he staggers back down the hall, reaches out and grabs the banister, stays on his feet. I hit him again, close the door behind me. I hold back, don't put all my force into the punches. Have to be careful. Wells doesn't have a clue who I am. I can see it in his face. So I tell him. Hold up the 'God Save The Queen' badge he ripped off Smiles, and which I've kept all these years. He knows now, but it's a tiny part of his life, not one of his priorities. And I'm in his house, in his hallway, trespassing, blood down his shirt from my fist. I stand back and he comes at me, so I punch him again, and this time it's textbook but packed with anger, and I know I've done some damage. He hits the floor and rolls over. Then he's still. I remember this from before, and don't worry too much.

The bell rings and I stand still. The hall is dark, light creeping in under the living-room door. I crouch down, look at Wells's face inches away, the features hidden. I take the badge out of my pocket and open it up. Pull the pin out so it's straight and push it into his cheek, just like he did to Smiles all those years ago. The skin resists, then pops. I push harder so it goes right in. Same badge, same action. He doesn't move. There's a trickle of blood. I wipe it with my finger, stay crouched as the bell rings again. Once, twice, three more times. Don't know who's on the other side of the door, but I wish they'd fuck off. I stand up and go to the kitchen, look out of the back window, move around in the darkness, past a rack full of dishes, spotting the silver blade of a carving knife. I hear someone come down the side of the house and move back into the hall. I think of Alfonso with a knife in his hand, surprising burglars, except I've got no argument with whoever's out there. I've come for Mr Wells.

I can smell curry and realise he's only gone and called Chapatti Express. They must make a mint down there. Everyone's tucking in. I can hear the kid round the back of the house knocking on a window. He probably thinks Wells has fallen asleep, pissed and tired. Maybe he'll try an open door and waltz right in, and I'll have to stand and face a boy earning pennies ferrying lumps of chicken tikka around. Just doing his job. The chicken skinned and diced. Pink meat and Bangladeshi spices. It's the little people who get blamed for everything and end up in trouble, and I always thought that was true about Wells, that he made a mistake, but the truth is he never learnt his lesson and kept picking on easy targets. I stand over him, looking down, in charge now.

A minute later I open the front door and go outside, click it shut. The street's empty and I step forward, knock into the Chapatti boy's plastic bag. I look inside and see a familiar greaseproof bag on top of the silver containers. I grab it and quickly walk along the path, head down, start running when I'm in the shadows, run till I'm out in the lights again, open the bag and take out an onion bhaji, rip into it, my hands covered in grease, a strange blood-like colour under the lamps, keep my face hidden as I hurry home.

I get up early and go down the cafe, order my breakfast off Tracy Mercer who runs the place with her boyfriend Terry. She's looking fit in Umbro tracksuit bottoms and a loose T-shirt struggling with the fading smile of Diana, wrinkles creasing the face of a dead princess, the Union Jack logo on Tracy's trainers smudged with oil. We have a chat about nothing in particular, and when she mentions the mutilated body that's been on the news I stare at the counter. She says the police have questioned a youth who works for a local takeaway, but he's been released without charge. I shrug my shoulders and tell her I don't watch telly much, can't stand all that doom and gloom, nasty little back-stabbing reporters shit-stirring for a living, stitching people up for a handful of silver, making up stories. She frowns and says she knows what I mean, don't they have souls, don't they ever think what it must feel like having your life spread over the front pages, but according to the news the head was cut off.

I feel sick, see my order scribbled on her pad, and when I say I'm starving she smiles so her teeth catch the light, sparkle they're that clean, a perfect line off *Baywatch*. She pops a tea-bag in a mug and covers it with boiling water, takes a spoon and presses it against the side, counts to ten and flicks it in a saucer. There's a small stack there, colour fading as they dry and show the pores, bleeding dry. Tracy leans through the hatch and passes my order to Terry, and I choose a table by the window where I can sit and watch the street pick up, adding sugar and stirring well, creating a whirlpool with my spoon, the tea spinning faster and faster. I take my spoon out and the mixture keeps twisting, slowing down.

I place my hands around the mug and see how long I can keep them there. I want to burn my fingers off, show I can do anything I want and get away with it, believe that I'm invincible and will never get caught out. Rain dots the window as a bus accelerates towards a puddle, splashing three boys in black puffa jackets. They hop back, kicking against the water soaking their jeans, shaking their heads and shouting after a bus that's quickly gaining speed, on the run, the bulldog jaw of the bald driver fixed in a big grin. I have to smile, can't help it, laugh out loud so Tracy looks over and nods, goes back to the paper she's reading. Now the boys are laughing, seeing the funny side of things as they push each other into the puddle, sunlight warming the pavement, mist rising from tarmac. And I was back in the tropics last night, with the rain hammering on the roof, sheet lightning cracking the sky apart, rain taking the hard edge off life, easing the pressure with a quick monsoon rinse. In summer it's even better, when car fumes hang in the air and people are tense, and those storms they had in Hong Kong were so special I used to go up on to the roof of Chungking Mansions and watch the sky light up, killer blades stabbing into the city, chopping and hacking away at the skyscrapers, showing where the real power lies.

The smell of cooking food starts my mouth watering and I think about ordering an extra round of toast. Money in my pocket means I can have anything I want. The person before me has left a paper behind, the front page taken up by a story of a public face being gay. I laugh and look outside, watch the people pass till Tracy brings me my breakfast. This woman is an angel, a girl from another planet, from Planet Reebok. Steam hisses behind the counter and Tracy tells me to enjoy my breakfast as I add salt, and looking out of the window there's this rush as I realise life doesn't get much better than this. It can't do, sitting in a hideaway stuffing your face, in familiar surroundings, everything sorted, justice done, in among the houses, pubs, shops, patches of grass you know and love, miles away from the scum who try to control us. Fuck them. I'm topping up on life, buzzing like I've been at the charlie with my old mate Dave, except I'm not on anything, trying to slow down and stay in control, riding the old dodgems of life, electricity cracking right there above my head, tapping into the generator that keeps the light shining.

I go to the counter and pay Tracy, who punches the till, Terry out back frying bacon for a couple of pensioners, and she leans over for her pad, forgetting the tea for a moment, the gentle curve of her tits pushing into the Umbro top, her teeth perfect in the light. She's always been a friendly girl, salt of the earth, and it's people like Tracy who keep the world going, a constant smile on her face never mind what happens. I pay my dues and put a pound tip in the saucer, say goodbye and leave the cafe, start walking.

I pass the police station and try to remember the times I've been in the cells. Once for knocking a man out in a fight outside a pub. Another after I was stopped and caught with some sulphate in my pocket. Once for putting a brick through the window of a bank. They did me for being drunk and disorderly for that last one, criminal damage thrown in, a fine I paid off at a tenner a week. The fight when I ended up inside. It's best forgotten now, silly arguments, stupid coppers worried about harmless drugs, and I smile when I think of the bank window, the years of bricks, superglue and low-key damage. Can't remember how much I was fined. Don't care. Don't give a fuck, turn and follow the road, cars blocked by a hole in the tarmac, men gathered round a bald navvy shaking with the drill, chips of concrete spitting back into the street, craters in his head, thick insulated cables with the sort of voltage that will burn a man to the bone, wires under the surface of his skin, veins on bone, down the back of his neck. I keep going and turn left, past the cemetery, my eyes drifting over, catching movement in among the gravestones, but I keep going, keep walking. I pass the mosque and go over the railway bridge, into the dip, two old women in saris at the top of the next bridge looking at the canal. They turn and walk away, so I keep going, don't have to wait, go down the steps to the banks of the canal.

I take off my clothes and put them in a pile next to the water. For some reason I fold them. I don't know why. The wind blows across my skin and I keep my pants on, dark clouds smothering the sun, shafts of light feeding through the cracks. Light, dark, warm, cold. Doesn't matter. There's nobody around. No kids fishing for tadpoles or old men walking the dog. Traffic crosses the bridge, and I can see the tops of the lorries with their messages blazing out, moving on. If there was anyone by the canal I'd keep walking, wait till they've gone and come back. The water ripples from a breeze, and I'm not going to hang around, flash back to a summer night when I was a fifteen-year-old boy, a kid who thought life was straightforward. The memories have hardened, but the feeling is still in me, part of what I became. I sit down on the edge of the canal, shivering, the lining of the Grand Union ice-cold on the back of my legs. I dip them into the water, let my feet sink down till it's halfway up my shins. The canal is freezing.

A thick block of cloud shuts out more light. Goose pimples pock my skin and I see a woman plucking a white cockerel, the chilli-seed pattern of its featherless body, the pink flesh that a civilised country smothers with the Colonel's secret recipe. People talk about headless chickens, and I've seen one with its throat cut, running in circles flapping its wings on the ground, beating its soul into the dust, blood vanishing in front of my eyes. These things make an impression, affect what you become, how you behave, seeing boys lined up outside a Chinese station with plaques round their necks. And I suppose when I came out of the canal all those years ago I was never going to be the same again. The world was different now, and everything had an edge. The colours were different, the smells, the way I felt inside. There's a Coke can on the opposite bank, its logo slowly rotting away, changing colour as it melts down to a gold rust.

I lift up and lower myself into the canal. The water's cold and smashes into me, the shock racing through my heels to the back of my skull, stabbing into my brain. I keep moving, slowly, so I don't go under, not yet, dipping my shoulders below the surface, like I was taught as a kid, head up, moving my legs. I swim to the middle of the canal, do a slow breaststroke, same as a frog. My movements are easy and I see thousands of peasants lining up early morning in China, before sunrise, dressed in the green and blue cloth of Chairman Mao, doing their t'ai chi for a party official with a loudspeaker, the same old cunt wherever you go in the world, doesn't matter if he's communist, fascist, anarchist, democratic, there's always some wanker waiting to tell you what to do, what to think, telling you that you've never had it so good, never had it so bad, and the difference in approach depends on how much he can get away with. I see the faces of the Chinese peasants, clever enough to keep their peace, quietly dodging the authorities, staying alive as they flow this way and that, mouths shut, doing nothing that will give them away.

I reach the middle of the canal, paddle for a few seconds, looking along the surface of the water which is smooth and grey. The canal's been cleaned up, but is more dead than the last time. It used to be busy, when the brickworks were booming and there must've been ovens and kilns everywhere, I wonder if they're still there, probably levelled and built over, and that was a long time before I was born, horses breaking their backs on the towpath wishing they were in a field, worked to death and sold off to the knacker's yard, slaughtered for dog food, hooves ground down and soaked in jelly. And I can feel the slime covering the water, even though it's not here any more, the tangled weeds long gone but the water still unused at the end of the Slough Arm. There's nothing here, not even weeds, no life, everything ripped out, and when I listen I don't hear anything except traffic on the road. There's no frogs croaking, nowhere for them to live. And this is the moment.

I take a deep breath and duck under the water, turn over and pull myself down, reaching with my arms and stretching the muscles as far as they'll go making sure I use my legs right the long legs of a frog with his popping eyes and croaking gossip baby frogs picked out of the ditches and skewered on a bent piece of wire legs clicking electrical currents charging the muscles legs eleven in the social club middle-aged women tapping their biros on halves of lager thrashing frog legs and pierced little hearts broken valves drowning in blood a jam jar full of spawn turning into tadpoles sprouting big bubble heads growing feet and we sit and watch them swim around the jar trying to escape getting bigger day by day the pressure building up inside me a heavy load to carry as I try and get deeper into the water leave everything behind dig into the water and when I've gone far enough I turn so I'm the right way up and get ready, 1–2–3–4, blow the air out of my lungs slow and steady then when I get to the end and think I'm going to bottle out I blow hard as I can so I choke and have a split second before I suck water back in open my eyes the lull before the flood my eyes misty as I look along the tunnel the light from up above broken and bent curving through the years and if I bottled it and went back up I'd come out at night during summer find the Major at the side of the canal waiting to help and there's this big burst of joy that says this is my second chance and Smiles is still alive and I can do things different now the chance to change history and then quick as a flash faster than the happiness comes the horror knowing the impossible doesn't happen and there's no second chance no turning back the clock and my mouth is open and the water bursts in the pressure in my head growing as I remember now what it felt like when Wells threw us in the water and we got stuck the moment when you know you're going to die think you're as good as dead but I know it this time and this is the end of everything and because I never listened to the television and radio when I was young I never worried about the arguments going on around me life was about what I saw and did the voices loud now there's no getting away from them Smiles and me sitting in the station cafe pretending we've got tea in our cups because we're skint and he's telling me he's going to be a dad and while he's feeling sorry for himself the girl he's got in the club is carrying Luke around in her belly a foetus clinging to the walls of another child's womb he was just a possibility and now he's a young man beaten up by scum after spending the best years of his life in a home and institution what a fucking liberty-taker Wells is – was – and I can feel the lager in my belly cheap drink from the social club special-rate lager light and bitters cheese rolls behind the counter mushy dough from the slice of tomato that leaks juice into the bread the trickle of lager down the sides of a mug blowing the dregs against a car-park wall a bursting feeling in my bladder a Russian railway worker naked as we cross the world a local girl turning her head away from the mirror a lovely woman and my lungs are stretched ready to explode feet on the bottom of the canal airware soles of ten-eye Martens dragging me down boots I worked hard for saving the money I made stacking shelves with all those tins working for a manky cunt who treated me like shit and I got away from all that did my own thing and I'm drowning filling up a bloated corpse and this is the real thing back where I started struggling for life with my brother the rubber band twisting through Mum's water my twin brother tangled up in his own umbilical cord and this time I'm staying behind want to die with him so neither of us ever have a name go in the oven together and Smiles isn't as important as my own flesh and blood but I have to die to make what I did right the knife cutting into Wells and the thing is . . . it wasn't me . . . it really wasn't me who did the mutilating, and suicide is for the insane, I'm not mad, know I did nothing wrong, didn't mean to kill the bloke just did what I thought was right, some sort of justice, and I push stretch pull towards the surface each split second thinking I'm almost there giving up as the light burns my eyes and a rush of oxygen races into my lungs big gulps of air roaring into my chest as I sink back coughing and spewing water, reaching for the side of the canal, try to pull myself out of the water, wait for helping hands that don't come, do it myself second go, lie down in the long grass, sharp blades around my head, and I cough up water, get my breath back.

The clouds blow away and light bursts out. The sun hits me and warms my skin. I watch the long trailing fizz of a plane trickle across the sky. My breathing gets easier and settles into some sort of proper pattern. I try to find a tune, but there's nothing. No music. People forget quickly and I had to remember what it felt like being in the canal. Memories fade and I killed a man, or at least I think I killed him, but I never cut him up. Don't understand any of that. And I have to remember what he did if I'm going to stay solid and get away with it. You have to know that what you've done is right. Life is too good to throw away, and imagine if there was no music in heaven, if you had to go to hell and burn for ever so you could hear a decent tune, surrounded by Stalin, Hitler and that cocky little fucker Mao off the Trans-Siberian Express. I put my clothes on quickly, before those women come back and see me, get upset and call the police, send for the dredgers and social services, the men in white coats, their syringes loaded and needles primed.

I walk back up to the road and the Major is sitting on the wall on the other side. He knows everything that happens in this town. He has to be the man with the knife, embarrassed in a court of law, a boy without a dad, a copper's son with a sense of justice, standing at his table slicing up slugs. He smiles and nods. He's in my head. Knows what I'm thinking. He must have been out on patrol and seen what happened. I don't want to know the details. When I get in I'll wash my clothes and clean up, go down the pub and have a drink. I turn away from the Major searching for a tune, but there's just the sound of lorries rumbling past, and if I'd died in the canal when I was a kid, held down by a pair of heavy boots, the leather rubbed raw with a brick and polished till they shone, I'd have missed what came next. I lived and my brother died. He was stillborn. He never had a name. Smiles was a mate who went mental. Neither of them dying was my fault. Wells was an accident. If I'd drowned just now, I wouldn't go round and see Sarah tonight, find out what happens next.

I follow the road, the minaret and dome of the mosque up ahead on the right, the Co-op out of sight on the left past the pub, the greyhound stadium long gone, racks of bleach and tinned tomatoes filling the space, shelves packed with tinned carrots and tinned peas, tinned pears and tinned pineapple, tinned pork and tinned fish, workmen drilling at the foot of the railway bridge in their yellow tin hats, the sweet smell of diesel in the air. Someone sounds their horn on the other side of the road. I look over and see Dave stopped at the bus stop, and he's hanging out of the window waving me over. I want to keep going, be on my own, but he starts shouting and the workmen turn round. I cross to the central reservation, climb over the railings and wait for a gap in the cars, fumes blowing into my face.

The passenger door opens and I get in.

– Why's your hair all wet?

He doesn't wait for an answer, indicates right and inches

forward, lorries barrelling past. When he sees a gap he accelerates away.

– You're a thick cunt signing your name like that, he says. Prints all over the badge and Wells half dead. He'd have grassed you up. They'd have given you five years, specially as you've already been inside. Probably a lot more. Sticking the badge in his face would've got you extra.

He laughs and cracks my head with his knuckles.

– You daft fucking cunT.

The traffic slows down to a crawl.

– You were right what you said about chopping people up.

We reach the hump of the bridge.

– Someone had to finish the job. You couldn't leave it half done. I never cut his head off either. That's just lies. But we'll be alright. He was scum anyway.

Dave's talking to himself.

– It's a good job I followed you.

Dave's a good mate, the best friend I've ever had. He laughs long and hard.

– We're brothers, you and me, just like brothers.

He reaches over and puts a badge in my hand. I look at the cut-out tabloid letters spelling GOD SAVE THE QUEEN, a dayglo background for a world that turned dayglo years ago. He's turned the cassette down, but I can hear Black Grape's 'In The Name Of The Father'. I turn it up so the speakers vibrate with the heavy vocals. Dave's killed a man. Cut him to ribbons for me. The police are after a drifter, an outsider, a maniac who acts without rhyme or reason.

I couldn't handle prison again, banged up on one of their stinking blocks, every last bit of freedom stolen. It's no way to live. I'd rather top myself than rot away in prison. Dave's saved my life.

The sky's jammed with jets queuing to land at Heathrow, suntanned passengers looking down on the glass, bricks, streets of our town, the people invisible, toy cars on the move. Dave puts his foot down and we race down the slope, the bright gold dome of the mosque sparkling in the sunlight, clouds washed away, and we have a laugh trying to match the ragga vocals of the song, the boom of the bass blowing everything into the past.

We beat the red and slow down, circle the roundabout, the lights in our favour, moving faster now, the road ahead straight and empty.

It's good to be alive, don't care what anyone says, and when it comes down to it we're nothing special, just two ordinary blokes trying to do the right thing, going with the flow but keeping our eyes wide open, like you do.

John King

THE FOOTBALL FACTORY

'The best book I've ever read about football and working-class culture in Britain in the nineties'
Irvine Welsh

The Football Factory centres on Tom Johnson, a seasoned 'Chelsea hooligan' who represents a disaffected society operating by brutal rules. We are shown the realities of life - social degradation, unemployment, racism, casual violence, excessive drink and bad sex – and, perhaps more importantly, how they fall into a political context of surveillance, media manipulation and division.

Graphic and disturbing, occasionally very funny, and deeply affecting throughout, *The Football Factory* is a vertiginous rush of adrenaline – the most authentic book yet on the so-called English Disease.

'The most savagely authentic account of football hooliganism ever seen. The book's veins pulse with testosterone and bellicose rage, effing and blinding throughout the warzone of macho culture'
Blah Blah Blah

'Bleak, thought-provoking and brutal, *The Football Factory* has all the hallmarks of a cult novel'
Literary Review

VINTAGE

Also available in Vintage

John King

HEADHUNTERS

'King loads his characters up with enough interior life, but it's the raw energy of their interactions – the beano to Blackpool, the punch-ups, the casual fucks, the family skeletons and the unburied fantasies – that make this excellent book run'
Time Out

Following on from his best-selling study of violence, *The Football Factory*, John King considers Britain's other obsession – sex. Formed in the chemical mists of New Year's Eve, The Sex Division sees the once-sacred act of procreation at its most material, as five men devise a points system based on the sexual act. In this lager-soaked league, the most that Woman can offer Man is 4 points – unless, that is, she leaves her handbag unattended.

'*Headhunters* is sexy, dirty, violent, sad, funny: in fact it has just about everything you could want from a book on contemporary working-class life in London...If John King can keep doing this sort of thing, he'll wind up top of the pile'
Big Issue

'The realism and political edge echoes Alan Bleasdale's *Boys From The Blackstuff*'
GQ

VINTAGE

Also available in Vintage

John King

ENGLAND AWAY

'If every nation gets the football fans it deserves, what does that say about England? For an answer you might try John King's brutal novel, *England Away*'
Daily Telegraph

Having examined England's twin obsessions – violence and sex – in *The Football Factory* and *Headhunters*, John King completes his trilogy with *England Away*: sex and violence *abroad*, under the Union Jack. The novel works on three levels - past, present and future - as pensioner Bill Farrell remembers his war experiences in a London pub, Tommy Johnson fights his way through Holland and Germany for an England football match in Berlin, and Harry considers the future fuelled by doses of Dutch skunk and German speed. John King's powerful new novel looks at notions of what it means to be English. Exploring stereotypes of language and nationalism, the primal pulls of lust and aggression, *England Away* culminates in a unity of the tribes and a blitzkrieg in the streets of Berlin.

'Easy to read, finely balanced and often brutal in its sexual and physical imagery. There was never any serious doubt, but this book confirms John King as the nation's finest writer of football fiction...immense'
Total Football

VINTAGE